Dear Reader:

Mail-order brides in the old American West have always intrigued us. What would make a woman move halfway across the country to marry a man she had never seen before? Did these women find happiness? What were the unexpected consequences? When I asked three authors to create mail-order bride stories, it turned out that the reasons they picked for their women marrying strangers were as individual as the writers themselves.

In HEARTS ARE WILD (April 1993) by Teresa Hart, deLacey Honeycutt is a clever female card sharp who is down on her luck. Desperate to get enough train fare to once again gamble with gentlemen in their private cars, she signs up with a mail-order bride agency only to get a free train ticket. Unfortunately, she runs across the very man she was expected to marry—with unforeseen consequences.

SWEPT AWAY (August 1993) by Jean Anne Caldwell is a delightful story about a girl who can't quite make up her mind whether she wants to go through with a marriage to a stranger . . . so she pretends to be the maid who is hired through the mail, not the bride. Of course she is soon unmasked.

SCOUNDREL (December 1993) by Pamela Litton is the story of a dreamy woman from Boston who has always longed for adventure. She travels west after corresponding with a man who writes proper and respectful letters. But when she arrives, she finds a different, much more compelling man waiting for her. How she turns the town, and her life, upside down will charm you.

All three of these stories start in Saint Louis, where the women meet for the first time. Though strangers, the women know that the choices they've made have bonded them as sisters of the heart. I hope you enjoy these romantic stories.

Best wishes,

Carrie Feron

Carrie Feron
Jove Books

P.S.—Turn to the back of this book for a special sneak preview of *Swept Away,* the next romantic adventure in the ''Brides of the West'' series.

BRIDES OF THE WEST

HEARTS ARE WILD

TERESA HART

JOVE BOOKS, NEW YORK

BRIDES OF THE WEST: HEARTS ARE WILD

A Jove Book / published by arrangement with
the author

PRINTING HISTORY
Jove edition / April 1993

ISBN: 0-515-11079-5

Jove Books are published by The Berkley Publishing Group,
200 Madison Avenue, New York, New York 10016.
The name ''JOVE'' and the ''J'' logo
are trademarks belonging to Jove Publications, Inc.

PRINTED IN THE UNITED STATES OF AMERICA

10 9 8 7 6 5 4 3 2 1

PROLOGUE

St. Louis, Missouri. The Gateway to the West. For those seeking a new land, a new life beyond the mighty Mississippi, this was the bottleneck through which all hopes and dreams were filtered.

The crowded depot at the St. Louis train station was a testimony to that fact, for people, men and women of every design and description and every station in life, could be found on any day of the week eagerly awaiting the call to board and ride the rails to their future.

The three young women sitting restlessly on a long, hard bench were no exception. There was something about them, perhaps the forward tilt to their shoulders, that captured his attention. Or perhaps it was the careless way the one on the far end with the inordinate amount of baggage left herself open to his scheme. Wait, wasn't she the one who had been his easy target before?

The man, quite disheveled, and in need of a bath and a good meal among other things, sidled over to stand as near to his chosen prey as he dared without being seen by the dark-haired one. From his vantage point he could hear the conversation, even as it erupted.

"Can you believe it?" the rather plain blonde wearing gold-framed glasses and clutching a book began as if she

1

were speaking to anyone who cared to listen. "The West."
She heaved a romantic sigh. "We're truly in the West. Can
you believe it?" Sitting between the other two women, she
glanced from right to left to see if she would get a response.

The one to her left, his target, tilted her head so that he
caught a glimpse of her pretty face and dark hair beneath the
expensive silk bonnet she wore.

"I can believe it. I just wish the long train ride was
over." Worriedly she scanned her mound of luggage. She
had already been robbed once here in St. Louis. She didn't
want to be a victim again.

"And where are you going?" the blonde asked with
sincere interest.

The dark-haired girl hesitated for a moment before
answering. "Colorado. I've taken . . . employment there.
And you?"

"New Mexico. Starlight, New Mexico," the enthusiast
replied, smiling. "I have a handsome man waiting for me.
He owns a silver mine. We've been corresponding for
several months. I plan to marry him."

"A mail-order bride?" The question came from her other
side, from the woman in the simple calico and ugly slat
bonnet.

"Yes, isn't that the most romantic thing you've ever
heard of?" the blonde replied.

"Well, don't get your hopes up, miss," the cynic warned.
"There's nothing romantic about a man who can't attract a
woman except on paper. I'm not expecting much."

"All aboard for Denver, Colorado," came the monotone
call of the stationmaster.

"Oh, that's my train." The woman on the other end, his
mark, stood and began to gather up her baggage.

It was then, when all three of the women's attentions
were distracted elsewhere, that the man made his desperate
move. Reaching down, he grabbed the closest bag, a small
one to be sure, but he was optimistic.

Dashing away, he heard the indignant screams, but he
ignored them.

The gateway to hopes and dreams. By damn, he had a

right to have some, too. With any luck today's take, already successful, would be great. If not, tomorrow he would simply try his hand again.

And did he feel even a twinge of remorse for robbing a woman? Robbing her twice, in fact. Why should he? From what he could tell, those three young ladies had not a worry in the world. Their futures were set. So why should he feel guilty for dipping his fingers into the plentiful pie of good fortune?

CHAPTER 1

May 1, 1888
St. Louis, Missouri

"Pardon me, Miss Honeycutt, but before you board the train I want to check to make sure that your paperwork is in proper order."

With an unbecoming slat bonnet concealing her eyes, deLacey reluctantly looked up. Brushing aside her apprehensions, she stared up at Mr. Shockley, swooping down over her like an indignant stork.

Ichabod Crane. Yes, that was the character that came to mind whenever she contemplated the ungainly Ebenezer Shockley in his stiff white collar and severe black suit. In all of her travels she had never met anyone who reminded her more of that nervous schoolmaster. His spectacles teetered on the end of his long, thin nose and looked likely to tumble off at any moment.

"I'm all squared away, Mr. Shockley," she reassured him, patting her reticule. A wisp of a smile bowed her well-formed lips as she touched the slight bulge of the deck of playing cards stashed inside. Yes, she was more than ready. With relief she watched him walk away and resumed her surveillance of the station door.

For all his Good Samaritan facade Ebenezer Shockley, organizer and director of the Foundation for Unification, was no better than she was. Hidden behind his lofty title and sanctimonious airs was a fellow sharp, pure and simple. No doubt he managed to make a most comfortable living feeding off the needs and miseries of desperate people—just as she did. But at least most of the time her marks were far from innocent. She did feel a slight twinge of guilt over her most recent plan: deceiving the poor clod foolish enough to send for a wife sight unseen.

Lowering her lashes for just a moment, she took a deep breath to calm herself. Only several more minutes—a half hour at most—and she would be safely on her way out of St. Louis. Being spotted, dressed as she was in simple calico and posing as a mail-order bride, was most unlikely.

The front door of the station house swung open. Stiffening, she chided herself for growing lax even for a few seconds. If she'd been discovered . . .

Her eyes darted to the left. There was an exit that led to the boarding area. If the situation warranted it, she could always bolt in that direction.

Unfortunately, her predicament wasn't that easy to resolve. Mr. Shockley headed back toward her as if struck with a sudden inspiration.

"Now, you are sure, Miss Honeycutt, that you have all of the necessary tickets to make your train connections?"

"Yes, yes," she insisted, trying to hide her apprehensions and annoyance, wishing only that whoever lingered in the train yard entrance would come inside.

"And your copy of the contract and letter of introduction to Mr. Abrams . . ."

"Right here," she assured him once more, patting her purse. Every muscle in her body tensed when two men, one tall and powerful and handsome to a fault, filled the empty doorway.

Oh, God, they *had* found her. In her heart she just knew it. Cattleman Will Hockett, the rich Montana rancher she had attempted to clean out last night at poker, had sent his henchmen after her, and she could well imagine what they would do to her if and when they got their hands on her. "Cheater," the rancher had called her, and she had been lucky to get out of the hotel with her life. She'd left her winnings behind on the table. Looking around Ichabod Crane, she prepared to run.

"Hup, hup, not so fast, Miss Honeycutt." Shockley's spidery hand clamped down on her shoulder. "Though I must admit I am tickled with your obvious eagerness to be on your way to your new future. Just remember what I told you this morning when you applied for this once-in-a-lifetime opportunity to meet such a suitable husband," he offered in a sales-pitch singsong. "I have wired ahead to let Mr. Abrams know your arrival time, but you're under no obligation to marry him. Your contract requires only that you *meet* with him at least three times and be willing to listen to his proposal. He expects a lady of good breeding and in return will treat you like one."

She stared at him blandly. He really believed she was going. What could a man who was hard-pressed enough to mail order a wife possibly expect, much less have to offer? One eye? A hunched back? Some such awful deformity must be a part of the bargain. But even if he were an Adonis, she had no intentions of marrying Mr. Silas Abrams—or anyone else for that matter.

In fact, she planned never to reach the town of Medora in the Dakota Territory. Unbeknownst to Mr. Shockley she had already cashed in her connecting tickets for a poker stake. If things went well she would be altering her route long before the train ever left Missouri, on her way to Kansas City and Denver where the pickings were much more lucrative—miners with gold in their pockets to gamble away, no more manure farmers with mud between their toes.

However, before she moved on to more fruitful orchards there was one last cowpoke she wanted to entice to her table. Joss McRae. It was said he had more money than the government, and if her information was accurate his private car was attached to the rear of the train. Right now she could do with a sliver of his wealth, and chances were he'd never miss what little she might rook him out of.

Frowning, she recalled that just such a plan had gotten her into her present fix. But, she reassured herself, *this* time it would be different. This time she was prepared. As long as she managed to evade Cattleman Will.

Shockley's hand still on her shoulder, she cringed as the pair she'd spotted earlier at the front door led by the handsome, raven-haired man surveyed the depot and its occupants. For the briefest of moments their eyes collided, the strangest feeling ricocheting through her.

Don't let them recognize me, she prayed inwardly, lowering her head and holding as still as she could, even though she could feel the stranger's eyes boring into her bonnet-covered skull and her heart pounded so hard it threatened to jump its tracks like a runaway train.

Endless seconds trickled by, each measured by the erratic flutter in her throat. Realizing that she was holding her breath, she inhaled and swallowed down the sick feeling churning in her stomach. Any minute now the two men would come up to her, say something, demand that she go with them.

What would she do then?

Unable to stand the tension another heartbeat, she sneaked another peek at the doorway. Discovering the entranceway empty, relief in the form of a sigh escaped her lips.

Thank goodness. Whoever the men were didn't matter as long as they were gone. Once again she was safe—at least for the time being—at least long enough to get out of town.

"All aboard."

Like a cleansing rain the conductor's summons washed over her. Still shaking from the close call, she rose, collecting her carpetbag containing all of her worldly goods—most importantly the tools of her trade and a burgundy velvet gown that had cost her a king's ransom in New Orleans. Keeping her apprehensions under firm control, she took a step toward the door leading to the waiting train.

"Miss Honeycutt, you'll remember to write to me and let me know the outcome of our arrangement, won't you?" Mr. Shockley called to her just before she disappeared.

"Remember? Of course," she lied, thinking for just one moment that it might possibly be sincerity that shone in his wire-framed eyes. But no, that wasn't likely. Surely no one would actually agree to such a farce—would they? Of course not. Honesty was not part of the game people like she and Shockley played.

Steady in her course, she turned and hurried toward the boarding platform, her fingers clutching her reticule that held the deck of cards, the money from selling the tickets, and the note she had painstakingly penned in her room at the hotel just before sneaking out the back stairs, the bill unpaid—a challenge to one Mr. Joss McRae to test his gaming skills against "the King's."

Oh, Lord, let this particular Dakota cowboy be as arrogant as most self-made men she'd encountered in her travels, for it was the overbearing ones who always succumbed to her duplicity so readily.

Stretching out his long, denim-encased legs, Joss McRae made himself comfortable, accepting the Waterford crystal glass from Henry's gloved hand.

"And did you find the woman you were seeking, sir?" the servant asked in that stoic tone that even now drove Joss to distraction. A gentleman's gentleman Henry called himself. That might well be, but no McRae had ever claimed to be a gentleman, nor would they have wanted to be so mislabeled.

For generations the McRaes had been men willing, even eager, to take a long shot whenever one presented itself, setting their goals high, determined to have all or nothing. For the most part nothing had been what his ancestors had received for their trouble and ambitions—men who had pushed on looking for their golden opportunity and been beaten by the odds or by others more ambitious and ruthless than they were.

Not much different than his forefathers, he supposed,

he'd gotten lucky and his gamble had paid off. Stock in the Northern Pacific Railroad, cattle, and the harsh winter of '86 that had destroyed so many of his fellow Dakota ranchers had made him rich beyond his wildest dreams. Now there seemed nothing further to strive for, unless one considered revenge a worthwhile goal.

Worthwhile or not, it was all he had.

"We located her, Henry," he replied, lifting his glass of the finest rye whiskey money could buy to offer up a somber salute to those who had gone before him, and a vow to the interfering bastards he would topple before he was finished.

"We made it, by damn, and nobody is ever gonna take it away from us," he murmured, then he gulped the amber contents of the glass and closed his eyes, savoring the liquor burn as it trickled down his throat. Dropping his head back against the soft contours of the couch, he conjured up an image of Silas Abrams's cruel face, a vision of the son of a bitch standing over his father's dead body, his lips curled in a sneer, declaring that the world was better off minus one more loser.

Frowning, Joss shook his head to clear it of the reoccurring nightmare, one that had haunted him for as long as he could remember, turning his thoughts instead to the task at hand. Where in the hell was Jackson? By now the detective should have returned with the woman.

"Would you care for another drink, sir?"

Joss's lashes lifted revealing the most incredible gray orbs, smoky as a battlefield sky, the carnage and pain just as evident.

"Not now, Henry. Why don't you go sit down or something?" he grumbled. "Your hovering is goddamn annoying."

Henry never flinched, but then he never did no matter how outrageous Joss acted.

"As you wish, sir," the servant replied, and slipped away. Joss had no idea where, nor did he particularly care. All he wanted was to get this whole sordid scheme in motion as quickly and efficiently as possible.

At the moment when the train began to roll forward, the wheels grinding beneath his feet, metal to metal, grasping the rails and picking up speed, when the acrid smell of the engine smoke drifted through the open window behind his head, the staccato of a knock sounded upon the Pullman door.

Jackson had arrived at last, and Joss's well-laid plans for revenge were beginning to take shape.

"Henry!" he shouted in annoyance. Pulling up from his slouch, he brushed a lock of coal black hair out of his eyes and glanced about. Where was that servant when he wanted him?

The rapping grew insistent, urgent.

Rising, he crossed to the door and flung it open, fully expecting to find Randall Jackson, the detective he had hired to track down Abrams's mail-order bride and round her up, waiting there, the plain little miss he'd spied in the station in tow. Instead a moon-faced lad stood in the doorway. Beneath the floor the clatter of the wheels was so loud, and his disappointment so intense, that Joss shouted, "Yeah, what do you want?"

"A . . . a m-m-message for a M-M-Mr. Joss McRae," the boy stuttered, his slight frame swaying with the movement of the train. In fingers that visibly trembled, he held out a folded piece of paper.

Joss eyed the note, one dark brow arching as he assessed the messenger's offering. Fine linen—not cheap. Definitely not from Jackson. Reaching out, he accepted the missive, dipping into his vest pocket to retrieve a coin, four bits, a substantial tip in any circle.

Eyes widening to emulate the roundness of his pie-shaped face, the boy caught the money tossed to him and scurried away.

Watching as the kid slipped through the door on the other side of the coupling, Joss frowned. Who knew he was on this train? He slammed the door shut, determined to find out why Jackson wasn't back and how the secret of his identity had become common knowledge.

"Henry. Damn it, Henry, where are you?"

Filled with impatience, he ripped open the note's seal and scanned it, noting the florid penmanship, the way the *s*'s curled, the tails of the *y*'s and *g*'s curlicued, very fine indeed. Then he read it once more, slowly, smiling at the memory of a long-ago experience. As a boy he had watched a dapperly dressed gambler do amazing things with a deck of cards. King Honeycutt was a childhood idol never to be forgotten. Now he was being given the unexpected opportunity to face the legend man to man.

"Henry, you lazy good-for-nothing . . . !"

"Yes, Mr. McRae." Completely unruffled, the servant materialized in the room. "Did you page me, sir?"

How did Henry constantly manage to do that? All the time, appearing, disappearing into the thin air. No matter how Joss tried, it was something he just couldn't get used to and probably never would.

"Set out the silver decanter and the deck of gilded-edged playing cards Teddy Roosevelt gave me," he ordered, his smile deepening as he contemplated the unexpected challenge issued in the note. "We'll be having a guest tonight. One, I think, who will be most stimulating."

As far as Jackson's mission, there was no need to worry, at least not yet. The detective had a reputation of always tracking down his man—or his woman—whichever the case might be.

Gone was the atrocious slat bonnet, the unflattering calico dress, the serviceable shoes—the meek little mail-order bride on her way to join her "intended" groom. In her place stood a seductive siren in an outfit that put the finest ladies of leisure in New Orleans to shame.

DeLacey couldn't have been happier or more at ease as she stuffed the discarded clothing into her carpetbag. There was no way Mr. Joss McRae, or any man for that matter, could resist her charms so carefully contrived and displayed. A smile curved her discreetly tinted lips as her fingers, long and tapered just like her daddy's, lifted to smooth the row of lace outlining the deep décolletage of her bodice. Sleight of hand. Every cardsharp knew the only way to success was to keep the mark distracted elsewhere. What better ploy than giving him a little cleavage to contemplate?

Enough dawdling, missy. That was what her daddy used to say to her whenever she stood daydreaming before a mirror. Dismissing her reflection, she lifted her skirt to inspect the small derringer strapped to her right thigh. Secure and loaded, the gun would be handy for anything that might happen. Never again would she be caught unprepared like last night with Cattleman Will. Turning her attention to the small device attached to her left leg just above her garter, she checked to make sure it functioned properly. Seated at a table she merely had to slip her hand under her skirt, tap the concealed lever with a fingertip, and voilà! Whatever card she desired popped up into her waiting hand, no one the wiser.

The contraption was one of her father's clever inventions, but he had used it to retrieve cards out of the cuff of his shirt sleeve and only for parlor tricks—not nearly as convenient or profitable as the way she put it to use. Merely a small adjustment had been necessary to make it suit her needs.

However, filling her daddy's shoes had been another matter altogether.

Kingston Honeycutt had been one of the finest riverboat gamblers of his time, and *The Caddo Belle,* the paddle wheeler that had plied the muddy Mississippi River from New Orleans to St. Louis prior to the Civil War and even during the first few years of Reconstruction, had been legendary—not only for its fine facilities and excellent cuisine, but for the opportunity it gave its passengers to watch the gentleman from Louisiana display his unbeatable skills with a deck of cards. Quite the showman, her daddy had performed amazing card tricks for the crowds, much to their delight. No one ever walked away disappointed. It was an honor to face King Honeycutt across the *vingt-et-un* table and a privilege never to be forgotten to lose money to such a famous gambler, making a story to pass down to your grandchildren.

However, unbeknownst to the rest of the world, King had spent his final days as a pauper, his hands trembling, his eyes sightless, the two greatest terrors of the gambler. It seemed so unfair that his death had gone unnoticed. Even so, his legend continued to reign. To this day there were still reports of "the King" in mining towns all across the West, the tobacco he smoked allegedly laced with gold dust because he had more than he knew what to do with.

Dropping her skirts and smoothing out the wrinkles, she flattened her mouth at her own mirrored image. That was the way she wanted it, had carefully planned it over the last couple of years. Long live "the King." It was her due, after all. Unlike her father, she was not too stiff in the neck to use every available resource to her best advantage. Let the world think her daddy still lived and ruled the gaming tables. Eventually, as the daughter of King Honeycutt, she would acquire the respect her talents deserved. Perhaps she wasn't as skillful as her daddy, but she was much more resourceful, an opponent to be reckoned with across the poker table.

Men like Joss McRae were easy to woo and bilk, and most times they never realized what had happened to them. Or if they did, she could usually count on their male pride to keep them from doing anything about it, too ashamed to admit a woman had gotten the best of them. There were few men in the world like Cattleman Will who had so little self-esteem. But then she supposed his determination to get revenge stemmed not only from the money she had attempted to cheat him out of but from the way she had teased him, making promises she had no intention of fulfilling. Never again would she allow the situation to get so far out of hand.

Let 'em look, missy, but never let 'em touch. Those final words of instruction from her daddy had become her motto, had seen her safely through many an adventure. A master of the fine art of seduction, she recognized the risks involved. Good timing was necessary to slipping out of the noose before a man could tighten the knot.

Retrieving her beaded reticule from the counter beside her in the ladies' lounge, she gave her image a final inspection, wondering what this Joss McRae would look like. Would he be old or young? Old men were more likely to have the money. Handsome or ugly? From her experience rich men usually weren't much to look at. Kind or cruel? Neither were particularly hard to handle. The nice ones were the easiest to lead by the nose, but the mean ones, though a little more difficult, were much more deserving. Joss McRae would be old and ugly and incredibly naive, she decided to her satisfaction, flipping a stray lock of golden hair out of her face before turning away.

Cracking open the door to the lounge, she peeked up and down the corridor. It was empty for the moment, so she slipped out, clutching her carpetbag and purse close to her body. They were all she had in the world—at least for now—and she needed to find a place to stuff her belongings until she could come back for them after she'd completed the job at hand.

She could not return to her seat. That nosy old biddy who had been sitting next to her would without a doubt note the change in her appearance and set up a clamor. It was essential to her plan that no one realize that the plain little mail-order bride and she were one and the same.

So where could she hide her baggage and be sure she could retrieve it later? Glancing around, she took in her surroundings.

Just ahead and to her left she spied a small window. Pausing, she cocked her head and studied the situation, noting the way the sash swung outwards, the latch low on the framework. Perhaps if she opened it, hung her bag by one handle on the lever, and closed it again, the bag would be out of sight, safe from anyone tampering with it. It was certainly worth a try.

A few frustrating moments later she managed to relock the window, and though she could see the carpetbag handle, she doubted anyone who wasn't looking for it would. Satisfied, she dusted her gloved hands and moved away, clutching her reticule to her side, looking back over her shoulder only once to make sure her luggage was still all right.

From one coach to the next she wove her way down the

moving line of the train toward her destination—Joss McRae's private Pullman. Each car replicated the next, the hard wooden seats one after the other like church pews, the occupants no more than a blur as she skirted by them.

What if the next car she encountered wasn't for passengers but carried freight? How would she ever get around it or over it? The thought of climbing up the side and crawling on hands and knees across the top wasn't that appealing, but that is what she would do if she had to. Trying not to think about the dangers and the possibility that she could be swept off and never be missed, she reached for the next door and paused there on the small platform between the cars, the wind belling her skirts about her ankles.

At last, she had reached her objective. Confronting the ornate door with Private stamped across its face in bold black letters left no doubt in her mind.

Just behind that barrier was Mr. Joss McRae and enough money to last her for a lifetime. Well, at least enough to suffice until she could reach Denver and beyond.

Lifting her fist, she didn't hesitate to knock, although she had to admit there was a tight knot in the pit of her stomach. That incident with Cattleman Will had shaken her confidence a bit—but only a little. Joss McRae would be nothing like that cagey old Montanan.

Taken by surprise by the immaculately dressed man who greeted her summons, if one could call the way he stared at her down his long nose a greeting, she eyed him back.

"Mr. Joss McRae?" she finally demanded when she realized he had no intention of initiating the conversation.

Only then did his countenance reveal his thoughts. From the tip of her dainty burgundy slippers to the array of pink and burgundy feathers artfully arranged in her hair, he inspected her, apparently drawing his own conclusion as he tried to close the door in her face. "I'm sorry, madam, but Mr. McRae did not . . . request . . . the services of . . . a lady."

The implication of his words didn't really take her by surprise. People often treated her abruptly, assuming she was *that* kind of woman.

"You are mistaken, sir." She stuck out her hand to keep the door from shutting. "I haven't come to offer my services," she announced with a smile sweet enough to dilute the most bitter of dispositions. "Please inform Mr. McRae that King Honeycutt has arrived as arranged."

That certainly made the pointy-nosed stiff sit up and take notice—as well it should. Obviously shaken, he eyed her again, this time with a little more respect, or so she'd have liked to imagine. But at least he opened the door a bit more.

"Mr. McRae anticipated a *gentleman.*"

"You stand corrected. I believe Mr. McRae is expecting a *gambler.*" Reaching into her reticule, she drew out the deck of playing cards, waving them under his nose as evidence.

"Henry, what's the problem over there?"

From deep within the Pullman car the resonant voice thundered like a bass drum. Attempting to catch a glimpse of the speaker, she darted a look around the figure in front of her. When the servant glanced over his shoulder to respond to the question put to him, she took advantage of the situation, skirting past him.

Mission accomplished, she skidded to an abrupt halt. The richly appointed interior of the car caught her completely by surprise, although it shouldn't have, as she had been exposed to opulence most of her life. She'd just not expected to find such wealth displayed in a train car. All of the windows, including the large one that encompassed nearly an entire wall, were hung in velvet that put to shame her clothing that she had thought so expensive. Leaded glass lamps accented fine pieces of authentic Hepplewhite furniture. A massive chandelier hung from the ceiling, the crystal pendants of the finest quality and cut, shimmering and tinkling with the motion of the train. But it was the man draped across the hand-carved bar that made her catch her breath.

Wasn't he the man from the station? The one she had assumed worked for Cattleman Will? Flicking up and down his large, impressive frame, her gaze settled on his handsome face.

If this was Joss McRae, then she was in a peck of trouble. Neither old nor ugly, he was no doubt about the most handsome example of manhood she had ever come across. He was so tall she had to tilt her chin to look up at him. She guessed his age to be in his midthirties. His jaw was classically square cut, his cheekbones as rugged as if a sculptor had taken a chisel to them, his hair gloriously black and thick, and yet there was nothing oily about it like so many men with such dark hair. Exposed from the elbows down, his arms were bronzed and bulging below the casually rolled-up sleeves of his shirt. But it was his eyes, smoke gray, that—God help her—seemed to penetrate right through to her soul and her every intention, holding her spellbound.

She swallowed so hard her throat refused to cooperate. Ruthless and smart, Joss McRae would be an adversary like none she'd ever confronted before, and if she wasn't so desperate for the money she would do what her instincts told her to do—run for her life.

"King Honeycutt." Skepticism filled his smoky gaze as it skimmed down taking in all of her, practically stripping the burgundy gown from her petite body. Like a besotted fool she just stood there unable or perhaps unwilling to stop his flagrant violation. "Somehow I pictured such a legend would be much taller and . . ." Pointedly he stared at the swell of her bosom. ". . . much broader in the shoulders."

"Funny," she countered on a great rush of indignation. "I had the same thought when I first laid eyes on you. The wealthiest man in the Dakotas should have a more imposing stature." What a stupid thing to say. If he were any taller or broader in the chest it would be immoral.

"So you like your men big, do ya?" There was no question as to what he insinuated. A grin, so cocky she wanted to slap it off his gorgeous face, widened his sensuous lips. Once more assessing her well-displayed attributes, his gaze never wavered.

"How I prefer my men is quite frankly none of your business, Mr. McRae." Pink splotches tinted her cheeks, already hot with embarrassment.

"Then suppose you tell me, honey, just why you're here." Like quicksilver the amusement altered, replaced with a look so fierce and demanding she recoiled.

Every wile, every trick she'd ever mastered, she would need them all now as never before. Trembling inwardly, she refused to let him see how much he unnerved her. Joss McRae might be a tough opponent, quite possibly the most difficult she'd ever encountered, but that didn't mean she'd be defeated. Not by a long shot, and long shots were her forte. Arranging her expression to give an air of complete innocence, she softened her lips into a pout that never failed to affect men. One thing she could make a sure bet on, Joss McRae was all man.

"Why, Mr. McRae," she drawled in her best New Orleans accent. "You *did* receive the invitation from my daddy, didn't you?" Batting her long lashes, she widened her eyes to display their alluring blueness to full advantage.

"Yes, I did." His gray eyes never wavered for a instant. "But he didn't indicate that he was sending a mere slip of a girl to meet the challenge."

Her attempt to beguile him didn't seem to be working, not one iota. Confused and battling an odd sense of breathlessness, she glanced away.

"Don't worry, Mr. McRae," she snapped, irritated at his lack of gullibility and the way he insinuated that being female might be worse than death. "You'll get a fair run for your money."

Damn, she had to be more careful not to reveal so much about her true feelings. A gambler always presented a poker face, that was the number one rule, and right now she was doing a lousy job of that. Gathering her composure, she once more disciplined her features.

"My money's worth is all I ever ask for, honey."

Again she felt as if he saw right through her to the core of her deception. Impossible. If that were the case, if he suspected that she planned to cheat him, surely he would show her the door and be done with it.

Narrowing her eyes, she studied him as if he were an interesting specimen beneath the lens of a microscope. Joss

McRae might be handsome and smart, but he was not nearly as clever as he gave himself credit for. Men like him always possessed a barrelful of male conceit, and she had no qualms about using his overinflated pride to her own best advantage.

"Then I suggest, sir," she challenged with a smile, "we waste no more time and begin our game."

CHAPTER 2

In all of his born days Joss had never met a women to compare with the sassy female who stood before him, her hands propped on her hips issuing a challenge, so fearless, so damn reckless—so obviously conniving, and yet . . .

If he had half a brain in his head he would spin her about and swat that most enticing backside right out the door and slam it before she managed to do whatever it was she'd come to do.

However, his curiosity—as well as other factors—was thoroughly aroused, although he had to admit he was somewhat disappointed that the real King Honeycutt wasn't there. Whoever she was, he instantly recognized that they were two of a kind, he and the lady, the ace of spades and the ace of diamonds, both heartless and irredeemable gamblers willing to risk it all merely for the thrill of the game. As nothing else had in one hell of a long time, she presented a challenge. A most interesting one.

"By all means, Miss Honeycutt, won't you have a seat." With a gesture, he indicated one of the two chairs drawn up to the game table positioned in the middle of the room. "I assume it is Miss Honeycutt."

"Yes," she replied, eyeing the seat as well as her surroundings with a calm, critical assessment that left no

20

doubt she found them to her liking. "Miss deLacey Honeycutt," she expanded, accepting the chair and staring up at him expectantly with eyes so blue he thought he would drown in them if he didn't look elsewhere.

"Henry, get the lady something to drink." Glancing away, he took his place opposite her, planting his elbows on the felt tabletop, and lacing his fingers together in front of his chin. To think that some half-pint female attempted to take advantage of him was laughable. Watching her try—well, that might be most entertaining.

"No, thank you, Henry," she declined the offer, never taking her eyes off Joss, as if judging the effect she was having on him.

"And what of your father?" he demanded, riveting her with an iron glare, refusing to let her get the best of him.

"Ill," she retorted, her gaze as steady as a surefooted mule, and he suspected she could be just as stubborn and unpredictable. "Taken to his bed. It must have been something he ate . . . before we boarded the train, of course."

"Of course." Such a pat excuse, and well rehearsed. "If that's the case he should have simply postponed our game. I would have understood. In fact . . ." He made a movement of dismissal.

"Oh, no. There's no need for a delay, Mr. McRae," she volleyed so quickly that it confirmed his suspicions of her story. "I am every bit as proficient as my daddy, perhaps even more."

Still angled forward, half risen from his chair, Joss searched her beautiful face. Yes, he imagined she was quite capable in many ways. Just what did she want from him? The answer was only too obvious—money. Wasn't that why most people sought him out?

"Then shall we begin?" Dropping down onto his seat, he snapped his fingers at Henry, discreetly stationed behind the bar. Bringing out a loose deck of playing cards, the servant placed them in Joss's outstretched hand—the gilded deck Teddy Roosevelt had given him that night so long ago in Medora. With the memory still vivid, he smiled.

"Oh," she gasped as Joss held them out to her. "No need, sir. I've brought my own." From her reticule she pulled out a pack of cards, brand new, still sealed in their box.

"That's all right, Miss Honeycutt." For emphasis he riffled the cards in his hand and frowned. "I'd rather use these." He didn't trust her one bit.

"And I prefer a new deck," she insisted. Apparently she didn't trust him either.

Well acquainted with the ways of professional gamblers, marked cards and aces up their sleeves, he studied her a moment, not as a woman but as an adversary, oddly enough finding her show of spunk most intriguing. Since she didn't have sleeves, just those tiny, wine-colored puffs that made her shoulders look so delectable, and she wore gloves that prevented her from making marks with her fingernails, he decided that it really didn't matter what deck they used.

"Very well, Miss Honeycutt, if you insist," he conceded, setting his aside. With a show of nonchalance he watched her tear open the seal and shake the cards from their carton, shuffle them with expertise, and offer them to him for the cut.

Obliging, he then drew back, but when she reached out to scoop up the two stacks, he dropped his hand over hers, trapping it like a white dove, his thumb slipping beneath the glove to press against the pulse point in her wrist—oh, so very slender—that seemed to jump with apprehension. Just what was she afraid of?

"Five-card draw poker. No limit," he stated for the record.

"Of course," she replied in a strangled whisper that had nothing whatsoever to do with the rules of the game. It was his touch that set her nerves on edge. There in her eyes he could read that as she tugged at his grasp, insisting that he release her.

But he wasn't ready to let go, not with her pulse frantically fluttering against his fingertip, a frail-winged butterfly snared by a spider's web. It was comforting to discover that she was human after all, not just some ice-veined gambler—but a woman, warm and passionate. Then before he could stop himself he envisioned what her flesh would feel like without the glove, heated and smooth, skimming along the corded muscles of his back, down, down until . . .

As if he'd suddenly been scorched, he jerked back his hand, rubbing it, unseen, down the side of his pant leg to eradicate the overpowering sensations that radiated from where he had touched her. It seemed he was mortal, as well, just as vulnerable as the next man to a woman's calculated charms.

Indignation wrenched at his gut. Was that what the lady counted on, that he would be so enamored with her amply displayed femininity that he would be unaware of her actions?

"Deal the cards, Miss Honeycutt," he snapped, tossing out his ante in the middle of the table, wondering if the stakes were too high for her, almost wishing that they would be, knowing he would be disappointed if they were.

Without a bat of her lashes she reached into her cleavage—for his entertainment, most likely—took out a roll of money, and matched his hundred. Then she picked up the cards and began divvying them up, first to him, then to her, back and forth.

Smooth and detached, her features were unreadable and so beautiful in their iciness that he had to fight down the urge to jump up, knock the table out of his way, and snatch her hard against him—uncap the passion bottled up within her lovely body. Instead he watched her with steady eyes, and not until she had set the deck down and gathered up her own cards did he follow suit, raking in his hand and straightening the cards before he fanned them out with a slow deliberation that hid the conflict roiling inside of him.

A pair of jacks—diamonds and spades. One dark brow jutted upwards in amazement. How interesting that his first hand should conveniently contain the cards necessary to open the betting. Eyes flashing a challenge, he glanced up at deLacey, who stared back with relaxed indolence. Chances were that she held a better hand than he even though her expression, or lack of one, gave no such indication. Damn, if she wasn't a cool one, putting "the King" himself to shame.

Over the top of their cards their eyes met, held—and probed.

"Your bet to open, Mr. McRae," she said in a voice devoid of any emotion.

His bet, all right. He'd be willing to wager that she knew exactly what cards he held and had already calculated just how he would play them. Let her think him an overconfident, beguiled fool. That way he would snare her in her own trap. With bravado he tossed out another hundred, which she matched, and then he raked her with a hungry look, which he highly suspected she also expected from him.

"How many cards?" she asked, never once looking away as he assessed her attributes.

Three. She would assume he would ask for three cards. What would her reaction be if he didn't do the obvious? A slow smile tugged at the corners of his mouth. Keeping only one of the jacks, a ten, and a queen, he shoved the other two in her direction. "Two."

Her surprise was fleeting, but it nonetheless had been real. Then she snapped her features back into place as a turtle withdraws into its protective shell. She dealt him two cards, then after a moment's hesitation, one for herself. Her hands trembled ever so slightly, just enough that she had to realize he'd notice it.

He glanced down at his cards, his grin widening. Nothing. Nothing, that is, except unpredictability. But then he suspected her hand was no better.

"Bet's to you, Mr. McRae."

Try as he might, he couldn't suppress the chuckle that erupted from deep in his chest. Why, she expected him to bluff.

"I'll pass to you, Miss Honeycutt," he answered.

How beautifully she covered her confusion, studying her cards, looking up at him once with an expression that would melt wax and cloud most men's ability to reason.

"I find I must do the same," she offered prettily,

spreading out her hand to reveal a four flush of clubs and the jack of hearts, a jack no doubt she had drawn and had been intended for him to give him three of a kind. He would lay a wager that the next card on the deck was a club.

"Beats me," he declared, throwing his cards face down on the table and turning expectant gray eyes on her.

To demand to see his openers was her right. Would she ask? Indecisive seconds clicked by, but then she scraped up the jackpot in front of her.

Miss deLacey Honeycutt might think she had control of the game and of him. Well, let her think what she wanted, but she was in for a mighty big surprise.

What had gone wrong? Anxiety churned in the pit of deLacey's stomach, leaving uncertainty in its wake. A professional never acknowledged insecurities, especially not in the middle of a game, and yet as hard as she tried not to, she found herself succumbing to her worst fears. Chances were, she might not pull this caper off.

No. No. That wasn't true. Just the way her daddy had taught her to do it, she had shuffled the new deck of cards. And even though it hadn't been in quite the fashion she'd intended, she had managed to distract the mark. Fool that he was, Joss McRae had obligingly created his own diversion long enough to make sure that the cut deck had been returned to its original order. But still, something had gone awry, although she couldn't quite put her finger on what had occurred.

Those nagging doubts swooped in on her once more. Searing as a branding iron, his touch had unnerved her. That's what had happened. The unexpected surge of heat had confused her long enough that she had made a crucial mistake, unwittingly stacking the deck wrong.

Impossible. The cards she had dealt herself had been the ones she'd expected, and had he discarded three as he should have, she would have had her flush. So why had he drawn only two if he held the pair of jacks, and then claim to have lost? It took all of her willpower to avoid flipping over his cards to confirm what they were.

Calm yourself, Lacey, she chided inwardly. *What's important here is that you won the money.*

Flashing Joss a probing look, she took in his turbulent gray eyes that scrutinized her just as steadily, the slant of his lips that grew more arrogant with each moment that passed. She had won, hadn't she? He hadn't thrown the hand—or had he? Confusion whipped up the tempest inside of her once more. Why would he intentionally allow her to beat him?

Why, indeed? Narrowing her eyes, she experienced a sudden rush of clarity.

Why else, but to throw her completely off-guard, which is exactly what he had managed to do. Irritated, she narrowed her eyes. No one hoodwinked the daughter of King Honeycutt and got away with it. No one, damn it. For if it came to playing by skill and wits alone, she was as good as, if not better than most—better than some rustic from Dakota, no matter how handsome or slick he might appear.

But what if she had lost her touch? There *had* been the disaster with Cattleman Will, and now . . .

Get a hold of yourself, Lacey. Too much was at stake, her very future, to lose her nerve.

"Aren't you going to deal, Miss Honeycutt?"

DeLacey jumped at the curtness of the question.

"Deal? Of course." Scooping up the scattered cards from the previous game, she pushed them aside and took up the remaining deck as of yet unused, preparing to count out a new hand.

"Aren't you going to reshuffle the deck?"

Ah, now, there was a question she had a ready answer for. At last Mr. Joss McRae did something predictable.

"If you really want me to, Mr. McRae, I will," she replied sweetly. "However, it might change the luck of the cards." Picking up the discarded stack, she slid it beneath the rest of the deck, confident that he would stop her before she had the chance to mix them. Men like Joss McRae always did.

He had better do it soon or else . . .

The knock on the door came at the most convenient

moment. DeLacey let out the deep breath she'd been holding in her lungs when Joss's riveting glare focused on the door rather than what her hands were doing.

"I'll get it, Henry," he announced, rising to his feet so fast she thought for sure he would knock over the table in his haste.

Using a trick her daddy had taught her, she went through the motions of pretending to shuffle the cards, pausing once Joss was out of sight. Glancing up, she discovered the servant, Henry, still standing behind the bar, watching her intently. Did he realize the ruse she employed? Smiling up at him, she hoped to put him at ease. Nosy, cold stiff, he merely stared back at her.

From behind her came the murmur of an excited voice.

"What do you mean she's gone?" That was McRae speaking, and she could tell he wasn't pleased with what he'd been told.

The answer was too faint to hear clearly.

"That's impossible. How could she have gotten off the train without you seeing her?"

Again she couldn't make out the reply.

A strange sensation washed over her, a feeling that it was in her best interest to eavesdrop. Wanting so badly to see who it was Joss spoke with, she instead grew perfectly still, straining to listen to the private conversation.

"Damn it, Jackson. It's important you find her. She has to be somewhere on this train. Did you check with the conductor and get her name?"

Memories of the poker game in St. Louis and how she had seen Joss in the station, mistaking him for one of Cattleman Will's henchmen, crowded her thoughts. Could he be looking for her? Not likely. If that were the case he knew exactly where she was—right here with him in his private car.

"Are you sure, Jackson?"

A chill rushed through her igniting the feeling that McRae had turned to stare at her, but then she couldn't be certain for suddenly he was standing behind her, so close that the heat of his male presence permeated the back of her velvet dress. Glancing up, she found him leaning over her, his face just inches from hers. A foxlike expression that was meant to pass as a smile creased his handsome face, setting her nerves on pinpricks and her heart to racing like a cattle stampede.

"Sorry for the interruption, Miss Honeycutt. Now, where were we? Ah, yes, I believe you were about to shuffle the cards and deal." Hard and unrelenting, his hand closed over her bare shoulder.

An unexpected thrill mixed with apprehension gushed through her.

"Shuffle and deal, Miss Honeycutt, " he instructed when she failed to move.

Everything she'd ever learned about the art of gambling vacated her brain like wharf rats deserting a sinking ship. Clumsily her hands did as they were told, riffling the cards and straightening them, once, twice. What was she doing? By actually shuffling the cards she had ruined the run, and now . . . now . . .

Her hands shook so hard she didn't dare deal them.

"Perhaps you were right, Mr. McRae, we should postpone this game to a better time." Popping up like a cork, she dropped the deck on the table.

Inching across the line of her neck, his fingers paused on her collarbone, pushing her back down into her chair. "Sit, Miss Honeycutt, and deal the cards."

Fear lodged in her throat, as unpleasant as if she had swallowed a fish bone. Joss McRae was onto her scheme. This time she had gotten herself into a hell of a pickle the likes of which she would never escape.

Then she smiled slyly. Getting out of this might not be as difficult as one might think. All she had to do was keep calm, use her head and all of her skills—and every ounce of femininity she possessed. This time her natural instincts and preparedness for just such an incident wouldn't fail her.

Amazing. Of all the blind luck. He had plotted and planned to get the future Mrs. Silas Abrams in his grasp, and here she had simply waltzed into his private car and sat herself down as pretty as you please.

According to Randall Jackson, who he had just spoken to, the woman he sought was none other than the daughter of the famous King Honeycutt. Now, why would such a fine-looking, capable female choose to become a mail-order bride? And why had she been dressed earlier like some mousy spinster? Only one possibility came to mind. Desperation. DeLacey Honeycutt was running from something or somebody. Somehow he would use that knowledge to his best advantage.

Raking in the cards dealt him, Joss stared at deLacey across the table, watching as she arranged her hand to her satisfaction, wondering if Silas Abrams had any inkling of the kind of wife he would be getting for his efforts. Oddly enough a spurt of hot, angry resentment rocketed through him. The thought of Abrams putting his grimy paws on something as pretty as deLacey Honeycutt . . . well, it just didn't seem right, even if she was an underhanded little schemer. Nobody deserved the likes of Silas Abrams.

His fist curled about his cards, bending them.

DeLacey shot him a suspicious look, as if she thought he was attempting to mark the deck.

Hell, he hadn't even taken a look at them yet.

Relaxing his grip, he glanced at his cards, noting the bobtail straight. An eight or a queen would give him a hand tough to beat. Once more he lifted his gaze to study the cool countenance of his opponent. Could she best him? If given the opportunity he had a sneaking suspicion she would do her damnest to beat him.

Hit hard, heavy, and ruthless. That was the only way to keep the odds in his favor. DeLacey Honeycutt must be forced into a corner that gave her no choice except to do what he told her to do. Money, his endless supply and her lack of it, would be the key to his success.

Fingering his cash, he tossed his bet into the pot. A slow grin widened his mouth as he glanced down at the tidy stack of bills beside her left arm resting on the table.

"Five hundred to you, Miss Honeycutt."

Would she match it, or would she fold? Her hands didn't twitch, her face as impassive as the hangman's watch at high noon and just as deadly. Then her eyes, flashing and incorruptible as blue flame, swept over him, meeting his challenge with one of her own.

"I'll see your bet, sir, and raise you another five hundred."

He had to admire her bulldog determination, a trait worthy of a McRae. The lady had her fair share of guts, but she also had a hell of a fine knack for bluffing. There was no way she was going to outplay him, not unless she had a couple of aces tucked up her sleeve. Still smiling, he matched her wager and her arrogance, thoroughly enjoying the competition and the inevitability of winning.

When she folded her hand and laid it aside, retrieving the deck to deal him the one card he asked for, he thought nothing of her actions. One card. Did she surmise that he drew to a straight or a flush? Yet she never flinched. Dividing her own cards, she pushed away her discards and replaced them. Then without looking at them, she relaxed her arm on the table, her other hand clutching the edge, her fingers long and tapered.

Even then he found nothing that unusual about her actions. All gamblers had their quirks and rituals when it came to the final showdown, especially when the stakes were high. Some did as he did, squeezing out each card, searching for, divining the one he needed to be there. Others, like deLacey, waited until the last moment when the bet was to them before confirming their hand.

Slowly he revealed his last card. Holding steady, he relaxed. The queen of hearts. He'd gotten what he needed.

"Your bet, Mr. McRae."

When he looked up she was staring at him, her oval face reminiscent of the royal lady in his cards, her eyes as wide and pristine as the rolling carpet of wild blue sage framed in the window beside them. She was so breathtakingly desirable, he wanted to toss down his hand and forget all about the game—concentrate instead on her lips, full and pouty, the soft contour of her neck, the swell of her breasts revealed by the low neckline of her gown, the sweet smell of her perfume that suddenly seemed to fill the air and every nook and cranny of his brain.

Mentally, he shook himself. That was exactly what the little minx wanted him to do, wasn't it? Fall victim to her alluring charms so completely that he wouldn't notice, or if he did, he wouldn't care that her left hand was nowhere to be seen.

Just what was she up to? Cheating, perhaps? A smile spread across his face. *Ah, deLacey, honey, you just made your first big mistake.* Little did she know it, but she played right into his hands.

As fast as a striking rattler, he lunged across the table, manacling her slender wrist with fingers used to roping and wrangling a thousand pounds of angry steer. She struggled, admirably so, but he held tight, squeezing, her pulse wild and erratic beneath his thumb.

"Show me your cards, Miss Honeycutt," he demanded.

"Take your hand off of me."

If not for the thundering palpitations in her wrist he would have been fooled by her outward show of calm defiance. He might even have had his doubts about winning a battle of wills with her, but in a war of physical strength, she was no match.

Applying more pressure, he saw her grimace with pain, and though it brought satisfaction, it gave him no pleasure. Finally, she gave in. With a whimper her fingers jerked open, and she dropped her cards on the table.

Three of them. Just three, not five as there should have been. Wordlessly he spread them out to make sure, then checked her discards—three there also, which meant she had only dealt herself one from the deck. Anger shot through him at her flagrant attempt to cheat him.

"Where are your other cards?"

"I don't know what you're talking about," she insisted in a harsh, frightened outburst. Once more she took up her struggle, her free hand reappearing, empty, clawing at his merciless grip.

Standing, he forced her to rise with him. Then he skirted

the table until he towered over her, a mountain of determination to her spitfire resistance. Encircling her waist, he
pushed her down on the table to keep her from escaping,
while he searched for evidence of her cheating. Breasts, full
and soft, pressed against his heaving chest, melting his
resolve into a puddle of raging desire.

Open in protest, her mouth demanded kissing in the worst
way. Closing his eyes, he angled his face. A hairsbreadth
away he checked himself.

No. He wouldn't allow her to wiggle out of this by using
her most persuasive female charms. Many men had been
gunned down for doing less than she had done to him. At the
very least, she deserved to have her cage rattled a bit.
Reaching down, he jerked up the hem of her skirt, revealing
the length of her shapely left leg from knee to ankle.

"W-W-What do you think you're doing?" she demanded
in a strangled whisper, her gaze casting about as wildly as
her thoughts must be at the moment.

"I should have you arrested."

Her brows worked with concern, but her reaction wasn't
nearly enough.

"Or we could always go find Daddy and tell him what his
little girl has been up to," he threatened.

"No, you can't do that," she choked.

Now, that was a halfway decent response. Chances were
Daddy was nowhere around. Still he wanted more from her,
wanted her so scared she would be willing to agree to his
terms no matter how she felt about them or him.

"Better yet, Miss Honeycutt, I'm willing to settle this
between us here and now." Suggestively his hand slid
further up her leg. "Nobody will ever attempt to cheat me
and get away with it." *Not even Silas Abrams,* he vowed
inwardly.

Her struggle became one of desperation. Kicking out, she
caught him on the shin with the hard toe of her shoe. Pain
flared, igniting his determination into full-blown wrath. Just
how many besotted fools had the little witch cheated and
laughed at afterwards. Dozens, maybe more? Well, this time
she had met her match.

Seeking evidence, his hand continued its search, her soft flesh beneath the silk stocking so warm to the touch, he found it impossible to squelch the desire flooding through him. Screaming and twisting, she curved the fingers of her free hand into talons to tear at his face and neck. Then he found what he was looking for just above her lace garter so close to her woman's treasure his fingers ached to continue their climb. It took all of his willpower to hold himself in check.

Her profiled face was pale, her eyes squeezed so tightly shut he could barely make out the moisture spiking her long, thick lashes. Tears of defeat and fear. Fear of what would happen to her, as if she'd been through it all before. Even if he had the power and the motive, he knew then he would never take such unfair advantage of a woman, not even if she deserved it.

Nonetheless he needed her cooperation, and he harbored no gallantry about forcing her to help him get even with Silas Abrams. Grasping the small device that held several cards to match the "new" deck she had insisted they use, he wrenched it free from her leg. Then he straightened up, his breathing still harsh and raspy, his resolve so shaken that he had to tear his gaze away from the sight of her shapely thigh still exposed to his view.

She gasped, her hand groping to push down her skirt, her gaze filled with suspicious disbelief as it darted to the damning evidence he held, then back to his face. "What are you going to do now?"

Good question. What should he do? Politely ask her for her help? Demand it? This wasn't going at all the way he'd planned it. Releasing her, he stepped back, needing the time and space to make up his mind.

DeLacey showed no such qualms or hesitation. Jumping up from the table, she darted for the exit. He easily outdistanced her, trapping her against the door with the length of his wide body, the breadth of his solid arms.

"Let me go," she pleaded softly, one hand stealing up the front of his shirt, suggestively, so stirring, her lips opening, offering an unspoken bargain. But just how far was she willing to go? Not likely as far as he had in mind.

Make a pact with the devil and expect to honor it. That was the lesson he intended to teach her. Twisting his head, he laid claim to her parted lips.

But the lesson was his to learn. All he'd ever imagined or known a woman to be, deLacey was more. So open at first in the game she played, thinking she had control of the situation, but then when the kiss became serious, deepening, his tongue slipping into her mouth, soft and untried, she stiffened in his arms, attempting to wiggle away.

God help him—and her. Her show of innocence and resistance made him want her that much more.

Dragging her forward, his hand moved down her spine, cupping the feminine roundness of her bottom that fit so well into his palm. Through the rising fog in his brain he heard the train's whistle blow, two short blasts announcing their arrival at the first stop on the long journey home as the wheels beneath the flooring began to slow down. Sensing her sudden alertness, he knew the event was important to her. Important enough to agree to help him?

"Please, Mr. McRae, I'll do anything if you'll just let me go."

Pulling back, he glanced down at her upturned face. As prettily as the promise was made, he knew she didn't mean it. DeLacey Honeycutt was a consummate liar and a desperate one at that. And yet he wanted to believe her.

Pushing himself away, he searched for the right words to convince her to help him. Then when he turned back around, determined to just lay the story out to her, he came to a sudden halt.

Though she hadn't moved from her position at the door, in her hand she held a derringer, small yet deadly, aimed directly at his heart.

Taking a step toward her, he felt the anger billow up inside of him, as much for his gullibility as with her.

"I wouldn't do that if I were you, Mr. McRae."

The click of the hammer being drawn back sounded like thunder. Then the tension was shattered by the blast of the train's whistle as the locomotive came to a standstill, wheezing and puffing in protest. He couldn't allow her to get off the train. How would he ever find her again?

"You'll be sorry if you try and stop me," she warned as if she'd read his thoughts, groping behind her back for the door handle.

Helplessly he watched her slip away, slamming the door in his face.

"Damn." Gathering up his Stetson and holster from the hat rack, he glanced about the room. That's when he noticed the top of the game table. It was empty except for the scattered pack of playing cards she had brought with her.

Not only had the little witch managed to slip through his fingers, but she had stolen his money. All of it. Ten thousand dollars as well as his deck of gilded cards. And he hadn't even suspected.

He rushed to the door, his pistol already cradled in the palm of his hand.

"Mr. McRae, sir." Henry stood calmly in his way.

"You tell the conductor the train is delayed until I get back."

"But, Mr. McRae."

"*Tell* him, Henry. I'll have his job and yours, too, if he doesn't obey."

With that he stormed out of the Pullman. There on the platform he stared out into the teeming Missouri town and caught a glimpse of burgundy velvet slip behind a distant building. He had a sneaking suspicion where she might be headed. If he was right, deLacey Honeycutt was in for one hell of a surprise when she got there.

CHAPTER 3

Daddy had always said that money slips through butterfingers. This axiom took on a special meaning as deLacey raced away from the train and the tiny shack that served as the depot. Just as she tore down the platform stairs outside the private car a hundred-dollar bill escaped the wad she had hastily stuffed into the front of her gown, to fly beneath the great iron wheels, irretrievable and no doubt bound to make its finder's day a memorable one. Then as she rounded the first street corner another greenback fluttered to the ground. This time she paused long enough to recoup her loss.

Ill-gotten gains.

Tucking the bill back into her cleavage along with the others, she gathered up her purse, tossing the derringer into its depths. A twinge of guilt pricked at her conscience. Dear Lord, she had stolen money—robbery at gunpoint! If her calculations were right, there had to be several hundred, maybe even a thousand dollars or more. And just to spite Mr. High-and-Mighty McRae she had also pilfered the pack of gilded cards he had taken such pride in.

What had gotten into her? What terrible notion had possessed her to do something so . . . so completely out of character? It was one thing to relieve a well-deserving gentleman of a little ready cash with the skill and talent acquired over a lifetime, even if it was considered cheating. In her opinion, there was a certain self-respect and even pride in doing so, but to just snatch it up, to wave a gun in someone's face, to revel in a vulgar crime of outright thievery . . .

How could she have stooped so low?

But she had, and now there was no going back. If he got his hands on her Joss McRae would never let her off easily. Of that she had no doubt. Oh, he would take back his money, take it back with vengeance, but then he would demand . . .

DeLacey swallowed so hard it pained her. Not really sure just what he would extort from her, instinct told her he wanted something, all right—something more than she dared give.

Breathing hard, she paused at a cross street to get her bearing. Hammons, Missouri, was one of those little river towns like so many she had been to as a child with her daddy. There was an establishment only a few blocks away, Sadie's, if her memory served her, where the Honeycutt name would carry weight and gain her entrance and safe haven, at least for a little while. At least until the train rolled away taking Joss McRae with it. She was banking on it.

And the money she had taken? If the truth be known, she needed it desperately. Besides, feeling guilty wouldn't exonerate her, wouldn't change the facts. And it wouldn't feed her. The best she could do was to swear that she would never repeat such an outrageous act.

Never again would she allow a man like Joss McRae, with his handsome face and devastating smile, to confuse her. And that is what he had done—no doubt on purpose—totally flustered her until she'd not been able to think straight. His hand skimming up her leg had been like liquid fire evoking not only fear but excitement. And his mouth—she could still feel the potency of his kiss, her own lagging willpower that had seemed to seep from every pore in her body until she had wanted him never to stop.

Yes, Joss McRae had no one to blame for his losses except himself.

In the distance the melodic tinkling of a piano caught her attention. Lacey sighed with relief. The song was familiar, one often played in gaming houses by players who all seemed to have the same repertoire, more effective than a signpost pointing the way to Sadie's. She followed the sound until she stood in front of the swinging half doors staring into the smoky, well-lit interior of the saloon.

Somehow she'd thought it would look different. Her memory of Sadie Farrell was of a soft-spoken woman who relished pastel watered silks over the gaudy sateens that the females on the other side of the door flounced about in among the clientele, men who looked to be dirt farmers and store clerks for the most part. She also remembered elegant gaming tables covered with soft green felt manned by professionals like her father, not the battered furniture and has-been dealers she saw now.

Her plans now hinged on Sadie Farrell's ability to help, and in this it seemed she may have miscalculated. She could only hope the woman's memory was better than her own, and that she would be willing to give her sanctuary, even temporarily.

Knocking the dust from the hem of her burgundy velvet gown, deLacey also straightened her feather-bedecked hair as best she could. Then she stepped forward, chin lifted, to be met by the piercing looks of the women and the curious ones of the men. She wished then that she'd had time to change into her drabber clothes in case Joss McRae came looking for her.

But surely he wouldn't do that over a few measly hundred dollars and a pack of playing cards.

"If it's the opera house yer lookin' for, dearie, you ain't found it."

DeLacy ignored the smirks and laughter that followed the snide remark. The woman who spoke was most likely in her fifties, her eyes were hard and assessing.

"I'm not looking for the opera house, but for Miss Sadie Farrell."

"And what would you be wantin' with Miss Sadie?

Surely you're not another one of them desperate but delicate souls wantin' a handout.''

"No," deLacey replied, although "desperate" did describe her situation quite accurately. "Tell her . . ." She thought for a moment. "Tell her King Honeycutt sent me."

The woman instantly straightened, her tired eyes taking on an interest and a youthfulness that had not been there before. "Kingston? Why that sly old fox." She tittered like a girl. "Is he back in town?"

"Sadie?" deLacy asked, surprised at how different the woman looked. "Don't you remember me? I'm deLacey. Kingston's daughter."

"Lacey? Little Lacey?" Sadie rose from her seat and held one aged hand at breast level indicating a size.

True. That was about how tall she had been the last time she and her daddy had been to Hammons. She had been an innocent, wide-eyed child. And Sadie? Well, she had been a beautiful, worldly woman. They both had changed—so very much, it seemed.

She smiled and nodded. And then Sadie's arms that smelled of talcum powder were about her, drawing her close.

"Sadie," she whispered. "I need your help."

The older woman leaned back to study her face. "You're in trouble, child?"

DeLacey nodded.

"And I bet you need a place to stay for a little while." Her brows knitted knowingly but there was no animosity, no accusation, in her look.

Again deLacey dipped her head.

A deep sigh issued from the woman's brightly painted lips. "There are only a couple of people in this world I could never say no to. One of them was your father. Is it legal trouble, Lacey? If it is . . ." she trailed off somewhat doubtfully.

DeLacey gave the notion serious consideration. No, Joss McRae would never go to the law—that was the kind of arrogance he possessed. If he wanted her, he would come looking for her on his own. Confidently she shook her head.

"It's not the law, Sadie. Just a persistent man who simply won't accept no for an answer."

"Ah, I know the type, and they're never the ones you wish would be so determined, are they?" Sadie said, a touch of nostalgia in her voice. "Come. There's an empty room at the end of the hallway. Not much bigger than a cracker barrel, but it's clean . . . and private." Her arm still about deLacey, she led her toward the stairs off to one side. Once they reached the top landing, Sadie faced the crowd below. "If anyone comes snoopin' about lookin' for this poor child, none of you has seen her."

There was a polite murmur of agreement.

"And for your cooperation a round of drinks on the house."

Now, that was met with enthusiasm. She hoped it was enough to assure her safety if Joss should show up asking questions.

No more or less than promised, the tiny room was barely large enough to accommodate the bed, dresser, and washstand, but deLacey was only too glad to have it. Sinking down upon the sagging mattress, she closed her eyes and, allowing her chin to settle on her chest, she sighed her relief. She was tired, so very exhausted from the ordeal of the last few days.

"There's so many questions I have for ya, child, but git some rest first, and then we'll talk."

"Yes, Sadie, thank you. We can talk later," deLacey murmured. Turning, she felt the wad of bills she had hastily stuffed into her cleavage poke against the softness of her breasts. Reaching down, she drew one of them out, and taking up Sadie's hand, she pressed it into the dry, rough palm.

"Now, what's this for?" the older woman inquired with a lift of one penciled brow.

"I'm not looking for a handout."

Unfolding the money, Sadie showed surprise upon seeing how much it was. "I didn't mean what I said downstairs. I would never consider the daughter of King Honeycutt a moocher."

"I know, Sadie." Once again deLacey pressed the woman's hand. "Let's just say this is to help cover your . . . generous gesture with your customers downstairs."

"Your father was always one to buy a round of drinks."

"A Honeycutt tradition, then." DeLacey smiled tiredly, her eyelids drooping over her blue eyes.

"There's a nightie in the dresser if you would like one."

"Thanks, Sadie."

"And clean water in the pitcher."

"I'll keep that in mind."

"You can lock the door after I leave if you want, but nobody's gonna disturb you."

"I'll do that."

The door closed softly. DeLacey's last thought before she drifted off to sleep was that she should really get up and remove her shoes so as to not soil the pretty patchwork quilt upon which she lay. And the money—she must find a safe place to stash it until . . .

Yes, she would see to all of that and more in just a moment.

"A thief, you say. Aboard the train." Lonnie Horton, the sheriff of Hammons, was a likely sort with a comfortable job, not in much of a hurry and definitely unwilling to stir up trouble if he could avoid it. "I'm not sure, Mr. McRae, that the railroad is in my jurisdiction." Pushing back his battered hat, Horton scratched his balding head and gave Joss an unhappy look over his boots propped up on his desk.

Exasperated, Joss pointed out the door toward the depot. "The tracks out there. Are they in town limits or not?"

"Well, yes, sir," the lawman drawled, shifting in his chair. "Once you get past the bluff, technically you're in Hammons, I suppose, but the railroad . . ."

"The train was already beyond the bluff when my money was stolen, Sheriff. I was in Hammons," Joss insisted, "and it's your responsibility to go after the culprit."

A staring match ensued, one Joss had no intention of

conceding. Hell, he had too much at stake—not just the money—to buckle under to some two-bit tin star.

"Did you see which way the suspect went?"

The question was asked perfunctorily, and Joss doubted that the man cared.

"My guess is that the little thief headed to Sadie Farrell's place."

"Sadie?" The sheriff frowned, his expression closing up as tight as a brothel on Sunday morning. "Then you didn't actually see him go in there, did you?"

"No." Joss didn't bother to correct the lawman. "Look, Sheriff, I'm willing to offer a reward—a substantial one."

Ah, yes, the monetary lingo understood by one and all. The sheriff of Hammons would be no exception.

"Can't take no reward, McRae," Horton replied, much to Joss's frustration. "You know that. I'm an officer of the law."

"I'm not offering a reward. Call it a . . . donation to the fair town of Hammons." Joss glanced about the shabby office. "Use it to make some much needed improvements around here."

"Well, I suppose I could check it out." Rising from his chair, he revealed a leather seat worn by constant usage. "You wait here, McRae," he said when Joss attempted to follow him.

"I'll go with you."

"I don't want no trouble."

"There won't be any as long as you do your job."

"How much are you offering?"

Joss sized up his adversary. How much would this man think was a lot? "Five hundred dollars."

It was obviously more than enough.

Adjusting his hat to sit squarely on his head, the sheriff smiled. "Let's go see what Sadie has to say about all of this."

"Get up, girlie. Sadie says ya gotta git out as fast as ya kin."

DeLacey jerked awake at the soft knock, the sound of the

feet in the corridor outside her door, the whispered warning. Stiffening, her heart bucking in her chest like a corralled bronco, she eased up off the bed, gathering up the money that had spilled out of the front of her dress as she had slept, and moved to the door, cracking it open just enough to verify the woman's face—one of Sadie's girls.

"What is it?"

"The sheriff's come snoopin' around. Sadie says you have to get out before . . ." The woman glanced over her shoulder, down the corridor where the sound of booted feet could be heard on the hardwood planking. "Now," she hissed, pushing deLacey back into the room and pulling the door closed, the sound of her footsteps diminishing as she hurried on down the hallway.

Get out? But how? Blinking in the darkness, deLacey glanced about the tiny room, her eyes settling on her purse tossed on the table. Wadding up the money she clutched to her heart, she started to stash it in the handbag, then changed her mind, shoving it deep into her bodice. Then she spied the one small window. She brushed back the bit of curtaining to stare out across the steep slope of the roof's overhang. The darkened street below was quiet except for the solitary clip-clop of a horse moseying along.

Not even the muffled plink of the piano sounded below, or the chatter of Sadie's clientele. Could it be that late already?

She looked around in the gloom, but there was no ticking of a clock. No way for her to confirm the time—nor the extent of the danger.

Then she heard the quiet shuffle of boots right outside her door—much too quiet. As if they hoped to surprise someone. Her pulse darted like a rabbit's.

"Come, now, boys, you know I'd never take in no train robber."

That was Sadie; she recognized the woman's husky, assuring voice. Bless her. She was cool as icehouse sawdust in the middle of July.

Then deLacey frowned. Train robber? A terrible fear shot through her. Could the sheriff be looking for her? Had Joss

McRae really sunk so low as to blow this whole thing so completely out of proportion?

She had to figure out a way to get out of the room before . . . before . . .

Glancing about, her eyes lit once more on the solitary window, and she swallowed so hard she knew for sure that whoever was outside her door must have heard the sound. God help her. The steep rooftop offered the only avenue of escape. Pushing up the window sash as high as it would go, she snatched up her reticule and squeezed through the narrow opening, gasping as her foot slipped on the slick shingles.

Don't look down, Lacey. Just don't look down, and you'll be all right, she told herself as she struggled to regain her balance. *Oh, God,* she prayed, *for once, let me know what I'm talking about.*

"You know, Joss, honey, there's only a couple of men in all the world I could never say no to." Sadie Farrell reached up and twirled the top button of his shirt, giving him one of those looks that better suited a younger woman. "Won't you believe me when I say I'm not hidin' some ol' bank robber?"

Joss stared down at her lined face and saw it as it once had been many years before, etched with the wisdom of hard-learned lessons, perhaps, but nonetheless pretty. Sadie had known him in his traveling days before he had returned to the Dakota Territory to face his past. But more important, she had believed in him—before the cattle ranch, before the railroad stock. Before he had discovered his own self-worth. Smiling wistfully, he chucked her gently under the chin.

"Only a couple, Sadie?" he asked, wondering as in the old days just who that other man might be who claimed the same privileges that he'd once had. More likely, he'd suspected then and still did now, she said the same thing to every male who swaggered through those swinging front doors with a little money to spend. Not that he particularly minded. Hell, Sadie had to survive just like the rest of them. She was doing it the best way she knew how—just as he did.

"Of course, Joss, honey," she purred, her very red lips puckering suggestively.

The suggestion didn't interest him.

"Then step aside and let me look for myself."

Darting a nervous glance at the closed door, the last one in the hallway, the woman shot him a compelling plea then complied, although her restraining hand never released its grip on his arm.

Sorry, Sadie. And he meant it, but he kept his thoughts to himself, brushing past her and through the doorway.

The moment he entered the tiny room, empty and appearing with a first glance to be unused, he knew that the Honeycutt woman had been there. He could smell her. The winsome wildflower perfume she wore filled his nostrils evoking brief flashes of a shapely thigh, breasts as soft as a down-stuffed pillow. Besides, in the middle of the bed, slightly rumpled, lay a single burgundy feather the exact hue of the ones that had adored her silken hair.

Yes, deLacey Honeycutt had come to Sadie, all right, just as he'd suspected. Birds of a feather.

"Where did she go, Sadie?" He glared down at the visibly nervous woman.

"Wh-Who?" she stuttered in denial, her eyes widening with calculated innocence.

Joss wasn't fooled. "DeLacey Honeycutt."

"I thought you said you was lookin' for a train robber, McRae, not some barroom hussy," interjected the sheriff.

Joss turned to the lawman, his hands clenching at his sides. Odd. DeLacey Honeycutt was a conniving bit of baggage, to be sure, but to hear her labeled hussy by some paunch-bellied tin star did something most unpleasant to his insides.

"Your job is to make arrests, Sheriff, not to pass judgment."

Had Joss been anyone else, say some drifter passing through robbed by a nimble-fingered thief, no doubt the sheriff would have then and there escorted him to the edge of town and told him never to return. But he had money, influence, and in his case the law worked differently—to his advantage. He smiled wryly at the irony of it all.

"You failed to mention that you were lookin' for a woman, Mr. McRae." Though he was exaggeratedly polite, the sheriff was clearly livid.

"You failed to ask." Joss made no attempt at civility. He didn't have to. "Since when does gender made a difference when it comes to crime—or rewards?"

Before the sheriff could reply the tension was cut by a shriek, almost mouselike but definitely human and female.

Joss looked back into the room, noting the wide-open window for the first time, and knew exactly how the little witch had managed to elude him. He muttered a curse at his own stupidity as he grabbed up a lantern, lighting it on his way back to the window. That woman was like some fleet-footed feline who always landed on her . . .

Pretty little ass.

Amusement parted his lips, laughter erupting from the pit of his belly when he spied her. Halfway down the sloping roof deLacey Honeycutt sat craning to peer over the eaves only a few feet away. Her arms and legs were flung about a protruding stovepipe, her purse swinging like a pendulum from her elbow; her face, although he couldn't see much of it, was mashed against the metal as well.

"Why, Miss Honeycutt, whatever are you doing out there?" he called to her, still chuckling as he indolently rested his elbows on the window sill. The lantern in his hand cast its light in a great circle on the rooftop, highlighting the woman, accenting her predicament.

She looked back at him, her incredibly blue eyes leveling on him with an intensity that heated his blood and sent it surging in his veins. A wide smudge streaked her cheek where it had been pressed against the pipe, but even so she was incredibly pretty. And although there was fear etched in her gaze, it sparked with unwavering indignation.

"Checking for leaks," she said with a surprising amount of spunk considering her situation. "Care to join me, Mr. McRae?"

She reminded him of a storm-battered bantam. Her

colorful maroon plumage was now disheveled, flapping about her head in the breeze. She appeared ready to do battle, no doubt to the death—and yet she looked so . . . comical.

"No, thank you." Joss laughed, amused by her audacity. His mirth served only to ruffle her more.

Sputtering, she scrambled to her knees, the dangling purse tripping her as she attempted to push herself up from her precarious perch. Losing her footing, she slid to the next row of shingles, almost out of the circle of light, with a loud thump. Now only her arms clung to the stovepipe, her pumping feet unable to gain traction on the slick rooftop.

"DeLacey?" Recognizing the danger, Joss straightened, all amusement gone. "Don't struggle." He turned, pressing the lantern into Sadie's hand. Then in his haste to hoist himself on the ledge he bumped his head on the bottom of the window sash. "Damn."

"Stay away from me." Hearing him curse, probably she thought he swore at her.

But he was already flat on his stomach stretched across the slanting roof, the fingers of one hand inching forward until they encircled one of her wrists, about which the strings of her purse were wrapped.

"Let go, honey, I have you."

"Why? So you can send me plunging to certain death?" Glancing up at him, she narrowed her eyes to mere slits, her fingers clutching the stovepipe even harder.

"No, you little fool. So I can pull you to safety." He felt himself slip.

"Joss, be careful!" he heard Sadie cry behind him.

With his free hand he clung to the roof peak. "Damn it, woman, do as I tell you before it's too late."

Stubborn minx that she was, she refused to listen. Instead he was forced to wait until her fingers could no longer maintain their grip. With a lurch she slid another few inches, the suddenness putting extra strain on Joss's hand. Losing his grip on her wrist, he managed to hang on to the twisted cord strings of her silly beaded handbag, the only sturdy part of it.

"My purse!" Staring up at him in accusation, there was no doubt in his mind that she thought he intended simply to take the bag and let her go.

Not that the thought hadn't crossed his mind, for it seemed they were indeed stuck, the purse string digging excruciatingly into his flesh. In order to reel her in he needed his other hand, the one holding on to the peak of the roof. If he let go of it, chances were they would both plunge to their deaths.

Well, probably not their deaths. They were only on the first-story roof—but let her think what she would. It could be to his advantage if she assumed his heroics would save her life.

"DeLacey, grab on to me with your other hand."

Valiantly she tried. No complaints, no typical female whining. Amazing. He admired her courage. But then her struggle ceased.

"I can't," she declared in a flat voice. "Just let go of me and be done with it."

Noble of her. But then a strange suspicion wormed its way into his thoughts, squelching his sense of chivalry. Noble or incredibly conniving? Perhaps it was her game plan all along to fool him into letting her escape.

An overwhelming need to win, to show her he was no fool, brushed aside all thoughts of the risks involved. If she was so willing to gamble, then so was he. The stakes were incredibly high, but wasn't that what made it worthwhile? And it was not just the ten thousand dollars she had stashed somewhere on her that spurred him into action.

Releasing his grip on the roof peak, he reached down with his free hand, grasped her wrist, and began pulling her up.

"No, let me go," she protested. "Don't you see . . ."

"Let you go? Not on your life, lady." Inch by inch he dragged her toward him. Odd that she clung so tightly when at last she could reach him, but he put that down to another not so convincing display of her acting ability.

Once he had her secure, straddling the roof peak facing him, his wide body between hers and the window, he encompassed her slender shoulders in his large, work-roughened hands and shook her.

"Where's my money?" he demanded.

"I don't know what you're talking about." She gathered up her purse by its strings and swung it at him, hitting him across the shoulder. And again. This time it glanced off, catching him on the collarbone. It was as if she vented all of her frustrations on him.

The blows didn't hurt him, although the glass beads on the handbag scratched the tender flesh of his neck, the side of his face.

Blast her vicious hide. Reaching out, he snatched the purse out of her hand and considered tossing it to the ground. It would serve her right.

"Is that why you saved me?" she cried, her breasts heaving as she tried in vain to retrieve her property that he held high above her head. "To get back your precious money? You could have just as well let me fall and plucked it undamaged out of the street below."

The admission of guilt was no more out of her mouth than she clamped her teeth together and reddened with embarrassment.

"So you admit you took it." Joss eyed her with satisfaction as he stuffed her purse under his arm. "Sheriff, did you hear Miss Honeycutt's confession?" he called over his shoulder.

A look of panic crossed her face, her pretty mouth working as she debated her limited options. He realized then that she was capable of almost anything, even something as foolish as . . .

Joss took no chances. He grabbed her by the arm, and ignoring her protests and well-aimed fist, dragged her toward the window. Then he shoved her through the opening as if he were stuffing a cork into a bottle.

"Lacey, child, you never told me you robbed a train." Sadie's softly spoken accusation sliced through the silent uneasiness of the tiny room and wafted out to the rooftop.

"I didn't, Sadie," deLacey whispered back, shooting

Joss a glare of hatred as he slid through the window and joined them. "He's the one who should be arrested."

"Search her, Sheriff. You'll find my money on her." Remembering he had her purse, he took it from under his arm and jerked it open. Sticking his hand in blindly he rummaged around and came up with the evidence he was looking for, at least some of it.

"These are mine." He waved under her nose the deck of ornate playing cards Teddy Roosevelt had given him, then tossed them on the table beside the bed. Again he delved into the bag, his hand molding about and recognizing the derringer she had pointed at him with deadly intent. "And this," he announced, "is what she used to hold me up."

"That peashooter?" The sheriff didn't conceal the mirth in his voice.

Joss glanced down at the weapon in his hand. He had to admit it did look awfully small. Frowning, he leveled an assessing gaze on deLacey. For that matter, she looked awfully small, too. Humiliation rose up inside of him.

Tossing down the gun and the empty purse onto the bed, he took a step toward deLacey. Regardless of her size, she had still stolen ten thousand dollars from him, and he had a good idea just where she'd stashed the money. He eyed her chest, which appeared fuller than he remembered.

"If you won't search her, Sheriff, then I will." Encircling her tiny waist, he was surprised when she went limp in his arms, issuing him a dare to be so bold, even as his hand slid along the front of her dress.

"Now, just a minute, McRae," stammered the lawman.

Sadie was not so hesitant. "Joss McRae, just what do you think you're doin'?" she cried, flying forward to slap at his probing hand as if he were an errant child.

This wasn't going at all as it should. Somehow deLacey Honeycutt, conniving baggage that she was, had managed to get them all on her side. Staring down at her upturned face, he could see the arrogance, the mute satisfaction etched in the sensual curve of her lips, the awareness of exactly what was going on in the glint in her blue eyes.

She was making him look the fool and was enjoying every minute of his disgrace.

He wouldn't let her get away with it.

Forcefully he shoved her down on the bed. The edge of her skirts flipping up, revealing the expensive lace on the hem of her petticoats and one shapely calf. With a cry of modesty that he knew was as much an act as all of the rest of it, she brushed it down, giving him a challenging look. Oh, yes, she thought she'd bested him for she banked on him being a gentleman.

Once again Miss Honeycutt miscalculated. No McRae had ever claimed to be a man of honor, including himself, and he wasn't about to start now.

As fast as lightning, he slid his hand into her cleavage and came up with the hastily balled wad of bills.

"Here," he said, tossing the money onto the bed in front of where the sheriff stood. Rising up, he didn't relinquish his hold on her arm. "You'll find it's almost ten thousand dollars."

"DeLacey," Sadie gasped, a look of pure horror crossing her lined face. "That's a fortune."

The sheriff scooped up the evidence and carefully counted it. "Can you prove this is yours?" he demanded of Joss.

"Honestly, Sheriff. How else would a woman like her have gotten her hands on so much if she'd not stolen it?"

The sheriff sighed his agreement. "Miss Honeycutt, you're under arrest." Stepping forward, he snapped a pair of handcuffs about her delicate wrists and led her out of the room.

Joss watched her go, her back stiff and proud, her chin raised in arrogance. Little bitch. She didn't even glance over her shoulder to plead with him for a reprieve.

Even so, he knew she had to be praying for one. What would her reaction be if he offered it to her? Would she concede to his demands? There was a good chance she might not. But there was just as good a chance she might.

CHAPTER 4

Being arrested was horrible. To be led away like some hardened criminal to a fate she could only imagine, down the stairs to the saloon below, out into the street where people stopped to gawk and point and decide for themselves just what she had been accused of was the worst thing that had ever happened to deLacey. Stripped of her pride. Stripped of all dignity. And now it seemed she was to be stripped of what little remained, including her meager possessions.

Dear God, what was going to happen to her?

Fear manifested itself in the tears that gathered in her sky blue eyes. Fighting down the urge to cry, to turn around and plead with that despicable Joss McRae to give her a second chance, she instead held herself erect. She looked neither left nor right, not at the sheriff who had clamped the cold metal cuffs about her wrists, nor at Sadie—poor, dear Sadie—even when the woman touched her arm, the tears she so wanted to shed herself glistening in the older woman's eyes.

"I'll do what I can for ya, Lacey. I promise."

But there was very little Sadie could do for her. Even less she could do for herself except refuse to allow Joss McRae to see that he had her almost to the point of compromising herself to get out of this scrape.

Dear God, if just one more time You'll only see fit to provide me with a way out, I swear . . . But what could she promise that would make the heavens sit up and take notice of her? *I swear I'll give up cheating, I'll . . . I'll give up gambling altogether—forever.* Surely that would be sacrifice enough. At the moment she could think of nothing more noble.

Reaching the far side of the street, she stumbled when the sheriff pushed her a bit gruffly up the steps to the plank sidewalk in front of his office.

"Best pick up yer feet, miss," he mumbled belatedly.

Over her shoulder deLacey shot him a belligerent look. To her surprise she saw him level an equally intense glower on Joss, who was keeping pace with them. Could it be that the lawman didn't care for McRae any more than she did?

Sensing Joss's eyes gravitate to her, she glanced away, aware that he was assessing her in turn. He did that a lot, it seemed, and she didn't like it one bit. He had his money back, and his way—she was under arrest. What more could he possibly expect from her?

A lot more. A whole lot more, some inner voice whispered. The prospect made her very uncomfortable indeed.

But there were some extremes even *she* wasn't willing to go to in order to save herself from imprisonment. Besides, she doubted that God intended that she use her femininity for such a purpose. If He expected her to give up her sole means of making a living, surely He would balk at her taking up another, much older profession.

Once inside the sheriff's office, the door closed on the curious faces of the citizens of Hammons. Escorted to a cell behind another set of barred doors, she found herself locked inside, still handcuffed—and forgotten.

"Sheriff," she implored to his retreating back.

"Sit tight, Miss Honeycutt," the crotchety old lawman growled, "and keep yer mouth shut, will ya? And I'll see what I can do for ya. Believe me, miss, I don't want ya here

any more than you want to be here. A woman in my jail just
don't sit right with me.'' He turned to leave.

"But, Sheriff."

This time his irritation was evident in the matter in which
he pivoted to confront her.

Without a word she stuck her still manacled hands
through the bars palms up in a silent plea to be unfettered.
Was that so much to ask?

The keys jingled when he unhooked them from the belt
loop on his pants. No apology, no words of encouragement
as he released the cuffs from her wrists and turned away
once more.

"Thank you, Sheriff."

But he ignored her words of gratitude, slamming the door
to the cell block area behind him.

Unsure what to do, deLacey inspected her prison and was
appalled by what she found. There was a bed, more of a cot
with a dirty blanket tossed over it. She could swear that she
saw a cockroach slither beneath one corner. Under the bed
was a chamber pot. Most disgusting and not very private
considering that there were two more cells, one on each side
of hers, that fortunately were empty at the moment. In the
far corner was a spittoon, black stains darkening the
tarnished brass and the floor all around it—the most
revolting thing she had ever seen or smelled.

The tears that she had held in check for so long welled in
her eyes and slipped from the corners, but even though she
couldn't control them she kept silent. She would not break
down and allow them to hear her weeping with the despair
that clawed at her insides. Nor could she bring herself even
to sit down on the cot though her calves and knees were
bruised and sore from her near fatal escapade on the roof. So
she huddled by the cell door and waited, wondering just
how long she would have to stand there. However long
would be a lifetime in her opinion. But the waiting didn't
frighten her as much as what would surely come after it.

"I cain't keep her here, Mr. McRae," the sheriff announced, tossing the cuffs and keys on the empty surface of

his desk and dropping down into his chair with a familiar, insolent air. "As soon as I have to arrest some rowdies or drunkards I couldn't leave her back there with them. Wouldn't be decent, or very peaceful."

"What are you suggesting, Sheriff?" Joss perched on the edge of the desk as if he had every right to do so, and folding his arms over his chest, frowned down at the uncooperative lawman.

"You got yer money back. Let it drop."

Joss shook his head.

"Then surely there's something the little lady can do to smooth your ruffled feathers," the sheriff said in exasperation.

The implication of the man's statement was only too obvious, and even if he didn't realize it, he had just played right into Joss's corner. Joss frowned as if he were thinking about it, and then he agreed with a great show of reluctance.

"I suppose I could talk to her."

"Good." Without bothering to rise, the sheriff stretched across his desk, retrieved the set of keys, and tossed them up to Joss. "I just don't want no screamin' and yellin', ya hear me, McRae?"

It seemed barbaric to think that a man of the law would give license to another to take advantage of a prisoner, especially a female one. Joss's fist curled about the key ring so tightly that it cut painfully into the palm of his hand. What if he had been someone else, some unscrupulous bastard more than willing to take advantage of the sheriff's not-so-subtle offer? What would have happened to deLacey then? Would she have been raped and then turned loose, penniless, with nothing but the clothes on her back?

Then it struck him. Here he was defending the little witch and her honor—which he doubted she possessed. He should be only too happy that the sheriff gave him the opportunity to "talk" to the Honeycutt woman alone and undisturbed. It saved him a lot of time and trouble. Now he could go in and tell her just what he wanted her to do—to help him with his plans to trap Silas Abrams—in exchange for her freedom, no one else the wiser.

But what if she refused to cooperate? The sudden thought stopped him in his tracks, for he didn't put it past her to do just that. He didn't dare leave her here, even overnight, not even to give her time to stew over her dilemma and her only option. He didn't trust the sheriff to protect her for even a few hours.

She would have to be agreeable from the start. He suspected that wouldn't be an easy task to accomplish, not with the feisty . . . greedy . . . Miss deLacey Honeycutt. Then he smiled to himself. Money was the language she understood, and he spoke it fluently.

DeLacey had been anxiously watching the outer door of the room that housed her cell and two others for so long her eyes began to blur. She refused to acknowledge that it might be tears taking control again. No, her relentless vigilance had just tired her vision, that's all. She blinked rapidly several times, but the clearing of her sight was negligible.

Then, unexpectedly, the door handle turned, and she jumped, scooting backward to the rear of the cell, her palms flat against the cold stone wall. Sniffing, she wiped her face in the crook of her arm to erase all signs of her distress. At least she hoped that she did.

To her surprise it wasn't the sheriff who entered, but Joss McRae himself. There in the austere surroundings of blank white walls and dark bars, he seemed so much taller, his shoulders much broader, his demeanor more . . . threatening than she'd remembered. Once he closed the outer door, he stood there, just on the other side of the bars of her cell, staring at her in cold-eyed silence, the only sound the clank of the ring of keys he spun round and round in his hand.

Staring back—for what else did she dare do?—she swallowed hard and waited, still huddled against the far wall. She wished for all the world that she could simply melt into the surface that pressed against her spine and held her prisoner. She was only too glad the bars were between them.

He edged toward her, and if she could have she would have matched his steps in retreat, but there was nowhere for her to go.

"The sheriff suggested that we work something out between us." The statement didn't really sound sinister, yet there was something very frightening about the way he said it.

Her eyes darted left, then right, looking for a way to escape even when she knew no path would suddenly open up to her. Glancing back, she conquered her show of fear, at least outwardly. Work something out? What did he mean by that? Clamping her mouth into a thin, determined line, she had a pretty good idea just what it was he considered his for the asking.

"I'd much rather take my chances with the law." How steady and confident her voice sounded although her insides were quivering.

He frowned as if her declaration had struck a sensitive chord, but then he laughed. It didn't sound like humor, more like a short, derisive bark. "I think you'll find that's not your best course of action, Lacey, darlin'."

It was the first time he had called her by the shortened version of her given name. How familiar it sounded, yet oddly enough a thrill rushed through her at the way his deep, masculine timbre projected the syllables, drawling out the "darlin'" that followed.

"My best course of action is whatever I see fit to do." As much as she wanted to, she couldn't bring herself to call him Joss and tag it with a derogatory "dear."

"Face it, honey." He made a sweeping study of their surroundings, then his gaze, like lead—hard and gray and uncompromising—settled on her face, on her mouth. "Your judgment hasn't been too good of late."

Spurred by bitter resentment—for was he not the one responsible for her situation?—she pushed off from the wall and flung herself against the bars, her hands outstretched and curled like claws aimed at his handsome face.

He was just out of reach, the bars between them, and it was obvious he had planned it to be that way, as if it was his intention to rile her up and watch her fling herself against her cage, strictly for his amusement.

"Damn it, just what is it you want from me?" she

demanded in an angry, impotent cry. The moment she
spoke, she knew she had given him precisely the uncon-
trolled response he wanted.

"It's not what you think."

She flushed to match the color of the remaining pink
feathers drooping in her disheveled hair. "You couldn't
possibly know what I'm thinking."

"Don't I, Lacey?" The intensity of his smoky gaze,
raking her from head to foot, left no doubt that he knew
exactly the thoughts that had crossed her mind, and had
even considered viable for a moment. Reaching through the
bars, he clasped her wrist.

She gasped, pulling at the strength of his grip, but with
very little effort he turned her hand palm up and squeezed
until she was forced to relax her arced fingers or risk having
the fragile bones in her arm crushed. He studied the surface
like a Gypsy about to tell her fortune. Then he flipped her
hand over to examine her knuckles as if they were some
kind of oddity.

And weren't they? The hand of an accomplished bunco
artist was not an everyday sight.

For a moment she thought he was going to stoop and kiss
her fingers like some dashing gentleman of old. The prospect excited and revolted her at the same time. Instead he
merely released her and stepped back. Her hand tingled as
if she had allowed it to fall asleep and now the blood came
roaring back into circulation once more. Confused, she
pulled her arm inside the protection of the jail cell, rubbing
it as if that might erase the strange, unnerving sensations.

"Silas Abrams has been boasting all over Medora that he
has a beautiful, hardworking woman on her way to become
his wife. Now, I suspect no hardworking woman has hands
as soft as yours."

"*You* know Silas Abrams?" She couldn't have been
more surprised than if he had thrown a bucket of cold water
in her face. Dropping her hands to her sides, she clutched at
the soft velvet of her skirt to hide the fact that they were
beginning to shake. Dear God, the last thing she'd expected
or needed was for Joss McRae to be acquainted with the

man who had paid her passage to the Dakota Territory. No doubt it was his intention to see that she paid for that deception as well. The hole that she had dug for herself only seemed to be getting deeper and deeper and more impossible to escape.

"I know him. Too well."

Could it be that she heard a touch of contempt in his voice? Latching on to that possibility, she ran with it. "Is he your friend?"

Joss was silent for a moment, but there was a tenseness about his mouth that answered her question before he ever spoke.

"Can't say that he is."

Then if he wasn't a friend, could that mean he was an enemy? "Look, Mr. McRae," She forced herself to focus on his face as she perfected a wide-eyed plea. "J-Joss. I never actually agreed to marry this Silas Abrams. I was desperate and needed a way out of St. Louis, that's all. I . . ."

"Just another besotted fool to take advantage of, huh?"

"No, it's not like that," she defended. "Not at all."

"Then you planned to go on to Medora?" He was baiting her and she knew it.

"I . . . I planned to write him a letter and explain that I just couldn't go through with the marriage."

"And were you gonna send him his money back as well?"

"Yes, eventually." What a barefaced lie, but she never blinked or flinched as she spoke it.

"That's a cock-and-bull story, Lacey, and we both know it." As fast as a coiled rattler strikes, he reached through the bars and seized her by the shoulders, pulling her hard against him. And even though the cold metal separated them, protected her—odd that she saw her prison as a safe haven now—she had never been so close to a man. His mouth was only inches from hers, the hard plane of his chest pressing against her breasts making the bars seem like nothing, his hand heated steel about the small of her back.

"What do you want from me?" she asked again, the

question a breathless plea. She lowered her lashes in anticipation of the brush of his lips on hers.

"Oddly enough, I only want your help."

"Help?" Her eyes flew open. That was the last thing she'd expected him to say. "What could I possibly do to help a man like you?"

What, indeed? His mouth was still only inches from hers, and she focused on his lips, finding herself unable to look away, so perfect were they in their moist fullness, barely able to keep herself from leaning forward to end this torture of incompletion.

"Silas Abrams is expecting a blushing bride. I don't want him to be disappointed."

Lacey jerked back. The arrogance to suggest she might be throwing herself at him. So he wanted her to marry some Dakota oaf, did he? Not on his life—or hers. Even she was not fool enough to play such a dangerous game. She began to struggle, her hands prying at his arm still wrapped about her.

"No chance, Joss McRae. I refuse to become the wife of some backwoods . . . ."

"You don't have to marry him, Lacey." He held her tightly regardless of her attempt to escape his clutch. "Just think of this as the biggest gamble in your life. I think you'll find the stakes worth it."

"Never."

"Do what I ask and you can have the money back."

"The money?" Ceasing her struggle, she strained against his arm and eyed him suspiciously. "You mean the money from the train?" Then she shook her head. "A few measly hundred dollars. So what?"

"Try more like ten thousand, Lacey."

"Ten thousand?" Surely he lied. She'd assumed as much at Sadie's.

"Didn't you bother to count it? Yes, ten thousand, honey." It was as if he dangled the most delectable carrot before her eyes.

"What did Silas Abrams ever do to you to make him worth so much?" she asked incredulously.

"What he *did* is none of your damn business," he

snapped. "It's what he's doing now that I want you to find out."

Ten thousand dollars. Her mouth began to water to think that she could earn that much—legitimately. Well, it was only a bit underhanded. And all she had to do was . . .

She frowned. "I don't have to marry him, right? And I don't have to allow him to . . . touch me?"

Joss chuckled. "That's strictly up to you, honey. I have no intention of being your moral watchdog."

She allowed that remark to go unchallenged for all she could think of was the money—enough to see her through months without having to watch over her shoulder constantly. There was only one catch. She would have to trust Joss McRae.

Trust him? Lord, she didn't even like him.

"What guarantee do I have that you will follow through with your end of the bargain once I find out what you want?" If he said "You'll have to trust me," she would tell him to go to the devil.

"There's never a guarantee in any gamble, Lacey, not for either side. You know that." He let her go with a suddenness that made her stumble backward. "The choice is yours." He shrugged his wide shoulders with arrogance. "Stay here and rot, or take a chance on my offer. What will it be?"

There was very little to choose between. Her odds, however risky, were much better agreeing to his scheme, at least up front. There would be plenty of time to put her own twist to the plan—once he dropped the charges against her—once they were out of Missouri.

"Just what is it you want me to find out from Silas Abrams?"

"Are you saying we have a deal?"

After a moment of soul-searching hesitation she nodded.

"Good girl." Taking up the key ring, he slipped the appropriate one into the lock on her cell door. Then with a take-charge attitude he laid claim to her arm and pulled her along. "You'll get back on the train."

"I don't have my tickets anymore."

He paused to look at her, demanding an explanation.

"I sold them for my poker stake."

"You know, Lacey, you're amazing." He shook his head. "As luck would have it, you won't need tickets. You'll be riding with me."

At that she dug in her heels and tried to pull away. "I don't think . . ."

"Don't give me a hard time, honey, or I'll march you right back into that cell."

There was no doubt in her mind but that he meant his threat, and right now she had to agree to anything just to get out of jail. Holding her tongue, she allowed him to direct her through the door that led to the front office.

Once there, Joss barely paused before the sheriff, who gave them a perfunctory once-over before accepting the set of keys from Joss's outstretched hand.

"I see you worked it out," he commented dryly, apparently coming to his own conclusions.

Joss nodded, picked up Lacey's reticule, obviously minus her pistol for it was less bulky, and shoved it into her hand. Then he steered her out the door.

In the distance she could see the locomotive, sitting idle, puffs of steam occasionally emanating from underneath its belly. An entire train just patiently awaiting one man's return, unmindful of missed schedules or all the other passengers aboard. Would the engineer have stayed all night if necessary? No doubt he would have, she concluded.

Staring up at the tall, handsome man who had suddenly taken control of her destiny, Lacey felt the apprehension knot in her stomach. No one man deserved such power over so many, but regardless, Joss McRae had it.

Dear Lord, she had been foolish enough to play with the deck stacked against her. Even a greenhorn to the gaming tables knew better than that. But worse, she still had no idea exactly what it was she'd gotten herself into. Information about Silas Abrams. That was all Joss McRae claimed he wanted, but somehow she suspected fulfilling her end of this devil-made bargain would not be easy.

CHAPTER 5

Amidst a grumbling air of discontent from the horde of passengers that had disembarked the train to mill about the depot "until necessary repairs were made," Joss steered the Honeycutt woman down the long line of cars toward his private Pullman at the very end.

The Honeycutt woman. Yes, it was definitely best to think of her in those terms only, not as Lacey or even deLacey. Somehow giving her a first name made it that much harder to maintain his distance and to keep his wits about him.

As they moved along the platform they passed one of the many conductors. Oddly enough the man was struggling with a small carpetbag over his head trying to untangle it from the latch of an open window on the side of the train.

"Stop, please," Lacey cried, pointing as Joss dragged her by. "That's my luggage."

"Your luggage?" Unsure of just what she was babbling about, Joss did as she requested, coming to a halt before the poor man, who grew quite flustered in the presence of his employer. "What's going on?" Joss demanded.

"I don't understand it, Mr. McRae," the man began to explain. "Somebody reported seeing this bag hanging out the window, but nobody seems to know how it got there."

Joss continued to stare at deLacey. His short acquaintance

with her made him quite confident that she would have some sort of bizarre explanation.

"I put it there for safekeeping," she offered, as if nothing further needed to be said, as if everybody hung their luggage from the windows of trains.

He nodded. If the truth be known, he didn't want to know more. Snatching the bag from the confused conductor's hands, he merely ordered, "We can leave now, Mr. Hollingsworth, whenever the engineer is ready."

"Yes, sir."

Jerking Lacey along, Joss realized that his long, quick strides were forcing her practically to run to keep up with him. So much the better.

"You are just chock-full of surprises, aren't you?" he muttered, not bothering to look back at her or to check his speed.

"No more than you are," she retorted. "And if you don't slow down this minute, Joss McRae, you'll find yourself obligated to pick me up off the ground."

Halting abruptly, he faced her just as she came crashing headlong into his chest. "You would like that, wouldn't you, Miss Honeycutt?"

"No, but I suspect you would."

They stood there glaring at each other, their breath coming in equally short, indignant huffs.

She was so petite, and determined, he had to admire her. His eyes traveled down the length of her in a lingering fashion. Oh, *how* he admired her, every feminine curve and hollow of her.

"Well, then, if you don't want me hauling you around, make it a point to keep up with me."

He marched on, yet contrary to his threat, he shortened his strides a little. Reaching the steps of his private car, he pulled her in front of him, forcing her to precede him.

"Henry," he bellowed as they climbed the stairs and mounted the landing before the entrance.

The servant appeared at the door with his usual unruffled composure.

"I see you found her, sir." Without being told, Henry

took the carpetbag from his hand and held the door open as Joss ushered the woman inside.

There were no signs of their poker game or ensuing tussle. He'd expected no less from the fastidious old valet.

"Show Miss Honeycutt to the bedroom, Henry."

He was surprised at how docilely she followed the servant's lead. Such acceptance just didn't suit her at all. It made him nervous.

"And Miss Honeycutt."

DeLacey stopped but didn't turn to face him, her spine as rigid as well-stretched barbed wire.

"I suggest you forget any ideas you might be harboring about sneaking out through another window. You'd only get stuck halfway through. And then I would be forced to rescue you once more."

The tightening of her shoulders indicated her irritation, and he chuckled inwardly at the manner in which she marched out of view. No, it was more like a strut with her hips swaying back and forth with indignation.

His gaze settled on those sensual curves. Fine hips. A mighty fine woman. How much easier this would be if Silas Abrams's mail-order bride had just been a pasty-faced frump.

Joss sighed at his sudden lack of purposefulness. How much easier, indeed.

The dark masculinity of the room deLacey was shown to was softened only by the hodgepodge of vibrant colors on the patchwork coverlet of the big bed that dominated the space. A maternal hand had stitched that quilt. She wondered if the seamstress had been Joss's mother, but such sentimentality didn't quite suit him—at least not the man she had come to know over the last twenty-four hours.

However, there was no doubt that she was in Joss McRae's bedroom. It spoke of an opulence and comfort she had not encountered since the heyday of her daddy's career. The walls sported a wainscoting of the finest walnut and hand-painted wallpaper of subtle fleur-de-lis. A rich Aubusson carpet covered the floor, muffling the rumble of the wheels beneath her feet. On the dresser was a casual array of engraved decanters, some empty, some half full, all made of expensive cut glass.

The room spoke of pride. The oil painting over the velvet-covered settee in the corner was of a great, sprawling ranch, more like some Eastern estate really, the likes of which most men only dreamed about. No doubt it too belonged to Joss McRae.

"Thank you, Henry," she said softly as the man dropped her battered bag on a straight-back chair beside the bed.

"If you have need of something, miss, you have only to call me." He opened another door she'd assumed was a closet. Instead it was a bathroom that contained every possible modern convenience.

She edged forward and peered inside. She was impressed, both with the furnishings of the small room—tub, sink, and water closet—and the ornate fixtures adorning them. Studying them intently, she widened her eyes. That couldn't possibly be gold—or could it?

"You have only to turn these knobs"—Henry's hand curled about a gilded swan's neck—"and water will . . ."

"I'm quite familiar with the workings of inside plumbing, Henry."

"Yes, miss. Of course." He bowed with servility and stepped backwards.

It did her heart—and self-esteem—good to have this worldly servant treat her with a measure of respect. And Joss too seemed to be making reparations for the horrid way he had acted upon their first encounter.

But she was suspicious. She didn't trust the stiff, unreadable Henry. Not one bit. It would be necessary to keep an eye on the old servant at all times.

After he departed, closing the door quietly behind him, she realized there were a thousand questions she should have asked him. Bent over the tub, she stared in dismay at the drain in the bottom. How did one plug that up to contain the water for a bath? And soap and towels? She glanced about. Where would she find such toiletries?"

It seemed a lifetime since she had luxuriated in a bath, not just swiped at the grime with a moist cloth and small basin of water. Not since . . .

Lord, not since the night she had tried to stack the deck against Cattleman Will in St. Louis, and the hotel facilities couldn't begin to equal her present surroundings. She closed her eyes and sighed. Cattleman Will. A tame pussycat compared with her current opponent.

A loud click issued from the bedroom and broke into her musings. She stiffened, knowing precisely what had made the sound. Someone had locked the door. A pleasurable experience was about to become a prison.

Joss McRae. Damn his arrogant hide. She tried the doorknob, vainly. Just as she suspected. Secured from the outside.

Well, two could play that game. She marched toward the bathroom, snatching up the handmade quilt from the bed and the stopper from one of the crystal decanters that looked about the right size to her as she went. Once inside she locked that door, ensuring her privacy and no doubt the irritation of her jailor once he came to realize what she was about.

"What in the hell is she doing in there?"

Before the sedate Henry, Joss paced the stateroom of the train car, now and then stopping to glare at the closed door of the bedroom. His bedroom. Somehow that woman had turned the tables on him, making him feel like the one whose movements had been restricted.

"No doubt taking a bath, sir." The way Henry pronounced "bath" made it sound as if he were following a doctor's instructions to open his mouth and say "ahhhhh."

"A bath?" Joss jerked to a halt, a disconcerting frown creasing his jet black brows.

"Yes, sir. The lady was inspecting the facilities quite closely when I left her."

Joss started to laugh, an image of the mercenary Miss Honeycutt stooped over the gilded fixtures busy trying to figure out how to remove the faucets and spouts, no doubt thinking them solid gold, not just plated. But then he quieted abruptly. He wouldn't put it past her to attempt to do just that, steal him blind once again.

To hell with the Honeycutt woman's privacy. It was *his* bedroom. Unlocking the door, he opened it and burst inside. The room was empty, the entrance to the lavatory closed. Crossing the space in quick strides, he reached for the knob and halted, discovering that the lock was secured from the other side. But that was no surprise.

"DeLacey, open the door." Using the heel of his hand, he hammered on the wooden panels, and placed his ear against it, listening for a response.

There was no sound of activity, no running water, no patter of bare feet, nothing.

He pounded once more, knowing full well she had to be within as she could be nowhere else.

"Go away." Her order was brisk and irritated.

"What are you doing in there?" he demanded.

"What do you *think* I'm doing in here? Stealing the fixtures? Now, leave me alone."

The truth formed a contrite knot at the base of his throat. Wordlessly he backed up and dropped on the settee, casually draping one long leg over the arm of the couch in total disregard of its expensiveness. He would wait for her, for eventually she would have to come out of the bath or else pucker up like new leather left in tanning solution too long. He chuckled to think of how surprised she would be to find him sitting there.

He didn't have long to wait. Like a toga-clad Roman she waltzed into the room. He arched one black brow. That was his grandmother's quilt she had wrapped about her lithe body. Head bent, humming under her breath, she was using one end of the heirloom coverlet to towel dry her hair, those long, golden strands that rivaled the brilliance of the golden swan fittings. Apparently she didn't see him, or if she did, she didn't care.

But then she brushed the wet tresses from her eyes and spied him, a little gasp issuing from her parted lips. Fresh from a bath, a rosy tinge highlighting her fairness, she was more beautiful than ever, paganlike wrapped in those patchwork colors that revealed the naked skin of her shoulders and throat, the gentle swell of the creamy white tops of her bosoms, the toes of one bare foot. She looked earthy and wild—a temptress to make any man recklessly cast aside all rational thought.

Joss swallowed down the raging desire, and, to hide the fact that his fingers were shaking, he dug them into the cushioned arm of the sofa on which he lounged. It was hard to judge her reaction to his presence for she merely draped the free end of the quilt across her neck and shoulders to cover them as best she could. Then she tossed her head and glared at him indignantly.

"There truly is no limit to how low you're willing to sink, is there?" Her hand was curled about some object, and she threw it at him without warning.

He caught the missile easily, recognized it as the crystal stopper of the Waterford decanter he had left on the dresser the night before. There were flecks of gold on one end. Apparently she had had the audacity to use it to plug up the bathtub.

Regaining his composure, he rose from the settee, and flipping the stopper in his fingers with casual unconcern, he crossed to the dresser. There he dropped it into the neck of the decanter, turned, and examined her with a distaste to match hers.

"Just as there is no limit to your disregard for the property of others."

She glanced down at the quilt about her and shrugged, the draped corner dropping down to reveal those delectable shoulders once more.

"One must make do with what one has." Her statement was certainly no apology but a challenge, deliberately issued—one he wasn't about to let slide.

As fast as the cougar that preys upon Dakota cattle, he snatched up the dangling end of the coverlet and wound it about his arm. She gasped and struggled, but in the end she had no choice except to be reeled in with it or let it go. Neither option was to her advantage, and he relished the look of helplessness that crossed her pretty face. Holding back as long as she could, she tried desperately to maintain her dignity as well as her modesty but eventually her sense of decorum won the battle. And even as he hooked his free arm about her tiny waist, the majority of the coverlet bunched over his other, she never lost her courage. It was as if she were confident that he would do nothing to her. Joss McRae was all bluff.

And it was true. Up until now he had never crossed the boundaries of true decency, not when it came to a woman— this one at least. But she was drawing a line in the dirt and daring him to step over it.

Well, maybe it was about time that deLacey Honeycutt learned that she was dealing with a man—in every way— unpredictable and authoritative.

He felt her tense in his arms when he claimed her mouth, at first soft and open in surprise. But by the time she could convey any hint of displeasure, his invasion was complete. He was taking a risky gamble, he supposed; she could bite his probing tongue. And yet he suspected she wouldn't. For whether she acknowledged it, or even realized it, she found the intimacy most enjoyable.

And perhaps that was a bit conceited on his part, but he had known enough women in his lifetime to be able to read female receptiveness to his advances.

He pulled back, discovering her face lifted, her eyes closed, her lips parted as if the kiss had not ended, as if she were still savoring the feel of his mouth on hers—all classic signs of submission if he'd ever seen them. But this was ground they had trodden before—safe, explored territory. A kiss, nothing more.

Grabbing her once more, he again covered her warm, moist lips. She stood quietly, her arms dangling at her sides as if useless.

Then he began an exploration of a different kind, nibbling at the corner of her mouth, moving to the peak of her jawbone and downward to the soft underside that led to her earlobe. Her breathing became irregular, little gasps, and then she would hold her breath, the pulse there beneath her ear jumping and racing whenever he ran his tongue over it.

Still he was treading in a temperate zone, only skirting the edges of impropriety. But still she was much too confident in her enjoyment.

With a mighty sweep he plunged forward, stripping away the last of the quilt, so moist and scented where it had pressed against her freshly washed skin, leaving her naked in his arms. His mouth swooped downward as his hand moved upward cupping the velvety flesh of her breast, his tongue enveloping the jutting nib as sweet as a summer-ripened raspberry.

A reeling shock wave rolled over him. An unexpected hunger tightened every nerve in his body. It was more than mere lust that shook him to the very foundation of his being. Much more.

It was in that moment of self-discovery when his defenses were down that she began to fight. Her palm came flying up to catch him full on the face with a loud whack that was as thunderous as gunfire in his ears—and as painful.

He released his hold on her and stumbled backward, his fingers moving up to explore his smarting cheek. Through the blur of pain he had a moment to peruse her lithe body, one nipple still wet from his caress, before she managed to gather the quilt up to cover herself.

"You, sir," she hissed in a voice quivering with indignation, "are despicable and depraved beyond words."

"And you, darlin'," he retorted in a slow, deliberate drawl, "are a delectable feast for the deprived." Taking in the way she fearfully clutched the coverlet to her hot little body, he grinned at her, knowing that he had accomplished his goal even if he had paid for it. "Besides, you enjoyed it as much as I did," he boasted, knowing that her confidence was shaken, her arrogance squelched. She wouldn't be so quick to defy him again, at least not anytime soon.

Then she raced back into the bathroom, slamming the door, catching one end of the coverlet.

He heard it rip and grimaced. Old Granny McRae would flop in her coffin to see how her handiwork was being abused. Old Granny would spit on the floor and call him a fool for not going after what he wanted.

Joss frowned. For the briefest moment he was no longer sure just what it was he *did* want. Somehow his desire for peace and happiness in his life and his goal for revenge had all gotten jumbled up, and that Honeycutt woman was in the dead center of the turbulence.

He left the room more unsettled, more unsure, than he had ever been in his life.

Still clinging to the damp quilt, deLacey watched him go through a tiny slit in the bathroom door, aware only of the wide expanse of his shoulders beneath the polished cotton of his shirt, the tautness of his buttocks encased in tight trousers—his hands, his large, masculine hands clutched at his sides like fists of steel.

He had touched her in a way no man had ever attempted before, had fondled her, tasted her, and left her wanting more. DeLacey swallowed down the strange, burning desire clogging her throat. No wonder her daddy had repeatedly warned her to "let 'em look but never let 'em touch."

It was as if his hand had torn down the carefully constructed barriers of her innocent body, his mouth ravishing all sense of right and wrong. She was smitten and tainted and no doubt lost. Lord, her first instincts had been right. She should have run the moment she laid eyes on Joss McRae. Run and never looked back.

But now she couldn't tear her eyes away, not even when the outer door closed between them, separating them, making her feel—she groped about trying to understand what it was she was experiencing—as if she'd been led to some kind of brink and left teetering on the edge.

"Look, Lacey, if you're going to survive this one," she muttered to herself, forcing her feet to carry her out of the bathroom, her eyes to look elsewhere, "you had better pull yourself together and be quick about it."

Spying her battered traveling bag perched on a chair, she crossed the room and opened it. Then as if the heavens had opened up and dropped the answer at her feet, the way to handle Joss McRae became only too evident. Her tactics with him had been all wrong. Making herself look desirable was exactly what she shouldn't do. She had to look plain and pious, something to be pitied and protected, to be repulsed.

Reaching into the gaping carpetbag, she pulled out the shapeless calico dress she had been wearing when she had first boarded the train, the serviceable shoes, the concealing slat bonnet. And she began to laugh.

Yes, she knew exactly how to handle a man like Joss McRae.

"Henry, did you tell her dinner was ready?"

It was nearly nine o'clock at night, and Joss had been sitting at the table waiting for nearly half an hour.

"I informed her, sir, and Miss Honeycutt said she would be out presently."

Joss didn't like to be kept waiting, not by an employee, and certainly not by a woman, and not when he was hungry. But it seemed everything that had to do with the Honeycutt woman, who was now in his service—for had he not hired her to do a job for him?—required that he do just that.

Irritated, he rose. He had thought she'd learned her lesson, but it seemed that thick-headed woman forgot much too easily. But as he started to cross the room, the door to the bedroom opened and out popped . . .

What was it?

Joss stood, mouth agape, blinking in shock at the transformation in deLacey.

The calico dress hung like a shapeless flour sack on her slim body. The shoes. They looked as if they belonged to somebody's decrepit old grandmother. Her complexion was pale and pasty, her lips nonexistent, and he couldn't imagine what she had found to put on her face to make it look so ghastly white. Her hair, that glorious gold filigree that had held him enraptured only hours before, was drawn back and knotted so severely against her scalp that it had to be painful.

"DeLacey?"

"I'm sorry to be tardy, Mr. McRae," she said, so sweetly and solicitously that Joss shot her a skeptical look, "but as you can see I broke a shoelace." She lifted the edge of her skirt to reveal where she had tied the two frayed ends of the black string together just over her instep.

What ugly shoes, deserving only of some female evangelist, but there was no disguising the shapeliness of her ankle. Somewhere beneath all this . . . this getup . . . was the feisty siren he had briefly held naked in his arms. His gaze swept up as she lowered the hem of her dress. But one wouldn't guess it to look at her now.

Just what on God's green earth was she up to?

She was standing next to the empty seat at the table waiting, her fingers laced across her stomach. Waiting for what?

At that moment Henry stepped forward and pulled out her chair.

"Thank you, Henry," she said matter-of-factly, and settled on the edge of the seat. Then she pinned Joss with a prim look that made him feel like a wayward schoolboy caught putting a mouse in the teacher's desk drawer.

Just what did she think to accomplish with all this rigmarole?

"I see you changed."

As Joss spoke Henry poured a red wine in the stemmed glasses in front of them. Picking his up, he took a sip and scrutinized her through the Bordeaux. She'd gone to a whole lot of trouble to look her worst.

"It's what Mr. Abrams is expecting." She in turn eyed him quite boldly but ignored her drink. "You remember. Hardworking and innocent, I think you said."

Frowning, he swallowed the mouthful of wine and returned his glass to the table.

"Ah, yes, Silas." Odd that he should feel anxiety at the mention of his rival's name. As he evaluated her and her motives, he mulled over the exact meaning of rival. "Don't you think this is all a bit severe even for the likes of Silas Abrams?"

Lacey slowly glanced down at herself, then back at him, her blue eyes heavy with sarcasm and conceit. "What's wrong, Mr. McRae? Do you find the way I'm dressed offensive?"

"Not at all." He gave her a lazy smile and lounged back against his chair. "But then, I know what lies beneath it. Silas, on the other hand, will judge only the surface like he does everything else. You wouldn't want to run him off before he can get the chance . . . to know you like I do."

Just as he expected, up she popped, indignant as a ruffled biddy caught in a sudden downpour.

"You, sir, are insufferable!"

He rose with her and skirted the table until he stood towering over her. For a moment he thought she would stand her ground, but then she began to back up, one step at a time. He pursued her, giving her no reprieve until he had her cornered against the back of the sofa.

"Don't try and pretend with me, honey." He eyed her with contempt. "You and I both know there's not much you wouldn't resort to for the promise of money. I'm willing to admit that there's no limit to what I'm willing to pay to get what I want. That's why we're perfect for each other's needs."

Reaching down, he unpinned the golden banner of her hair, releasing it from its tight knot and running his fingers through the silky mass. Though she never flinched he could nonetheless feel her tremble when he touched her.

"And because this covenant we made in hell and signed in blood is so damn ideal for both of us, I have no intention of spoiling it. Though it's damn tempting. But don't worry, Lacey. Even when you beg me, just as you are doing now, you're safe with me. I want Silas Abrams a hell of a lot more than I want you."

He knew then just what she would do. Had she not slapped him for his impertinence once already? So before she could gather the momentum to carry through with her intention, he shackled her wrist and squeezed until she relented. Then forcing her upturned hand to his face, he drew the tip of her pinkie into his mouth and sucked it gently, his eyes never once releasing hers.

"Most tempting," he murmured, his tongue gliding along the finger to the sensitive core of her palm.

With a squeaking protest, she jerked her hand free,

ducked beneath his arm, and scurried toward the safety of the bedroom. Once inside she slammed the door, and he could just picture her, spine pressed against the barrier, her breathing erratic, anticipating his next move.

His next move? He didn't have one. Muttering to himself, he turned his back to her and sat himself down.

"I'm hungry, Henry."

"Yes, sir." The servant placed a covered dish before him, removing the lid with a flourish. "And the lady's dinner, Mr. McRae?"

"You eat it." He shot a dark look at the closed bedroom door, and caught a glimpse of the valet's face. Why, the old man was frowning with worry and disapproval. How unlike the normally expressionless servant. "I don't think she'll have much appetite for it."

"No, sir." Once again the wizened face was as impassive as the mantelpiece clock.

"And Henry."

"Yes, sir?"

"I don't want you taking her a tray later when you think I'm not watching."

"Me, sir?"

But Joss didn't bother to answer. The old fraud was succumbing to the Honeycutt woman's charms just as easily as he was himself.

DeLacey Honeycutt. Joss glared once more at the closed door, his lips thinning. Tossing his fork down, he found suddenly that he wasn't hungry anymore. Why did she have to be the one to hold the key to all his years of plotting and planning in her tiny, conniving fist?

Why, indeed. He suspected that even God, in all His celestial wisdom, every now and then had to get a hankering to try His hand at a game of chance. How better to sweeten the odds than to call His opponent's bet with an enticing woman.

He'd done it to Adam, hadn't He? So why would He have qualms about doing the same to Joss McRae?

CHAPTER 6

Long into the night, deLacey tossed and turned in the big bed. The bed that belonged to Joss McRae. Even the rhythmic lullaby of the wheels beneath her did little to ease her turbulent thoughts. Her stomach growled a protest. Hunger she could ignore. But it was the insistent throbbing at the crux of her being that made it impossible to sleep. And at the very center of that tidal wave of feelings loomed an image of the man himself, his gray eyes bearing down on her, penetrating to the very core of her soul, his hands . . .

Oh, damn those skillful hands of his!

Trying to escape the sinful path her thoughts took, Lacey turned over to face the other way. But that was even worse.

Like a great, sorrowful soul lingering outside the window, ever following, the moon, round and silvery, cast its beams on the wall before her. Illuminated was the picture of the ranch, and the magic of the moonlight seemed to make the landscape come alive. The line of cottonwoods behind the house took to dancing as if a breeze rustled through them, the windmill off to one side seemed to turn and squeak. The painted shadow cast by the huge, rambling house created the illusion of depth and hinted at the secrets that no doubt abounded in its corridors.

She could almost imagine Joss McRae standing in the

front entrance, one shoulder propped against the door frame, his arms crossed before his broad chest, a challenge to anyone brave enough—foolish enough—to step forward and enter his domain.

She wondered if she would ever have the chance to see it all for herself. Did she really want the opportunity?

Yes, she decided unequivocally. She yearned to discover everything there was to know about this man who dared to match her brashness, measure for measure. No man had ever done that to her before, not successfully—no man, that is, except her daddy.

But Joss McRae was nothing like her beloved father. Nothing at all.

Kingston Honeycutt had been kind and generous to a fault, had possessed a sense of honor and decency that made her suddenly feel terrible about the turn her own life had taken over the last couple of years. Once she remembered when he had beaten a man out of considerable money in a game of cards, fair and square, and had sent the loser on his way like so many others. Late that night, a small child nearly asleep in an alcove of her daddy's hotel room, she had heard that same man's wife appeal to him, willing to beg or barter for the money back. It was all they had, she had sobbed, and without it she and the three kids would be put out on the streets come sunrise. She would give him whatever he demanded if only he'd return at least enough to make the mortgage payment on the farm. Kingston Honeycutt had not questioned the woman's integrity, and had asked nothing from her except that she and the children consider leaving such a worthless provider. And then he had given her back the money threefold.

Until now, deLacey had never fully understood the sacrifice that woman had been willing to make nor how benevolent and truly noble her daddy had been in return.

On the other hand, Joss McRae probably would have had such a woman shown to the door and promptly forgotten her plight. Or if she were pretty enough, taken what she'd offered in exchange for the money.

No, Joss McRae could never be called anything closely resembling kind or generous or noble.

Arrogant, and self-centered, a man who found material things more important than people. A man filled with vengeance. What could Silas Abrams possibly have done to him to make him so vindictive?

Probably nothing more than he deserved.

With that final thought, she tossed once more to stare out the window at the waning moon, wondering just what she could do to get even with Joss McRae for the way he treated her, for the way he made her feel.

Vengeance. A most comforting sentiment. Not bothering to stifle a huge yawn, she closed her eyes and focused on the clackety-clack of the train wheels and on how best to wreak havoc on this man who had managed to do the same to her life.

It was amazing just how imaginative her mind could be so late at night.

''Mr. McRae, sir.''

Joss pushed aside the summons, wanting nothing to do with it or the world from which it came. Muttering something foul but undecipherable, he rolled over to escape.

The bed was too short and narrow to accommodate his movement, and against his will he found himself awake, his neck sore, his right arm asleep and beginning to sting as the blood surged back into it. Disoriented, he opened his eyes to the semidarkness and the insistent voice. Where was he?

And then it all came back to him. Last night he had finished off the bottle of Bordeaux served with his untouched dinner and then had tackled something stronger. With nowhere to sleep and no way to freshen up or even change his clothing since that Honeycutt woman had taken over his bedroom, he had stripped down to his trousers and drowsed off on the sofa.

Someone had covered him, and that someone was now demanding his attention.

''What time is it, Henry?'' The shades were still drawn so he couldn't be sure how early it might be.

"Five-thirty, sir."

Joss frowned his impatience and brushed back a lock of dark hair that had fallen into his eyes and glared up at the immaculately groomed servant. This had better be good. And it had better not involve deLacey Honeycutt.

"There's a conductor outside the door with a very strange message," the servant explained without elaboration.

"Is something wrong with the train?" Instantly alert, Joss sat up. Had the boiler blown? A car derailed?

The even rhythm of the wheels beneath his bare feet assured him that such was not the case.

"It seems the engineer reports seeing a steady stream of . . . items flying off the back of the train."

"Items?" Joss demanded, somewhat confused. "What items? Bolts and rivets?" He could just picture the train coming apart piece by piece.

"No, sir." The servant hesitated for a moment, then continued. "Clothing and other household goods."

If Henry hadn't said it, Joss wouldn't have believed it. "I don't understand."

"Neither do I, sir. But that apparently is the message."

And then the cream began to clot, and a strange knot of apprehension gathered in the pit of his stomach. Somehow this had to involve deLacey Honeycutt.

Barefoot, dressed only in his pants wrinkled from sleeping in them, Joss stumbled to his unsteady feet. What was she doing now? He was tired of her antics. Sick to death of them.

Without prelude he burst into the bedroom, not sure what he would find. What he did discover brought him to a blinking halt.

The furniture was strangely devoid of knickknacks. Every book gone. The decanters and other personal items had disappeared. Bedding, pillows, curtains missing as well. And the doors and drawers of his wardrobe were thrown wide open, the invasion of his privacy complete.

Sitting on the window ledge, her lap piled high, deLacey didn't look the least bit upset or surprised to see him. In fact, if he read her impertinent expression correctly, she was pleased to be finally discovered. Wordlessly she took up one of the shirts from the folded stack on her knees—his shirt—and casually trailed it out the open window. Then with what he could only describe as a giggle, she let it go.

She had just thrown one of his best cambric shirts out the window! He stood there, unable to believe what he had just witnessed, and yet the fact that she had done it didn't really surprise him. Nothing deLacey Honeycutt did surprised him anymore.

"Good morning, Mr. McRae. I hope you had a good night's sleep." She spoke the greeting cheerfully, even as her vicious hand reached down and grabbed up another one of his shirts and held it up for his inspection.

"Well enough," he replied, his response automatic and no reflection of the truth. In fact his night had been wretched, but he wasn't about to admit that to her.

"Good. You'll need it." With that she tossed the shirt out the window, the wind snatching it from her fingers to whip it away like the previous one.

When she took up the next one from the stack, he knew it was destined to follow in the wake of the others. Brazen little witch. Was there nothing she wasn't willing to do to rile him up?

He had to stop her. Now. His eyes began to rove about the room looking for an answer. Or the next thing he knew she would be hacking up the furniture and tossing it out piece by piece as well.

He could easily force her to stop, for now, but that wouldn't teach her a well-deserved lesson. There was only one good way to handle the situation. Tit for tat.

Wordlessly he crossed to the chair where her carpetbag sat. Taking it up, he joined her at the window, and though it took a little doing he stuffed it through the opening and sent it flying.

DeLacey never flinched. Just as resilient as he, she raised her chin and dumped the remaining shirts out the gaping window.

But he was not to be bested. Not by a little snip like deLacey Honeycutt. He reached for her.

This time she was ready, and she slapped his hands away, darted across the room, and came to a halt in front of the open wardrobe.

"Stay away from me, Joss McRae," she warned.

With calculated caution, he advanced like a stalking mountain lion, one step at a time, expecting her to flee at any moment.

But she had planned her strategy well. A barrage of shoes, his of course, pelted him, but the supply wasn't endless. When the last one sailed past his left ear, he resumed the pursuit.

Just before she managed to slip into the bathroom and ruthlessly slam the door on his bare, unprotected toes, he caught her.

She was a handful, kicking and fighting, those shoes of hers, more like clodhoppers than something a woman should wear, wreaking havoc on his shins and knees. But he persisted, for his cause was just. DeLacey Honeycutt had a thing or two to learn about overconfidence—and paying the consequences of her actions.

It didn't take him long to unbutton the back of her gown. He'd done his fair share of disrobing women over the years. Down to her white lace petticoat and camisole, she was like a spitting feline, her eyes, wide with disbelief, fastened on the calico dress in his hands.

Having her full attention, he sauntered over to the open window and held up the dress just as she had his shirt.

"You wouldn't dare," she challenged in a voice fraught with emotion, her little fists planted on her curvaceous hips like handles on a teapot.

Oh, but he would. Just as she had earlier, he let the wind snatch the god-awful dress from his fingers, and he watched it whirl away with a sense of satisfaction.

That seemed to take the wheeze out of her bellows of defiance. Slumped down on the couch, she looked like a lost little orphan, her eyes wide, and could that possibly be tears he saw sparkling in their blue depths? If they were, most likely they were contrived.

"How could you do something so . . . barbaric?" she whispered.

For the briefest of moments he was struck with regret. Perhaps he had gone a bit too far. But then he glanced about the barren room, remembering that *she* had begun this farcical line of attack, and changed his mind.

"You started it, honey. All I did was finish it."

"If you think this is finished, Joss McRae, then think again." So indignant was the way the tops of her barely covered breasts rose and fell against the lace of her camisole as she stood to confront him. So distracting.

Why couldn't she just accept defeat with the grace and dignity God gave all women? It was as if her resistance knew no bounds. Would he be forced to strip her naked to make her bend to his will?

The idea wasn't all that unpleasant or farfetched.

Appalled at the lurid path his thoughts dare tread, he tore his hungry gaze from her scantily clad body. He had better leave—now. In fact, if he had any sense at all he would see to it that the impetuous Miss Honeycutt was escorted from the train at the very next stop and be glad to be rid of her.

But then all of his well-laid plans for revenge against Silas Abrams would come to naught. Plain and simple, he needed her. And he wanted her. And no doubt both deficiencies forebode disaster.

Turning away, he made as if to depart.

"What am I supposed to wear, Joss?"

The question was softly asked, and the sound of his first name upon her lips spoken with such familiarity did strange things to him, destroying all previous notions he had entertained regarding deLacey Honeycutt, although he knew it was foolish of him. His heart skipped several beats, his palms began to sweat, and his mouth went dry as the prairie in August. Without turning about, for he feared if he did he might make a buffoon of himself, he replied, "I'll buy you whatever you need before we reach Medora." Then he left before he lost complete control of the emotions she so readily played upon.

What a lame resolution. But it was all he dared give her
for the moment.

From the time Joss stormed out of the bedroom leaving
her stripped to her underclothing and thoroughly degraded,
deLacey saw nothing more of him. Henry became her only
visitor, bringing her meals, and when they passed through
Omaha, finally crossing the Missouri River, he even presented her with a current newspaper.

Something, anything to read, for if she regretted one
aspect of that fiasco, it was throwing out all of the books
that had once lined the glassed-in shelves over the tambour-
fronted bureau in the corner.

But the biggest surprise had come not long after Joss had
so brutally tossed out everything she'd owned. The train had
stopped for what seemed an inordinately long time in a
moderate sized town she was never to learn the name of.
After an hour of delay the boxes began to arrive, a steady
stream of them.

At first Henry said nothing, just delivered the packages
without so much as an explanation, and she, in turn, had
refused even to peek under the lids to see what they
contained, although she had her suspicions. Joss McRae
couldn't buy her cooperation with trinkets and frills. They
had made a bargain for cold, hard cash. And if he thought
she'd sit by quietly and allow him to deduct the cost
of . . . of whatever he had bought for her . . . from their
agreed-upon payment of ten thousand dollars . . .

With a discreet knock, Henry entered again, his arms
ladened down. Pinching the masculine robe—the one she
had found hanging on a hook in the bathroom—tightly
against her throat, she watched in silence as he piled the new
arrivals atop the others.

If Joss didn't stop soon the room would be overflowing.

And then something happened that she could only think
of as miraculous. Henry smiled at her. What prompted the
unexplained expression, whether it was something she did
to encourage it or if it was self-motived, she couldn't be

sure. Nonetheless, the normally undemonstrative servant beamed at her.

"It seems Mr. McRae has finally run amok."

The unexpectedness of his statement said so matter-of-factly struck deLacey as funny, and she began to laugh with unrestrained freedom. After a short hesitation he too joined in, his chuckles much more sedate, but nonetheless they became comrades-in-arms sharing a common opinion of the enemy. Ah, yes, perhaps Henry wasn't so bad after all.

"Shall we look and see what he found so irresistible?" she asked, unable to stop laughing.

"I must confess it would be most entertaining to view his conception of female fashion."

Henry's unerring calmness and air of propriety swept away any lingering reservations she harbored, not only about him but regarding the packages. It was as if they were no longer intimate gifts to her from Joss. She could now step back and view them with a different eye. Making a game of it, she tore away the paper from the first box and tossed the lid aside.

She had to admit the powder blue gown was exquisite and most tasteful, not too bold for a woman on her way to meet a husband and yet not too modest. It suggested style and grace and a background of comfort. It was perfect.

"Do you think he picked it out himself?"

Henry shook his head knowingly. "No doubt he left it up to the clerk's discretion."

A sense of disappointment speared through deLacey. She would have preferred to think Joss had selected it for her all by himself. But that was a crazy notion. Why would she possibly care one way or the other?

It took them nearly an hour to sort through all the packages. There were dresses for every occasion and every color as well as a wide array of accessories from shoes to hairpins and even an assortment of unmentionables and a large portmanteau to pack them all in. Odd. She didn't feel embarrassed with Henry there. In fact, she found his input invaluable.

"Fine Belgian lace," he commented, picking up a frilled

camisole and inspecting it with a critical eye. "Expensive. The stitching is very good. Mr. McRae has outdone himself." Giving her a curious look as if trying to decide what she was all about, he then glanced away and began folding the clothing and stacking it according to category.

Guilt nipped at the edges of deLacey's conscience when she thought back on the way she had maliciously set out to wreak havoc in Joss McRae's life from the very moment she had learned he was aboard the train. And in retaliation— what had his final gesture been? Why, he had lavished on her a wardrobe most women could only dream of possessing. Just what had she been thinking about when she had thrown all of his stuff out the window?

Somehow in the early morning light, it had seemed a most satisfying and ingenuous way to seek her vengeance. But when he had tossed out her baggage and then her only dress—well, she had experienced a terrible sense of helplessness and violation. Had he felt that same way, too?

She glanced at Henry, busy organizing the clothing, and she wondered why the servant had decided to cross over to her side of the fence.

"You didn't like me much when you first saw me, did you, Henry? Why?"

The old man paused to study at her, his steady gaze never flinching. "It's my duty, miss, to fend off suspected riffraff for Mr. McRae."

His duty? Riffraff? Yet, oddly, she wasn't offended, instead she was impressed with his sense of loyalty, for had the servant not accurately judged her original purpose? She had appeared at the door looking to bilk Joss McRae out of a little . . . a lot of money.

"So what do you think of me now?" It was a fair question, yet she wondered if he would reply with honesty.

"Mr. McRae is a most troubled man, in need of a woman's soothing touch." The valet abandoned his task and sat down opposite her, tempering his sense of propriety with a sigh she found most endearing. "He rails a lot. At everyone, mind you. Especially at me, for I am usually around. But whether he admits it or not, he depends on me."

She found it difficult to believe that Joss McRae might depend on anyone or need anything, especially a woman's soothing touch, but she kept her opinion to herself.

"It seems Mr. McRae tongue-lashes those closest to him. Even Miss Annie, whom he adores, receives her unfair share."

"Annie?" deLacey asked, surprised at the way her heart leapt jealously into her throat.

"His young sibling. A sweet child, much your own age I would guess, miss, who suffers terribly from her brother's brisk manners and attitude of self-importance."

Self-important? Yes, that described Joss McRae to a T. But it was satisfying to discover that he was human after all—with a family. He probably even had a pet dog he kicked around on his better days.

"He cares for you, Miss deLacey."

"Me?" DeLacey sat back. "Hah. Why would you think that? Because he yells at me so much?"

Henry smiled in silent confirmation.

"Well, you're mistaken," deLacey stated emphatically. "We have a business arrangement, nothing more. And that's the way I plan to keep it."

"Of course, Miss deLacey."

The curtains of propriety dropped down between them once more, but she sensed she'd not convinced Henry of her intentions.

Then an outer door slammed, and the servant rose and departed even as the sound of Joss's angry voice reverberated through the train car.

"Henry!"

Alone, deLacey took stock of the new dresses, selecting the one she thought most attractive.

Odd. If she cared so little for Joss McRae, why did she want to look her best for him?

For him? Not at all, she told herself as she listened to him make his usual barrage of unreasonable demands from the ever-patient servant. But in spite of him.

* * *

DeLacey Honeycutt was becoming an expensive, risky liability. That's what Joss's intellect told him. His heart, on the other hand . . .

Would she accept his generous invitation to dine with him? Which of the gowns he had so meticulously chosen for her would she decide to wear to the occasion? Had he calculated her size correctly? Would she be gracious or contrite in her gratitude? Either would do quite nicely.

He rubbed his hands together in anticipation, then chided himself for the uncharacteristic display of schoolboy impatience.

But then he laughed, quite pleased with himself, really. And no doubt deLacey would be just as delighted with the way things were turning out. So far she had lost so little and gained much more in exchange. If he could be so sporting about it all, surely she would be as congenial.

Henry stepped from the bedroom, closing the door behind his back before Joss could catch a glimpse of the woman beyond. Eagerly he rose to meet the servant.

"Well, did she agree to join me?"

"Quite so, sir." Henry made a move to step around his employer.

Damn the old codger for never elaborating when asked a question.

"Has she opened the packages?"

"Indeed, sir."

"Well, what did she think?"

"I couldn't venture to say, sir." Henry looked him straight in the eyes without flinching. It was only too obvious the valet had no intention of revealing anything more, not without the threat of torture.

He would just have to wait.

But he didn't like to be kept waiting.

Oddly enough, he found that deLacey Honeycutt was worth waiting for.

DeLacey was ill prepared for the transformation without. Not only with the setting, though the table was overlaid with fine white linen, expensive china, and crystal. Two silver candlesticks, the flames dipping and weaving as if alive, offered the only illumination except for the spectacular display in the western sky that streaked through the picture window to bathe the room with a golden aura.

Highlighting the man. Tall and darkly handsome in his well-tailored gabardine suit, he appeared bronzer and broader in the shoulders than she'd remembered him to be.

She couldn't help it. Catching her breath, she allowed her gaze to travel down the length of him, and she sensed he was doing the same to her. Did he approve of what he saw?

Glancing up, she found him staring back at her, inordinately pleased.

"You look lovely this evening, Miss Honeycutt."

"So do you," she murmured. Then she reddened when she thought about what she'd just said, her eyes skipping about the train car, finally settling on her own hands clasped in front of her, so pale against the blue of her skirts. The dress he had bought for her.

The muted moment of tension was broken by the creak of a chair as it was pulled away from the table. Alerted, she glanced up to find Joss standing behind the Windsor, apparently waiting for her to sit down. Still unwilling to look at him, she glanced about once more. Where was Henry? Odd that the wily servant was nowhere in sight.

And Joss did seem to be growing impatient. Either she must sit down or flee back into the sanctuary of the bedroom. She swayed in indecision.

The thought of being alone was not one she particularly relished.

Spurred by her need for company and conversation, she glided over the plush carpeting on silent feet to settle into the seat. His hands, so close, resting on the fluted back just behind her head, exuded a heat she found hard to explain and to ignore. The urge to drop back against them was just as difficult to combat, but she held herself erect and allowed him to scoot her closer to the table. Relief tinged with disappointment shot through her when he sat down opposite her. Like two glowing embers covered in a thin layer of gray ash his eyes held her transfixed.

Oh, dear, did he plan to stare at her like that all evening as if he were waiting for her to say something?

And she imagined he was.

"The c-c-clothing," she stammered. "I suppose I should thank you."

"It was nothing," he countered before she could close her mouth. He smiled. "You had to have something to wear."

"But the cost," she protested, wondering if he did indeed plan to subtract the money he had spent from the amount he'd agreed to pay her.

"Not for you to worry your pretty head about."

Just like something a man would say, slick and noncommittal. She frowned.

"They're a gift, deLacey," he explained as if he could sense her vexation.

A gift? No, that wasn't what she wanted either. It obligated her to him. "I could never accept such charity from you."

"I wouldn't quite call it charity, honey." Settling back in his chair, he crossed his arms over his chest and stared at her for a long, hard moment. "Call it additional compensation. Part of our agreement."

Now, that should have satisfied her. But the way he said it, so condescendingly. "I don't think . . ."

"Face the facts, deLacey. You have to have clothes, the right ones to impress a man like Silas Abrams. Believe me. That getup you had on," he said with a chuckle and a shake of his head, "that hat, the flour-sack dress, the shoes." He rolled his eyes. "Those god-awful shoes. Abrams would have taken one look at you and sent you packing."

"How can you be so sure of what Silas Abrams would have done?"

"Because I know him, honey, probably better than he knows himself. I know what he's capable of—what he wants." He gave her a shrewd, piercing look. "He thinks to surround himself with things of taste and quality. He thinks it will rub off on him, gain him entrance into certain circles.''

DeLacey glanced about the room, the expensive furnishings, the very clothing he had on. What a hypocrite Joss McRae was. ''And you're so different?'' she demanded.

If she thought to irritate him, she was in for a letdown. Joss merely laughed at her cutting remark and raked her with an insolent look. ''Unlike some people, I make no pretense of who I am or what I am, what I have . . . or what I want.''

DeLacey knew that comment was aimed directly at her and the way she had attempted to deceive him, but she kept her face blank.

''Power, Lacey, influence, the kind of respect and recognition only money can provide. That's what I want. I couldn't give a damn about social acceptance or community standing.''

DeLacey recoiled at the honest venom she heard in his voice. The very foundation of her disdain for him and all she thought he stood for began to crumble under her feet. Were they so very different, Joss in his arrogance, she in her pride? Were not the things he claimed he wanted the very goals that she had been striving for since her daddy's degradation and death? And yet somehow coming from a man like Joss McRae such ambitions sounded anything but honorable.

Did that mean that she too was so . . . reprehensible?

Rising, she swayed for a moment in indecision, wishing for all the world she had never met Joss McRae, that she had never been forced to confront her own possible shortcomings.

''Sit down, Lacey.'' The command was softly spoken but nonetheless irrefutable. His gaze, gray and steady, revealed not a trace of regret for who he was or what he was, nor what he planned to do to another human being even if Silas Abrams was as culpable as he claimed. ''There's a lot we have to discuss and get straight before we reach Medora tomorrow morning.''

Defeated, not so much by him but by the gnawing need

within her to obtain her objectives, to keep the Honeycutt honor alive even if it was only a facade, she sank back down. Make a pact with the devil. . . .

Too late she realized her mistake, and for the life of her she couldn't think of a single way to extract herself from the undeviating path she trod, short of throwing herself from the train in sacrifice. And she was much too cynical to entertain such a noble notion.

She was stuck, for it seemed this demon, with his smirking gray eyes and generous mouth, was much too handsome and persuasive a cad to deny—even if she wanted to. Simply said, she would just have to play this hand out and hope he was bluffing.

CHAPTER 7

When the train chugged into the town of Medora the comparison that came to deLacey's mind was that of a dried-up prune. It was obvious that the community had once been a thriving plum of civilization surrounded by patches of grasslands, wild and untamed, and framed by fantastic buttes of turbulent color that went on as far as the eye could see. But now there was little left of the boomtown except abandoned buildings, some so large she couldn't imagine what kind of enterprise they had housed. All that remained was a shriveled nucleus of what once must have been grandeur and prosperity, an oasis of civilization bordering the famous Badlands.

Why would a successful man like Joss McRae want to live in a place like this? Could it be that he was one of those people who chose to see what used to be in a crumbling world about them rather than what truly was? Such a vulnerability seemed incongruous with the man she'd come to know over the last few days. Nonetheless, it was an interesting conjecture.

Lacey sighed. Chances were, she would never get the opportunity to find out. Last night the final details of their business agreement had been hashed over and the arrangements made, via Henry, for her to resume her place in one of the public train cars. Before the sun had risen, the kindly servant had awoken her in plenty of time to get dressed and make her way to her assigned seat.

For the most part the train was relatively empty as Medora was near the end of the railroad line. The few remaining passengers were asleep, and couldn't question her sudden appearance. No doubt they would assume she had come aboard during a late-night stop.

Gathering the gray serge skirt of her dress about her, the same one she had worn the night before, deLacey watched the sun rise in the far corner of the train window. She experienced a flutter of nerves like she had never felt before. Deception was nothing new to her, heavens no, but this time . . .

This time was different. This time it would not be a quick in and a quicker out, taking what money she could in a few hands of poker. This time she would have to court her victim, milk him for information, and keep him at bay for who knew how long.

That was one thing she'd forgotten to quiz Joss about. Just how long *would* she be expected to keep up this masquerade? How long before he would pay her what he owed her and let her be on her way?

Her only source of comfort was in the fact that Silas Abrams, if what Joss had told her about him was true, would be most deserving of what was to happen to him.

She tried to imagine what someone capable of stealing cattle from his neighbors would look like, this man who had been willing to accept a bride sight unseen. If she listened to Joss, she imagined he would be tall, overbearing, probably much like McRae himself.

Joss. Eyes flashing, she glanced away from the scenery outside the window to stare at the exit at the far end of the aisle. Where was he? There had been no sign of him in his private parlor when she had crossed through it earlier that morning en route to her present position. Somehow through all of this . . . ordeal, she had assumed he had spent his nights stretched out on the sofa. But the room had been empty—no sign of him at all. Almost as if he didn't exist.

She shivered, wondering if perhaps that wasn't the case. Joss McRae was no more than a shadow in the night, a figment of her overactive imagination, a finger of conscience to point out her own long list of shortcomings.

Then hours later, the sun high in the sky, reality made its presence known. The awful metal squeal hurt her teeth as breaks were applied time and again to the thundering wheels beneath her. Her wild musings were brought to an abrupt halt, much quicker than the train itself.

So this was it. Reaching up, she fiddled nervously with a curl on her forehead, smoothing it down. Then she tested her bonnet strings to make sure they were still tied in the big bow underneath her chin. Clutching the hard seat beneath her, she stared out the window, wondering if Silas Abrams was in the small crowd that was framed in her window for just a few moments before the car rolled on past the depot platform. Knowing his nature as it had been explained to her, would Abrams even bother to meet her himself? She doubted it seriously.

When at last the metal serpent came to a complete halt, she remained in her seat even after the other passengers had slipped from theirs and had threaded past her to disembark from the train. She could put it off no longer. Rising, she took up her reticule and traveling bag and moved down the narrow aisle to the exit at the rear of the car.

"Ma'am." The conductor doffed his square-billed cap and helped her descend and then promptly forgot her as if he had not once seen her in the company of Joss McRae.

There on the platform she set down her luggage and glanced about. The sun, although well beyond its zenith in the vast Dakota sky, beat down mercilessly on her. A thin sheen of moisture beaded her upper lip, another trickled between her breasts, and she knew then that this land would not be a gentle one. Touching her gloved hand to her face to absorb the perspiration, she sighed.

And then a strange prickling feeling skittered down her spine—a sensation that had nothing at all to do with the heat of the sun or her apprehensions of who was going to meet her. Joss McRae, damn his unredeemable soul, was watch-

ing her, no doubt out the window of his lavish private car.
She could feel his piercing gaze upon her back, scrutinizing
her actions, almost as if he waited for her to make a mistake
so he could go about rectifying it in the way he enjoyed
best—humiliating her.

Just what did he expect her to do? Go tracking down this
monster who would claim her as his bride? It was not her
fault if Silas Abrams wanted nothing to do with her. Not her
responsibility to find him. Not . . .

"Miss Honeycutt?"

DeLacey turned and found herself face-to-face with one
of the most disgusting men she had ever encountered. He
was not very tall, only a few inches more than she, and the
enormous cowboy hat and flapping leather chaps he wore
made him appear even smaller. Tobacco juice browned the
corners of his mouth, which had a cruel downward turn to
it, and he reeked—just of what, she couldn't be sure, but his
smell was most unpleasant. Oh, surely this couldn't be Silas
Abrams.

"You couldn't possibly be Miss dee-Lacey Honeycutt,
could ya?" There was an expression of pure amazement on
his stubbly, dirty face as he pronounced her name improp-
erly. Then when he grinned at her, he revealed a row of
stained, crooked teeth.

If there had not been so much at stake, so much money in
the offing, she would have denied who she was then and
there, fleeing back into the safety of the train car. But the
railroad was Joss McRae's domain and no doubt he would
never allow her to escape so easily.

"Yes," she murmured, the dread a giant knot clogging
her throat, hating the situation but especially hating Joss
McRae for putting her in this position. "I'm deLacey
Honeycutt." She flashed a wooden smile even as her gaze
slid down to the holstered pistol strapped to the man's hip.

"Well, I'll be a 'pecker on an ironwood post." Laughing,
he swept off his hat and slapped it against the side of his leg.
A flurry of dust rose from his filthy clothing, heightening
the awful smell. His brown eyes, full of cruel merriment,
swept over her with obvious approval. "Sy is about the

luckiest damn son o'a bitch this side of Missouri . . . Sorry, miss, didn't mean to oh-fend.'' But his look said otherwise as he spat on the ground just inches from the shiny toe of her shoe.

However disgusted, deLacey sighed her relief. At least he had said Sy, not I—which meant this wasn't Silas Abrams. Thank goodness for small wonders. For if it had been, she would have never been able to adhere to her agreement, not for any amount of money.

"No offense taken, Mr. . . ."

He stared at her dumbly for a moment as he wiped the residue of tobacco from his chin.

"Oh, Billy Howell, ma'am," he supplied. Then contrary to good manners, he dropped his battered hat back on his head and tapped it, stirring up the dust once again. "At yer service. I work at the Rocking A Ranch. Mr. Abrams asked me to see that you was picked up with the weekly supplies."

DeLacey felt the hair on the back of her neck stiffen. A package to be delivered, was she? Well, she would just have to do something about that false impression—on the part of everyone—Billy Howell, Silas Abrams, and Joss McRae. Especially Joss McRae, who was probably still watching her. The daughter of King Honeycutt was not an incidental to be treated as if she were nothing more than a sack of flour.

Without a word, she bent down, retrieved her baggage, and began walking away. Not once offering to relieve her of her burden, Billy Howell followed her across the platform, the jingle of his spurs marking his stride through the small, rickety building that served as a depot. Only when she passed out of the front door and veered to her left toward a hand-painted sign that read Medora Hotel did he finally speak up.

"The wagon's over yonder, miss."

She didn't bother to pause, even to slow her determined pace one iota. She was almost to the front door of the hotel before he stopped her. The shot fired into the air caused even the dozing horse hitched in front of the building to flinch in surprise and jerk back.

If he thought to scare her, then Billy Howell knew nothing of the Honeycutt mettle. Turning about, she confronted him.

"Thought maybe you was deef or somethin'." His gun still aimed skyward, he grinned and spit on the ground.

"Mr. Howell." She called him that begrudgingly and with little respect. "I am not deaf, nor am I something to be picked up and delivered. You tell your employer, Mr. Abrams, that if he would care to come and present himself to me, I will consider receiving him. But in the meantime I will be staying at the hotel, not at his ranch." With that she continued on toward her destination.

"Well, if she ain't the prissy li'l heifer."

Ignoring him and his muttered insults, she marched on.

"The train back East leaves in the mornin', miss. If yer smart, you'll be on it."

She didn't stop to ask him why he would say something like that to her, almost as if he were trying to warn her off. Yet, as much as she despised the cowboy with his dirt, and smell, and tobacco juice, he was right. If she had a brain in her head she *would* take his advice to heart and get out before she got further involved. But that option wasn't open to her—at least, not at the moment.

Just what kind of a crude bumpkin would send a man like Billy Howell to meet his intended bride?

And what about Joss McRae? He had to have seen what she had been forced to deal with. How could he just stand by and watch? Knowing his as she did, she suspected he had not only watched but found her predicament most amusing.

Once inside the hotel, she dropped her bag in front of the reception desk in the lobby and took a look around. A room just beyond, though not that large, was crowded with tables and chairs all occupied to overflowing. Apparently the place served as a gathering place for locals. She received several curious stares, but she ignored them, returning her attention to the hotel clerk.

"I would like a room, please." Removing the glove from her right hand one finger at a time, she prepared to sign the registry.

Almost as if he hadn't heard her the clerk, a little man whose head with its large, protruding ears looked like a sugar bowl, merely stared at her, as if her reason for wanting a room needed explanation. Of her own initiative, she turned the book around and scripted her name in big, bold letters. He angled it back around.

"Miss dee-Lacey Honeycutt," he read slowly, and looked up at her once more over the wire rims of his spectacles. "You the mail-order bride Silas sent fer from St. Louis?"

Couldn't anyone pronounce her name properly in this godforsaken town? But biting off the sharp retort, she nodded, unsure how her acknowledgment would be received. She was not to find out. The man simply reached behind his back and took up a key without much contemplation and placed it on the counter beside her ungloved hand.

"Twelve. Up the stairs and at the end of the hall near the facilities. But use 'em early if you plan on usin 'em at all."

Ignoring the gruff innuendo, she scooped up the key. As she swept up the stairs she could have sworn that every set of eyes in the hotel was trained on her, and the buzz of conversation concerned her as well, but she didn't turn around to confirm her suspicions, refusing to allow them to get to her.

Let 'em look.

It was her daddy's familiar drawl that spoke to her, a bolster to her flagging spirit.

But don't let 'em touch.

That warning took on a very different, special meaning to her. She knew then that it was her heart and her conscience that she so fervently had to protect from violation, not just the outer shell. So long as she kept herself distanced from all the players in this game of deception and bluff—especially Joss McRae—and kept her head squarely on her shoulders, her purpose and goal in the foreground, she would get through this minor scrape like all the rest.

Like all the rest. DeLacey took each step of the staircase with single-minded determination and the confidence of an alley cat that always managed to land on its feet, somehow, no matter how long the fall.

Joss hit the rear entrance of the hotel like a dust devil. Plowing up the rarely used back stairs to the rooms above, he gathered speed spurred on by the powder keg of emotions waiting to explode just below the surface of a calm facade. She had done it again, that Honeycutt woman, blatantly ignored his explicit instructions. Just what in the hell did she think she was doing?

He didn't need to stop and ask the clerk what room she would be in, for there was only one the man would dare to give her. The only one decent enough to house a woman. Twelve.

In spite of its history of wealth and far-reaching vision, Medora was now no more than a cow town, one with a reputation for rowdiness and not just on Saturday nights when the outlying ranch hands came to town to squander their week's earnings and blow off a little steam.

Room twelve, actually a small suite, was a monument to that once glorious past. No, more like a mausoleum for a grandeur lost, not once but twice over. Nobody ever came to Medora anymore who would appreciate the dainty Eastern furnishings, the fine Aubusson carpeting. Only he and Teddy Roosevelt, perhaps—and Silas Abrams, not that the son of a bitch could appreciate anything of subtle class or quality even if it slugged him in the mouth. But rarely did one of them have the urge to stay in town—there was nothing here anymore. And yet room twelve remained intact, waiting, a reminder of what had once been.

Now Miss deLacey Honeycutt would park her pretty posterior on the rosewood sofa in the sitting room and think herself royalty to hold court. She was supposed to have met with Abrams, not sashayed off on her own, even though he couldn't quite blame her. What had possessed Abrams to send Billy Howell to town to escort his bride-to-be back to the Rocking A Ranch? Obviously something important had kept the prospective bridegroom from coming himself, and Joss could well imagine what that something was.

Cattle. It seemed of late that small herds, in particular his own, were disappearing from the range. He was sure Silas Abrams had something to do with it.

Reaching the top of the stairs, he glanced down the long hallway, pleased to find it empty. He had to be careful that no one saw him traipsing after deLacey. It would never do if word got back to Silas Abrams that the two of them had gotten together. Abrams would then be suspicious of her and never would she be able to gather the proof he wanted that Abrams was a cattle thief.

It took him only a few steps to reach the door to room twelve. His knock was soft, yet insistent.

Without bothering to inquire deLacey opened the door and immediately slammed it upon seeing who was standing beyond. But before she could throw the bolt, Joss forced his way inside.

"Damn it, Lacey, you have to be more careful about who you open a door to."

"What are you doing here, Joss McRae?" she demanded in a strained hush. Stepping behind the rosewood sofa, she put its bulk between them. Her hair was down, its lushness a cape about her slender shoulders, a brush clutched in her fist and held up as if it were a weapon.

"I should be asking you that question, honey, for it seems you forget instructions much too easily." Joss fought down the unaccountable surge of jealousy that flash flooded through his veins. "You were supposed to be on your way to join Silas Abrams."

"No, he was to have met me at the train station. Instead he sent some . . . horrid man to cart me off into the wilderness . . ." Her face turned up to him with a look that, although it was a plea, displayed a hint of determination. "Did you, or Silas Abrams for that matter, really expect me to go off, no questions asked, with someone like . . . Billy Howell?"

No, he couldn't say that he did, yet it wasn't safe for her to remain in Medora alone. And what if Abrams took offense at her refusal to travel with his escort—and Joss wouldn't put such callousness past his enemy—and sent her packing before she could ever set those delicate hooks of hers in him?

Even now he could feel the tug of her tentacles that she had somehow managed to entangle him in, stirring up an unaccountable need to protect her. He brushed aside the concern and sympathy creeping into his heart and took on an authoritative air.

"I'll admit that Billy's a little rough around the edges, but he's basically all right."

"All right?" She bristled like a cat with its tail caught under a rocking chair. "He smelled and spit tobacco juice at me and . . . and . . ."

"This is me you're talking to now, deLacey." Frowning, he glared at her and her little act of priggishness. "So don't try and tell me you've never dealt with men like Billy Howell before."

She sputtered, her small fists mounted on her hips in defiance, but she made no denial.

Oddly enough he was disappointed at her lack of defense. "I'll make arrangements for a buggy and driver to take you out to the Rocking A, so you can make your amends to Abrams." The matter was settled, at least in his mind.

"No."

"What?" This final show of defiance on her part was unforgivable. "What do you mean, no? We have an agreement, Lacey, and you'll damn well stick to it."

"No," she reiterated with a saucy air and a knowing smile. "He'll come to me. Just you wait and see."

"How can you be so sure?" He knitted his brows in uncertainty.

"You're the one who said it." Dropping her hands from her waist, she clutched the back of the sofa.

He watched the movement, and against his will he remembered how her strong little fingers had felt similarly wrapped about the muscles of his arms.

"He craves things of class and refinement," she continued. "A lady would expect him to court her."

What she said made sense, and yet he suspected she had ulterior motives for wanting to stay in town. To be frank, deLacey wasn't a lady, not by his standards, anyway. Not that it made a difference about how he felt about her. It was just that he didn't trust her, and even the lure of the money he had agreed to pay her might not be sufficient to hold her long enough to get what he wanted from her.

If she roomed in town, then he would have to stay as well, not only to make sure she remained put but to make sure no one bothered her. He didn't relish the idea of spending even one night in Medora, but what choice did he have?

"You had better be right, Lacey." It was a way of giving in to her without really conceding. Turning away he headed toward the door.

"Joss." She spoke his name with a heart-stopping softness that did crazy things to his insides.

Without answering, he paused, but didn't look back at her, almost afraid of what the sight of her would do to him and the hard edge of his determination to do whatever he had to do or use whomever he must to get what he wanted.

"If you were Silas Abrams, wouldn't you want to court me?"

That was a loaded question, blast her, one he could take a dozen different ways, and yet he knew what she was asking even if she didn't know it herself.

"I'm not Abrams; I'm not looking to get roped and branded by a female," he answered gruffly. "I have no need or inclination to court you or any other woman."

It was a malicious thing to say, he supposed, but it was the truth. There was no room in his life for the sacrifices and artful glibness that wooing a wife would undoubtedly require. Yet, oddly enough, for the first time in his life, he wished he had told the Honeycutt woman a deliberate lie and spared her feelings.

And even if he should ever consider a binding relationship, it wouldn't be with a difficult snip like deLacey. No, indeed. The best kind of woman was the one who asked for nothing and demanded even less. That kind of woman . . .

Well, that kind of woman required little effort and no commitment.

Joss frowned as he marched out of the room. It seemed he had put out and put up with too much already when it came to deLacey Honeycutt. Here and now it was going to come to a stop.

Leaving the building the same way he had gone in, by the back entrance, he made his way around to the front. Then as if he had not seen deLacey only moments before he entered the hotel and approached the front desk.

"Give me a room, Otis," he said to the clerk, confident that no one would think it odd for him to stay one night at the hotel before heading to his ranch.

"I'm s-s-sorry, Mr. McRae. Had I known you were comin'," the horrified man trailed off. "Twelve's already occupied."

Joss pretended to be surprised. "Then give me the key to eleven." He stuck out his hand.

"Eleven's a shambles, sir. How about number three?"

"Eleven," he insisted. He wanted to be directly across the hallway from Lacey, so he could watch her—watch over her, he justified—but he didn't want the clerk to know that. "I want to be next to the bathroom." His request was not unreasonable or unusual.

"Eleven." Otis didn't argue further. Just like everybody else in Medora, he knew better. Whatever Joss McRae wanted he got. Taking the key from the slot behind him, he dropped it in Joss's hand.

"Have a good night, Mr. McRae."

Joss sincerely doubted that would be the case.

DeLacey blinked back the mounting tears and swallowed down the ridiculous hurt scalding the back of her throat. Damn his insufferable hide. Joss McRae was a cold-hearted bastard, as cold as they came.

She swiped at the gathered moisture on her lashes with the back of her hand and sniffed with indignation. Her daddy had been right. Let 'em look, but never, *never* let 'em touch. Against all advice she had allowed Joss McRae not only to touch but to grab ahold of her inexperienced, vulnerable heart. She had let him. No. He had forced his way into her life without ever asking "if you please."

Well, she didn't please. Not one bit. Again she sniffed back the resentment that manifested itself in her rebellious tear ducts, which seemed to have sprung simultaneous leaks. Stripping off her travel-stained gown, she tossed it over a chair.

Yes. Revenge. Getting even with him. That notion put a stopper in the waterworks. And the way to do it was so easy she couldn't believe she'd not thought of it sooner. Joss wanted information about Silas Abrams. Well, she would see that he got exactly what he wanted, and what did she care if it was true or not? Abrams meant nothing to her, and Joss even less. Duping him—both of them—for the money would be easy. . . .

And richly satisfying.

And most ingenious. A feat worthy of a Honeycutt.

Collected once again, she took up where she had left off brushing out her long hair before Joss had so rudely disturbed her. Staring into the gilded mirror over the dressing table, she studied her face, noting the puffiness about her eyes that even the few moments of crying had caused, and vowed not to let it happen again. She had a big day ahead of her tomorrow. No doubt Silas Abrams would come calling, and she had to look her best to greet him. She knew exactly how she would handle him.

As a prelude to any discussion about matrimony she would ask him pertinent questions about his business. As a prospective wife she had a right to know, didn't she? Then with her inventive mind it would be easy enough to concoct a story that was innocent sounding and yet alluded to wrongdoing on Abrams's part and feed it to Joss, collect her money, and be gone before either of them had the chance to figure out that she had deceived them.

Yes, it was a good plan.

Thinking no more about it, she turned away from her own reflection and set about deciding just what she should wear for the coming interview with Silas Abrams. She considered several selections, and as she eliminated the possibilities

one by one, she tried not to dwell upon the fact that the only
reason she had so many outfits to choose from was because
of Joss McRae's generosity. But it was no more than she
deserved for the horrible way he had treated her.

She was down to a sea green faille with a darker green
sash with tassels on the ends that would wrap about her
waist several times, then fall low in the front in a casual
knot. She picked it up, held it in front of her, and turned to
face the mirror once more. Very stylish, and it would accent
one of her best assets, the smallness of her waist.

Pleased with her final selection, she hung the dress over
the vanity to allow the wrinkles to fall out of it overnight
and gathered up her soap and toweling. She slipped on a
loose-fitting dressing gown that tied in front with a wide
sash. The clerk had warned her that if she wished to take
advantage of the communal bathroom two doors down, then
she should plan to use it early. She couldn't imagine why,
for if her room was any indication, only those of good
breeding stayed in the Medora Hotel. Well, perhaps later the
facilities would be in great demand, so she decided to take
the man's advice and bathe now before going down to get
something to eat.

When she stepped out of the door of her room and bent to
lock it behind her, she was relaxed, humming under her
breath, really quite pleased with herself and her plan of
action. Then she turned and started down the hallway.

She had taken only a few steps when something latched
on to her arm and jerked her into the room directly across
from her own. It happened so quickly and unexpectedly that
she didn't have time to scream before the door closed.

"Just where do you think you're going, Lacey?"

Even if she had been shrouded in total darkness she
would have recognized that voice. Joss McRae. What was
he doing back here, apparently camped out in the room
across from hers? And what a horrid room it was, with a
sagging old bed and a stained and faded carpet. Nothing like
the fancy suite she occupied.

Why did she owe him an explanation? She didn't.
Besides, he could figure out the answer for himself if he

would only bother to look at the items she had clutched to her chest.

Still holding on to her arm as if he had every right, he towered over her, glaring down at her with that look of his that was halfway between a scowl and indolent amusement. How many times had she wanted to wipe that expression from his face?

"I asked you a question, honey." His eyes, so steely gray, pierced her, demanding an answer.

He wanted a response, well then, she would give him one—one he would never forget—one that her daddy had taught her would get the attention and respect of any man bent on harassing her. Dropping the items in her hands, she brought her knee up with as much force as she could muster. To her surprise, and his as well, she caught him squarely in the groin. He sucked in a loud breath and doubled over. For a moment Lacey thought he would fall to the floor. She'd had no idea such a simple action would cause him so much pain.

"Joss?" She bent over him with concern, her hand cupping his shoulder.

Grabbing her by the wrist, he straightened, wrenching her arm behind her as he pressed her against the door so hard it knocked the breath out of her. For an instant she thought he was going to strike her back. The anger on his face gave every indication that he would. Finally, she had pushed him too far, and she regretted her impulsiveness.

But then, she changed her mind and lifted her face, practically daring him to reciprocate. What gave him the right to bully her so? Always it seemed he was an obstacle she had to get over or around or through, even just to take a bath. Quite frankly, she was tired of his never-ending interference in her life. If she had hurt him, then he deserved it. So let him hit her if he wanted to. Perhaps then he would go away and leave her alone.

But his plans for her were not to be so simple. He began by groping the waistline of her dressing gown. Finding the single pocket, he turned it inside out.

"Where's the key to your room, Lacey?"

"I don't know." Even if she did, she refused to tell him. "I dropped it." And she was glad of it.

"Then find it." Pulling her back to the spot where she had thrown down her toiletries, he pushed her to her knees.

He was doing it to her again. Treating her like so much dirt under his feet. The last thing she was going to allow him was entrance into her room again.

"It's not here. I can't find it." Shuffling the articles on the floor about, she shoved the key into the folds of the towel. Then she gathered the items up and clutched them to her heart.

"Woman, you are trying my patience." As if she were a sapling he was attempting to defoliate, he shook her so hard her teeth chattered. The key slipped from its hiding place and clattered to the floor.

Joss said nothing, but his eyes pinned her with an accusation that made her feel like a complete fool. Never releasing his painful grip on her arm, he stooped and retrieved the key. Powerless to do much to stop him, she nonetheless dragged her heels when she realized his intent. Just as determined, he lifted her bodily and carried her into the hallway, quickly unlocking the door to her room.

She dared not allow him access to her quarters as she could well imagine what would come of his anger and her stubborn resistance. As lightning strikes the lone tree on the prairie, they were destined to collide. Once the sparks were ignited, she knew only too well what the inevitable heat did to her apathy. It charred it, turning it to passion, into an aching need to throw herself into the flames no matter how badly she might get burned.

"Let go of me, Joss McRae, or I swear I will scream so loud it will bring the rafters down." The threat was barely out when his hand clamped over her mouth.

Forcing her inside, he slammed the door and pressed her against it. He glared down at her with that arrogance of his she knew well and had confronted and fought futilely so many times in the last few days. Already the air was crisp with the electricity his nearness inevitably incited. Gasping for a breath that didn't seem to be there, she flattened her spine against the solid wood and opened her mouth to follow through with her threat.

And then it happened just as she had feared it would— lightning struck and sizzled clear to her curling toes. His lips were hot, searing, demanding. Her heart began to race out of control; her resistance tucked tail and ran, abandoning her when she needed it most.

She knew she was kissing him back and was powerless to stop herself, and was just as incapable of halting the way her heart, that traitorous beast, slammed against the prison of its cage when his hand slipped into the front of her dressing gown to cup her breast covered only by the thin material of her chemise. A garment he had purchased for her, she reminded herself, and no doubt had touched numerous times before.

She knew not how it happened, when he broke through the barrier of her resistance, but the next thing she knew she gladly allowed him to scoop her up into his arms. But then he just stood there in the middle of the room as if undecided, staring down at her in a way that renewed the frenzy of her heart.

Somehow her arms had found their way about his powerful neck. But now with him staring at her so, she jerked them away and splayed them against his chest, a last gesture of defiance. His heart. She could feel it hammering away beneath the thinness of his shirt, just as violently as her own.

She looked up into his face, saw the mirror of her own conflict taking place on his handsome features. Joss McRae had human failings, after all. The discovery left her reeling. Somehow she had imagined that nothing could stir the calculating ice in his veins, and especially not her. But there it was, the proof, pounding away beneath her palm.

Such revelation was reassuring and at the same time unnerving. Then when he turned, his decision made, and he strode toward the bed, the fear swept over her like an arctic wind. She might be innocent, untried in the way of love, but Lacey was no fool. She knew exactly where this was heading. Others might indulge lightly, including Joss

McRae, but the Honeycutt passion was no less famous than their skill with a deck of cards.

The devotion of her parents to one another had been vollied from one gaming house to another, yet everyone had respected their commitment to each other. And even after her mother had died, her daddy had remained faithful to her memory for so long. When he had finally accepted his loss, deLacey remembered how discreet he had been. Though he had never committed himself to another love, he had treated the few women in his life very specially.

Would Joss McRae treat her specially?

It was too much to hope for.

And yet, his mouth covering hers was warm and giving, offering her a haven, if only a temporary one, from the storm her life had become over the last few years since her daddy's downfall and death. She didn't deceive herself. There was nothing offered in the emotions he evoked, except the passion itself, but neither were there thoughts of revenge, or ambitions. No pain, no disappointment. No shame. Only a wild, wonderful opportunity to express that lost little girl buried deep within her who so desperately wanted to be loved and sheltered from reality, if only for a while.

As if he sensed her secret longings, Joss placed her gently in the middle of the bed. On bent knees, he towered over her, removed his Stetson and tossed it on the nearby chair. Then with one crooked finger he traced the contour of her jaw line, his touch as soft as silk.

"I only wanted to protect you, Lacey," he murmured, swooping down closer as if testing the waters of her acquiescence.

Wanting desperately to believe him, she lifted her arms. He instantly filled their emptiness, blotting out the doubts and uncertainties with the weight of his masculine body over hers. What he thought to protect her from, she hadn't a clue, nor did she care to know—not now. There was nothing, no one who could harm her at this moment.

Then there was no more thought, only the feel of his mouth, heated and demanding, the trace of bearded roughness on his face, prickling and yet so exciting as he nuzzled her ear, her neck, and across her throat that convulsed beneath his caress. She heard a sigh, soft and unrestrained, and wondered where it came from.

"Joss." There it was again, more of a susurration this time that went on for eternity like the wind, and she realized the sound had come from her own throat raw with need.

The sweetness of his name upon her lips spurred him on. He parted the dressing gown, brushing the two panels to the side. Almost as if she were a spectator standing on the sidelines, she watched him as he untied the ribbon of her chemise and pushed it down as well, freeing up her breasts to his perusal, releasing her inhibitions where she had tucked them down so deep that she had thought they could never be unveiled.

A wonderful shudder coursed through her. He found her beautiful. His devouring eyes, softened to the color of the gentlest gray mourning dove, assured her of that.

At that moment she was the focus of his universe, and he in turn became the only world that existed for her. There he hovered, his face so close and yet so far away, the anticipation so intense she closed her eyes and arched upwards, striving to shatter this final barrier between them.

Oh, but the wait had been worthwhile. His lips as they encircled her tender, untried flesh unlatched the floodgates of desire within her. Rushing down, they swamped her with a giddiness. That another passion deep down inside, so overwhelmed her that she gasped and cried out, not caring who might hear her. Nothing could be more important.

Then when his hand slipped into her drawers, she opened to him and discovered how wrong she had been. There was so much more to experience and savor—and strive for. Only Joss could give it to her.

The gentle rhythm of his fingers was easy, knowing, just as his words of encouragement were, carrying her up, up. . . .

"Show me where, Lacey, where you like it best."

Then, when it seemed she came so close to that inexperienced something, he came to a sudden, unexplained halt.

Crying out her frustration—oh, why would he stop now?—she lifted her hips against his hand, trying to recapture the lost moment.

''Jesus Christ, Lacey. I didn't know.'' He withdrew his hand and pushed up, and stared down at her as if someone had stamped Leper across her forehead.

What was wrong? What had she done to displease him?

''Don't stop now,'' she whispered as she ran her hands inside his unbuttoned shirt and across the thick mat of chest hair, marveling at how different he was from her, how gloriously masculine. She felt him twitch under her caress. Her touch stirred him, she knew it did. . . .

Yet he pushed her hands away and rose up off the bed and turned away.

But not before she saw the evidence of his arousal.

''Joss?'' Pressing up on her elbows, she didn't care that her clothing was in disarray, her body wantonly displayed. If only he would look at her—really look at her.

He refused, and she recognized that the moment was over before it had truly had a chance to begin. When he finally turned to stare down at her, she felt her throat convulse with pain. Gone from his eyes was the passion. In its place was the cold accusation she knew only too well.

There was only one answer for his strange behavior.

The hard-hearted bastard had done this to her on purpose. It was a game he played, one to show her that he held the upper hand, and she had fallen for his ruse like a tenderfoot with a tinhorn gambler.

''Get out,'' she cried, pulling her clothing about her as best she could, feeling cold, used, and soiled.

He didn't argue. He didn't even look back. He just gathered up his discarded hat and stalked toward the exit.

The door closed so softly on his departure that she hardly heard it. And yet, it was as if he had slammed it on her fingers, so intense was the agony in her heart.

The heat died within her, hardening as molten lava turns to stone. Joss McRae thought to toy with her, did he? Well, she knew a thing or two about using people, more than he could even begin to imagine. He had made up the rules. She would play by them. The slate was clean between them. She owed him nothing, not consideration—not even the truth.

He would lose, and she would be ten thousand dollars richer. Then she would be the one leaving him behind.

She vowed that she too wouldn't give him the satisfaction of looking back.

CHAPTER 8

Bright and early the next morning an insistent pounding on
the door to deLacey's hotel room refused to go away. She
woke with a start, bleary-eyed and exhausted, for her sleep
had been haunted by a vision of Joss McRae, of his body,
hard and sleek, his knowing hands, his mouth that had
pulverized her willpower, turning her into a whimpering
female willing—no, eager—to do whatever he demanded.
And then when she thought about him getting up and
leaving without so much as an explanation, it renewed her
determination to get even—to prove to herself that her
defenses, though battered, were still intact.

"Yes, yes. I'm coming. Who's there?" Dragging herself
off the bed, she stumbled to the door. However, after the
fiasco the evening before, she refused to open it until she
was certain who was on the other side.

"I've a message for ya, miss."

The hotel clerk's voice. She cracked open the door just a
little bit, enough to see into the dimly lit hallway. To have
found Joss lurking in the shadows wouldn't have surprised
her, but there was no one behind the bespectacled clerk. The
door across the way was closed. Was Joss behind it, asleep?
Or perhaps he was gone. Oddly enough, deLacey experienced a moment of panic to think she might be on her own.

"Yes, what is it?" she demanded with a curtness that stemmed from self-contempt.

"From Mr. Silas Abrams." He offered her a folded piece of paper.

She accepted it, then quickly closed the door. All hints of grogginess dissipated when she opened the note and began to read. Quite pleased with herself, she giggled. She knew she'd been right about Abrams. However, she had to admit she'd not expected him to jump at her beck and call so swiftly.

The paper was expensive linen, the handwriting amazingly florid and refined for some backwoods cowpoke even if he was rich. DeLacey frowned as her eyes skimmed over the invitation once more. And the words he chose—they really were quite poetic, even if they were a bit overdone.

Could she, his dearest Miss Honeycutt, find it in her generous heart to lunch with him at eleven of the clock in the hotel dining room? Signed, The Honorable Silas A. Abrams.

Honorable? The words leapt out at her from the page. If it had had fingers they no doubt would have encircled her slender neck and squeezed, strangling her.

How silly. It was just a word, and Silas Abrams probably didn't deserve the title especially in light of what Joss had said about him. But then after last night, who was Joss McRae to judge another when it came to honor?

At the rat-a-tat-tat of a follow-up on the door, deLacey jumped.

"Pardon, Miss Honeycutt? What do you want me to tell Mr. Abrams?" It was the clerk again, apparently waiting for her answer.

"Tell him . . . yes," she called out and set about getting dressed for that most important meeting. For even if she didn't plan on giving Joss what he'd bargained for, she still had to go through the motions.

At five of eleven she was ready, but she held herself in check. It would not do if she arrived too early in the dining room as that would make her appear overly eager, and heaven forbid that she should arrive before he did. No, it

was best to allow Mr. Silas Abrams to wait on her just a few
minutes. Just enough to put him off-balance, so he would
experience a moment of relief when she finally decided to
join him.

Confirming the hour once more at eleven fifteen, she was
satisfied that her luncheon companion had stewed long
enough. Taking her time, she left the room, after again
glancing up and down the hall for signs of Joss McRae, and
carefully locked the door behind her as she did.

The dining room was beginning to fill when she arrived
downstairs. In the doorway, deLacey glanced about the
occupied tables. There were only three that had single men
sitting at them.

The first surely couldn't be Silas Abrams. The diner
looked more like some ancient miner who had been in the
hills much too long and would be more comfortable with a
pick and pan than china and silver. DeLacey dismissed him
immediately.

The second possibility was just as unlikely. Rather small,
almost dumpy and balding. Although he wore a tailored
suit, she chalked him up as some kind of drummer.

Her gaze slid to the third and final choice. This had to be
Silas Abrams. The man was dressed as a rancher should be,
denim pants, a clean although well-worn checkered shirt.
Hanging on the chair beside him was a Stetson that looked
a lot like the one Joss McRae wore. In fact, he looked about
as arrogant—just the kind of man to send someone like
Billy Howell to pick up a prospective bride.

She smiled at him, and he, in turn, examined her rather
pointedly, but he made no move to rise and greet her. How
irritating. Just what did he expect? For her to come up to
him and introduce herself?

"Miss Honeycutt?"

DeLacey turned, discovering the drummer. Although she
had to look up at him, she still considered him short for a
man.

"I didn't mean to startle you."

Out of the corner of her eye she watched the third man.
Still he made no move to intercede.

"You didn't startle me," she replied and looked away, dismissing him as forward even though she had to admit that he was very polite about it.

"Then if you would care to join me." He swept his hand toward the table where he had been sitting.

"*You're* Silas Abrams?" She knew the surprise she experienced, and hadn't meant to express openly, tainted her voice anyway. But he was nothing like the formidable enemy Joss had made him out to be.

"Sorry to disappoint you, ma'am." He laughed, and she had to admit it was a rather pleasant sound.

"Oh, oh, no. I'm not disappointed. Not at all," she assured him quickly, but in truth she had expected her adversary at least to look worthy of her contempt. This man was anything but contemptible. In fact, he was almost pitiful. Sweet. Soft-spoken. And if his face was any indication—and she prided herself, at least up until now, in being able to read men's faces—he was really quite kind and mild-mannered. That made what she planned to do that much harder.

"Good, I'm glad to hear that." He took her arm with confident fingers and guided her toward his table and saw to it that she was properly settled before returning to his own chair.

Busying herself, she studied him across the tablecloth and the single rose in a vase between them. This was truly Silas Abrams?

"Apparently I'm not what you expected."

"No, you're not," she admitted truthfully. Adjusting her napkin in her lap, she slid her eyes away. She thought of all the awful things Joss had said about this man—well, not really said, but insinuated. "I expected someone of a greater . . . stature, perhaps."

"I am big, Miss Honeycutt, in ways that really matter."

She looked up, wondering just what he meant by that remark. Had Joss McRae said something so boastful, she would have had no doubt of his crude innuendo, but Silas Abrams was gazing at her with such an open, unthreatening countenance she knew he spoke of quite decent things.

"Of course you are, Mr. Abrams," she murmured her assurance, chiding herself for her own inappropriate line of thought.

Then, as if he suddenly realized the implications of his words, the poor man reddened.

She had never seen a man blush so profusely before, but that is what he did—turned a shade to rival the rosebud in the center of the table.

The strangest urge seized her, almost a maternal instinct to reach out, squeeze his hand, and tell him not to worry, that she knew he'd meant nothing by his comment. Or worse, to pat his balding pate as if he were some gentle beast that needed such reassurance.

But then he took control of the situation, much to her relief. Lifting his hand he signaled to the waiter, and soon he was placing an order for both of them. He never inquired into deLacey's preference when it came to the food. Yet oddly enough she wasn't offended by his take-charge attitude—something that made her furious whenever Joss McRae did it. But now, she was only too glad that the disconcerting moment had passed.

Inevitably the menu centered around beef, as it seemed all meals did in this cow town, even breakfast. The eggs she had ordered up to her room earlier had been served not with the traditional bacon but with a slice of cold beef, which she had found unpalatable. Lunch wasn't much of an improvement, and if she hadn't known better she would have sworn that the roast beef on her plate was the same piece she had refused to eat that morning and had thrown out to a band of wandering dogs beneath her window.

She picked at the corn and side of tomatoes that had obviously come from a can and nibbled at the slice of bread, hot, homemade, and really quite delicious.

"We have a vegetable garden out at the ranch, you know."

"What?" DeLacey glanced up at Abrams and found that he was intently watching her and apparently had been doing so for some moments. She abandoned all attempt to eat the dull fare.

"Fresh produce—potatoes, snap beans, shell peas, and when the weather gets a little cooler, cole crops. I have an old German cook, Laura Bell, who can make the best sauerkraut and bratwurst served with a potato salad with crispy bits of fried bacon . . . umm-umm." He kissed the ends of his fingers and rolled his eyes.

"I swear, Mr. Abrams, if I didn't know better I would think that you were trying to tempt me." DeLacey laughed, she couldn't help it, and her eyes sparkled with an easy-going challenge. She was beginning to like this man and his gentlemanly ways.

"Tell me, Miss Honeycutt." He leaned forward conspiratorially. "Is my plan working yet?" His reciprocating smile, so disarming, gave his rather bland face a pleasantness she found hard to resist.

And that was what he was attempting to do, she realized, to persuade her to return to his ranch with him. But that didn't fit into her plans—not at all. That was exactly what Joss McRae wanted her to do, and she was determined to thwart *him* at every possible turn.

"Look, Mr. Abrams . . ." Taking up her napkin from her lap and draping it beside her uneaten meal, she pushed back her chair.

"Please, Miss Honeycutt," he cut in, his hand, amazingly strong for such a soft-looking man, cupping her wrist. "I have no ulterior motives for wanting you to come with me to my ranch. It's just that staying here in Medora, a woman all alone, isn't really safe for you."

That was precisely what Joss had tried to tell her—and even Billy Howell in his own coarse way had suggested the same thing. Speaking of Billy Howell . . .

"Quite frankly, I didn't find your choice of escort reassuring," she offered in defense, frowning.

"Forgive me, Miss Honeycutt." How quick he was to appease her. "I asked Billy to see that the housekeeper was brought to town to meet your arrival in my absence. Billy meant well enough. . . ."

Again he echoed the same sentiments Joss had spouted to her yesterday, and yet coming from Silas Abrams she tended to believe him. Somewhat mollified by his excuse, she resumed her seat.

"The Rocking A is quite extensive. You would have separate quarters in a private wing," he said. "The housekeeper, Mrs. Symthe, is always there, along with the cook. You wouldn't be the only woman present, if that is what concerns you."

"I'm sorry, but . . ."

"Miss Honeycutt, you must be reasonable. Last night when Billy returned to the ranch without you and told me you insisted on staying here, well, I immediately set off for town. That's why I arrived so early this morning—I've been traveling all night. I was so afraid some ruffian would accost you."

"No one bothered me," she protested, trying not to think about what had nearly happened with Joss, his mouth and hands taking liberties that no man had ever taken before.

"Then you were lucky, or else you have some guardian angel watching over you." He issued a loud sigh of relief. "Medora is not a . . . civilized place after dark."

Guardian angel? DeLacey's thoughts raced back to the sight of Joss in the dingy room across the hall. Could that have been why he had been there—to watch over her? She remembered him saying something about wanting to protect her, but she'd thought nothing of his proclamation. Besides, given what she knew of Joss McRae, he was there only to guard his investment.

But it was true. She had been in her share of unsavory places, boomtowns, mining towns, even cattle towns, although not on her own. Her daddy had been there to protect her. She could even remember him posting a guard at her door when he was not with her.

If she stayed in town what would happen tonight? Would Joss be there again? She didn't want a repeat of last night. She didn't trust him, but worse, she didn't trust herself. For whether she liked to admit it or not, when Joss came around, she found it hard to resist him. Perhaps it would be better to take Silas Abrams's advice. At the Rocking A Ranch at least she would be safe from succumbing to the advances of Joss McRae.

"Very well, Mr. Abrams, I will go with you. But my concession does not mean I've consented to anything else."

"I understand that. I know the terms of our agreement, I'm an honorable man. I fully intend to abide by them."

He made the statement with such sober good faith that deLacey felt rotten all over again, hating herself for her own lack of conviction and honor. She decided then and there that she would somehow find a way to beat Joss at his own unsavory game. Never, never would she let this man learn of her pact with his nemesis. Silas deserved better treatment—much better. At the least, he deserved a chance to present his side of the story.

"I can be ready to go in an hour," she announced, and rose from her seat.

"Perhaps, Miss Honeycutt, it would be best if we waited for the coolness of the early evening to travel. I wouldn't want you to be uncomfortable. The Dakota sun can be quite brutal to fair, delicate skin like yours," he warned her, his gaze sweeping down for the first time to assess her as a woman. However, she felt nothing of the slow burn she experienced when Joss looked at her in that way.

His thoughtfulness and concern for her comfort, as well as her own cool response, convinced her even further that she was doing the right thing. Smiling with an easiness and sweetness she had never felt before around any man except perhaps her father, she covered his hand with hers and squeezed.

"No, I would rather leave right away. I'm not some hothouse flower. I won't wilt, Mr. Abrams, I promise you." Not unless the heat came from Joss McRae. But she didn't dare tell him that.

"I'm so glad, Miss Honeycutt." His face lit up with approval. "So very glad you have come. It took a lot of courage to travel so far, to meet a man you didn't know. . . . Well, I just can't tell you how much I admire you." Taking her hand in his, he stood and escorted her through the dining room to the bottom of the stairs that led up to the guest rooms. There he paused like the gentleman he was.

"As soon as you are ready, just let me know, and I will get my men to carry your luggage out to the carriage. I'll be waiting right here for you to return."

She knew that he would. The moment she turned away the smile on her lips faded. He had called her courageous, but she knew better. Duping men, all kinds of men, was a way of life for her, but the thought of doing it to that poor little fellow waiting for her at the bottom of the stairs . . . it just didn't sit right.

However, it went against the grain to walk away from ten thousand dollars. She just couldn't quite bring herself to it. Besides, Joss controlled her with more than money. There was still his threat to send her to prison if she didn't cooperate.

Why did you have to have an attack of scruples now, Lacey? You've really gotten yourself into a fine how-do-you-do this time.

Stationed in an unobtrusive spot across the street from the hotel, Joss recognized deLacey's luggage as it was carried out of the front door and loaded onto the back of Silas Abrams's buggy.

Joss frowned. DeLacey. She was an enigma. She was a conniving little liar and a thief to boot, but last night he had discovered something else about her that had forced him to look upon her—and himself—in a different light. As incredible as it seemed, deLacey Honeycutt was a virgin.

Virginity wasn't something a man meddled with lightly. That was one of the first lessons of manhood he'd ever learned. Virgins were pure and innocent, what a man looked for in a wife. Virgins meant commitment, marriage— virgins meant trouble.

Oddly enough, deLacey's virginity meant the world to him, enough that he had been unwilling to take it from her even when she had offered it to him. Now, knowing that she was going to go off with Silas Abrams, he was so confused about what to think, just how he should feel.

To be sure, her acquiescence was what he wanted, what he had demanded of her, but that didn't quell the strange displeasure that coursed through him. DeLacey with Abrams. It just didn't seem right to him. Perhaps it was a mistake to send her on this mission.

He tamped down the urge to put a stop to this whole madcap scheme—even if it was of his own making. But no. It was too late to turn back now. The wheels were already set in motion. He needed the information that she alone could get for him, he needed to assuage his need for vengeance. It was important to allow her to proceed.

Lacey emerged from the hotel entrance. The brightness of the sea green dress she wore complemented her hair, the color of ripened wheat. And when she placed her small gloved hand in Abrams's and smiled up at him as he assisted her into the buggy, Joss felt the resentment grab hold of his common sense and squeeze.

The thought of Abrams just touching her . . .

Slimy little bastard.

Gritting his teeth against the whorls of dust the bright yellow wheels stirred up, he stepped into the street and watched the vehicle roll away until there was nothing left to see. Then he set off toward the livery stable where he had boarded his horse before setting off on the long journey to St. Louis to intercept a woman who had then represented nothing more to him than a means to an end. But now she had a face and a beautiful body to match, and hopes and dreams and ambitions to rival his own.

DeLacey Honeycutt was not a woman to be easily dismissed as trivial. How much she meant to him now was only too obvious—at least to himself. Had he not camped in that dirty room across the hall all night long to make sure some liquored-up cowboy didn't disturb her? No doubt she had slept quite peacefully in her ignorance while he had remained awake, listening, until the clerk had arrived in the morning with a message from Abrams.

He knew the missive was from the rancher for, stationed with his ear against the door, he had overheard the conversation between the two of them, at least the clerk's end of it.

It just didn't figure, the way Silas Abrams was acting, like some schoolyard puppy, so eager to acquire a wife—someone who knew nothing about him.

Joss found himself wondering how Abrams would react to such an independent woman as deLacey. What would he do when he came to realize how difficult she could be? Abrams was not a man who took kindly to being told no.

No, siree. He chuckled to himself, picturing it now. No was a word deLacey used quite liberally. Abrams would fume, she would refuse to relent, and then when the poor bastard least expected it, she would turn on him and use those feminine wiles of hers to get what she wanted from him. Was that not what she had done to him? Yes, he supposed he should be only too glad to let Abrams handle her for a while.

Striding down the wooden boardwalk he came to an abrupt halt before the telegraph office. Through the window he caught sight of none other than Billy Howell. Joss frowned. This wasn't the first time he had seen the Rocking A Ranch hand there obviously sending a wire. Not that the fact was that unusual, cowboys occasionally used the service, but Billy used it all the time. Just who was the man, who claimed to have no family, communicating with?

Torn, he continued to watch. When Billy turned and moseyed toward the door, Joss ducked back in the alley between the buildings and watched him walk away.

Billy Howell. Although he considered the man harmless, he made a mental note to keep his eye on him as he continued on toward the livery.

The cool confines of the stable emitted the earthy scent of the animals it housed, safe and familiar. Some didn't care for the smell, but Joss found it quite pleasant, more honest than a parlorful of perfumed high society.

Perhaps that was why he stayed here in the Dakota Territory, in the small deteriorated town, when he could have just as well resided in Chicago, or St. Louis, or even New York, or one of the other uppity East Coast cities.

"Joss. Joss McRae." Gus Causey, the blacksmith who ran the livery, dropped the hoof of the horse he was shoeing and straightened to greet his customer with the friendliness he used with everyone, rich or poor. Wiping his hand on his leather apron, he stuck it out.

It was still coated with the grime of good, honest toil, and Joss readily took it.

"Saw the train arrive," the farrier said. "Henry was in earlier and took the trap. Thought you'd be around soon enough. Got your buckskin all ready to go for ya."

"Thanks, Gus." Moving toward the stalls where the horses were kept, he stopped at one halfway down the line. The dun-colored gelding nickered to him.

His tack, hanging over the stall door, had a fresh coating of neat's-foot oil—the efforts of the conscientious blacksmith. The horse was just as well cared for, and when Joss automatically checked his feet before saddling him, he could tell Gus had recently reshod him.

"Did you hear about Sy Abrams gittin' hitched?" Gus Causey was a fine blacksmith, but he was also a bit of a gossip. He invariably knew what was going on in Medora and was always looking not only to pass along what he gleaned but to update his information. "Up and mail ordered himself a bride, sight unseen."

"I heard," replied Joss, trying to sound nonchalant as he tossed the heavy saddle on the buckskin's back.

"I hear she arrived on the same train as you did. You didn't happen to run into her, did ya?"

Joss's heart skipped a beat. It was important that no one connected him in any way with deLacey Honeycutt.

"Can't say that I did." Cinching the saddle, he checked it for tightness.

"I hear she gave ol' Billy what-for when he tried to take her back to the ranch." Gus laughed. "Billy said Sy's gonna have his hands full with that little filly."

Based on his own experience with her, Joss could attest to the accuracy of that statement.

"It wouldn't take much," he mumbled derogatorily. Then he waited to see how much more the farrier knew. But apparently the smithy was going to say nothing else without a little prompting.

"Saw Billy just a few moments ago coming out of the telegraph office." Joss unhooked the stirrup from the saddle horn and let it swing back into place.

"Again?" Gus asked, lifting his battered hat from his head to scratch his scalp. "Third time this week. Amos, the operator, says he's sending wires to Chicago. Don't know why. Amos won't tell me any more than that."

"Chicago, huh?" *Billy Howell and Chicago?* The two just didn't go together. He would have to check it out, but for right now he had more important things to think about. DeLacey Honeycutt.

Tugging on the girth strap one last time, Joss swung up into the saddle and spurred his mount out of the livery.

It shouldn't take long, he concluded as he reined the eager horse out of town toward home. In no time at all deLacey would have the information he needed, and then she would be out of his life, once and for all. He decided then and there, that was the best thing that could happen.

With the calash raised to deflect the glaring heat of the noonday sun, the interior of the carriage was stuffy and most confining. DeLacey perched on the seat, her throat parched from doing most of the talking. Silas Abrams sat right next to her. They had been that way for nearly two hours. Under the guise of merely giving her his undivided attention as she spoke, she knew he was studying her, rating her no doubt on a scale of one to ten as if she were a prize mare he had picked up for a song at an auction. She imagined she was not at all what he had expected to get when he'd sent for a wife, potluck.

"Your father was a banker in New Orleans, you say," he reiterated her final statement of the long oration she had just given him about her family history.

A history that was as close to the truth as she dared skirt. And if by definition banking meant providing the opportunity to give and take money, then her daddy *had* been a financier—of sorts.

"Yes, he was highly respected in the community," she embellished, remembering what Joss had said about Abrams looking to raise his social status. "My mother came from a very old and prestigious Louisiana family." Very old indeed. In fact, she could trace her maternal ancestry to French convicts who had arrived in the early seventeen hundreds.

Her final statement seemed to please him immensely for he straightened, and his eyes took on an illumination that reminded her of a bird preening its feathers.

"New Orleans society. That's excellent, Miss Honeycutt." The expression nearly encompassing his face, he smiled, conveying an almost schoolboy glee.

Silas Abrams was so gullible, so easily duped, and she felt terrible about taking advantage of him for he seemed to accept her at face value—without question.

"Yes, well." Shamefaced, she dropped her head, unable to look him in the eyes another moment. "That was a long time ago."

"Now, now, Miss Honeycutt." He reached across the carriage and patted her folded hands, apparently mistaking her show of belated conscience as humble regret. "You cannot blame yourself for unforeseeable circumstances. Good breeding is good breeding. No one can take that from you."

And no one can give it to you if you don't come by it naturally. But she didn't tell him that. Nor did she tell him that by a mere stroke of luck he had just played right into her hands. She could milk him for everything she wanted—if that was what she chose to do. But she couldn't. Instead she covered up her confusion with a doe-eyed look of innocence.

"You are very kind, Mr. Abrams."

His hand was still covering hers, his liquid brown eyes reflecting the same sentiments hers conveyed—only it seemed his were genuine.

Guilt washed over her, and she pulled her hands away. Opening her mouth, she was determined to stop, here and now, this insane imposture. "Mr. Abrams."

"DeLacey." He captured her hands once more. "Please, won't you call me Sy like all of my friends do?"

"You don't understand. I . . ."

"I know we will become good friends. I have so much to offer you even if I'm not as dashing and debonair as you might have wished for in a husband. But won't you give it—give me—a chance?"

His plea was so endearing and tempting. Dashing and debonair was not a requirement. Joss McRae had those qualities, and she didn't wish him for a husband. Not that he would ever ask her. Not that she would ever want him to. Silas was offering her an opportunity like no one had ever given her before. The chance to escape her past—the chance to be judged strictly on merits of her own invention—the chance of a lifetime. Ignoring that nagging voice in her head that warned her of the risks she was taking, deLacey swallowed down the confession and nodded.

"Mr. Abrams, please. Don't rush me," she pleaded. Then she settled back into her seat, and a strange notion struck her. She held in the urge to laugh. Joss McRae had thought to send her into his enemy's camp to spy for him. But what he failed to realize was that once she was there, under the protection of Silas Abrams, there was no way he could get to her. She was safe . . . from him and from her past.

But he held the ten thousand dollars. That was a lot of money to turn her back on. Besides, he knew the truth about her, and what would keep him from talking if she double-crossed him? Therefore he must never know he'd been duped. The wheels of her fertile imagination began to turn, churning out a most convincing story to feed him when he demanded to know what she had found out about Silas Abrams.

She was quite relieved to discover that the famed Honeycutt creativity and ability weren't dead yet. Not by a long shot.

CHAPTER 9

Early that same afternoon Joss arrived at the Lazy J Ranch, his oasis in the Dakota Badlands. Several hours before he had sped past the road that turned off to Abrams's ranch. The telltale dust cloud in the distance bore evidence to the fact that the carriage in which deLacey rode had almost arrived at its destination. During the long ride he had come to grips with his own feelings. DeLacey Honeycutt's apparent lack of experience in one department didn't change who she was or what she'd been pretending to be long before he'd come along.

A confidence artist posing as the future blushing bride of Silas Abrams.

Joss laughed aloud and slowed his horse as he rounded the high, circular corral with its snubbing post in the center and entered the front yard of the ranch house.

The poor fool's Achilles' heel was more like it.

The Lazy J Ranch looked nothing like the other spreads in the territory. The two-story house sported cornices and dormer windows reminiscent of buildings found back East. But the cost and labor involved to construct it meant little, for this was his home, the culmination of all his hard work and endeavors, not some place merely to hang his hat, prop his dirty boots, and pillow his head each night. He had built this house planning to live in it for the rest of his life.

Dismounting, he drew the buckskin's reins through the ring of one of the fancy hitching posts and vaulted up the steps to the wide veranda that was shaded by a line of ancient cottonwood trees. He was in a fine mood. It was cool out of the glaring sun, but more important, he was home and was damn glad to be there.

"Annie," he called as he strode through the tiled and wainscoted front entrance, the door already flung wide in the Western style to admit the bit of breeze stirring the bleak, wide-open Dakota landscape.

He wasn't the least bit surprised to receive no answer. Annie, his little sister, was not known for her prudence. Always on the hottest days she would choose to go riding on that uncontrollable paint she called Rastus. Then she would return at dusk, the end of her upturned nose as red as rare beefsteak, her cheeks just as colorful, for she always refused to keep her hat on her head for long. Her enthusiasm a bubble near to bursting, she would invariably rush into the house, ignoring her muddy boots, full of all kinds of information.

It seemed she knew more about the daily running of this ranch than he did, which cows had calved, what fences were down, which of the hands had gotten into trouble in town and were paying off their fines a dollar for every day in jail. She could ride and rope with the best of them, and once he had even caught her behind a hayrick smoking a hand-rolled cigarette as if she'd been born to it.

Annie's behavior put that of Calamity Jane's in the shade, but he loved his little sister dearly nonetheless. And if the Lazy J was his oasis, then Annie was the wellspring that fed it.

"Welcome home, sir." Henry looked as fresh and unruffled as always when he reached out to take Joss's dusty coat and hat as if they were a gentleman's cape and bowler. "Miss Annie went out at sunrise and hasn't returned as of yet. I fear she might not. The spring roundup began this morning, and you know it is impossible to convince the young lady that such an unruly environment is no place for her to be.''

No, there was no keeping his little sister from the hub of ranch life, for it seemed she was the core of it.

Joss sighed. Roundup. The very essence of running a successful ranch revolved about this semiannual event. In the spring it was necessary to gather up the stock from the range, count your losses—with luck they were few—and brand your gain. A good spring calving could almost double a man's herd and worth. Then in the fall, before the cold weather set in, it was time to bring in the three-year-old steers to be driven to slaughter.

Roundup was the time when all the ranchers by necessity teamed up on the open range. Maltese Cross, Elkhorn, and Rocking A, and hands from all of the other ranches worked beside Lazy J men, for a calf belonged to whatever mark its mother bore, and it was branded then and there. Sometimes it could be confusing and mistakes weren't that uncommon, but it did seem of late that some of Silas Abrams's men, unless they were closely watched, made more than were reasonable.

It had been that way since the spring roundup of '87. The previous winter many of the ranchers had been wiped out by the severity of the snowstorms. Even Teddy Roosevelt had sustained huge losses, and the Rocking A even more. Only Joss among the dozen or so ranchers had managed to survive with a minimum of loss, but then, he had warned them all that it was coming sooner or later.

Like the grasshopper that mocked the industrious ant they had laughed as he had baled and stored hay from the free-range prairie grasses throughout that entire summer. But when the debilitating storms had come Abrams had been the first to declare that the stored fodder should belong to all of the ranchers since it had come off the free rangelands in the first place.

The majority of Joss's herd had survived as he had managed to keep them close to home with the enticement of feed. And when Rocking A cattle had ventured into the protective coulees on his land, he'd had no qualms about running them off even though he had been much more lenient with the other ranchers' stock.

It was true, he had singled out Abrams to rebuff—but then Joss felt he owed the bastard nothing, and nothing was what he gave him.

And now it seemed Lazy J stock was mysteriously disappearing and the Rocking A herd increasing. However, unless he actually caught Abrams's men in the act there was no way to prove he was altering the McRae brand. It would be easy enough to do, the slanted *J* becoming one leg of the elongated *A* that Abrams used. If that were the case, and he suspected it was, then this was the opportunity he'd been waiting for all of his life to bring the son of a bitch down.

Joss sighed as he thought of the task before him. The idea of coming face-to-face with his enemy didn't appeal to him, and yet he knew he must join his men. If he was lucky Silas might not make an appearance—after all, he had his prospective bride to entertain. Joss couldn't imagine deLacey Honeycutt partaking in a spring roundup. It was just not her style.

"I'll be heading out as quickly as I can to join the cowboys."

"I thought as much, sir." Henry smiled and bowed from the waist. "I have taken the liberty of preparing something to sustain you on your way."

The Rocking A Ranch was nothing at all like what deLacey had pictured. It was large, to be sure. The house itself sat on a cliff, the wilderness seeming to come right up to the bit of barren ground that served as a front yard. No more than a few hundred feet away, the river ran through a wide, deep gorge and was anything but tame. And though the structure was low and sprawling with twin fireplaces on either end of the central structure, it was constructed of hewn logs. Rather crude, but at least it didn't have a sod roof, and she could only pray it didn't have dirt floors.

"I told you, Miss deLacey, it needs a woman's touch." Though his words were an apology of sorts, his face nonetheless beamed with pride.

In Lacey's opinion it needed a lot more than a mere touch.

She wondered if Joss McRae lived in the same manner. Having seen his opulent train car, she found it rather hard to believe that he would ever accept less than the finest his money could buy. Then she remembered the painting she had seen on the wall of his Pullman bedroom, the two-story mansion. But why did she care one way or the other how he lived? In fact, she didn't want to think about him at all. It was much too dangerous a practice to engage in.

"I'm sure it's quite nice, Mr. Abrams." She still refused to call Silas Abrams anything less formal if she could avoid it. It made her position much too vulnerable. After what Joss had done to her, she was wary of ever leaving herself wide open to another man again.

As soon as the carriage came to a full stop, Abrams was quick to descend and offer her a hand down. His eyes darted about. It was almost as if he were nervous about something, but of what it might be she had no idea, although she wondered if perhaps he was concerned that she might see something she shouldn't. Something clandestine, perhaps? She shook herself mentally. No. That was silly. She had to forget all the untrue things Joss had said about Silas Abrams.

But all was quiet—unnaturally so. The ranch was devoid of activity except for a couple of milling horses in the corral. No signs of life, not a ranch hand to be seen, no one but the man who had driven them out from town.

Poised on the buggy step, she considered refusing to descend for the longest moment, and demanding that Abrams return her to town immediately. The thought of being alone with any man, even though he had been nothing but polite, set her heart to racing. Murderers had been known to be just as seemingly well mannered.

But then her baggage was tossed down with a loud, decisive thud. Abrams began to berate the careless driver. The moment to protest was gone. Besides, she had to stop this foolishness. With a determined resolve she joined him in the barren yard.

The hot afternoon sun beat down on them, and Abrams took her hand and led her forth. Once in the house he paused, giving her the chance to look over the front room.

The interior, though adequately large, was furnished to the point of clutter. To her horror every item of furniture looked as if it had been hand selected for its opulence and cost, no doubt meant to impress. However, the combined result was a complete decorating disaster. Next to an imported buttoned-back sofa that belonged in a formal parlor of some fine Southern mansion was the most god-awful side table she had ever seen. The four legs were made from some poor beast complete with hoofs and dewclaws. There was even a pair of matching candlesticks.

Next to that atrocity was an ornately carved Burmese armchair, the game table beside it constructed of papier-mâché and mother-of-pearl inlay.

"Oh, my." DeLacey closed her eyes, unable to look farther.

"It's something, isn't it?" Abrams said, his voice tinged with pride. "I only bought the best, and picked it all out by myself."

He was waiting for her to voice her approval. DeLacey opened her eyes hoping perhaps she'd been overly critical. She hadn't been.

"I must admit I've never seen anything quite like it," she said carefully. "Is the rest of the house so . . . uniquely furnished?"

"Unfortunately, not yet. I can't devote near the time and effort I would like to the house, but I'm working on it."

DeLacey sighed her relief. Thank goodness. She couldn't imagine staying in such a disaster for very long.

"But come, Miss deLacey, let me show you to your room. There will be plenty of time later to tour the rest of the house and even the ranch if you would like." As if he thought she really wanted to see it. "I'm sure you must be exhausted and will want to rest awhile. I'll see that Mrs. Smythe, the housekeeper, brings you something cool to drink."

He led her down a long, dark hallway, past several closed

doors. At the last one on the left he paused and glanced back at her. "Like I promised you, you will have your privacy. None of these other rooms are occupied."

She wanted to ask him why the rooms were there if they were not used, but she didn't, suspecting that their very existence once again had something to do with his misplaced sense of what constituted good taste and style.

At least the bedroom was much more subdued than the living room.

However, she couldn't fault Silas Abrams's manners. He was the perfect gentleman. He opened the door for her, arranged for her baggage to be carried in by the driver and placed to her satisfaction. Without once crossing over the threshold he saw her properly settled in.

"Perhaps you will join me for dinner this evening. I'll have Laura Bell, the cook, prepare one of her famous German meals in honor of your arrival. And then tomorrow we can tour the Rocking A," he said on a hopeful note. "Spring roundup has begun, and if you feel up to it, we might even venture out to the encampment so you can meet some of the other ranchers." Then he pointed toward a wardrobe on one wall. "I hope you don't mind, but I took the liberty of providing some appropriate riding clothes for you."

Before she could formulate an opinion or an answer he eased away from the door, closing it with a quiet click.

DeLacey cocked her head. Silas Abrams. What an odd man. She didn't know quite what to make of him. But she had to admit she was finding it harder and harder even to think about betraying him to a rascal like Joss McRae. No matter how much was at stake.

The buckskin settled into a long-legged lope across the open country. As long as Joss would live there would be nothing quite like riding alone across the vast Dakota range in springtime. Interspersed among the lush grasses, short-stalked prairie roses carpeted everything as far as the eye could see with a wide spectrum of pastels. The thick vegetation dulled the thunder of the horse's pounding feet.

Ahead, a crop of buttes jutted up like posted sentries. But even they were not colorless. Tiny cacti fill every nook and cranny, shooting out an abundance of crimson flowers more than twice the size of the plants themselves.

Yes, these Badlands could be beautiful and brutal at the same time, just like a deceptive woman, but that did not lessen his enjoyment of either one's charm.

Just beyond the buttes he pulled up sharply to study the terrain. Hooves and wagon wheels had churned up the prairie before him not so long ago. He was headed in the right direction, and if the dust cloud in the distance could be trusted, the roundup would be found just over the next rise.

An hour later he rode into the meeting place and was greeted by the shouts of the spectators of an impromptu horserace. He wasn't the least bit surprised to discover his sister Annie clinging bareback to Rastus like some mythical centaur. Her long, dark hair flying out behind her, she was in the lead, shouting taunts over her shoulder at the poor suckers who had taken her on and thought to beat her simply because she was female.

Joss laughed. Annie had gained possession of more fine cow ponies, including his own buckskin, than he could count on these roundups, taking advantage of the newer hands from other ranches who knew nothing of her reputation.

His reins loose, his Stetson pushed back, and his arms draped over the saddle horn, he watched her win by several lengths and pull up so short that even some of the best bronco busters would have come unseated. But not Annie. It was as if her bottom was glued to her mount's broad back.

She was laughing and pointing. Joss gritted his teeth. Her language was as rough as, if not worse than, the other cowboys'. He would have to talk to her about her choice of words, for she was getting too old to swear. When she was little, it had been amusing, but not anymore.

"Joss!" she squealed, spying him on the sidelines. She slid off the paint's back in one fluid motion. Then like the long-legged curlews that followed the cattle herds, she darted across the encampment, her face saying it all.

He was just as glad to see her. Joss dismounted and caught her up into his arms and swung her around once before setting her back down on her feet.

"When did you get back, big brother?" she demanded, her face just as sunburnt and freckled as he'd known it would be after a long day in the saddle.

"This afternoon, tyke." Grinning, he pinched her pink and peeling nose between thumb and forefinger in a gesture of affection. "Who did you manage to con this time?"

"Con? I won fair and square," she insisted, punching him in the shoulder with her fist.

At that point a young, rather gangling cowboy, not much older than Annie herself, sauntered over and tossed the reins of his mount in her hands. Rusty Chapin. He recognized the youngster known more for his drawings than for his punching abilities.

"Ain't natural for no woman to ride like that," Rusty mumbled belligerently, eyeing Annie with a sweeping look before stalking away.

Annie was laughing but all Joss heard was the one word—woman—and all he saw was the way the cowpoke assessed his little sister.

He glanced down at her, noting the jutting breasts beneath her checkered shirt that quivered as she laughed, the fullness of her hips covered by denim pants. He frowned. Annie was no longer a girl. She was a woman. The evidence had been there for a while, but he had failed—no, refused—to notice it. He couldn't ignore the truth anymore, and neither could she.

Circling her slim shoulders with his arm, he guided her away from the crowd.

"Annie, I think you should go home. This is no place for you."

"What in the hell do you mean, Joss?" Like a stubborn jenny she came to a halt refusing to be led any farther.

"And you gotta quit cussing, honey."

"Then quit tryin' to tell me what to do." Pulling out of his reach, she raced away, a frisky filly left too long without proper training, wild and beautiful, but completely out of control.

"Annie!" he shouted, but she was already gone, leaving the reins of her newly gained trophy in his hand.

Mounted on Rastus's back, she galloped off across the prairie. It was as if she thought to escape the inevitable fact that she had grown up much faster than she could run away.

DeLacey stared at the pig-eyed sorrel who glared back at her with equal intensity. Even she could figure out by the way the horse pinned back his ears that he didn't like the situation any better than she did.

"I swear to you, Miss deLacey, he's as manageable as they come."

That was as empty a promise as she had ever heard, for she had no idea if Silas Abrams's definition of manageable was the same as hers.

Abrams stood there, dressed in traditional cowboy garb, a bright red bandana knotted at his throat, even a pistol strapped low over one hip, and that surprised her. It was hard to imagine a man like Silas using a gun. Ever so patient, his fingers interlocked into a foothold, he was waiting for her to slip her boot into his grasp so he could boost her up into the saddle.

Oh, she had ridden a horse all right, several times, in fact. It was just that this particular beast seemed—well, unpredictable.

"Perhaps you have a gentle mare. . . ."

He shook his head. "Mares are trouble on a roundup. Now, come on. This is something you'll just have to get used to if you plan on being my . . ."

She was certain he had almost said wife.

DeLacey frowned. Silas Abrams took way too much for granted much too quickly. She'd yet to agree to any kind of permanent arrangement. And the thought of marrying him, of him demanding conjugal rights, touching her in ways that Joss McRae had—it was unthinkable.

Nonetheless she succumbed to his insistent urgings and planted her booted foot into his waiting hands. Then she was airborne and in the saddle, her divided skirt making it easy to straddle the horse. There was no ignoring the fact that the gelding stiffened beneath her. And when he began to fidget and snort, she silently prayed he wouldn't just decide to take off before Abrams could climb onto the back of his own mount.

"There, see?" he assured her, reining his animal to take the lead. "I told you there's nothing to worry about."

She nodded, yet as they rode out of the yard, she was only too glad to allow the sorrel his head, hoping he would be content to follow the other horse.

The secret to wrangling was having a good mount. The buckskin was one of the finest cutting horses in the Dakota Territory, and so he made Joss's task that much easier.

However, the maverick they were attempting to round up had a mind of his own. Somehow the young bull had managed to escape branding and castration over the past seasons, and he was determined not to be caught now.

The buckskin knew his business; he countered every move the angry critter made, keeping him from darting away long enough for Joss to lasso his unwilling target.

Timing was crucial. The noose settled about the bull's horns at the precise moment that he decided to charge. The horse wheeled and braced himself, sending the maverick to his knees. Joss vaulted from the saddle, and as the buckskin kept backing up to keep the rope taut and the dangerous horns down, Joss managed to wrestle the mound of bellowing flesh to the ground.

It was hard, dirty, smelly work, for Joss had never in his life come across a sweet-smelling herd of cattle—but it was rewarding, this one-on-one contest with such a powerful beast, even though such labor was not required of him.

But his participation served as a reminder to the men who worked for him that he was as good as the best of them. Such respect for the boss went a long way on a cattle ranch.

The cries and whistles of approval mingled with the sound of his own labored breathing and the defeated blowing of the bull. Then when it seemed his strength would surely give out, the branders and wrestlers arrived to take over.

Retrieving his lariat, Joss limped away, sore, but the victor nonetheless. It had been a long time, but at the moment he felt good about himself.

"Nice wranglin', Joss." The compliment was accompanied by a resounding slap on his back that stirred up a cloud of dust thick enough to choke a steer.

"How much do ya want for that ol' buckskin?"

"A hell of a lot more than you got, Billy Howell," Joss retorted, knowing the cowboy's offer was only meant as a friendly gibe, a suggestion that the horse had done all the work, and he had merely gone along for the ride.

Unknotting the bandana from around his neck, he swiped at the dirt and sweat on his face and neck. Then he turned to spit out the grit in his mouth. . . .

That was when he spied her sitting atop her horse, her hat cocked jauntily to one side, the strings knotted under her jaw as if they were a big satin ribbon of a bonnet.

He swallowed, dirt and all, knowing that he looked worse than something a coyote might drag up from the river. This wasn't how he wanted deLacey Honeycutt to see him—filthy, sweating, debased.

"How long has *she* been there?"

"Purdy little thing, ain't she?"

The man had no idea just how pretty she could be, nor what a pain in the butt. But then he remembered Billy was the one Abrams had sent to town to meet her. Perhaps he did know how much trouble she could be.

"They say ol' Silas is plannin' on marryin' her. Ordered her up like a new suit from the Montgomery Ward catalogue," Howell continued, then snorted. "Personally, I'd much rather tangle with a nest of rattlesnakes. But she is purdy, as purdy as the first time I seen her, don't you agree?"

"I wouldn't know, as I've never seen her before," Joss lied, shooting Billy a hard, suspicious look. Just what did the old cowboy know or suspect? Nothing. There was no way he could tie him to deLacey.

He wiped the side of his mouth with his leather work glove. And to hell with what "they" said—he knew better. The ten thousand dollars he was going to pay her and the promise not to turn her in to the law assured him that she was planning on marrying nobody.

He glanced up to find her watching him, an angelic look on her face, fresh and beautiful, as if she'd been sitting on the porch sipping lemonade all day. But beneath her benign expression he suspected she was laughing at him.

Wordlessly he moved forward, for as much as he would like to ignore her, he wasn't about to do the same to her escort, Silas Abrams. The son of a bitch. His men were at it again, trying to brand calves that didn't belong to him.

He looked right past her as if she weren't there, concentrating his energy on his rival. Then a most amusing thought struck him. Just how good of a poker face would she have when it came right down to it?

Whether she realized it or not, she was about to be confronted with the ultimate test.

"Afternoon, Abrams."

Joss McRae's resonant voice washed over her like a flash flood leaving total destruction in its wake. Dressed in fine gabardine pants and a linen shirt he had been handsome enough, but in his checkered shirt, even with a rip in one elbow, his dark blue bandana, leather vest and tight leather chaps that drew attention to that most manly part of him, he was devastating.

DeLacey swallowed like a long-necked goose and felt about as foolish. She was staring, but she just couldn't help it. To see him again, to watch him ride that horse of his as if he were a part of it, working and sweating, subduing the fire-breathing, horned brute with his bare hands . . .

Dear Lord, she'd not realized how the sight of such masculine prowess could affect her, especially Joss McRae's. But whether it was the pageantry or the promise in his turbulent gray eyes that he could, and someday would, do the same to her that left her feeling as if her lungs had collapsed, she couldn't be certain.

DeLacey's mouth tightened with annoyance. He refused even to give her the satisfaction of a reaction to her appearance here where he had to have least expected to find her.

"McRae." Abrams frowned, and she sensed it was because of the insolent way Joss refused to show his respect and remove his dusty hat in her presence.

His insult was intolerable, but there was nothing she could do about it—at least not at the moment.

"Why is it, Abrams, that you're the only son of a bitch in the territory who can't seem to hire competent hands?"

Abrams ruffled like a prairie grouse. "If you're accusing me of something, McRae, then I suggest you come right out and say it."

Even a blind man couldn't miss the hate and animosity that sparked between the two men, the way their hands simultaneously settled on the handles of their pistols. She wasn't the least bit surprised to see Joss act that way, but mild-mannered Silas Abrams? Arching her brow, she turned her head to look at the unimposing little man.

It seemed that Joss McRae could bring out the worst in even the gentlest of natures. Her gaze slid to Joss, the agitator in all of this, and he looked as if at any moment he were going to challenge poor Silas to a gun battle, there and then. If somebody didn't do something, fast, the two of them would be at each other's throats like mad dogs fighting over an old bone. She feared Silas was no match for a brute like Joss McRae. No match at all.

Desperate situations called for equally desperate measures, even if it meant going against her earlier vow to call Silas Mr. Abrams.

"Silas," she interjected with a sugary Southern sigh, fanning her hand before her face, hoping it looked flushed enough to be convincing.

To her relief the sound of his first name for the first time voluntarily on her lips instantly caught the man's attention.

"Miss deLacey, whatever is wrong?"

"I do believe that the heat and the sight of such vi-o-lence"—she darted a searching look to see how her display of distress was affecting Joss—''has left me quite unable to catch my breath.'' She reeled and made as if to faint.

And even if she had laid it on a little thick, her ploy seemed to be working. At least on Silas Abrams. Truly concerned about her health, he scrambled down out of his saddle and reached up to assist her to the ground.

Joss—damn his devilish hide—merely watched the spectacle with an amused glint. He didn't believe her act, not for a moment. Well, what if she hadn't been faking it and had been about to faint? Would he have simply allowed her to fall in a dead faint at his feet without moving a muscle?

No doubt that was exactly what he would have done. Then he would have probably informed her, quite rudely, that she was blocking his way.

''Water, please.'' Abrams's forceful command, as he held her outstretched hand and led her toward the shade of a wagon parked not too far away, brought a volley of responses. Before she could protest she had her choice: a canteen, a tin cup, and a pewter dipper, all full of water—all splashing the front of her dress as they were thrust in her face.

''Why, thank you kindly, gentlemen,'' she warbled like some helpless bit of fluff. She accepted the tin cup—it looked the cleanest—and took an obligatory sip.

Again she shot Joss a glare out of the corner of her eye, knowing that she was a glutton for punishment. Yes, he still found the whole affair quite amusing.

Parked on an overturned barrel, she stayed quiet, trapping her tongue between her teeth to keep it under control, to keep from shouting at Joss all the things she yearned to tell him—how she despised him and the battery of feelings and desires he evoked deep within her merely with a look, with a promise of a caress.

How easy it would be to continue on with her charade, perhaps even feign a faint, just to see what everyone would have done then, to show him that others did care about her even if he didn't. But that would have been going way too far, even for her. However, she allowed Abrams to continue to fuss over her as if she would surely wilt away if he didn't do something quickly.

"Now, Miss deLacey, just rest your head on this." Slipping off her hat, he wedged a rolled-up blanket between the side of the wagon and the back of her neck. It felt strange to be pampered so. If the truth be known, she found such a show of concern over her well-being rather enjoyable.

Closing her eyes, as much to block out Joss's smirking face as to keep her own expressionless, she dropped her head back against the makeshift pillow. Abrams had taken up her hat by the brim and was attempting to fan her with it. His good intentions only managed to stir up the hot, stale breath of the men crowding around her.

Like Black Jack gum that is chewed too long and becomes tasteless, the insistent hovering and the terrible deception she'd agreed to stage and hadn't quite figured how to get out of, all lost their appeal to her. Assailed by a sense of panic, deLacey sat up and pushed the fanning hat out of her face.

"Let me up," she exclaimed.

"Now, Miss deLacey, you just take it easy. . . ."

But she had already brushed her way into the clear. She wasn't sure just what she expected to find. Joss still watching her with bemusement, or better yet, to catch him with his guard down showing some penitence, perhaps—anything to redeem him in her eyes, to assure herself that she could stay one step ahead of him. To her disappointment she found neither. He was gone, and so was his horse. She could see him in the distance, in the thick of the roundup roping another cow. His lack of concern was as powerful and painful as a slap in the face.

Her expression revealed every emotion she was feeling, and she knew the moment she let her guard down that she'd made a careless mistake.

"Miss deLacey, you must calm yourself." Silas Abrams grabbed her by the arm, forcing her to face him. "Don't waste your time on a man like McRae. He wouldn't think twice about using and then discarding you just to spite me."

He spoke gently enough but there was a determination about his stance and pain in the way his brows knitted together. It was only too obvious that he, too, had suffered at the hands of Joss McRae. What he didn't say, though she sensed it, was what he was thinking. *I won't lose you to him as well.*

Just what had Joss McRae done to this poor man? This flare of jealousy seemed totally out of character for Silas Abrams. But under the circumstances he had every right to chastise the behavior of a woman he thought was about to become his wife. Oddly enough she felt terrible about the way she'd acted, but not for the reasons he supposed. Although it wasn't fair for the poor man to be harassed by someone like Joss McRae, she was more worried about herself. As selfish as her concerns were, she couldn't help feeling them. As she'd done since her daddy had died, she had to look out for herself.

Joss had this knack of making her forget herself, of casting aside all rationality. That she didn't like, nor could she tolerate such erraticism in herself.

Her daddy would say she was losing her touch, the famous Honeycutt ability to control the deck, be it the game of life or cards. DeLacey swallowed hard. ''The King'' had lost it, and look what had finally happened to him. She could not allow herself to follow in her father's doomed footsteps.

She would not let Joss McRae, handsome and wealthy as he might be, continue to pull her strings as if he owned her.

What she had to come up with was an infallible story for him, one to turn his vengeance elsewhere and gain her the freedom she so desperately needed. The ten thousand dollars was becoming less and less important, for Silas offered her much more than that. He represented security, stability—respect.

If what Joss said was true, if someone was stealing his cattle, then the odds were that the culprit was here at this roundup among all these ranchers and cowboys.

Yes . . . that was the answer. Give Joss the person truly responsible. Narrowing her eyes, she glanced about the sea of masculine faces, looking for one that stood out among the rest.

If the real rustler was here then he had to be someone as rotten and unscrupulous as Joss himself. Someone in the position to carry off grand-scale theft without being caught. All she had to do was figure out just who that somebody was.

CHAPTER 10

If deLacey was looking for somebody different, then that evening she found him. At Silas's insistence, they were just getting ready to depart from the roundup when an approaching cloud of dust delayed them. Into the camp rode a slender gentleman trailed by an extensive retinue. She heard the epithet "the four-eyed dude from New York" bandied about by the cowboys.

The label fit the newcomer well. Slick and sleek as a carnival thimblerigger, he came off as domineering and opinionated as Joss himself. Although he was garbed in the traditional getup that the other ranchers and cowboys wore, he looked too new, too neat, to really be a part of this rather motley group. The fact that he wore eyeglasses didn't help his image much either.

But just as important, he was deLacey's last hope. Having spent the entire day getting to know the other ranchers and their cowboys, assessing them as prospective rustlers, not one of them had struck her as a likely suspect. They all seemed honest, straightforward men. This new arrival was without a doubt different. Apparently he had power and influence rivaled only by Silas and Joss—the perfect guise under which to hide a sinister nature.

Even Silas seemed to not like him much and whispered,
"You can always tell a real cowboy by his boots."

Skeptically deLacey glanced down at the stranger's feet
and then at the others all around her. What was so different
about his boots? They were exactly like the expensive pair
Joss wore except that they were brand new and spit-and-
polish clean.

"Ya aren't a real cowboy," Silas went on to explain in an
exaggerated drawl, staring down at his own dirty shoes with
an inordinate amount of pride, "unless ya gotta little sh—"
He paused. A grin edged up the corners of his mouth, and he
touched the brim of his hat. "I'm sorry, Miss deLacey. I
mean, cow droppings on your boots."

She glanced at him in surprise to see him express such
scorn. Could it be that here in the Dakota Territory a man
was truly judged by the amount of manure caked on his
shoes? How ludicrous. How like the male of the species.
Well, if that was the case then Joss McRae should be well
respected for he was full of it. She shot a contemptuous
glare at Joss, who had kept his distance on the other side of
the camp as he greeted the boisterous Easterner with
genuine affection.

Yes, if Joss thought highly of this boastful new arrival,
then that put him right on the tip of her list of suspects. She
could just imagine Joss's reaction if she could prove his
apparent friend was the one responsible for all the rustling
he was attempting to pin on poor Silas Abrams. She smiled
to herself. Yes, she would enjoy seeing that.

"Just who is he?' she asked, bending close to Abrams so
no one else could hear her question.

"Why, that's none other than Mr. Theodore Roosevelt
himself," he answered with a touch of disdain. "Adven-
turer, politician—more good breeding than sense. They say
one day he may well become the governor of the state of
New York. That may be true." He snorted. "But, if you
want to know my opinion, he rides a horse like an old-maid
school teacher and doesn't know one end of a cow from the
other."

A politician. She should have guessed. The name

sounded vaguely familiar—not that she kept up with Eastern politics or society. But watching the chummy way Joss acted with this Roosevelt only served to reinforce her determination to deflect Joss's vengeance away from Abrams and onto the person who really deserved it.

If this Mr. Roosevelt deserved it, then she was determined to find out as much as she could about him. The fact that he was considered a tenderfoot and an outsider by most of the men was a good place to start.

Then Roosevelt's intelligent gaze, the kind not likely to miss anything, settled on her. At first his attention unnerved her a bit, but then she remembered she *was* the only woman in camp if one didn't count that unruly girl who was apparently Joss's sister. Annie. To deLacey's amazement she cussed and acted more like one of the boys, and Joss did nothing to try to stop her. Any woman who could bowl over a group of men as well as that girl did deserved her admiration. Her methods might be crude, but they were quite effective. Frankly, she would love to learn just how the girl managed to control her brother so easily.

DeLacey smiled at the Eastern dude, and sitting atop her horse looking as pretty as meringue fresh out of the oven, she hoped he would be unable to resist her charms. It seemed the only man immune to her and her ability to captivate was Joss McRae. Just as she had wished, Roosevelt bent his head, no doubt to ask Joss just who she was. Joss's glower as he glanced at her confirmed her hunch.

She took a deep breath. Would the newcomer decide to maintain his distance the way Joss did because of her association with Silas Abrams?

Apparently this Mr. Roosevelt was his own man and was not restricted by Joss's prejudices for he stepped forward, aiming toward her with purpose. Good. Now she could assess him for herself.

Abrams turned on the congeniality, edging his horse forward to intercept the Easterner who strolled across the camp grounds as if it were a stage and he owned it.

"Teddy," Silas called with a warmth that belied his earlier private opinion of the man.

"Sy, you ol' dog." Roosevelt, too, was all smiles. "I should have known you would find the loveliest maiden for miles around and lay claim on her." Doffing his hat, he turned his attention to deLacey and waited to be presented. His etiquette couldn't be faulted.

It seemed that Abrams was going to ignore the friendly overture, but she wasn't about to let him. She wanted to see how he reacted to her, for it was easy to judge a man's character by the way he treated a woman.

"Silas, won't you please introduce me to your friend," she demanded so sweetly that he couldn't possibly sidestep the situation without offending her.

"Of course, my dear." He shot her a rather warning look similar to the one he had given her earlier in the day when she had been watching Joss with such intensity. "Mr. Theodore Roosevelt of New York, Miss deLacey Honeycutt . . . of New Orleans."

Roosevelt gave her the strangest look, and for a moment she feared it was one of recognition. Her heart skittered to a halt, her mind scrambling like ducks on a frozen pond, sorting through her recollections. Had she perhaps met him somewhere before? Maybe even played cards against him and forgotten his face? Her pulse accelerated until she felt quite light-headed and sick at her stomach. Or perhaps he knew of her daddy's reputation and had associated the name of Honeycutt? What would she do if he remembered and proceeded to divulge that information to Abrams? Dear Lord, she should never have told him that her family was from Louisiana.

"Ah, yes, the Honeycutts of New Orleans," Roosevelt finally said with a slowness that revealed nothing.

DeLacey caught her breath, waiting for the ax of doom to swoop down and strike her.

"A fine family. A fine Southern family, indeed," he expounded with a show of authority.

Relief rushed out on the stale air she'd been holding deep in her lungs. Why he would substantiate her claim, this stranger she was positive now she'd never met before, she couldn't fathom, but she wasn't about to question his unsolicited support. She owed him one, and she didn't quite like that idea, since she'd hoped to prove him the cattle thief. But it was a fact nonetheless.

At the same time she considered it wise to stop him before he carried his compliments any further, perhaps too far.

"It has been such a pleasure to meet you, Mr. Roosevelt." Her statement was meant as a dismissal, as was the hand she extended.

Either the man was dense or was merely toying with her for he just stood there staring at her outstretched fingers. Then when Joss approached, his stride confident and cocky as always, she was sure it was the latter, especially when Joss raked her with a contemptuous glare before turning on her escort.

"Headed out so soon, Abrams?"

"Yes, my fiancée isn't used to the rigors of range life yet."

She wished he wouldn't insist on referring to her constantly as his future wife. It made her feel so guilty and reminded her of how she'd gotten tangled up in this confounded situation to begin with. What was worse was that her heart wasn't in this deception—not any of it, all because she was doing it for the wrong reasons, she told herself. Because she was forced into it, because the plan was someone else's, not her own.

She didn't like being used, not one bit, but until she came up with evidence to the contrary she had no choice except to ride it through.

The thought of falling back on the ploy of delicate disposition once again didn't sit well with her, but she could think of no other way to escape the snide remark that was sure to follow such a statement from Abrams.

Mustering up a vapid look, she pressed the back of one limp hand against her cheek.

"I think you're right, Abrams, ranch life doesn't seem to agree with her at all." Joss laughed, but she could see from the corner of one eye that he was frowning at the same time. A paradox like simultaneous rain and sunshine. "Perhaps you should return her from where you got her and demand your money back—damaged goods."

She stiffened at the venom in his voice, as his hostility for Abrams for some reason focused on her. His laughter was ridicule for them both. He did not bother to hide that fact, not for a moment. With breath held, she waited for Abrams's reaction.

"You son of a bitch." As fast as lightning Abrams drew his pistol and aimed it at Joss's heart. She had never seen anyone so quick with a gun. And Joss. He was just standing there, his hand resting on his own gun, yet he didn't pull it from its holster, almost as if he hesitated to fight back. But why? Was he afraid? It seemed unlikely. And yet he was doing nothing to protect himself.

"Silas, please," she whispered, looking as wilted as she possibly could, although she wasn't sure it would stop him. What had made her do something so stupid as to interfere with a situation that should have had her gloating? Joss McRae at the mercy of another man? But it was almost as if she felt this strange need to protect Joss. Why? Why would she wish to defend a man she despised so much?

Then, surprisingly, Silas slid his weapon back from where it had come.

"This ain't over with, McRae." He took hold of her horse's headstall and led her away at a jarring trot that made her bite her tongue at the suddenness of the movement.

It was at that moment, tasting her own blood, that she glanced over her shoulder to see the steely glare of hatred harden Joss's handsome face even more. Ungrateful bastard. And a coward to boot. If somebody was rustling his cattle, then it was exactly what he deserved.

It was not her place to uphold the code of the West, or to see that justice was served. What did she care if someone was stealing from Joss McRae. No. Her goal—her only goal from this day forth—was to take care of deLacey Honeycutt, to see to it that she didn't get trampled in the stampede of events that she'd somehow managed to land in.

But, oh, how she yearned to make Joss rue the day he had thought to use her for his own paltry gain. She would never, never buckle under to his demands. Damn the money he dangled before her, so confident her greed would outweigh everything else. Well, he was wrong. All she had to do was figure out a way to keep his mouth shut.

"Take it easy, Joss. Abrams fell for her story, hook, line, and sinker. It's better to corner a calf-thieving coyote than to have to lasso him on the run."

Joss heard the words of wisdom, mulled them over slowly. Teddy was right. He didn't deny that, but his fists were clenched, his lungs pumping, his conscience the driving force of the frustration coursing through him. All he could think of was Abrams, his lightning draw, Lacey between them unknowingly shielding the bastard, her very life at stake, keeping him from reciprocating and meeting the challenge so blatantly issued. Could he beat Silas Abrams in a fair fight? He would like to think that he could, but it was yet to be determined. He suspected the opportunity to find out would present itself soon.

And Lacey. What had ever possessed him to think that she could handle the mission he had sent her on? Little fool. She'd not even been aware of how much danger she had been in a few moments ago. Would she know if it happened again? Probably not.

She had looked so pale, so vulnerable. At first he had thought she was faking her attack of frailness—she was damn good at pretending. But now he wasn't so sure.

But worse, he couldn't shake off this unexplained urge to protect her. When he had so curtly suggested to Abrams to forget his plans to marry her, he had meant it. That son of a bitch had about as much right to a woman like Lacey as a fox had to a chicken coop.

"You're right, Teddy, I know that, but it doesn't make it any easier."

"It's the woman, isn't it?"

Joss shot Theodore Roosevelt a surprised look. Were his feelings that transparent?

"You needn't worry about her, my friend." The Easterner chuckled. "That little lady can take excellent care of herself."

That was exactly what Joss had thought when he had initially met her, but the real deLacey Honeycutt was nothing like that first impression. She was a little girl lost, a street urchin that filched from the pockets of every passerby with righteous indignation, then pleaded for another chance whenever she got caught, thinking she deserved a break. Most men might succumb to her charms—hell, he had, but if Silas Abrams caught her . . .

Though it was true her stealing was no nickel-and-dime affair, and cheating at cards was nothing to be proud of, worse could be said of men like Jay Gould, James Fisk, and Daniel Drew who had bamboozled not only the rich but the poor out of millions with fraudulent railroad stock not so many years ago.

And to be truthful, could he say any better about himself? Building a profitable railroad or cattle ranch meant stepping on toes, mostly small ones. His victims had been nameless and faceless; he had never had to know them or what they might have suffered so that he could attain his goals. In truth, he had taken the coward's way out.

On the other hand, she had carefully selected her dupes, had faced them all bravely, and no doubt it had been their own greed that had cost them.

Ironically enough, her methods had to be respected.

Just as she had to be admired for her frank forthrightness.

That was just it. He admired the hell out of her, and felt responsible for her, for he had been the one to send her into the wolf's den with no chance of survival. Silas Abrams was a smart son of Satan. It wouldn't take him long to figure out what she was up to. And when he did . . .

He had to reach her. Had to talk to her. See that she got out before something happened to her. But how?

"I can't let her go through with it."

"There's nothing you can do to stop her."

"Isn't there?" Joss headed for his horse with purposeful

strides. Then he was in the saddle and galloping off in the same general direction deLacey and Abrams had taken only moments before.

DeLacey liked options, liked spreading out her hand to study her cards and figure out her best chance for winning. It was like wild cards in poker that opened up the game, changing the odds—this time in her favor. To her delight, she had a number of fine choices to pick from at the moment, and she was going to take her time selecting one—just the right one. Carefully she considered the pros and cons of the ways she could secure her future. She could keep up this cat-and-mouse game with Joss indefinitely, but she wanted more, she wanted something solid and permanent. There was only one way to accomplish that. One that suited her needs quite nicely, now more than ever, for it made the most sense.

Beneath lowered lashes she studied the little man sitting across the dinner table from her, watched the way he was careful of his manners as if they were a new suit he was still a bit uncomfortable wearing. Silas Abrams might not be the most handsome or sophisticated man she had ever met, but to his credit he was kind and considerate of her needs. A gentleman in every way, she concluded, at least when it came to her. She was comfortable with him. Just as important, he offered her a sterling opportunity to obtain the two things in life she wanted more than anything else.

Respectability and acceptance. The chance to escape who and what she really was and never again have to rely on her wits and skill with cards.

The Honeycutts of New Orleans. A fine family. A fine family indeed. Teddy Roosevelt's lofty words, bogus or not, definitely had a sweet ring to them. She liked the way they sounded, liked the image they conjured up in her mind, liked to think they did the same for others.

She glanced about the dining room of Abrams's house. The potential was there, the chance to show what she could do—with this man, in this house, in this very room, although the dining area was almost as much of a disaster as the front room had been.

The damask seat covers of the lovely Sheraton chairs on their own might have been acceptable, but they contrasted sharply with the gold brocade curtains that looked as if they belonged in a brothel, especially with the dying sun highlighting them.

Instead of the fine china that should have graced the glassed-in shelves of the ornate sideboard, there was an odd assortment of knickknacks—really quite tacky, even though she thought she recognized several pieces that might be Dresden or Wedgwood. Like every other room there were stacks of paper, mounds of it. She was determined to take it upon herself to sort through it all and throw most of it away.

Yes, she could give Silas Abrams everything he sought in a wife and more.

A sigh escaped her parted lips as she thought of all the work ahead for her. And yet, she couldn't help but look forward to the challenge.

"What is it, Miss deLacey?" Abrams wiped his chin with the sleeve of his shirt, then thought better of his automatic action, attempting to hide his momentary backslide of manners by lowering his hand into his lap. By the way his arm was pumping up and down no doubt he was attempting to clean his cuff on his pant leg.

He presented a challenge as well. It was not that she stared down her nose at his lack of social graces. Not at all. She too had had to struggle for everything she had learned in order to make the right impression. It was just that she felt sorry for him. She knew what it was to want something like respectability so much that it made you try too hard. With his money and her know-how, regardless that her daddy had been a famous gambler, they could combine their advantages to give them both what they desired. Unified, Joss McRae couldn't touch them.

This common goal united them as nothing else possibly could, at least in her mind.

"Silas," she said gently, knowing that for once in her life she was doing the right thing for herself, and hopefully for someone else as well. Setting down her fork on the edge of her plate, she extended her hand across the table in a gesture of reassurance.

At first he merely stared at her open palm as if it were an untouchable icon. Then finally he reached out, encompassing her fingers. But there was no fire, not like when Joss McRae had touched her, and her veins remained cool, her pulse steady. His hand was icy cold, and a little bit clammy, but it was much safer that way.

"You'll have to trust me, Silas." And she would have to trust herself to know what was best as well.

"Oh, Miss deLacey, I do. I do."

His eagerness made her wince to think that even as she demanded trust, she would deceive him.

Never would she tell dear, sweet Silas of her plans to strike back at the one man who made her blood boil and her heart race out of control all at the same time. He would never understand, and would no doubt try to stop her or interfere.

What she needed was something to distract Abrams's attention. She glanced about the room, realizing she had the perfect diversion at her fingertips—the redecoration of this house.

"There are some changes we'll have to make." She was trying hard to be gentle.

"Changes? W-W-What kind of changes?" A strange, almost bad-little-boy look of confusion clouded his face.

"The house," she clarified. She suspected that she was speaking of apples, he of oranges. "It just isn't . . . quite right."

His expression instantly altered to one of relief laced with a touch of defensiveness. "I know some of the rooms aren't completed yet, but deLacey, whatever you need—you want—it's yours for the asking."

He had dropped the Miss before her name, and missed completely what she was attempting to convey to him. Tightening her resolve she made a stab at explaining herself better.

"Unfortunately, Silas, we'll have to gut it and start all over."

At that he sat up and glanced about, a blinking owl of surprise. "You don't like what I've done so far?"

In that moment, on his round, open face, she caught a glimpse of what it would be like to be married to someone like Silas Abrams. Life wouldn't be perfect, not by a long shot, nor would it be as exciting as living with someone like Joss McRae. Instantly, she struggled to brush aside such taboo thoughts. She could think of far worse fates than being married to a rich rancher, had even considered them from time to time. Appeasing this man's insecurities, soothing his gentle, yet enormous, pride wouldn't be that difficult.

"It's not that I don't like it, Silas." She studied him for a moment, deciding on exactly the right way to tell him the truth about his misguided taste in furnishings. "It's just that it doesn't make the impression we wish to make."

If Silas Abrams had even a trace of petulance, he would no doubt reveal it now.

"We?" he mouthed hesitantly. "Did you say we, deLacey, my dear? Does this mean you've agreed to marry me?" he finished on a great rush of air. "How soon?"

Lacey caught her breath deep in her lungs. Ah, yes, the "we" was a bonafide clincher, and although she had used the word with calculated intention, she wasn't prepared for Abrams's unabashed response.

She tried to think of a way to avoid giving him an answer, bat her lashes maybe and act coyly. But why put him off? Why did she hesitate to take advantage of the best offer to come her way in a long time? Hadn't she just decided that this was what she wanted?

She ignored the response that her body gave her, the little jolt of repulsion that coursed through her to think of Silas Abrams doing the things Joss had done to her, touching her, kissing her. But that wasn't what Silas expected from her; he had never even looked at her in a way to suggest that he did.

Like right at this moment. He was waiting, breath held for

her reply, and yet there was no carnal glint in his eyes as there always seemed to be in Joss McRae's.

If it came right down to it, she could keep a man like Silas at arm's length. Well, at least most of the time. Many marriages—good ones by the day's standards—managed quite nicely with such an arrangement, didn't they? Why did hers have to be any different?

And yet when she opened her mouth to say yes, to agree to allow him to set the date whenever he wished, she found herself unable to spit out the words. Taking the safe way out, she fluttered her lashes and looked down to conceal her confusion. Why couldn't she just do what was obviously the best thing for herself?

"Please, Mr. Abrams, I . . . I need just a little more time."

But time wasn't going to change the way she felt about him physically. Nor would it eradicate the vivid images of Joss McRae making love to her that invaded her dreams night after night, leaving her wanting more of the one thing she dared not have.

"Time? Is that all?" he said with a spurt of delighted laughter. "Then you have time, as much as you want." He glanced about the room, and by the look on his face she could tell he was remembering the original point of this conversation. "And money, deLacey. You have that, too. All you need to make this house suit you. To make the right impression. And anything else. Just ask and it's yours."

Time and money—and the security they afforded. What more could she possibly ask for?

She brushed aside her nagging doubts before they could formulate into a tangible response, a reason just to get up and leave this house, this community, the entire Dakota Territory now before it was too late.

But what was out there for her? A life of uncertainty, loneliness? Of gambling, cheating, and no doubt eventually losing? Of conniving men like Joss McRae ready to take advantage of her? To end up like her father?

No, she would never allow that to happen. Now that she'd

hit on a streak of good luck, she'd better hang on to it with all that she had. As her daddy had told her time and again, take advantage of the moment when it presented itself. It might not come around again, at least not in this lifetime.

Cocklebur tenacity—self-preservation. Those were the two lessons of her youth that she had learned well. This was her golden opportunity, and she would not walk away from it.

After dinner Lacey wasn't the least bit surprised when Abrams excused himself, leaving her to her own devices— his way, no doubt, of giving her time to herself, time to make up her mind and give him the commitment he wanted from her. Well, in time she would give it. In the meantime, she still had to figure out a way to mollify Joss McRae.

Alone, she wandered from the dining room into the vast wasteland of the living room. It was as awful as she remembered it to be. And the mess. All the stacks of paper on everything. She frowned. She would just have to have a little chat with Mrs. Smythe, the housekeeper, about doing her job properly. The lack of good taste did not give license to be untidy.

Automatically, she stopped in front of the closest stack of paper. Scooping them up, she glanced about, looking for a place to settle and sort through them. In a dark alcove tucked off in a corner she spied a desk she'd not noticed before.

It had to be Silas's. Her heart skipped an unaccountable beat. This was the man's private sanctuary. She should respect it as such. But she knew so little about him really. Was it wrong before she agreed to marry him to learn a little more? Glancing over her shoulder nervously, she glided toward the tiny room, then came to a sudden halt. Her mind made up, she discarded her stack of papers on a nearby windowsill and sat down in the leather-bottomed chair. Like all of the other furniture, the desktop was littered. As with any monumental task, she wasn't quite sure where to start.

Reaching for the nearest stack, she began to thumb through the sheaves. Mostly letters, several contracts to buy

cattle, others to sell, nothing unusual for a rancher to have
on his desk, but the amounts of money indicated was
extensive. Silas Abrams was even richer than she'd first
imagined. The next pile revealed much the same, as well as
the next.

Muttering to herself, she sat back.

That's when she saw something that made her catch her
breath with a little gasp.

It was a small piece of paper with handwritten block
letters on it. "McRae returned. Branding accomplished.
Sioux Coulee. Awaiting further instructions." It was signed
BH.

"BH. BH. B-B-Billy Howell," she mouthed, not sure if
she was right. Just what did this mean? She wasn't sure, but
she knew it had to be important.

"Miss deLacey?"

At the sound of her name being called, she jumped and
hastily shoved the stack of incriminating papers back where
she had found it. Then scooting out of the chair, she paused
at a nearby window, arranging herself to appear as if she had
been merely looking out, enjoying the view beyond the pane
of glass.

"I'm here, Mr. Abrams."

If he was suspicious there was no indication on his face
when he joined her. Instead he placed a tentative arm about
her waist.

"The Rocking A, deLacey," Abrams whispered. "It's all
yours for the asking."

Hers for the asking. Yes. It was all she wanted. She would
do whatever it took to hang on to it. Tomorrow she would
make Silas Abrams the happiest man in the Dakota Territory. Tomorrow she would agree to be his wife.

CHAPTER 11

Even though the days were warm this time of the year in the Dakota Territory, the night temperature still had a tendency to dip down quite low. Joss turned up the collar of his work shirt, cursing himself for rushing out of camp and not thinking to bring his jacket with him.

Hurrying had done him a lot of good, he thought sarcastically. He still had a long wait ahead of him. A long wait, indeed, before he dared to enter Silas Abrams's house.

Pausing on a butte that overlooked the Rocking A Ranch and surrounding buildings, he watched the sparse activities below, the winking and blinking of the lamplight within the house, an occasional silhouette moving by the windows. There was only a handful of cowboys remaining on the premises, a couple of tired-looking ponies in the corral, as the majority were at the roundup.

All to his advantage. Fewer eyes to spot his approach, voices to sound an alarm. In fact, his main concern was the flop-eared hound stretched out asleep on the ground at the bottom of the porch steps.

Shivering, he twisted in place and reached into his saddlebags and took out a leather-covered flask with the initials JDM tooled on the flat face. A cowboy's only companion on a cold night. Unscrewing the lid, he took a long drink, then wiped his mouth on the back of his shirt sleeve.

He would circle around to the rear and come in from that direction with the wind to his advantage, he decided. With a little bit of luck the dog would never detect his approach.

Finally the lights went out in the main room, and Joss capped the half-empty flask, returning it to his saddlebags, and sat up straight to see where the flow of illumination went next. His stomach growled, and the horse beneath him began to fidget. They were both hungry, but that would have to wait a little while longer. At least the brandy had warmed his insides somewhat.

"Sorry, ol' boy," he murmured, reaching down to stroke the buckskin's silky neck.

A few minutes later he saw twin lamps flicker, each at the opposite ends of the house. That was good. For that had to mean that deLacey was rooming on the far end of the south wing all by herself.

With a touch of spur he set his mount into action, circling around the house to the rear. There the rise was not nearly as steep, and he had no trouble descending the gentler slope.

In a small clearing a few hundred yards from the main building he dismounted and dropped the reins. The horse wouldn't wander far, for like most cow ponies he was trained to stay put with trailing reins. With a final pat, Joss set off, moving on silent feet through the lush spring grass that the horse had already begun cropping contentedly.

Several yards from the bedroom window, he paused, caught his breath, and held as still as a puma mesmerized by fire. The shadow play against the closed curtain held him entranced as nothing else could.

DeLacey reaching to unbutton her blouse and remove it slowly, then bending to do the same to her skirt.

His veins became like dry gullies after a spring downpour, the rush of heated desire enhanced by the brandy he'd consumed almost more than he could handle.

And then her underclothing followed. He listed each one by name in his mind as she removed them, knowing the moment she had completely undressed, so close . . .

And yet, so far away.

"Lacey," he whispered in a voice roughened with need.
Then and there he knew what he wanted more than anything
else—more than power, more than revenge—a hell of a lot
more than Silas Abrams's head on a platter. He swallowed
so hard he thought for sure he would strangle on his own
Adam's apple.

Her arms lifted, and a nightgown floated down over her
head. The light was blown out, the show was over as
quickly as it had started. But not in Joss's mind. This night
had just begun. Moving to the window, he tapped lightly on
the pane, the brandy and the desire making him quite
reckless.

The curtain rustled and divided. Her face appeared on the
other side of the glass, illuminated by the soft glow of the
nearby fireplace, so beautiful and fresh he couldn't help
smiling his pleasure even though he knew he must look
rather foolish standing outside her window like some
Peeping Tom. Lifting his hand, he waved at her.

If she was surprised to find him there, her poker face
didn't reveal a thing, neither approval nor disapproval. She
reached up, and he thought she was going to open the
window for him without him demanding it. But then her
hand dropped, and the curtain whooshed back into place.

Slowly his grin faded to be replaced by an angry slash of
a frown. She was going to just leave him standing out there,
cold and hungry and . . .

He tapped again, this time more insistent. He didn't care
who might hear him.

No response.

"DeLacey," he called through clenched teeth.

Nothing. Not even the acknowledgment that she had
heard him.

Well, he'd be hanged if he was going to come all this way
to rescue her just to be thwarted by her uppityness.

Hopping up on the ledge, he put his shoulder to the
casement of the French window and pushed with all of his
might, fully expecting to find it bolted from within, his
efforts useless.

To his utter surprise, the two halves of the window parted like a Red Sea miracle, leaving him teetering on the threshold with nothing to break his inevitable fall.

"Lacey, darlin'."

He was lying on the floor, just lying there grinning up at her as if his presence in the house of his enemy were nothing out of the ordinary.

"Joss McRae, what are you doing here?" she hissed, clutching the front of the frothy dressing sacque she had hastily thrown on to cover the rather low neckline of her nightgown. Glancing over her shoulder toward the door, she wondered if anyone else had heard the commotion when he had come crashing through the window like a bull on a rampage.

"Why, honey, I do believe I came to rescue you." That foolish grin seemed permanent and . . .

DeLacey leaned forward and took a sniff. The smell of brandy on his breath explained quite a bit.

"Joss McRae, I don't need to be rescued."

"Well, you can't stay here." He pushed up to unsteady feet. "I won't let you," he declared.

"In your state, you can't stop me." Defiantly she planted her fists on her hips. Just what did he mean, he wouldn't let her?

"My state?" He frowned. "Just what *is* my state?"

"Don't deny it, Joss McRae. You've been drinking, haven't you?" she chided as if he were a wayward husband and she an old fishwife.

"Just been keepin' warm, darlin', while I figured out a way to sweep you up and carry you off." He flung his arm in a wide, dramatic arc.

"Keeping warm? You wear a coat to keep warm. Any fool knows that." Battling a smile that insisted on parting her lips, she turned away. Oddly enough, she rather liked his chivalrous display, even if it was fueled by alcoholic fumes—and even if she did despise him.

She couldn't begin to explain or excuse the unbidden joy that had gripped her when she had peeked through the curtains to discover Joss McRae standing outside her window. Especially in light of the monumental decisions she had come to less than an hour before. She was on the verge of agreeing to marry one man, yet the mere sight of the very culprit she'd vowed to protect him from turned her head so completely she forgot all about her determination to do what was best.

But she doubted he would have taken her refusal to talk to him lightly. He would have just forced his way in regardless. Such a commotion might have attracted attention, and she did not want Silas ever to find out she'd had anything at all to do with his sworn enemy. It was just best to let him in and get it over with.

Now that he stood here before her, she wasn't so sure she'd made the best decision. Joss McRae wasn't good for her. He brought out a side of her she didn't like to acknowledge. In fact, it seemed he brought out every aspect, every vulnerability of her personality she'd much rather think didn't exist. No, she couldn't fall victim to his charms, and she made up her mind to demand that he leave. Now. This instant.

But the heat of work-rough hands slid down her lawn-covered arms igniting waves of pleasure she could only compare to the phenomenon of static electricity.

"I can think of something much more enjoyable than putting on a coat to keep us warm." His mouth was so close to her ear, his heated breath reinforcing the promise of his words.

Her heart cried out to comply, just to give in and lean back into the protection of his muscled chest, if only this once in her life, to believe that he might care, might have really come to rescue her. Closing her eyes, she smiled sadly. Unfortunately, there was too much of the cool, calculated card player in her to succumb that easily.

"I'm quite warm enough, thank you." Pulling away from his grip, she put as much space between them as the room that now seemed so small afforded.

He seemed put off by her lack of instant response to his

show of tenderness. Narrowing his eyes, he studied her so intently she felt the need to squirm, although she controlled it, refusing to allow him to unnerve her, for no doubt that was what he was trying to do.

"Warm, Lacey?" he finally said with a humorless laugh. "Hell, you're about as warm as a snake in snow."

Just why such a venomous remark coming from a hateful man like Joss McRae would cause her pain made no sense, but it did. His comment cut her to the quick. But at least it brought her to her senses.

"Perhaps you're the problem, Joss McRae. Did you ever think of that possibility?" she cried, wanting more than anything at the moment to hurt him as much as he had hurt her. "I can be very warm when I choose to be. Just ask Silas Abrams."

The deafening silence that followed was accented only by the popping of the logs on the fire. Joss straightened, the disarming effects of the brandy fading away even as she watched. For a moment deLacey wished she had kept her mouth shut.

Then she reconsidered. True or not, she'd had every right to say what she'd said. Joss didn't have a monopoly on smart remarks. Besides he deserved to be knocked down a notch or two. He might be handsome and plenty of women might melt at his touch—but she would not be one of them.

The sudden, unbidden image of him in another woman's embrace set her blood to boiling uncontrollably. Just how many women had Joss McRae been with?

The jealousy her thoughts stirred was quickly capped by his unbridled reaction. His hand curled about her elbow, and he jerked her against his hard, heaving chest.

"Honey, you don't know what fire is."

She had forgotten how tall he was, how wide and powerful his shoulders were. Dropping back her head to gaze up into his burning gray eyes she remembered. Oh, how she remembered.

And she relived even more. The feel of his lips upon her own, his hand caressing her breasts, peaking them into hard mounds of desire, stoking dormant embers of desire to searing flames until she had not cared what he had thought of her, nor what she thought of herself.

"I don't want to know," she protested. But what she really meant was that she was afraid to know, to lose control, to put herself at the mercy of a man, especially one like Joss McRae who made no commitment in return. It meant the sacrifice of everything important to her.

"You lie."

His mouth came down hard and passionate, covering hers, validating his accusation, the taste of the brandy he'd drunk sweet and potent.

She yearned to conquer whatever it was that turned her resolve into mush, that made her heart race like a toy wound too tightly, just as it was doing now, so confusingly. But in order to best an enemy she had to know it first, didn't she?

Had to know if the thick matting of chest hair beneath her palms went on, down, down, forever. If his hands, his mouth—she sucked in a ragged breath when his tongue touched hers—if they knew other ways of drawing forth her untried passions. If in truth the enemy was Joss McRae or some lurking unknown within herself that she was unwilling to confront.

Then when he brushed aside her dressing sacque, forcing it down her arms and over her fingertips, she couldn't remember why it had been so important to put it on in the first place, why it was vital to resist him and the feelings he stirred up. His arm curled around her back, pulling her upward until she stood on tip-toes, her spine arched, her breasts pressing against the rough texture of his chest that the thinness of her nightgown did nothing to disguise. In fact it seemed only to heighten her pleasure.

Suddenly the scoop neck she had thought so revealing only moments before couldn't be low enough when his lips brushed against the row of lace stitched along the top.

"The fire, sweet Lacey," he whispered against her straining heart. "Don't hold it back. Let it go. Let it go for me."

The next thing she knew the restraints were no longer there, no longer binding her, no longer imprisoning her. The freedom, not only of her body but of her consciousness, was glorious, the fire a raging blaze that seemed to follow wherever his mouth and hands led, leaving no part of her unscathed.

The edge of the bed pressed urgently against the back of her calves, and for a moment she stiffened with panic, refusing to bend, to abandon her last stronghold, to go beyond that point of no return. But he hooked her leg behind her knee, drawing it up, up against his chap-covered thigh. With no strength of resistance left in her, she buckled and fell backwards.

She wasn't sure how he managed it, but somehow he caught her and eased her down on the bed, following, yet not crushing her beneath his weight as he covered her. He still had his hand curled behind her knee, drawing her leg still higher until it fit like a puzzle piece into the indentation of his waist. The fullness of his groin encased in denim and leather pressed almost painfully against her soft vulnerability. But the flames only grew hotter, engulfing all her senses, erasing the fears, the uncertainties, leaving only the desire.

Joss was like the finest blacksmith who could build and sustain the forge fires, never allowing them to flicker for a moment. With hands and mouth that knew no limitations, no modesty, he skillfully stoked her untried passions into an overwhelming need that had to be assuaged or surely she would die.

She moaned with impatience, dug her nails into the bare flesh of his shoulder blades as his tongue traced the contour of her ear, her throat, and lower. And she entangled her fingers in his hair when his mouth enveloped the hard nodule of her breast, easing the tightness somewhat and yet the evasive sensation merely traveled lower, beckoning, demanding to be pursued and conquered.

He knew. Somehow he knew what was taking place inside of her, the whirlwind that was wreaking havoc on her self-control. His hand, large and rough, was ever so gentle as it followed the burning desire to that part of her that was alive and throbbing with the elusive need. And then he touched her, and it was like magic, as if he had lassoed her passion as wild and untamed as a mustang, taking control of it, making it go where he wanted, where she fervently needed it to go. Opening to his exploration as a flower bud unfolds beneath the warming rays of the sun, she gasped her delight.

How was it possible that her body could have concealed such pleasures from her? How was it possible that he could draw them out so easily—with or without her consent?

She reached down, cupping her hand about his wrist, but whether it was to stop him or to guide him, she couldn't be sure. His knowing fingers continued caressing her in ways and places she had never even touched herself. Stronger and stronger the wondrous turbulence built until . . .

He slowed his rhythm just enough to allow her to collect her reason, steady enough to remind her that there was something more she had yet to experience. Lifting her lashes, she discovered him staring down at her, watching her.

And then she realized he was offering her a choice, to accept what he could give her or reject it. And in that moment of ambivalence she knew the decision was already made—to trust him.

To trust the one man she feared the most.

Bravely she unshackled his wrist, her arms moving up to entwine about his neck, her body twisting so that she could run her crooked knee along his still clothed thigh. With those few moves she not only gave her consent but had managed to ensnare him in the pleasure web he had spun for her benefit. Such simple actions would alter her life forever, be it for better or worse.

From that point it was mutual trust, shared giving and taking. His hands that had been so confident, so skillful upon her body only moments before, grew clumsy as he tried to unbuckle his chaps, his jeans, and she found herself helping him with fingers sure and capable. Somewhat surprised, he watched her progress silently, not daring to breathe, as if he were afraid to move lest she change her mind.

She paused and stared up into his handsome face for once so full of uncertainty. Just what did he think? That she would reject him?

And was that not exactly what she had done with her words earlier?

Where was the overconfident Joss McRae she knew so well? Perhaps it was merely a facade to mask his own insecurities.

Joss McRae showing human vulnerabilities? The possibility astounded her, confused her, set her pulse to racing. A slow warmth invaded her heart, the one part of herself she had carefully shielded from this experience, drawing her so close to him. Uncontrollably she began to tremble.

No, no, she couldn't, she wouldn't admit that she might possibly be in love with him. To do so would be more disastrous, more devastating, than losing confidence in her abilities with a deck of cards.

Murmuring an incoherent excuse, she withdrew her hands from the fasteners on the front of his pants and tried to extract herself from his embrace, as well.

"What is it, Lacey?" he asked somewhat hesitantly, grappling with her when she shook her head and tried to squirm away. Forcing her to her back, he straddled her, and with a grip of steel he pressed her wrists to the mattress beside her head, shackling them. Forced her to face him and that unnamed something inside of her that left her weak and defenseless, and confused at her lack of willpower.

His breathing was labored, just as her own was, and laced with a determination she struggled to match. Then his gaze turned hard, dipping down to devour her.

Now this was the old Joss McRae she knew so well. The hated enemy, someone her heart was safe from, someone she could willingly fight. And fight she would.

"What is it, Lacey?" he repeated in a cold, commanding voice. "A case of cold feet? Or is it that the game has gone a little farther than you meant for it to go."

"No," she denied, bucking to free herself of his domination. "Merely a dose of good sense. Now let me go." She twisted and thrust once more against the manacles of his fingers, turning her head with the intention of biting him if she must in order to escape.

"Oh, no you don't, honey." Avoiding her bared teeth, he spread her arms wide and held her that way until she ceased her wild, hopeless struggle.

Panting like the captured prey that she was, she watched him, mesmerized, as he slowly lowered himself over her, covering her from breasts to thigh with his much larger, much stronger body.

"This time, darlin'," he declared in a low animal growl, "I'm calling your bet. You can't bluff, and you're not going to fold on me now." His lips captured hers in a passionate kiss, taming them much too easily, then moved to her ear and down the column of her neck.

The flames that she'd thought safely banked flared once more, scorching hot, a wildfire racing across her senses, out of control.

This is not love, she swore to herself, even as she matched his ardor with equal zeal. Her hand ran down his belly to mimic his actions to discover that, yes indeed, the line of dark chest hair never ended, not until it reached . . .

And then his hand was there, doing those wondrous things to her once more, winding the key of rapture within her tighter and tighter until she thought for sure she would shatter into a million pieces.

To die so would be blessed paradise, and not caring that she ran blind, she raced selfishly on toward the yawning abyss, urging him to hurry.

But Joss was not about to be rushed.

"Easy, honey," he murmured though his breath was as hurried as her own. "It's like playing for the highest stakes of all and winning. Savor each triumph, each victory, each crest of the wave. Make it last as long as you can."

But, oh, this was better than any game of cards she had ever wagered on. She didn't give a damn about savoring. All she wanted was to know, to experience whatever it was she pursued to its fullest.

But Joss had yet to deal the final card. And when at last he did, filling her, guiding her through the moment of blinding pain and finally taking charge of the craving deep inside of her, she discovered that this was no longer something she could do on her own. She needed him, needed him to give it to her, to direct her up the path of ultimate pleasure. And that he did, taking her higher, giving her no choice except to follow his pace, slow but unrelenting.

Up. Up. One wavering moment that made her gasp.

"Joss." The sound of his name uttered with such joy seemed to come from all about her, as if there were no world beyond, just the unbearable waves crashing over her. And in those few seconds she saw clearly the enemy she so valiantly must defeat.

Loneliness, not only the aloneness created by the outside world but within herself, as well. She would have to learn how to give, how to trust, how to share at any risk. Through Joss McRae she had glimpsed that fleeting moment of truth. Only through Joss.

The overwhelming meaning of it all engulfed her, frightening her, left her trembling and close to tears. And yet lying there as the spinning world slowed and her blood no longer roared in her ears drowning out the reality beyond the flicker of clarity, she knew she was helplessly hooked.

No matter the dangers to herself, to her heart, to her future and security, she would come back for more. Much more. She would take any and every risk she must to get there. She would dance with the devil. She would flirt with death. She would compromise her ambitions. She would even face the truth about herself.

Glancing up into Joss's face, she saw that he too had been shaken by the wonderful experience much the same as she had. That surprised her somewhat for she had assumed him accomplished in the ways of love. And there was no doubt that he was when it came to the mechanics. Perhaps it was his heart that was as untried as her own. The possibility made her breathless.

And determined her to do whatever she had to do in order to give him what he needed most. Peace. To have that overpowering need for revenge swept away. But she was willing to admit that her purpose was not a noble one. Only by giving up his relentless pursuit could he love her as completely as she wished to be. If only she could convince him of a lie that had to be perpetuated. He had to believe that Silas Abrams was innocent.

"Joss," she said with a soft yet decisive sigh. Reaching up, she ran her fingers through his dark, damp hair, hoping to give credence to what she was about to tell him, praying that after what they had just shared, he would be willing to listen. "You are wrong about Silas Abrams. So very wrong."

Every muscle in his body tensed. As he pulled away from her she knew what it was to have an arm, a leg violently ripped from her body, so intense was the loss of his warmth, his strength.

"No, Joss," she cried, reaching to draw him back to her, to hang on to the little bit of heaven she had found and desperately wanted to keep. "You must listen to me."

But it was already too late. The division was complete, the intimacy sheathed, the animosity and distrust taking hold once more.

"I am many things, Lacey, but I'm no fool." His back to her, he had pulled on his pants and was hastily stuffing his unbuttoned shirt into his open waistband. "If you thought to seduce me, then convince me that . . ."

"Seduce *you?*" DeLacey sat up, clutching the corner of the rumpled coverlet to her breasts, unable to believe that he could accuse her. "You're the one who burst uninvited to my room, making promises. Spouting chivalrous nonsense about rescuing me."

"You didn't seem so surprised to see me. And like you said, you don't need rescuing, do you, honey?" Securing the last of the buttons on his shirt, he confronted her, and the look on his face could only be described as antipathy. "You never did. I should have known better than to let my guard down with you, even for a minute, to think of you as anything but the ambitious spawn of King Honeycutt, gambler, con artist. Tonight you do your sire proud."

Without a backward glance, he headed toward the still open window.

"You leave my daddy out of this," she cried, rising to her knees in protest, for the one thing she would not tolerate was someone speaking ill of the only man she had ever completely trusted, the only man who had ever been truly noble.

But Joss merely laughed at her outburst. "You know, you almost had me convinced that you were capable of feeling something other than greed." Crossing over to where she sat defiantly beneath the protection of the coverlet, he grasped her chin and forced her to look up at him.

"Know this, Lacey. The money I promised to pay you is incidental now. You're in this for your life, honey. Cross me, and not only will I spoil your little nest here, darlin', but you'll find yourself in a jail cell so deep in the legal bowels you'll never see the light of day again—much less a penny of that ten thousand dollars."

Greedy. How dare he call *her* greedy, he with his cattle empire and fancy train cars. Angrily she clawed at his restraining hand, the same hand that had given her such pleasure only moments before. Besides, she didn't want his money, but she didn't want to go to jail, either.

"Now, you listen and you listen real good," he warned her, squeezing her cheeks so hard it almost brought tears to her eyes. "I want that information about Abrams. And don't tell me you can't find it. You have just two weeks." He released his grip on her jaws.

Her flesh stung, and she reached up to rub where she knew there would be two red imprints on her face.

"Two weeks, deLacey. That's all. I'm not bluffing. And don't count on Silas Abrams or his money to protect you. It won't."

With that he slipped out of her window and was gone, gone before she could even murmur a protest.

Gone before she could tell him what she thought of his ultimatum. Before she could tell him just what she thought of him.

Two weeks.

She sucked her lower lip between her teeth and began to chew it. There was no doubt in her mind that Joss meant what he said, for only a callous, unfeeling man could do what he'd done to her, make love and then threats all in the same breath. But even for self-preservation, could she bring herself to point a finger at Silas Abrams? Poor, misguided little man. He deserved better.

Those pangs of conscience struck again, and her timing couldn't have been worse.

She considered her options, and for once she found the process most distasteful. Running wouldn't work. Joss McRae would only hunt her down and follow through with his threats to have her arrested and tried for crimes she couldn't even begin to imagine. He was determined enough to follow her to the ends of the earth to get his due. She knew then that she somehow had to deflect him from his path.

He wanted proof, did he? Two weeks didn't give her all that much time, but it would have to do. She would ferret out some kind of evidence, for more than ever she was determined not to lose her chance to have all the things in life she wanted. The things Silas Abrams was offering her.

She had to finger someone else, someone Joss would find likely.

Remembering that note she had seen on Silas's desk signed BH. Billy Howell. Of course. It made perfect sense to her now. The dirty, despicable man who had been so rude to her upon her arrival into Medora. He was somehow connected with this whole affair. If there was cattle thieving going on in the territory then Billy Howell was probably in the thick of it. In fact he might even be the mastermind behind it, using Silas and his hatred of Joss McRae to keep them all from discovering the truth. Hadn't the copy of that telegram she'd found on Silas's desk indicated as much?

Yes, the rough old cowboy was definitely involved. All she had to do was prove it.

CHAPTER 12

Two weeks. It seemed more like eternity to Joss. The roundup was over, the cattle branded and returned to the lush and green range, the summer ahead for them to grow and fatten.

But for Joss it was a time of restlessness. Time for the susceptibilities within him to brood and fester. There was no denying it, no matter how hard he tried. DeLacey Honeycutt had managed to turn him inside out. And she couldn't have done a better job of it even if she had stood him on his head and shook him up and down. Like change in his pockets the feelings had come tumbling out until there was nothing left concealed.

If it was possible for a woman to rape a man emotionally, then that was exactly what she had done to him. Stripped him bare and wrung him dry.

Like it or not, he was in love with a woman too calculating and cold to know the meaning of the word, and try as he might, there wasn't a thing he could do to alter his state of mind. But he'd be hanged if he'd just sit around and bemoan the injustice of the situation.

The only way he could escape it and her was to purge himself of her.

Two weeks. Then he would send her packing, either to

jail or on the train, her purse full of money. Either way he would be free, if not of the emotions then of their cause.

In the meantime on his own initiative he had dug up some interesting information regarding Silas Abrams's operation. It seemed the cattle thieves were on the prowl again, night riding, and they were especially interested in the where-abouts of the Lazy J stock, rounding them up, singly and in pairs. One of the rustlers had been spotted repeatedly by several of his line camp riders, but whenever they pursued, their quarry managed to get away. Then one of his men had turned up dead, found shot in the back on the range not far from Sioux Coulee. No doubt the cowboy had stumbled upon the rustlers in action, and it had cost him.

Joss didn't want his men risking their lives. So he had taken to patrolling the line himself in hopes of catching the culprits redhanded. For where there was one there were bound to be more.

Besides, line riding gave him an excuse for not sleeping at night, even though the truth of the matter was that thoughts of Lacey were what really kept him awake, night after night, hour after long hour. Closing his eyes meant giving in to his need for her, a burning, relentless desire to make love to her, over and over again. The images of her lithe body entwined about his own were seared into his brain like a permanent brand, inescapable.

How she had managed to bewitch him so thoroughly bewildered him, a confusion that always brought him around full circle. He was so angry at her, at himself if the truth be known, that he would do whatever he must to be rid of such a weakness.

McRae men might love their women to a point, but they never let them get the best of them and never, never would they allow a woman to make a fool of them.

It seemed deLacey Honeycutt had somehow managed to do just that and more.

So on he rode, a night phantom, scouting the range that in the moonlight became a different environment from the stark harshness of the Dakota Badlands by day. If he'd been the poetic type he would have been apt to describe the nocturnal world about him in those highfalutin phrases one read in leather-bound books. *The river ran like molten silver. The buttes stood out like glimmering sentries, unmoving, the deep gorges the black cloaks of their concealment.*

Joss sighed. *Her long hair shimmered like a ribbon of gold.*

At the inevitable turn of his thoughts, he frowned. As he had said, he wasn't one for fancy words or sentiments. Hair was hair. It didn't shimmer. He'd be damned if he would allow himself to turn into a lovesick puppy.

But such denial did nothing to stop the vivid, almost lyrical images from crowding his mind.

In the distance a coyote howled mournfully. Another one answered from an overhead cliff. Twisting in the stirrups, Joss paused to listen. The call of a coyote wasn't always what it seemed to be. And then he caught the sound of hooves, horse or cattle, or maybe both, around the bend ahead of him. Alert, he settled back into the saddle and dug his heels into the sides of the buckskin, urging him on.

Perhaps at last he had found what he was looking for.

Two weeks. The time was whizzing by much too quickly. There was still so much to do—too much. Where would she find the time or energy to get it all accomplished?

Under the guise of settling in, redecorating Abrams's house, and making friends, deLacey so far had managed to escape Silas nearly every day and had finally set in motion her plans to come up with the evidence Joss had demanded that she supply him with—or at least the proof she wanted him to have. At the first opportunity she returned to the desk in the alcove to search it more thoroughly. Her efforts were rewarded when she found copies of even more telegrams, all in the same handwriting, all signed with the initials BH, and they had all mentioned cattle and Joss McRae.

For the briefest of moments she had feared that Silas might be involved. Why else would he have the telegrams? And how had he gotten them? Had he perhaps bribed the telegraph operator?

One evening when they were alone she asked him about Billy Howell, conveying her feelings of mistrust, based purely on her initial confrontation with the man, of course, careful to mention nothing else.

Silas had given her a rather strange look and then had said, "Funny you should mention him. I've had my eye on that man for some time now. I'm beginning to think he's untrustworthy, so I've been doing a little checking up on him myself. I'm watching him, so don't you worry. If anybody around here is doing something they shouldn't, I'll get to the bottom of it."

His straightforward answer had served to confirm his innocence, at least in her eyes.

And so it had been necessary to set in motion the next step in her plan. To find this place so often mentioned in the notes, Sioux Coulee, and check it out for herself.

Under the guise of needing to get out and shop for the redecoration of the house and to make friends, she had asked for a carriage to be put at her disposal. In the beginning, Silas had insisted that she have a driver who knew the roads go with her, and so her initial trips to town had been limited to the mercantile under the pretense of ordering fabrics and china and even selecting furniture from the array of mail-order catalogues the storekeeper had supplied her with.

It was during such shopping sprees that she had had the opportunity to become acquainted with many of the other women of the community, ranchers' wives, the banker's wife, and Miss Bertalli, the seamstress and milliner who had assured her that she could make quality curtains and tablecloths to suit the future Mrs. Abrams's every need.

At first, she had thought these women condescending, but it didn't take long for her to realize that they were being quite sincere in their efforts to integrate her into the social structure of Medora. Soon she was invited to the afternoon socials, and she found herself looking forward to them.

Silas agreed to allow one of the other ranchers' wives to pick her up on the way, freeing up the ranch hand to do his neglected chores.

It was a whole new world to deLacey, this being accepted and catered to. She was no longer on the outside looking in. Such newfound respectability made her more determined than ever to hang on to her booty like a pirate with a treasure trove.

Yes, becoming Mrs. Silas Abrams was sounding better every day even though every day she put off making the final commitment until the next one.

It was during one of these frequent teas that she had the opportunity once again to run across Annie McRae. Harnessed in a dress and high-buttoned shoes the girl seemed much tamer. Either way, deLacey found herself drawn to Annie, the only other unmarried female to attend these socials, other than the spinster, Miss Bertalli. To her delight it turned out that Annie was only a year younger than herself.

From across the room Annie sized her up in much the same way as her brother would have done. Oddly enough deLacey found the girl's mannerisms sparked off an entire series of unexplained emotions, raw and overwhelming.

Since that night she had spent with Joss—she refused to label what they had done as making love in light of the way he had treated her afterward—she had struggled not to think about him, at least not in the ways her newly awakened sensuality wished to.

To love Joss McRae was not an option open to her—nor was desiring him. So Lacey pulled up from the depths of her being all of the discipline her daddy had ever taught her and refused to succumb to such impractical fantasies as possibly falling for the one man who would snatch away all that she had managed to attain for herself over the last few days. If these women were ever to find out the truth about her . . .

Yes, she had admittedly made a mistake by allowing Joss McRae to seduce her; one she would never make again. Life's missteps were the best teachers of all as long as they were never repeated. That was what "the King" had always told her. Now that she knew what traps lay ahead, she could avoid them. Of that she was confident.

But fraternizing with Annie McRae? Did she dare risk it?

She so wanted a friend her own age. And she admired Annie
for the way she held her own with the men in this
community. As long as she was careful, what harm could
come of getting to know the other girl a little better?

DeLacey smiled in return under Annie's intense scrutiny
and was quite pleased when the girl made an undisguised
beeline towards her. However, the initial chitchat she'd
expected was not forthcoming.

"I'm Annie McRae." The girl stuck out her hand in a
manly fashion, but didn't give deLacey a chance to respond
before rushing on. "You're Sy Abrams's mail-order bride.
Is it true you're really plannin' on marryin' him?"

The girl's frankness took her by surprise, but Lacey found
she could appreciate it.

"Why, yes, I do," she replied, renewing her smile, and
accepting the masculine handshake with a firm grip of her
own.

"Don't you find him old and . . . unattractive?"

Yes, Annie was definitely straightforward. Nothing like
her brother.

"I've learned in life, Annie, there are some things more
important than the way a person looks." How sage she
sounded. In fact, she rather liked this wise and knowing side
of herself.

"Like what?" the girl demanded. Pulling her hand away,
she planted it on her hip and cocked her head with obvious
curiosity. It seemed Annie was just as intrigued with her.

Such bluntness, although she should have expected it,
caught Lacey off-guard.

"Well . . ." The old deLacey instantly thought of
Abrams's money—the security it gave her, she rationalized
inwardly to soothe the involuntary self-criticism that raged
within her. But she did not voice that particular consideration. "There is kindness . . . and friendship . . . and
respect," she offered instead.

"And that's enough for you?"

She had to admit she was beginning to feel a bit
uncomfortable with Annie's insistent quizzing, as if the girl

were some inner voice perched upon her shoulder, forcing her to reconcile with her own suppressed misgivings.

"Annie, dear." It was Miss Bertalli come to the rescue, thank goodness. The spinster dropped one hand upon the inquisitive girl's shoulder and squeezed. "Miss Honeycutt might not care for such a grilling so early in the day, especially upon first meeting." Then she smiled at deLacey. "You must forgive her. Annie means no real harm."

"No offense taken." She smiled in reciprocation, then turned her attention to Annie, studying the girl, looking for just the right thing to say to put her at ease. "In fact I find your honesty most refreshing. And I believe this isn't our first meeting. I saw you at the roundup. You ride so well, Annie. I'm quite jealous, you know. I would love to be able to sit a horse the way you do," she said without thinking.

"Would you really like to learn? I could come over and teach you sometime."

DeLacey's smile never faded, yet she winced inwardly. Even though she admired Annie for her talents, the thought of attempting to ride in the same devil-may-care way caused her stomach to churn with anxiety. But once she did learn to handle a horse a little better she could take jaunts about the Rocking A, maybe even find her way to that place, Sioux Coulee. Her two weeks were already speeding by and she had yet to accomplish that goal.

"I would like that very much."

"Tomorrow morning, then," Annie offered.

"Tomorrow," Lacey echoed. *And the next day and the next*, she promised herself. *We will ride over every square inch of the area.*

She lifted her delicate china cup and took a sip, her gaze never leaving Annie. Although her tea might have turned tepid, her sense of accomplishment ran hot with the promise of success.

"Where does Annie rush off to so early every morning?"

Shirtless, shoeless, standing at the window, the curtain pushed aside so he could survey the yard in front of the house, Joss tossed a frown over his shoulder at Henry, who had brought a mug of steaming hot coffee up to his room. He was dead tired, the results of another long, fruitless night of line riding.

What he had hoped would be a lead to the Abrams's rustling operation had turned out to be Billy Howell. A pack of coyotes had cornered a cow and her calf—Lazy J stock—in a coulee. The Rocking A hand had rescued them and was attempting to herd them back onto open range.

The cow seemed to have other ideas. She thought the small canyon safer than the open, and kept doubling back.

Billy had been having a hell of a time when Joss had arrived and had been only too glad for the assistance. Odd, but that old cow had seemed eager enough to escape the confinement of the ravine when he had herded her into the open. Yet, if Billy was trying to steal McRae cattle for market, why bother with a tough old cow and her young calf? It was the three- and four-year-old steer he'd be after.

Billy Howell. He wasn't quite sure what to make of the wrangler. At one point or another he had worked most of the ranches in the area including the Lazy J. Though crude in his mannerisms, Billy was straightforward and honest as the day was long. Never once had he done anything to discredit his name. Even if Abrams was stealing cattle, Joss found it hard to believe that Billy was involved.

"It seems, sir, Miss Annie is giving riding lessons."

Pulling his thoughts back to the present problem, Joss plopped his cup of coffee down on the side table and turned to confront the servant.

"Just who in the hell would she be giving riding lessons to?" he demanded, but he had a sneaking suspicion already, and already he didn't like it.

"Miss Honeycutt, sir," Henry confirmed.

"DeLacey?" What was that little conniver up to now? No good, doubtless. "How long has this been going on?"

"For the last three days, sir." Henry fell silent, busying himself with rearranging several shirts in one of the dresser drawers.

Joss knew the man hadn't said all he wanted—not yet.

Somewhat impatient, he waited for the servant to finish his oration. He didn't like to be manipulated even by someone he trusted as completely as Henry.

"Damn it, man, if you have something to say, then say it."

"It has done the young miss a world of good, you know, sir."

"What?" Joss snapped, snatching one of the shirts from Henry's hands to put on. "Taking early morning rides?"

"The association with Miss Honeycutt."

Joss snorted. He knew better. Consorting with deLacey Honeycutt was good for nobody.

"You should see her. Miss Annie, that is," Henry ran on. "The other day she asked me if a particular bonnet befitted her complexion." He leaned forward. "And I haven't heard her use the *h* word or the *d* word in two whole days. And it seems she is even beginning to show an interest in the young men in the community."

If something or someone had managed to have a good influence on his little sister, it couldn't have been deLacey. That was impossible. But then it seemed Annie had been extraordinarily quiet at dinner last night—and she had still been in a dress.

Now that he stopped to think about it, his sister had been in rare form and fishing for compliments. And he did recall that she spoke incessantly about that young cowpoke, Rusty Chapin, the artist, the same one she had beaten in the horse race at roundup. Rusty this. Rusty that. She had even shown him one of the pictures the man had sketched of a herd of cattle. It had been a fine drawing, but he had merely shrugged it and her off. Thick-headed fool that he was, how could he not have noticed the changes in her? Changes he wasn't so sure he liked or approved of. At least he knew how to handle the cussing, devil-may-care Annie.

"Mr. McRae." Henry cleared his throat. "If I might be so bold as to make a suggestion."

"Not now, Henry." Joss brushed past the servant,

knowing just what it was he had to do and a good inkling of how he had to go about it.

"What do you call this place, Annie?"

Shading her eyes from the glare of the midday sun, deLacey surveyed the surrounding countryside. They were not far from town, perched high on a jagged butte overlooking the railroad tracks headed west toward the Montana border. In the distance she could see a large box canyon, a perfect spot for rustlers to load up stolen cattle and ship them off to market, no one the wiser.

"Sioux Coulee. They say that before the railroad came along, the Indians used to herd up the stock of the earlier ranchers and slaughter them here so they wouldn't compete with the buffalo for the grazing."

Sioux Coulee. Her heart began to race. At last she'd found the spot she was looking for, and now, it turned out, it was a natural place to gather up cattle, already had the reputation for it.

"Whose land are we on?"

"It's open range. The closest ranch is my brother's." Annie pointed over her shoulder. "Our land begins about three miles north."

Open range. Yes, that made perfect sense. Close enough to the Lazy J to be convenient, yet far enough away to be unobtrusive. How very shrewd of Billy Howell. As much as she wanted to go down and take a look around, she didn't want Annie to know why.

They were the best of friends now. DeLacey really found the other girl's company enjoyable. She had learned a lot about ranch life and cattle. But more important it was nice to be taken at face value and looked up to. In exchange she had given Annie the chance to begin the search for her own femininity, something the poor girl was sorely lacking in due to being without a constant female influence in her life. How could Joss have been so neglectful of his sister's education?

Joss. She shot a look at Annie—his little sister. So much like him and yet so very different.

"Tell me about your brother." The request slipped out before she could stop it. She reddened with confusion.

"Joss?" Annie seemed surprised at the turn of the conversation. "What do you want to know?"

"What's he like? . . ." She'd almost said "when I'm not around," but she caught her tongue just in time.

Annie shrugged. "Like any big brother, I suppose. But he is handsome, isn't he?"

A vivid picture of Joss formed in her mind. Ah, yes, he was devastatingly handsome. "I suppose."

"I saw the way you were lookin' at him at the roundup."

"Looking at him?" Annie's bluntness caught her off-guard. "What do you mean?"

"I mean, I know you think he's good-lookin'. And it's obvious that he finds you attractive, too."

This conversation was getting too personal—much too close to the truth. It was time to bring it to an end.

"Let's go down there," deLacey suggested, pointing toward the distant coulee.

"No. It's best we don't."

"Why not?"

"Too close to granger country. They don't care much for us, nor us them." Annie stared at her rather strangely.

"Grangers?" Lacey asked, a bit put off by Annie's lack of cooperation, yet realizing the girl probably knew what she was talking about.

"Sodbusters. You know, farmers. But up here on the plateau the land is flat and empty." The girl smiled. "I thought this would be a good place for our next lesson. To do a little barebackin'."

"Barebacking?"

"Yeah. Ridin' without a saddle."

For the past three days Lacey had managed to keep up with Annie fairly well and was quite proud of her accomplishments, even though her bottom and inner thighs were sore. However, the minor discomfort had been worth it. She had made a true friend and in the process had found the place she was looking for. She had also learned a lot about

Joss McRae and his obsession with Silas. It seemed the
hatred ran deep between the two men, between the Abramses
and the McRaes—more than the mere act of cattle rustling.
The girl had even hinted that Silas was somehow involved in
their father's death.

But she had to be wrong. She couldn't imagine Abrams
killing anything, much less another man, not unless he was
provoked.

And so in order to obtain all this information she had
galloped and clung for dear life, listening to the girl's
instructions, and she had to admit she had learned quite a bit
about the demanding art of horseback riding—at least in
theory. But riding without a saddle . . .

Lacey shook her head. "I don't think I care to do that,
Annie."

Annie snorted, and she sounded just like her brother when
he showed his impatience. "You cain't ever learn to ride
good if you're always dependin' on a saddle and stirrups to
do the work for ya." Already on the ground, she began
loosening her horse's cinch.

DeLacey decided she'd had enough. The thought of
climbing up on the bare, sweating back of an animal as
unpredictable as a horse scared the living daylights out of
her, but she so enjoyed these outings with Annie and she
didn't want them to come to an end.

Reluctantly she swung down on the ground and began
picking at the cinch knot in a halfhearted attempt to loosen
it. The pig-eyed sorrel, bless his ornery hide, sensed his
moment to take advantage of her. He began to fidget, laying
his ears flat against his skull to show his displeasure.
Moving backward, he began making strange high-pitched
squeals.

"Whoa," she said with little conviction and a lot of
hesitation. If the truth be known she wouldn't be all that
upset if the surly beast decided to bolt.

Annie, however, was much too attuned to the ways of
horses to let something like that happen. Shoving the reins
of her own mount into Lacey's hand, she took charge,

quickly unsaddling the sorrel and calming him down with a stern slap on his neck.

"Now," she said, turning her attention back to Lacey. "I'll give you a boost up—this time," she qualified. Interlacing her fingers, she bent and offered the makeshift footing to Lacey.

"Look, Annie." Unsure, Lacey stepped back. How had she gotten in this predicament?

"You have to—now. Otherwise he'll know he got the best of you."

Would that be so bad? If the stupid horse wanted to win, then she wasn't one to deny him.

"Up," Annie ordered.

"Only if you'll agree to go down to Sioux Coulee with me afterward."

Annie hesitated for a moment. "All right. I agree. Now get up there."

It was like trying to climb atop a rain-slick boulder. There was nothing to hang on to, no footing once Annie moved away. Draped over the back of that horse, struggling to swing her leg up and over without falling headfirst on the other side, she felt like an utter and complete fool.

Then finally she was astride, her legs curling, clinging like a clothespin to the broad barrel of the animal. His spine was so bony and the thought of bouncing up and down on it wasn't appealing. In fact, the prospect seemed downright painful.

"Good," Annie complimented, shoving the reins into Lacey's unwilling fingers. Then she dropped her hands to her hips. "You got a good leg on him. In no time you'll be racin' 'cross country without even havin' to think about it."

Grasping the tangle of reins, Lacey turned so that she could look down at the girl and tell her in no uncertain terms that she had no interest at all in racing anywhere, when she felt the sorrel tense at the loud, resounding whack on his rump.

Ill prepared, off they went, shot forth like a missile from a catapult.

"Annnnie," she cried, grabbing at the reins that were suddenly nowhere to be found.

"Hang on, Lacey. Hang on." Annie's exuberant voice rang out.

And hang on she did. Her legs were wrapped so tightly about the horse's middle that her thighs, even her ankles, began to cramp, but she dared not loosen them. Her arms were likewise fastened about the horse's neck so tightly that she was surprised she didn't strangle him. If only that were possible. Anything to slow him down. But it was as if he were chased by a swarm of stinging hornets. He seemed bent on going faster and faster, just like her pounding heart.

Oh, God. She could feel herself slipping, slowly but nonetheless inevitably, down along his spine toward his loin and over, sideways, like a top-heavy tower. The thought of falling off the thundering horse, of no doubt breaking her neck when she did, forced her into action. Reaching up she entangled her fingers into the flying mane and pulled herself back up on the bony ridge of his withers. There, at least, her legs could hang on a little tighter to the narrower girth—if one could call wrapping one's legs about something as big around and ungiving as a tree stump narrow.

When she managed to stop the accursed animal, if she ever got him stopped, she vowed never again to get on a horse. She should have known better than to bargain with Annie. Friend or not, she was still a McRae—just like her brother.

It seemed only logical to plop the blame where it so rightly belonged, on the broad shoulders of Joss McRae. Oh, what she would give for the chance to confront him now and tell him just exactly what she thought of him. Damn him!

Oh, damn this blasted horse. He seemed to possess an inordinate amount of stamina. Would he never slow down on his own?

Once again she began to grope along his neck hoping to find the reins. Not there. And then she began to remember all that Annie had told her the last few days about riding a horse—over and over like a drillmaster. *Squeeze with your knees only, not with your ankles and heels, not unless you want the horse to go faster.*

Knees. Just knees. Yet it seemed her legs were set like lockjaw, unable to respond to the command her brain sent to them. With a conscious effort, she loosened her ankles and clamped tighter with her knees.

Miracle of miracles. That pig-eyed sorrel began to slow down.

Giddy with success, she straightened and leaned back, just the way Annie had showed her she should do when she wanted to stop. Then just when she thought she had the situation under control she felt herself lifted up.

With a little screech, she flung out her arms trying to cling once more to the horse's neck, but it was as if she were being plucked from his back like a quill feather from a goose.

Time slowed to an oddly tranquil pace, every nuance of her predicament clear, and she could consciously mull over each one. Below her the ground whizzed by in a blur so close that her feet now and then brushed against the top of the vegetation. The horse, a buckskin—oddly familiar—ran with his great mouth open, huffing and grunting, and flinging saliva and sweat. Flecks, white and foamy, dotted her brown divided skirt, and even the front of her teal blue tailored blouse. Just she and that animal, or so it seemed to her.

But then she realized a leg, a human leg, dug into the side of her rib cage. An arm, thick and muscled, was hooked painfully about her midriff.

Something to hold on to. And that is exactly what she did. Hung on for dear life. At the moment she didn't care who or what the support belonged to, only that it was there.

They began to slow. Simultaneously the seconds quickened. Her feet struck the ground; her knees buckled, and she cried out, closing her eyes, fulling expecting to be thrown under the horse's thundering feet.

Tuck and roll. Tuck and roll, the voice of instinct ordered.

She drew her knees upwards, took a deep breath and clamped her jaws tight, as prepared as she could possibly be for the inevitable.

"Put your feet down, Lacey."

That was no inner voice speaking to her now. In fact, it was tinged with an oddly familiar sarcasm.

Slitting open her lashes, just a little, she saw the arm she clung to, tan and strong, the shirt sleeve rolled up above the elbow. It was covered with a fine layer of dark hair. Her eyes traveled up the length of the appendage, seeking just who it belonged to.

"Put . . . down . . . your . . . feet."

She turned her head toward the voice, so condescending as it pronounced each word slowly, as if she were dimwitted or some such thing.

Her eyes flew wide when they latched on to a thigh, encased in leather chaps.

She would never forget those leather chaps, nor her lurid thoughts the first time she had seen him in them.

Down went her feet, secure against firm, unmoving earth. Up went her chin, ascending on the strength of her indignation as she wrenched free and faced her foe.

Joss McRae.

She should have known that only he would do something so utterly stupid as to drag her from the back of a running horse and throw her to the ground.

"Damn you, Joss McRae. You could have killed me." Her fists lifted and came down with all of their might hard against his unprotected thigh, which was at her eye level.

"It looked as if you were doing a fine job of that, darlin', all by yourself." Gasping, he clutched the spot where she hit him. "Damn it, Lacey, you're merciless."

"And you are a self-serving pig. How could you do that to me?" She was breathing so hard, her chest, her very heart heaved with the pain of the emotions coursing through her. No longer was she speaking of his reckless attempt to rescue her, but of things much more important, and intimate—and irreversible.

"You blame me, Lacey?" He laughed, and it sounded almost like an animalistic growl. Then his eyes, gray and predaceous, devoured her from head to toe. "Can't recall that you put up much of a fight at the time."

Lacey began to sputter, her words a garble so intense was her frustration. True or not, he had no right to say something so mean-spirited, so downright cruel. And yet, try as she might, she could think of nothing to say back to him, nothing that would wound him as deeply as he had wounded her. Finally, her anger manifesting itself in a need for physical release, she lifted her fist with the intention of striking him again.

He caught her balled hand in midair, the sound of flesh against flesh creating a loud smack, stopping her downwards thrust, as if her strength—as if she—were insignificant.

They glared, he atop his horse, squeezing her small fist in his powerful hand, she on the ground, refusing to give an inch to his elevated height or his superior might.

And then it was as if reality came rushing in to slap them both on the face, to remind them just who they were and how deep their involvement.

"I didn't know you knew each other, big brother. And quite well, it seems from the looks of it." Annie chuckled, and it was the sound of the naughty urchin who had just caught the priest with his hand in the offering plate. "What *are* the two of you up to?"

At the same moment they both turned to contend with the girl's bold, but accurate, accusation.

Sitting a few yards away on her own mount, looking just as smug as her brother could at times, Annie had apparently witnessed the entire exchange between them. Amazement, laced with a Cheshire-cat smile—another familiar McRae trait—creased her youthful face.

A timeworn yet most appropriate cliché popped into Lacey's mind. Dear God, the cow was in the cabbage.

She confronted Joss almost fearfully, her eyes wide with a question and denunciation.

And then she reconsidered, realizing that Annie discovering them just might be to her benefit and to his disadvantage. After all, Annie was her friend. She was most curious to see what his reaction would be.

Well, Mr. You-think-you're-so-smart, she thought smugly, crossing her arms over her chest, *what are you going to do now?*

CHAPTER 13

Why was it that women always assumed that no matter what transpired, the man was responsible?

Joss scanned one feminine face and then the other, both staring at him as if they had every right to lay the blame on him. Well, there wasn't a female alive who could cow him into submission with a look. Not his sister, and definitely not the woman he . . . he . . .

The woman he what?

Joss glowered and set his teeth when his mind came back with an answer that didn't sit well.

The woman he found more exciting and irritating than any other, all at the same time. The woman he hated. The woman he loved.

Riding hard on the heels of the resolve he'd worked so diligently to perfect, to keep this thing between himself and deLacey strictly professional, came an overwhelming sense of panic. Love? That was impossible. He wouldn't be in love with a conniving bit of baggage like deLacey Honeycutt. And yet, it was those very traits that intrigued him the most about her.

She was as resourceful, resilient, as he would like to think himself to be. As much as she drove him crazy, he couldn't help but applaud her spunk.

195

But admiring her didn't mean he was going to give in to her.

"Just what did the two of you think you were doing out here on the range all alone?" he demanded. There were rustlers and murderers running rampant, one of his men had been killed not too far from that very spot, he wanted to say but didn't. Instead he drilled his sister with an angry look, and then he riveted deLacey with an equally uncompromising glare.

"I don't have to answer to you."

The simultaneous response, accompanied by hands on hips, was adamant, no more or less than he'd expected from either of them. But they were both wrong, for answer to him they would. He couldn't make up his mind which of them to light into first.

"Saddle up and go home, Annie," he ordered decisively, never taking his eyes off Lacey, finding suddenly he couldn't even if he'd wanted to. "I'll deal with you later," he murmured when oddly enough his little sister obeyed, saddling up her horse and dashing off without the usual tidal wave of smart remarks.

And you, I'll deal with now, he promised deLacey with an unwavering stare when at last they were alone.

His gaze flicked down taking in all of her, her defiant stance, her face, so beautiful, lifted fearlessly, her mouth, so kissable, puckered with determination. It was that same look she had given him time and again, each time just before she'd done something outrageous. Like pull a gun, or rob him blind, or throw his possessions out the window of a train. He had to give her credit. She never flinched, never even batted an eyelid, even when her accomplice scurried off without protest or apology. With a look that was as much a slap in the face as anything physical, she gathered up the reins of her own horse, attempting to scramble atop his broad, bare back, no doubt determined to follow the other girl's hasty departure.

Her efforts were valiant and most entertaining to watch. In fact, several times he was tempted to swat her strategically presented behind, or perhaps to cup it and give her a boost up. Instead, like a cat playing with a cornered mouse, he allowed her to struggle for quite some time and almost succeed in mounting the horse.

Then just as she was about to fling her far leg to the other side of the animal, he clamped her about her tapered waist and dragged her back to the ground.

Lord, but he had his hands full turning her around to face him.

"Just where do you think you're going, darlin'?"

She came up fighting, her claws bared, her blue eyes glistening. It couldn't have been worse had he cornered a shrew, a fierce combatant that never acknowledged defeat, even in the face of a much stronger adversary. DeLacey was not to be bested, at least not without a supreme effort on his part.

The challenge, so saucily issued, fired his virile blood. Against her protest and his own good sense, he trapped her fragile wrists in one of his large hands and pinned her arms over her head against the horse's solid flank. Flesh on flesh . . . on flesh.

God help him—what was he going to do with her now? Her breasts as she squirmed and bucked were pressure points of heat against his chest. Her mouth as it cursed him was so close he could almost taste the remembered sweetness of her lips. Leaning into her, he wanted to crush her and her resistance, to absorb her aliveness, to . . .

He struggled within himself to tame the out-of-control beast, but having had her once only made him want her all the more.

To his surprise she went limp, uttering a little cry of defeat, accepting his domination, in fact it seemed she issued an invitation as she pressed against him in return. Closing his eyes, he lowered his head, eager to claim his due. Besides, she did owe it to him even if he didn't have the right to demand it so brutally.

She tasted like the finest brandy that only a sophisticated palate could appreciate, tangy yet sweet. As sweet as any woman he had ever known. And like fine brandy, her lips had the power to intoxicate, to cause a man to use poor judgment or no judgment at all. They were spellbinding.

Yes, deLacey Honeycutt could easily become a bad habit, and he an addict unable to resist the lure of her charms.

But then he remembered. His father lying in a pool of his own blood, all because . . .

Pulling back, he stared down at her, eyes closed, mouth slightly parted and still moist from his pilfered kiss. So tempting. So convincing.

Consummate little actress. Did she really think him so naive that he would fall for her bluff again?

"Yah!" With his free hand he slapped the rump of the horse against which she leaned.

With a little screech of surprise deLacey tumbled backward as the animal shot forth and galloped off across the range.

Releasing her hands, he caught her about the waist.

"Why did you do that?" Fighting the circle of his arms, she flailed against his chest with her fists. "Let me go, Joss McRae," she cried. At last she was saying what she really felt.

Confident that she had nowhere to go and no way to get there easily, he turned her loose. Even if she did try to run away, she wouldn't get far.

"You stupid brute. How am I supposed to get back now? Silas is going to be so—"

"To hell with Silas Abrams." The mere mention of that man's name fired Joss's blood once more. Again he snatched her up hard against his chest. "Since when did you give a damn about anybody but yourself, and especially Silas Abrams?"

It was jealousy through and through that caused him to act so irrationally. He knew that, but he didn't care. The thought of Abrams so much as laying a finger upon deLacey, of her welcoming his advances . . .

"To hell with Silas Abrams," he repeated in a throaty growl, his mouth descending once more to stake his claim upon the woman who had lassoed his heart with just as much ruthlessness as he took her lips.

To hell with all of it, the injustices committed, the revenge he had plotted for so long and had lived his whole life to accomplish. What he wanted was deLacey, and he wasn't going to give her up—at least not to the likes of Silas Abrams.

"Listen to me, Joss." Panting, she pulled her face away, refusing to succumb to his lips even when he kissed a fiery path along her jaw to the lobe of her ear. "You're wrong about Silas. I swear to you he's not the one stealing your cattle."

The fog in his brain lifted just a little. Why did she keep saying that to him? What did she know? Withdrawing, he stared down into her open, earnest face. Was that sincerity he read in her eyes or was this merely another Honeycutt attempt to deceive him? He couldn't decide.

"I know who is," she hurriedly added in the face of his hesitation. "I . . . I can prove it, Joss."

"Prove it? How?" he shot back.

Her eyes darted about, and for a moment he thought she would refuse to tell him more.

"How?" He shook her mercilessly. "Damn it, Lacey. Tell me what you know."

"I-I-It's true. The cattle thieves are working out of the Rocking A Ranch," she blurted, her eyes still casting about wildly as if they were afraid to settle on any one spot, especially his face. "But Silas Abrams knows nothing about it. Nothing. I swear." When finally her gaze did settle on him, it was determined, steady, unreadable as any gambler's poker face.

"Then who is behind the rustling?"

The moment of silence hung like smoke in the air, stifling and thick.

"Billy Howell."

"And your proof?" He shook her again. If she was making this up, she wouldn't live to see it through.

"Only what I've seen in copies of telegrams Billy sent. I don't know how Silas got ahold of them. Maybe he bribed somebody. They . . . they spoke of a natural box canyon, a place rarely used, called . . . Sioux Coulee. I asked

Annie to bring me out here," she rushed on, "to look around, to see if I could find something to substantiate what I've learned, something to bring to you." Her eyes, unwavering, implored.

Billy Howell. Sioux Coulee. Abrams bribing telegraph operators. It did fit. Joss studied her face, looking for a flaw, a flicker of something, anything to give her away. Was it possible? He couldn't be certain if she was lying or not.

And then so many things, clues he had refused to see, fell into place. Running across Billy supposedly unmiring Lazy J cattle. Billy in town repeatedly sending those now explained telegrams to Chicago. Billy asking questions all over the territory—mostly about him.

Billy Howell, the son of a bitch, stealing his cattle and making up to him all at the same time.

Violently he pushed Lacey away, turning his back to her, to the evidence she presented. Staring across the plains to the gray peaks of the buttes that framed Sioux Coulee, he studied the surrounding terrain. Proof. Regardless of what she said, he wanted something tangible, more than just the word of a woman who had lied to him plenty of times in the past.

Facing her once more, he was mildly surprised to see her still standing there, watching him, waiting for a reaction, a testimony to her credibility. If she was lying, knowing her the way that he did, chances were she would have at least attempted to run while his back was turned.

But still, that wasn't enough. If in fact the rustlers were using this spot to corral their stolen cattle, it wouldn't take much to catch them in the act, just a little time and patience. But to prove or disprove Silas Abrams's involvement . . .

Decisively, he took her arm once more, this time a bit more gently, and steered her toward his own horse grazing peacefully a few yards away.

"I'll take you back." It was a noncommittal statement, and yet it reverberated with finality.

"What are you saying, Joss?" she cried plaintively, prying at his fingers that refused to release her, at least not until he was ready to.

"I'm saying . . ." He paused, staring down at her, deciding in his own mind, much more rational now that he had distanced himself from her, from the whole situation, just what it was he wanted from her. "I'm saying I'm taking you back to Abrams so you can come up with solid evidence to support your allegations."

"A-A-Allegations?" Digging in her heels, she frowned up at him, indignation etching her slender brows. "Then you don't believe me?"

"Whether I believe you or not is not the point. Either way I want proof. I want to see those telegrams. That's what I'm paying you for."

"Then keep your money, Joss. I don't want it anymore."

"Then don't take it. But I still want my proof. Don't forget there's the little matter of your attempt to rob me on the train. I can still have you arrested and hauled off to jail, no questions asked. Just imagine what Abrams would think of his mail-order bride then."

That infernal devil-made bargain. It rose up between them like an angry red welt, a reminder of all that had transpired between them. The mistrust, the hate, the virtual extortion he had used to make her do what he wanted her to do—the intimate encounter stolen in a moment of spontaneous passion. There was no doubt in his mind that it was sincere pain that marred her beautiful face. Pain and regret.

He couldn't help that, and he shouldn't feel responsible for what she felt, or for her, for that matter. But, God help him, he did. But this thing with Silas Abrams had been a weight about his neck for so long, he couldn't shed it that easily, not without tangible evidence.

Ignoring the stirrup, he vaulted up into the saddle. Reaching down, he offered her a hand up. For a moment he thought she wouldn't accept his assistance, the way she stared at his gloved hand as if it were poison, but would dart away instead. To be honest he wished she would take that course of action. To chase her down, to force her to comply with his will, somehow that seemed more satisfying than her meek compliance.

But then she pinned him with a look that spoke of

helplessness, as if she had no choice, and she placed her small, unprotected hand in his, so resigned, so unguarded that his anger turned inward at himself for being so weak that he couldn't walk away from the bitterness that had controlled his life for so long. With the toe of his boot he pushed the stirrup so she could reach it, and waited until she had placed her tiny foot into it before pulling her up to sit sideways in front of him.

Her bottom, round and well remembered, pressed warmly into his groin and only added to his self-flagellation.

He should never have come here looking for her, but should have waited for her to seek him out.

Digging his heels into the sides of his horse, he welcomed the spirited response, the need to concentrate on keeping the animal under rein rather than his runaway emotions and desires.

DeLacey Honeycutt. Petite and fragile as she looked and felt in his arms, she was enough woman to make any man lose sight of his goals. More than enough to cause a man to make irreversible mistakes and never once regret them.

For once in his life, he was beginning to understand what had driven his father to do what he had done.

Shamelessly deLacey clung to him, her arms wrapped about Joss's neck, her face pressed into the collar of his coat that smelled of man and horseflesh. His arms were a warm bolster about her waist, clutching her just as tightly.

And yet she knew the shared closeness meant nothing to him, nothing at all. He didn't believe her and he was taking her back.

Oddly enough she wondered just when it was that she had lost her gambler's edge—when had she started to care about the other players in this game—Silas, and yes, Joss, too. She had irrevocably forfeited her heart at the same moment she had squandered her innocence.

She wanted to cry. She wanted to rail. She wanted to shake Joss, to make him forget all the past ghosts and demons that drove him so mercilessly. Wanted him to love her back, even if it was just a little—even if it was only for a few fleeting moments in time.

But she couldn't bring herself to do any of those things, couldn't go against all that her daddy had taught her about the art of wagering. Winning was everything, and never show your cards until you're sure you have the best hand at the table.

Right now she couldn't be sure—not of anything. Not of what was truly important to her, what was best for her to do. The only thing certain was that if she bet on love the odds were that it was a losing proposition.

The most she could hope for was to play Joss card for card, calling his raises, pocketing her wins as they came, no matter how insignificant, weathering her losses just the same. She didn't dare let her meager bet ride for she was gambling with a stake she couldn't afford to lose—her heart. And that in itself was a crucial mistake. The number one rule her daddy had taught her was never to risk what you aren't prepared to part with.

Silas, on the other hand, offered her every advantage. A safe bet she was sure to win. But somehow the winning became incidental when there was so little challenge—so little joy—in it.

"The King" would say she had dangerously crossed the fine line from a professional to a compulsive gambler doomed to a losing streak, but like a hopeless, helpless addict she didn't know how to stop the downward slide.

With a sigh of defeat, she squeezed her eyes shut and pressed herself into the protective windbreak Joss's broad chest offered. The thunder of his heart so close to her ear grew in velocity, or so it seemed, the reverberation all about her now. And then the first drop of wetness struck her on the cheek.

Her lashes parted with a mixture of hope and disbelief. Weeping? From Joss McRae? Not likely.

Lifting her face, she saw that the leather of his coat, the brim of his felt hat, were dotted with moisture.

Raindrops, not teardrops.

"I think we're in for a hell of a storm."

His statement, murmured without emotion, did nothing to alleviate her forlornness. Beneath her the horse leapt forward when urged to greater speed in what seemed to her a reckless dash. What did it matter if they hurried? They would never reach the Rocking A Ranch before the storm hit, and foolishly she prayed that they never would. Just as she could never expect to awaken Joss's heart before the bitterness claimed him completely.

As if he too recognized the futility of the race against nature, he brought the horse to a wheeling halt. Never taking his arm from about her waist, he twisted in the saddle. She could hear the slap of leather ties being unknotted. And then the slicker descended over them, a protective canopy against the slashing rain, binding them together, separating them—at least for the moment—from the rest of the world.

''We can't go on, Lacey. I'm taking you to a place to wait out the worst of this.''

Huddled beneath the slicker as close to his heart as she ever thought to get, she accepted Joss's promise with a sigh of regret. If only that were so. If only she could step back, escape the gale that raged within her own uncertain soul. If only she could throw caution to the wind, declare that hearts—hers and his—were wild cards in this madcap game called love. If only she could toss aside her own need for security and acceptance, those two all-powerful requirements that Silas Abrams dangled before her like a carrot in front of a starving beast.

Was that why she felt this overwhelming need to protect the poor little man from the wrath of Joss McRae? To protect her own future? It was true, Silas Abrams was willing to trust her blindly, with no malice, no ulterior motive—no questions asked. He offered her a clean slate to begin her life again.

No. It was more than that. Even she couldn't be that heartless. Silas Abrams was innocent of the crimes Joss accused him of. She was so positive of that fact. She was just as certain Billy was guilty of them.

But the multitude of hurdles weren't conquered, not yet.

She still had to come up with some kind of proof. Proof that a cynical man like Joss McRae would readily accept.

The steady rhythm of the horse slowed, and the rain took up a loud rat-a-tat-tat that suggested they had entered some kind of shelter.

"Lacey, are you awake? We're here." There was an underlying tenderness to his deep timbre she had never heard before. Perhaps it was only her willful imagination.

She stirred against his virile warmth. His arm tightened about her. Was his action a protective gesture or merely to remind her that she was his prisoner? Either way she savored it.

Then he dismounted taking the slicker with him, leaving her atop the horse suddenly feeling stripped and bare, cold and damp. As he tied off the reins she glanced about the tiny, dark shed, the smell of hay and animals exuding warmth and dryness.

"Where are we?" she asked, glancing at the ceiling when the rain suddenly picked up, pelting the tin roof overhead like a thousand drumsticks.

"A seldom used line camp." Reaching up, he swung her down to stand beside him as he set about loosening the girth of the saddle, although he didn't remove it. Turning, he moved to the doorless entrance and glanced outside. "We could make a run for the cabin or we can just stay in here. It's up to you."

Peering out of the opening, she watched the sheeting rain twist and whirl at the whim of the bullying wind. The cabin he spoke of was no more than a hundred yards away. Even so, it was a blur in the storm.

"Let's stay here," she opted with an uncontrollable shiver.

She turned back around to find him emerging from a small room off to one side, carrying a pitchfork full of hay. How odd it seemed, at least to her, to see him do such a menial task.

Seeing him reconfirmed what she already knew. There was nothing soft or flabby about Joss McRae, regardless of his money, his self-indulgences, his extravagances. His chest was so wide and powerful, his arms, his shoulders straining at the seams of his clothing. His gloved hands still holding the empty pitchfork, so strong. She couldn't stop herself from practically devouring him with her eyes for he was nothing like Silas Abrams. And it was those very differences that attracted her, his ruggedness and virility, his uncompromising will.

"I've changed my mind," she whispered, and tried to dash out of the door.

But he stopped her, just as she knew that he would, his fingers like heated ingots of iron about her wrist.

"Tell me, Lacey. Why are you so afraid of me?"

"I'm not afraid," she cried, and yet she knew she was lying.

"Then prove it. Stay here with me." He released her, his hand sliding up her arm creating waves of chill bumps in its wake.

"I mustn't."

"Why not?"

Why not, indeed, her aching body echoed.

"It wouldn't be right." She looked away, unable to face him.

"It wouldn't be wrong." His other hand caressed the side of her neck and gently cupped her chin.

"You don't understand, Joss." Their eyes met, staring deeply into each other's souls, and for a fleeting moment it seemed she knew him better than she knew herself, but then it was gone. "I plan on marrying Silas Abrams." There. At last she had made the commitment aloud. A great relief washed over her.

His reaction was not what she expected. Anger, hatred, jealousy perhaps. Instead he threw back his head and began to laugh. "DeLacey Honeycutt, gambler, thief, now mail-order bride."

"I'm serious, Joss," she scolded, her own ire rising at his lack of sensitivity.

"I suppose I should let you. It would be the ultimate revenge against the son of a bitch, wouldn't it? The gambler's daughter passing herself off as blue blood. I can just see his face when I finally decide to tell him the truth.''

She knew then the barter she would strike with him. Her proof, the messages from Billy Howell, for his silence.

"You won't do that, Joss." She lifted her chin with confidence, pulling it from his searing grip.

"I won't? And why not?" His amusement faltered, a frown marring the perfection of his face.

"You won't if you want your proof. Plus you'll agree here and now never to threaten me again with arrest." She took a chance, a terrible risk that he would call her bluff. If he decided to tell Abrams what he knew about her anyway, there was nothing she could do to stop him.

"Ah, Lacey, darlin'." He smiled but it was mirthless. "You make a devil's bargain. A damn fine one." His finger curled about her jaw, caressing. "But it's not nearly enough for me."

"Then what more do you want?" She was desperate, and she knew it rang in her voice. "You can keep your money, Joss. I don't want or need it. And I will never tell Silas about the way you have treated me."

"Still not enough, Lacey."

She knew then, it was indeed a devil's bargain she must enter, and she despised the way her pulse leapt, her heart throbbed, at the mere thought of what he wanted from her.

"Please, Joss, don't ask this of me." She edged backwards. Then she realized with that simple plea and show of fear, she had revealed her cards, and she knew his hand was better. He had beaten her, and she could only stand there, helplessly, and watch as he raked in his winnings. Love was the stakes she had gambled with and lost. But the worst part was that it meant nothing to him. Nothing at all.

She closed her eyes in concession, for in reality was she not getting what she wanted deep in her heart? True, Silas would be good to her, and kind, and gentle, but he would never be able to give her this. . . .

Joss's mouth was on hers, a plundering marauder, bold and arrogant, stripping her of every ounce of pride and dignity she possessed. That something inside of her, the latent warrior woman that demanded a man like Joss to thrive and prosper, sprang forth, taking control, caring not that she held nothing in reserve. Without shame she kissed him back, their tongues crossed swords of passion, dueling for supremacy.

Then he scooped her up and carried her into the room from which he had just emerged. There in the fragrant hay, he laid her down, pressing her deep into its depths with his own weight.

Above them the rain battered the metal roof, an army of rhythm, a song as wild and turbulent as the world beyond, as the desire that claimed them both. It filled her heart, it filled her soul, and drove her passion like a battle march, fearless, undeviating, a conqueror's weapon.

She would take this chance to know love one last time, and then she would turn her back on it, without looking behind her. Passion had no place in her life, not if she was to remain in control of her destiny.

But for now she would succumb because she had no other choice. Joss had made it very clear; he would accept no less. That fact alone exonerated her from guilt and inhibitions.

His hand covered her breast. She arched against it, crying out in frustration that there was something, even so thin as the material of her clothing, between them.

Without thought of the aftermath he shoved the two halves of her blouse apart, pushing it from her shoulders. Several buttons flew off, but at the time their loss seemed such a trivial price to pay. The chemise beneath was just as quickly brushed aside, most of the delicate eyelets ripped beyond repair as he jerked the lacing ribbon from them.

Then his mouth, warm and welcomed, took their place, covering her bare flesh, loving, laving, driving her wild with want. She reached up, splaying her fingers in the soft, dark hair of his head that was cradled in the valley of her bosom.

"Oh, Joss, why must it be this way?" She spoke from the depths of her aching heart, the tears that gathered in her eyes springing from the hidden wells of her battered soul.

His answer was a kiss, deep and silencing, demanding that she not question the methods fate used to bring them together. As with the game of poker, never challenge the way the cards were dealt, just make the best of them and the odds to assemble a winning hand.

And perhaps that was what she must do now. Make this moment, this coming together, her unbridled response, something he could never forget, and never escape, the price he must pay in the end much dearer than her own sacrifice.

Yes, she would make him remember and regret.

With a moan she matched his fervor with equal ardor, throwing her leg over his, urging him to roll over. On top of him now, she snagged the front of his shirt, ripping it apart so she could run her fingers through the thick, dark matting of his chest. Lifting his head at the sudden fierceness of her actions, he watched her like a wary predator, no doubt wondering at her swift change of tactics.

She ran her tongue along the ridge of his breast bone, the taste of his skin salty and warm—intoxicating. To her delight he stiffened and sucked in a deep breath, his hand clamping down on her bare shoulder in surprise. So she did it again, dipping lower this time to the hollow of his ribcage. There she hovered, unsure. Against her ear the intake of breath into his lungs was ragged, his heart a runaway.

What would he do if she went lower still?

He never gave her the opportunity to find out. As if he sensed her purpose, he rolled once more, pinning her beneath him, his gray eyes issuing a knowing challenge.

In no time he had her divided skirt unbuttoned and off. Her drawers soon followed, leaving her naked to his perusal.

His hand, hot against her flesh, allowed no protest. He knew her well—as well as what he was doing to her. And as his mouth skated along the ridge of her ribs to the soft valley of her belly, the rising waves washed over her. Though she tried to struggle free of them, there was no escaping their strength or his as he moved even lower.

Lost in the maelstrom of love, there was nothing now for her except him and the glory ride he took her on. There was no modesty, no hesitation, no bets to call or raise, only the need to take all that he would give her. Higher and higher.

She reached for him, wanting to feel him stretched

against her as she neared the apex, but to her utter disbelief she discovered that it was no longer his hand that gave her such pleasure.

"Joss, no," she cried, her own body flushing with embarrassment as she attempted to clamp her legs shut.

"No?" He rose over her, filling her line of vision and her being with one great thrust. "Confess." He held perfectly still, causing a rising ache to spread throughout her body. "It was no more than you planned to do to me."

"It wasn't." She had never dreamed of being so bold, and yet thinking back, it now seemed the logical conclusion to her brazen exploration. But she didn't wish to think about that, not now, so she arched against him, wanting only to regain the mindless ecstasy.

He laughed, refusing to accommodate her demand, his mouth so close to her ear that his breath sent a shiver racing down her spine. "Admit it, you would love me under any circumstances, in any way that I asked you to."

He spoke of love, but she knew she didn't dare take it to mean what she so wanted it to mean. Love was a physical act for him, nothing more. And yet she found herself agreeing, willing to say anything if only he would continue, would show his love for her in his own way for these few moments of time.

"Yes, damn you," she sobbed. She would love him under any conditions, God help her, but it was hopeless to think he understood or even cared about the depths of her confession.

From that point on there was a gentleness about his lovemaking, ever so subtle. She clung to that, to him, her little cries and whimpers of delight each a reaffirmation of her wretched admission. Still she savored the wonder of it all, the joy his embraces gave her.

And then as she crested that long-awaited moment of fulfillment, her heart slamming to a halt, her body trembling with the aftermath of release, she felt him shudder, as well.

"Woman, you have undone me, and no doubt will be the death of me," he whispered, collapsing against her, his breath caressing her bare neck.

DeLacey squeezed her eyes shut and willed back the insistent tears. It was as close to a confession of love as she could ever hope to get from a man like Joss McRae.

She would take it, stash it away like a cache of precious gold, her only comfort on those cold loveless nights of loneliness she would no doubt spend as Silas Abrams's wife.

CHAPTER 14

Several hours later, the rain stopped. Wordlessly they had lain side by side in the sweet-smelling hay, listening to the musical patter overhead, but now it was time to rise and face reality.

Her chemise was ruined and hopeless. With the point of the pocketknife he lent her, deLacey managed to punch new holes and lace it together haphazardly. But worse, most of the buttons were missing from her blouse, and even if she could have found them she had no way of sewing them back on.

In despair she glanced at Joss, noticing that his shirt was in no better condition. He came up with some bits of twine, and using the tip of his knife once more, he helped her restore her modesty somewhat. She watched him as he worked, his head bent in concentration as he tied pieces of the string to her blouse and pulled them through the buttonholes. Bits of hay were threaded in his dark hair.

"Oh," she gasped, reaching up, wondering if her own was as disheveled. It was, and was probably worse, for it had come undone and now hung down around her shoulders in scraggly disarray.

What was she going to do? How would she ever face Silas looking . . . as if she had had a tumble in the hay?

"No doubt your horse has made it back by now," Joss said as if he had deciphered her worries, pulling together the last of the fasteners on her blouse as best he could. "There will be a search party sent out to look for you." Without glancing up at her, he moved off through the doorway to the other part of the shed where his horse was tied off.

"Are you leaving me here?" She followed in his wake, forgetting the state of her clothing, her hair, thinking only of the possibility of being left alone.

"No." He scanned her slowly, then turned away, setting about tightening the saddle cinch. "There would be a hell of a lot less to explain, but it might take them days to find you out here in so isolated a place. I won't take that chance."

"Go on. I'll be all right," she insisted with more conviction than she felt. But she knew only too well the risks he would take by showing up with her in her present condition at Silas's door.

"No, since you've made up your mind to marry him, I'll take you back." The girth tight, he unhooked the stirrup from the saddle horn, allowing it to drop in place, a finality as much as his spoken words.

It was as if the last few hours had never happened, as if they had not given each other the ultimate in pleasure, had not known each other in a way that should have bound them together for all eternity. It was as if they were strangers once more. She wanted to cry out, *No, please, don't make me return. I want to go with you, instead.*

But she didn't say it, for that did not fit into her plans for the future. Just as important, she didn't have the courage to face Joss's rejection—not openly.

She followed him out the door of the shed into the glorious afternoon sunlight. Blinking like an owl, she glanced about. One would never know that so violent a storm had passed through only hours before. She gazed at Joss's expressionless face as he mounted the horse and reached down to give her a lift up. One would never suspect such passion lurked within such a stonefaced man.

Settled in front of him once more, Lacey watched that

tiny shed grow smaller and smaller and then disappear as they crested a small rise.

It was gone, and so was the moment, most likely never to be recaptured again.

But he would remember those wonderful hours, remember and regret just as she had planned it. Just as, God help her, she would too for as long as she lived.

An hour and a half later they reached the Rocking A Ranch home place. On the same rise where he had sat days before watching the goings-on below, Joss brought the tired buckskin to a halt. He knew then what his father must have felt so long ago.

The main yard was a hubbub of activity. Horses and men grouped and organized into search parties. All meant to look, no doubt, for Lacey. Beautiful, passionate Lacey. Calculating, cold-hearted Lacey.

She had made love to him, and yet she chose to marry Silas Abrams, his sworn enemy, by her own admission. How could she be so ruthless?

More than once on the long ride to Abrams's ranch he had considered turning around and heading home, taking her with him whether she wanted to go or not. To hell with what *she* wanted. But what good would it do if she resented his interference, if in truth her heart belonged with another man? He didn't deceive himself into thinking that love and lust were the same thing. They weren't, for love went much deeper than the desires of the flesh.

And much deeper than the demands of the justice-seeking spirit. Ironically, he no longer cared about Silas Abrams, or the evidence, for or against him, that had been so important to him not so long ago.

He glanced down at the top of deLacey's fair head and felt his heart break in two as if it were truly something fragile. Once again a McRae was giving way to the finer side of his emotions. But he didn't give a damn if he was just another fool to make love all-important. If only she would give him even the slightest indication that she didn't wish to return to Silas Abrams. But her desire was made obvious by her silence.

And then someone below spotted them. A cry went up as they were recognized and pointed out. There was nothing he could do now but press on. Fearlessly he urged the horse forward, moving into the enemy's camp.

Cowboys were never ones to be subtle, to conceal their compulsions or reactions.

"Lookee there, it's Joss McRae," one of them announced.

"He's got nerve showin' up here," another said, turning his head to the side to spit tobacco juice on the ground.

"Hell, anybody can see what the two of them have been up to."

"Like father, like son."

Someone laughed.

Joss rode on, straight at Silas Abrams, looking neither left nor right, the crowd parting in front of them like water before the bow of a ship. A few yards away from the man he had sworn to obliterate any way that he could, he brought his mount to a standstill. He still held Lacey tightly to him, even though she struggled to pull away—he didn't want to let her go.

"Abrams." There was not a drop of emotion, friendly or otherwise, in his greeting.

"McRae." Abrams's beady eyes swooped down over the pair of them, taking in their disheveled appearance. His swinelike face contorted with anger and disbelief, turning the same shade of red as the bandana he wore about his neck.

Joss knew what was coming. In response his own hand moved down to the pistol at his side. God help him and the McRae name, but it was all happening again.

"Silas, no." Lacey's cry of protest echoed through the yard as she wrenched herself free and tumbled to the ground, throwing herself bodily against Abrams even as he drew his gun and aimed it.

A long silence ensued. There was a moment when Joss, who had held himself in check, thought the man would shoot him down in cold blood, there in front of all those witnesses, in front of Lacey.

Not here, not now—not yet. The silent understanding passed between them as real as an electrical charge.

Abrams slid a protective arm about deLacey's shoulder, though he didn't lower his gun. The sight of that man touching her, just touching her, did strange things to Joss's insides. If she had shown any repulsion, the slightest indication that she found him distasteful . . .

But she didn't.

"Silas, please," she beseeched, turning to confront the man as bravely as any warrior, her hand forcing the barrel of the pistol downwards. "He rescued me. My horse threw me. And if it hadn't been for . . . Mr. McRae . . ." She shot Joss a quick, uncertain plea not to contradict her. "I would have surely been lost to the elements."

Could he do less than keep his mouth shut if that was what she wanted them all to think? Was that not the bargain he had made with her? His silence for her love, if only for a few short hours?

"So what in the hell are you waiting for, McRae?" Over her head Abrams sneered at him. "A reward?"

"There's nothing you have I want or need, Abrams." With that he turned his horse around, set his spurs to the buckskin, and galloped away.

Nothing, except the only thing that truly mattered.

DeLacey Honeycutt.

He rode off, never once looking back, riding out of her life as if he had never forced his way into it. Stifling a sob, deLacey felt the tears well behind her eyelids and threaten to spill over. She refused to allow herself such a luxury—not here, not now. Besides, he had done no more than what she had asked of him.

"What happened to you?" Abrams's anxious voice as he shook her cut into her desolation. Something snapped inside of her, something very basic.

"I told you, Silas," she said in a voice devoid of any emotion, staring at the red bandana about his neck instead of his face. It seemed he always wore a red one. Red, the color of vengeance. "He found me wandering on the plains." How easily the lies came now. Now that truth, the real truth that tore her heart asunder, could never be spoken.

"That doesn't explain this." Frowning, he pointed at the makeshift fasteners on her shirt.

"I . . . I fell. When the horse threw me, it tore my blouse."

"There was no saddle on your horse when it returned."

She scrambled for a defense, one that he would accept. "The cinch. It broke. That was why I was thrown."

That seemed to mollify him somewhat.

"And the saddle? Where is it now?"

Her mouth went dry. She couldn't afford for him to go looking for the evidence of her lies. "I'm not sure. Out there, somewhere." She waved off into the vague distance.

"And this, deLacey?" He reached into her hair, plucked out a bit of hay, and shoved it under her nose. "How do you explain this?"

How indeed?

"It was raining so hard, we were forced to take shelter in a small shed." Her gaze darted downwards, unable to look him in the eyes for the next lie was the biggest. "I . . . I fell asleep on a pile of hay, waiting for the storm to subside." Now that it was said she looked back up to gauge his reaction.

If he believed her, it didn't show on his face, but neither did outright skepticism. She was safe, at least for the moment.

Silas snagged her once more by the arm and started pulling her toward the front steps of the house.

"No more, deLacey, do you hear me?"

Meekly she followed, unsure exactly what he meant by his statement, but what choice did she have at the moment except to go along with it?

"No more gallivanting all over the territory, not without me or a proper escort," Abrams continued, slamming the door behind them once they entered the house. "You were lucky this time. Joss McRae is not known for his good reputation or intentions, but for his ill-bred manners, especially when it comes to women.'' He turned on her, pinning her with a look of pain that made her feel guiltier than ever. ''Please, Miss deLacey. You have got to understand. I couldn't take having a McRae sullying anything else in my life—especially something as important to me as you are.''

What was this terrible vendetta between Joss and Silas that drove them both to the point of obsession? She knew it had to be more than the theft of a few cattle. Whatever it was, she was determined to ferret the truth out, for she refused to remain blindly in the middle of it, a prize to be won and then either be discarded or flaunted.

It came to her that perhaps she should just tell Silas what Joss had tried to do, how he had used her to try and prove that he was stealing Lazy J cattle. She owed Joss no allegiance, for had he not deserted her as callously as a cowpoke in a brothel? *He's known for his ill-bred manners with women.* To learn that she was not the only female he had so mistreated should have made her feel better— comrades-in-arms—but it didn't. Instead a flaming red streak of jealousy ripped through her.

Damn Joss McRae.

Silas deserved to know the truth, all of it, but she just couldn't bring herself to tell him even part of it, ignoble or not. What purpose would it serve now except to assuage her need to come as clean as she dared without risking the loss of everything he offered her. It was a chance she couldn't take. Now that she had negated the original agreement between herself and Joss, she had forfeited the money he had promised to pay her for her help. Not that the money was important, not at all, but it had been her buffer if she'd decided against marrying Silas Abrams. And now, should Silas turn her away . . .

''I'm sorry, Silas. I promise you, it will never happen again.''

And she meant it. Once she delivered to Joss those messages written by Billy Howell that she had seen on Silas's desk, she would steer clear of him. Go on with her life, become Silas's wife. But she must take action as soon as possible and be done with it.

Tonight she would gather them up. Tomorrow evening there was to be a community social at the Roosevelt place, Elkhorn Ranch, and even if Joss was not there she was fairly confident Annie would attend. She would give those papers to the girl and ask that she pass them on to her brother. Annie would do it, for she owed her that much, especially in light of the trouble she had caused today.

Then she would have fulfilled her end of the bargain, buying Joss's silence at the expense of her integrity. But so be it. At least her future would be secured and her past buried, for she was confident that there was nobody else for miles around who knew the truth of her identity.

It was quite late that evening by the time the household settled down. Silas walked deLacey to her door and saw her safely inside.

"I'm glad you're back and all right, Miss deLacey." He was much calmer now. "Tomorrow I will be the proudest man at the Roosevelt party, having you on my arm. Perhaps you'll agree to making our announcement." With a chaste kiss on her cheek he turned and marched away. He was hurting, she could read that on his face, yet he never once stopped being the perfect gentleman.

"Perhaps. Good night, Silas," she called to him, pleased to see him turn and offer her a smile.

Issuing a deep sigh of relief, she closed the door, savoring the solitude of her own bedroom. If Silas only knew the true depths of her betrayal he wouldn't be so proud of her. For the longest time she sat on the window ledge, on edge and indecisive, watching the flicker of a torch just out of her view. The night air was cool, but refreshingly so, and she pushed open her window, hoping to clear her mind as well as glean an insight into what was taking place out by the bunkhouse and stables.

There was laughter and cheering, and it seemed so strange to hear such rambunctious activity after dark, as up until today the bunkhouse had usually been quiet. The men woke early and worked long hours, and by the time it was dark, they sought their beds, exhausted, looking to get plenty of rest before the next morning.

But today had been a holiday of sorts for them. Their normal chores and routines had been pushed to the side, many of the men rounded up from the range, to form search parties to go looking for her. Her arrival, so late in the afternoon, had left most of the men idle until the following morning. Yes, they were celebrating, cowboy style, with an impromptu rodeo by torchlight. Chances were there were even a few poker games in progress.

DeLacey licked her lips. At one time in her life her prime goal would have been to figure out how to sneak out and join them. There was money to be made by the right gambler. But no more. Her life had changed so much over the last few weeks. That was part of her past—one she would never revive. Besides, Silas might be among them.

Perhaps this was her perfect opportunity, now when he was out of the house, to search his desk for those papers, those precious papers that would free her from the manipulative power of Joss McRae. Determined to be finally done with it, she rose, yet her heart began to race at the mere thought of what she must do. She might be many things, even unscrupulous, but up until now she had never resorted to being an outright burglar in the night. Yet she had learned a long time ago, she was capable of doing a lot more than she'd ever thought possible if it meant her own survival.

Slipping out of her bedroom, she darted to look down the hallway, although she was relatively sure no one would see or hear her activity in that part of the house, unused except for her. Once she reached the end of the corridor, she paused in the doorway to the living room. Someone, Mrs. Smythe no doubt, had left a lantern burning on a table near the front entryway. That confirmed her suspicions. Silas must have gone out to join his men.

She glanced about the newly decorated room with pride, for this was her creation, and she had done a good job of it, even if it wasn't complete. There were several pieces of furniture due to arrive from back East any day now. Even so, the room exhuded an air of sophistication yet warmth that had to be admired.

A sudden movement across the room caught her attention, and she jumped, unnerved. Still hidden, she hoped, in the darkened corridor, she strained to put a name to what she had glimpsed from the corner of her eye. With a sigh of relief she realized it was only one of the new curtains Miss Bertalli had sewn for her, billowing in the wind of an open window.

How odd that Mrs. Smythe would leave a window open, but perhaps she, too, had found the evening breeze quite pleasant. DeLacey thought no more about it.

Instead she glided across the room to the alcove that served as Silas's office. The desktop was tidy now, at least relatively so, and for once deLacey wished the dear man hadn't so easily succumbed to her insistent badgering to clean up his mess.

In the shadows once more, she surveyed the office looking for the most likely place for Silas to have stashed those messages. Quickly she rifled through the drawers of the desk and came up empty-handed. Frustrated, she leafed through the couple of stacks of papers on the work surface. Nothing.

She turned to the bookshelf behind her. The lower part was an enclosed cabinet. Pulling open the doors, she began thumbing through the jumble, smiling to herself. Silas was an incurable pack rat. He never threw away anything, but at least now he hid his clutter just to please her.

Her heart accelerated. She was on the right track, for many of the papers in her hand she remembered seeing on the desktop along with the telegrams the last time she had snooped in there.

Then a small sound caught her ear. Her exhilaration melted to apprehension. The curtain that had frightened her earlier was less than a hundred feet from her. It came alive again, a sail collecting the breeze and snapping whenever the wind died down.

It was time she shut that window. Rising from her post, she slipped along the outside wall. The curtain was as round as a pregnant woman, and she brushed it aside, reaching for the casement.

Eyes, hard and determined, glared back at her.

Jerking back, she opened her mouth to scream, but she was spun about and a hand clamped over her face before she could utter a sound. Her first thought was that Silas had been waiting for her, had known what she was about, and would now demand an explanation. Her hopes and dreams were surely lost. Oh, what could she tell him, what lies could she concoct to protect herself?

The man grunted, and it was a man, she could tell by the roughness of the palm over her face. Yes, it was very rough, too rough. Her captor couldn't possibly be Silas, for he had hands as soft as a woman's.

A wave of temporary relief washed over her only to be replaced by another fear.

It it wasn't Abrams, then who was it?

Joss? Could it be that he had come back to take her away?

"All right, little lady," her captor growled, so close that she could smell his unpleasant breath, "you wanna tell me just what it is yer lookin' for that's so important?"

That wasn't Joss, but she recognized the voice nonetheless.

Billy Howell.

She shook her head. It was all she could do, for he hardly let up his hand to allow her to breath, much less reply.

"Accountin' books, maybe? Bills of sale?"

She shook her head even harder.

"Or maybe you was just lookin' for money." He chuckled low in his throat. "Silas Abrams ain't no fool. He never leaves cash layin' around."

DeLacey held perfectly still, in fact she went limp. Better to let the man think what he wanted than to know the truth of what she sought. Evidence that would label *him* a cattle thief.

At her lack of response, he let up the pressure of his hand, just a little. "Ah, hell, you ain't up and fainted on me, have ya?"

As quick as lightning Lacey shot forward toward the front

door, not caring how much noise she made. But she had only taken a few steps when Howell grasped her arm and jerked her back, pressing her against the nearby wall with his own weight, his hand grasping her chin painfully.

"Yer one slick little filly, ain't ya, Miss Honeycutt?" His ill-shaven face was so close she could see his grimace in the flicker of the lantern light on the nearby table. "I've done some checkin' on you, ya know. Know all about ya and yer gambler daddy. How you posed as a mail-order bride just to git outta St. Louis."

"You're wrong," she quickly denied. Unsuppressed anger shot through her. If he knew about her past there was only one person around here who could have supplied him with that information. "I don't care what Joss has told you. It's a lie."

"Joss? Joss McRae?" He pressed her harder against the wall. "Then you *are* in cahoots with him, just like I figured."

"No. No. That's not true." What kind of trouble had her foolish mouth gotten her into now?

The way he looked her up and down as if she were a prize side of beef, it was obvious he didn't believe her.

"Lady, if the truth be known, I don't give a hoot what yer up to." He ran one finger along the side of her face, temple to chin. "You can hoodwink men like Silas Abrams all day long, and I ain't gonna stop ya. Not as long as you give me a little cooperation in return."

What was he asking her for in exchange for his silence? The same as Joss had demanded from her? No, no, she would never submit to such degradation again, especially not with a man like Billy Howell. She raised her chin a notch.

"I would rather give myself to a wallowing pig," she exclaimed through clenched teeth.

"I don't rightly care who ya give yerself to. What I want from you is help gittin' to Joss McRae."

"Joss? I don't understand."

"I want you to help me prove he's rustlin' cattle."

"Joss? A rustler?" She almost burst out laughing at the

irony of it all. But then she thought she understood. If in truth Billy was behind the stealing he would now find it convenient to pin it on someone else. It was no more or less than she was trying to do, but to him.

"Seems logical, don't ya think? How else could he have been the only rancher to come out on top from the devastating winter of '86? How else, unless he lay claim to cattle that didn't belong to him in order to keep his herd intact?"

This wasn't the first deLacey had heard of the hard-hitting winter Billy mentioned. It was the subject on many lips, even the women she had met. Many of the other ranchers were having a hard time of it, even Silas, although his money supply seemed endless. Whereas Joss, on the other hand, was prospering.

Joss. Was he capable of stealing from his neighbors for his own gain? From what she knew of him, it was very possible, indeed. Yet she couldn't believe she had been so wrong about him.

Joss pointing a finger at Silas. She looking to implicate Billy Howell. And now, Howell causing it all to come full circle, suggesting it was Joss who was behind the scheme, all along.

It seemed incredible. But now those messages from Billy she had been so diligently searching for began to take on a whole new meaning. They suggested that Billy had been watching Joss, and might even have caught him in the act.

A deep resentment welled in her throat. Joss had used her and now he had lied to her as well. He was the cattle thief. Those telegrams incriminated him as much as anyone. No wonder he'd demanded that she get them for him.

Yes, she would give Billy what he wanted, but not for the reasons he thought. At last this was the way to escape from Joss McRae's manipulations. To free herself finally of the terrible longing and lack of self-control. Then she could live her life the way she wished, with whom she wanted. With the only person who truly seemed to care about her.

An inner voice cried, "No. You are wrong." But she ignored its sentimental protest. This was survival.

And nothing—nothing was more important. Somehow she had temporarily forgotten that. But not anymore.

"All right," she conceded, closing her eyes, squeezing shut her heart as well. "Just tell me what it is you want me to do, and I'll do it."

"Damn you, big brother, you're a bigger fool than I figured." Dressed in a plain but quite feminine calico, Annie McRae took on the air of an indignant female.

"Watch it, Annie. That mouth of yours . . ." Joss pointed an ineffectual finger at his defiant sister. Somehow she had managed to turn his intention to chastise her for her reckless ways into an opportunity to scold him instead.

"How could you just take her back there and dump her off? She's in love with you, you big, dumb ox." Arms akimbo, she stared at him. "Can't you see that? Or are you just as stupid and insensitive as our father?"

"Damn you, Annie, mind your own business, and stay away from deLacey Honeycutt. She's nothing but trouble." Fists clenched, he headed toward the door and the freedom it offered. What did a kid like Annie know of complicated issues like love? What could she possibly know about men and women, the lust, the betrayal? It had destroyed their father. He wouldn't allow it to do the same to him.

Lacey didn't love him, for if she did she wouldn't marry Silas Abrams. It was as simple as that. But what did it matter? He didn't love her either. He couldn't.

Stepping out into the coolness of the evening, he jabbed his hands into the pockets of his jacket and sucked in a lungful of cleansing Dakota air. If he didn't love her, then why in the hell did she occupy such a large portion of his thoughts? It was a question he didn't want to probe any further.

Then he remembered what his father had told him so very long ago, the words of advice that had driven him relentlessly over the years. His father. Annie had called him insensitive, but he had just been a poor deluded fool who had gotten in over his head—all because of a woman.

Thomas McRae had not been a sophisticated man, not by

any means, but he had managed to get through life with a little laughter and just enough money in his pockets to survive. "Don't follow in my footsteps, son. Don't make the same mistakes I've made. Instead make somethin' better of yerself. And when it comes to women, never let 'em git the upper hand on ya." He had grinned in that easy way of his, and that had been the extent of his fatherly advice.

That had been just two days before he had died, all because of a woman. A lying, cheating female who had used him to gain her own ends. A woman quite like deLacey Honeycutt.

Now that he had distanced himself from her deceptive arms and influence, he could see his way much clearer. This time it was a McRae who held all the cards. He would use her to get what he wanted. Revenge. Sweet, satisfying revenge against the man who had caused his father's death . . .

Silas Abrams.

"Joss?" Annie moved out to join him on the porch, her hand plucking at his shirt sleeve. "I didn't mean what I said."

There was a softness about his sister's voice he'd never heard before. Where had it come from? He frowned and tensed at her touch. Was it softness, or beguilement learned from an excellent teacher?

"Let it be, Annie." He shrugged her off. "Just let it be."

Instantly regretting his gruffness, he turned to take it back. But it was too late.

Annie, her face wet with tears, had already taken off toward the barn. Annie crying?

Moments later he saw her ride away.

Maybe she was right about him after all. He was an insensitive son of a bitch. But, it was too late for him to change now.

CHAPTER 15

DeLacey's gown for the Roosevelt affair was quite simple, really, a soft twilled silk of pale yellow that Miss Bertalli had proclaimed would set off her eyes and hair exquisitely. The way it fastened just off her shoulders with matching bows, then draped across her bosom in folds meant to conceal yet accent, it gave her an air of refinement and innocence, but it was merely a sham. She could claim neither of those qualities—one because she had not been born with it, the other because she had foolishly squandered it in a moment of heated passion. And yet the seamstress had clapped her hands with delight and declared the ensemble perfect. If the woman had only had an inkling of the truth. . . .

But Lacey didn't want to think about that at the moment, not now when she was finding that all the attention heaped upon her by so many felt so wonderful.

"Miss deLacey!" Silas stared at her in rapt adoration when she entered the living room.

He was dressed in a most dapper fashion himself. Sack coat and nankeen trousers were set off by the ever-present red neckerchief knotted at his throat. In the style of a dandy, his pants were tucked into the tops of his new and shiny boots.

Remembering what he had once told her about real cowboys and the condition of their boots, deLacey covered her mouth with one gloved hand to stifle a giggle.

"What is it?" Silas frowned, touching the front of his pants as if he had neglected to fastened them.

"Your boots are clean." She pointed down.

He blushed, and she found it quite endearing.

"In your honor, Miss Lacey," he said with a bit of dash, bowing from the waist like a true gentleman. Then he looked up at her rather sheepishly. "Besides, it's a Medora tradition. Theodore Roosevelt and his city ways demands that no one track range fertilizer into his house."

She had only made the acquaintance of Mr. Theodore Roosevelt that one time, several weeks before at the spring roundup. The thought of meeting him once again made her somewhat nervous, for he had substantiated her story of good breeding, and she had never understood why he had done that.

No one did anything without a self-serving reason. That was a lesson she had learned a long time ago. But perhaps she was being too cynical. Silas was not that way, not really. Even though he wanted a wife who would elevate him in the eyes of society, there was no harm in such straightforward ambitions. Who did it hurt? Together they could play their charades of respectability indefinitely without anyone ever being the wiser.

That would be the case once she fulfilled her obligation to help the despicable Billy Howell. Her hand grasped her reticule, winding the strings about her fingers as if she feared losing it.

The part she had agreed to play in his scheme against Joss McRae would be tricky. She had to be most careful that Joss never learned, until it was too late, that she was the one to betray him. If he ever did, he wouldn't hesitate to expose her for who she really was, ruining all of her well-laid plans for the future.

Her nervousness intensified. If only she could think of a way to circumvent her predicament, but her keen imagination, her normally sharp instincts for survival, failed her for the very first time in her life.

"Are you ready to go?" Silas turned and gathered up his gun and holster from the mirrored hall tree in the foyer where he always hung it, and strapped it about his hips.

DeLacey debated asking him to leave his weapon behind. If Joss should be at the party . . . With the tension that already existed between the two men . . . She chewed her bottom lip, doubting he would oblige such a request, so she didn't ask. Instead, taking a deep breath, she nodded.

Silas took her by the arm and led her out the front door into the yard where the yellow-wheeled buggy awaited them. As he handed her up onto the seat, Lacey tried to ignore the dread lodged in her throat. If only they would never reach the Roosevelt party. If only it were over, the deed done.

But the inevitable loomed before her like dark clouds on the horizon. Billowing, threatening, filled with possibility of eventual disaster.

The only thing she could fall back on was the Honeycutt luck. But lately it seemed even that had proved unreliable.

It had not been Joss's intention to attend the annual stock-growers' gala at the Elkhorn Ranch. He was not in a festive mood, not at all, but Annie insisted that he had to take her. Otherwise, she would be unable to go. This was the first year she had wanted to attend, and he couldn't imagine what had prompted her change of heart. But after the heavy-handed way he had treated her yesterday, could he do other than accede to her wishes?

How could he, in all consciousness, put a damper on her newly awakened femininity? She looked so pretty in her ruffled bodice and skirt, satin slippers on her dainty feet that he was used to seeing encased in muddy boots, her face flushed with excitement. Could that be a touch of rouge he detected on her cheeks?

What would those young sons of the nearby ranchers think when they saw her? Would they even recognize the hellion on horseback who had outridden, outroped, and outcussed the best of them?

Then he frowned. What would he do if he caught one of those unbranded mavericks attempting to steal a kiss from his innocent sister? Would Annie even understand the implication of such rashness? He doubted anyone had ever talked to the girl about things like . . . boys and their insatiable persistence.

"Joss, don't you like my new dress?" The uncertainty on her youthful face tugged on his untuned heart strings.

"Aw, tyke, you look real nice." He chucked her under the chin in a brotherly fashion, rather awkwardly for a man who prided himself in his worldliness. But somehow it didn't apply to his relationship with Annie. "You just be careful, you hear? Don't you let any of those overeager, untried colts get too close, or too familiar with you." Living on a ranch most of her life, it was a comparison he could only hope she comprehended.

"Why would I?" Annie savvied all right. Rolling her eyes and crossing her arms, she jutted her bottom lip with a stubbornness that reminded Joss of himself. "Besides, if I want to, you can't stop me. And don't call me tyke in front of anybody at the party. Understand? I can take care of myself, big brother."

Could she? If she were faced with the hardships of life—the way deLacey Honeycutt no doubt had been over the years—could she manage to survive? Why did he have to think about her just now? Why did he think of her constantly?

"I know you can, honey." His verbal reassurance did nothing to alleviate his own misgivings, not only for Annie, but for himself.

It had been a long time since he had escorted a real lady to a highfalutin shindig. Perhaps he should have paid closer attention to his own appearance. Although his boots were clean as was required, he had not bothered to dress up, but there was no time to change out of his checkered work shirt and denims. Hesitantly he stuck out his arm, and she took it, almost seemed to cling to it, as if she felt as insecure as he did.

Insecure? Again the name deLacey Honeycutt popped into his mind. No, it was as if it seized him by the throat and shook him, refusing to let him go.

Once Annie was settled in the accordion-roof gig, he climbed onto the seat beside her, taking up the reins in his well-worn work gloves.

''Ready?'' he asked. The question was directed to himself as much as his sister.

She smiled, as bright as sunshine after a thundershower. ''Ready as I'll ever be.''

Perhaps they both were.

With a click of his tongue Joss set the horse into motion. As they drove out of the front yard with its manicured lawn and well-trimmed hedges, he knew Lacey would most likely be at the party, escorted no doubt by Silas Abrams. That was the real reason he hadn't wanted to go. Would she dance with Abrams, his arm about her waist possessively? Would she laugh, her eyes, her beautiful blue eyes, alive with pleasure all for someone else—not for him?

Would she remember those stolen moments they had shared, the line camp shed, the rain, or would she prefer to forget them? Somehow that was the hardest for him to bear—the thought of her choosing to ignore him and all that had passed between them.

And then he knew what it was he had to do, had known all along and refused to acknowledge. And do it, not for himself, but Lacey. Release her from the terrible demands he had placed on her. Set her free to do with her life whatever she wanted. How simple and yet how hard to uncage the lovely bird whose song infiltrated his every thought, whose beauty filled a void he'd not even known existed until she'd come along.

DeLacey deserved a little happiness, even if that son of a bitch, Silas Abrams, was the man who would eventually give it to her.

Lacey was surprised. The Elkhorn Ranch was nothing like she expected, for it was every bit as rustic as the

Rocking A. There were the standard corrals, bunkhouses, and outbuildings, the rutted dirt yard in front of the low-slung log house crowded with every imaginable kind of vehicle from practical buckboards to a frivolous gig. Most unpretentious. Not at all like its owner.

Dressed in brand new denim pants, his large, jangling spurs as ostentatious as his ten-gallon felt hat, Mr. Theodore Roosevelt met them at the front door himself.

"Silas. Welcome, neighbor," he greeted, his voice as boisterous as she remembered, his presence confident and smooth. He instantly settled his attention on deLacey. Then, without really asking Silas's permission, he took her by the arm and whisked her away, leading her into the house.

"Lovely lady, it *is* good to see you again. You look as if the Dakotas have agreed with you very well, not like the first time we met."

What did he mean by that?

"Very well, indeed," he emphasized. Patting her hand, he smiled down at her. He winked at her, his brilliant blue eyes, magnified by his thick glasses, sparkling with an unnamed something, a camaraderie—a shared secret.

Her past.

Had he been the one to betray her to Billy Howell? It was quite possible, for she was sure he suspected at least part of the truth, if not all of it.

Through the house, simply yet elegantly furnished, he led her out onto a large veranda, already crowded with many of the local ranchers and their wives, most of whom she already knew from the weekly socials. Their smiles and greetings of welcome and warmth caught her a little off-guard. Lacey was still not used to being so totally accepted.

Responding to the call of her name, she glanced to her left and caught her breath. A line of old cottonwoods stood sentry just beyond the restraining porch rails. Behind them was a cliff that overlooked the Little Missouri River, a gleaming blue ribbon far below. Drawn forward, she found herself leaning over the balustrade, mesmerized by the raw beauty. She could see how a man could be attracted to these so-called Badlands, could be challenged by their vastness, to want to stay and conquer. Men like Teddy Roosevelt and Silas Abrams and . . .

No, she refused to think about the one man who had bullied his way into her life and left a void in it all at the same time.

She turned to share her newfound appreciation with her host. But Roosevelt had moved off just a little and was talking to someone else. She found herself the focus of a brooding appraisal from just a few feet away.

Joss McRae.

She had known he would probably be there, had prepared herself to watch him from a distance, but to be so close on that rather crowded veranda made her extremely uncomfortable. A nervous smile parted her lips, but he made no move to reciprocate. Her hand caught at her purse strings, and she remembered what it was she had come there to do.

She couldn't look him in the eye, not another moment, so she glanced instead at Annie standing next to her brother, her hand draped possessively in the crook of his muscled arm, her youthful eyes darting about, looking for someone. Apparently the McRaes had only arrived moments before, for they were still exchanging greetings among the other guests.

Between Mr. and Mrs. Anderson, the banker and his wife who were talking to Joss, Annie smiled at her shyly, lifting her hand in a tentative, unobtrusive wave. The girl looked breathtaking, her coal black hair caught in an upswept style that deLacey, on one of their many rides, had suggested would be most flattering. What a difference from that wild hoyden she had first encountered at the roundup.

Lacey stared back unable to forget that Annie had run out on her, leaving her at the mercy of her brother, of her own weaknesses if the truth be known, and she wasn't so sure she was ready to forgive her friend for the part she'd played in her downfall. She still hadn't forgiven herself for betraying Silas's trust. To do so twice was inexcusable on her part.

She glanced once more at Joss and found him staring at

her in return. Nor could she pardon him for his part in all of this as well.

Her line of reasoning made what she had to do all that much easier.

Looking away, she refused to further acknowledge Joss and his overt rudeness. The moment his attention was distracted and Annie's again turned to her somewhat pleadingly, Lacey tipped her head to indicate she wanted to talk to the girl—alone.

Before she could see Annie's reaction her view was blocked by the wide body of the banker as his equally round wife led him forth to introduce him to Lacey.

However, she was quite confident that Annie would meet with her at the first opportunity. She also knew there was no going back now. If Joss was truly guilty of stealing cattle, it would soon be public knowledge. And if he wasn't . . .

But he was. She had seen the circumstantial evidence with her own two eyes, the telegrams linking his name with stolen cattle, had heard Billy Howell's explanation. And now, she had her own future to look out for.

Lacey and Annie. As thick as barn flies on a white-faced heifer. That was the analogy that came to mind as Joss watched the secretive exchange between the two of them. They were up to something. Something, no doubt, he wouldn't like.

"She's really lovely, don't you think?"

Joss heard the question, but didn't respond.

"Don't you think, Mr. McRae?" the speaker persisted.

"I beg your pardon?" Joss glanced down at Miss Bertalli. Just why this woman had chosen to corner him and enlarge upon her hopes and fears for Medora, he could only imagine.

"Why, Miss Honeycutt, of course," the seamstress chided as if she found his lack of concentration tedious. "I couldn't help but notice the way you were looking at her just now. I designed and made that gown she is wearing, you know," she explained as if the dress was what made Lacey beautiful.

Joss knew better. DeLacey Honeycutt would be beautiful in a potato sack.

"She has brought such gentility and grace to our community, hasn't she, Mr. McRae? . . . Mr. McRae?"

That seemed to be the common consensus. It irked him to think that she had somehow managed to hoodwink the entire community. Even Annie. She, as well, had deserted him for the opposition's camp. As illogical as such reasoning might seem under the situation, that was what she was doing by associating with Silas Abrams's mail-order wife. It didn't matter that he, too, had committed such traitorous actions—consorted with the enemy. Annie didn't know that. She couldn't. And she never would. Although she might suspect that there had been something more than met the eye between himself and Lacey, she would never learn the truth of it, not unless Lacey had told her.

Lacey. Joss narrowed his eyes, observing her as she mingled, nodding, shaking hands, smiling—never once looking his way although she had to realize he was staring at her. What was she up to? Using his little sister, the whole town, no doubt, to get at him.

He had been worried about his sister being taken advantage of by the young bucks. Well, maybe his concern had been misdirected.

At that moment he caught another exchange between the two of them, very quick and meant not to be obvious. But that wasn't all. Wasn't that the artist boy, Rusty Chapin, who worked for Teddy, the one Annie had beaten in the horse race during the spring roundup? Damned if that cowboy wasn't making eyes at his innocent little sister. And she was making eyes back. Annie, Rusty, even deLacey.

As determined as Joss was to find out what was going on, he gave no indication when Annie slipped away and headed into the house not far behind deLacey's lead. He still didn't move when the cowboy followed. But once the three disappeared, he abruptly cut off Miss Bertalli, who had been chattering steadily for the last five minutes.

"Well, I never," the spinster sputtered to his retreating back.

No, I suppose you never have, Joss thought sourly. *And if you did, it was probably not very good.*

Well, he had known he wasn't in a festive mood. And now after what he'd just seen—and what he suspected—it was blacker than ever.

"What is it, deLacey?" Annie's gaze roved about as if she were expecting someone else.

"Ssh." Lacey placed a finger over the other girl's lips and glanced about the vehicle-crowded front yard of the Roosevelt ranch house. She could have sworn she'd heard a sound—something other than the milling horses in the corral.

"What's wrong?" the other girl mouthed, looking eagerly around as well with a wide-eyed innocence.

"I think we were followed."

"Is that bad?" Annie demanded.

It wasn't exactly good.

"Here." Lacey reached into her reticule and grabbed up the folded piece of paper, shoving it into the girl's hand.

"What's this?"

"For your brother," she whispered. "But don't give it to him until you get home."

"A tryst." The strangest look came over the girl's face, almost dreamy, as she pressed the missive to her heart.

"Annie, you must promise not to give that to Joss before you get home this evening." Worriedly, Lacey grasped the other girl's arm. Was she making a mistake by entrusting so much of her plan into such inexperienced hands?

"Don't worry, Lacey. Your secret is safe with me." Annie stuffed the note in her own purse. Then she glanced about once more. "If I tell you my news will you promise to keep it to yourself, too?"

"News? What news?"

"You're right." Annie bent close and whispered. "We are being followed. Rusty Chapin."

"The artist?"

Annie nodded. "He's sweet on me—and I'm sweet on him."

"Oh, Annie," Lacey cried, relieved to learn her fears of being spied upon were unfounded. "I'm truly happy for you."

"Well, you can't tell Joss, 'cause he may not like it."

"Don't you worry about your brother. He's just a big old sourpuss." Lacey laughed. Yes, that was a most accurate description of how he looked standing by the railing, discussing who knew what with Miss Bertalli.

"So what happened out there after I left?"

DeLacey glanced back at Annie. How much did Annie suspect?

"Nothing."

"That's what my brother tried to tell me, but I didn't believe him for a moment." Annie flattened her mouth in a way that reminded Lacey of Joss.

"If you were so certain something might happen, why did you run off and leave me alone out there with him?" Lacey demanded, hoping to change the subject.

"Why?" The girl seemed genuinely surprised at the venom in Lacey's voice. "It was obvious that was what you wanted me to do."

"No, it wasn't," Lacey denied. "I would have much preferred to have . . ."

"Miss deLacey. Whatever are you doing out here?"

DeLacey turned at the sound of her name. Much to her surprise Silas Abrams stood propped in the doorway of the house. How long had he been there? How much had he heard?

"Silas," she blurted, attempting to convey relief, not the fear she really felt at his sudden, unexpected appearance. "There you are. I've been looking all over for you. I wasn't even sure you had made it into the house."

He seemed satisfied with her explanation, as lame as it sounded to her. Claiming her arm, he led her back inside and out onto the guest-filled veranda. As they left the front yard she noticed that Rusty had appeared as well, taking Annie's arm and leading her toward the barn. She was

happy for the girl. She only hoped Joss didn't make a fool
of himself and interfere. But a few moments later she saw
Joss, a very unhappy Annie in tow, emerge through the
same door she and Silas had just used.

What had happened? What had Annie told him? Had the
girl broken her promise and already given him the note
against her explicit instructions not to?

She was not to know. All through the long day, Silas
never left her side, not even for a moment. He was
faultlessly courteous and attentive, and yet something didn't
seem quite right. His hand upon her arm was a little harsher
than it should have been, his voice a little sterner when he
spoke to her. And whenever they drifted too close to either
of the McRaes he steered her away.

Joss, too, kept his distance, and if he had received the
note he made no indication, for his dark, brooding surveillance never faltered. Annie was impossible to pin down.
Every young man at the affair was crowded about her. It
was as if they had discovered her for the very first time. But
she only had eyes for the young cowboy who drew pictures.

Then when the afternoon waned, and the early evening
brought torchlight and dancing, Silas remained steadfastly
next to Lacey, leading her out in reel after reel. Graciously
he handed her over to their host, and then the banker, and
then every rancher in attendance, all except Joss McRae.
Joss remained in a corner watching her, just watching her, a
great brooding beast. And then he was gone. After that she
had not been able to locate him or Annie the rest of the
evening.

"Please, Silas, I'm exhausted," she announced breath-
lessly when he again tried to take up the lively steps of yet
another polka.

He seemed pleased to hear her say that, and there was an
urgency to the unrelenting pressure of his hand on her back
as he led her to the sidelines.

"Then I suppose you are ready to go home."

Yes, she was more than willing. She had danced and
glowed in all of the attention and flattery. Accepted as she
had never been before, it was something she didn't ever

want to give up, but she needed to step back from it and catch her breath.

Then she remembered what she had done to secure her position. Joss. Her plan, already set in motion to betray him. And although he deserved to be caught in his own trap, she didn't like being the bait. As they departed, she glanced about, but still could not find him. She would have liked to see him one more time, to reinforce for herself that she was doing nothing wrong—nothing more than what he had attempted to do to her.

But once the buggy was rolling along and she was alone with Silas Abrams she began to regret her involvement in Billy Howell's scheme. Not so much for Joss's sake but for Silas's. She should have stood her ground, dared Billy to tell Abrams whatever he wanted, and believed that Silas, gentle, caring Silas, would have understood.

And he would have protected her for he cared for her, not who or what she was, as no one else in her life ever had, except her daddy.

Sitting in the buggy beside him, the darkness all around them except for the yellow of the sidelights Silas had lit just before leaving the Roosevelt ranch, Lacey wished she could go back to the beginning, to the moment she had read that handbill advertising for mail-order brides, when she had stepped aboard that train in St. Louis, and do it all over again. If only she had never met Joss McRae. If only, for once in her life, she had played the game honestly, and had set out to fulfill her obligation to marry the man who had sent for her, instead of trying to cheat everyone she'd met along the way. Yes, as hard as it was to face, it was the truth. She had never been honest in her life—not even with herself.

Once they reached the road that turned off to the Rocking A Ranch, and the lights from the house could be seen in the distance, she finally made up her mind. She would tell Silas everything—now.

She scooted on the seat to face him, confession on her trembling lips, integrity her spur, the steady clip-clop of the horse's feet the encouragement to finally do what was right, if only this one time in her life.

"Silas, I have something I have to tell you."

"How interesting, my dear," he said, never once looking at her, "for I have something to ask you." Then he pulled back on the reins and brought the horse and buggy to a standstill there in the middle of the deserted road, the house at least a half mile ahead. There was no chance of anyone else coming along to interrupt.

Alarm, nurtured by the gambler's instinct that had guided her all of her life, took hold of Lacey. Then when he confronted her, the sidelight casting its yellowish illumination, she caught a glimpse of his face, but only for a moment. Was that a look of accusation on his pudgy features, an expression he had never shown her before? She couldn't be sure.

"What is it?" she asked, containing her apprehensions as best she could, for they were still unproven. Nonetheless, a frown drew her brows together.

Slowly, meticulously, he wound the reins about the footrest in front of him but didn't reply.

"Is something wrong?" Lacey's heart began to race uncontrollably, but still there was nothing to justify her fear.

He stepped down, came around the back of the buggy, and paused beside her, lifting his hand. "Get down, deLacey."

DeLacey? Not Miss deLacey? Something was terribly amiss. She considered refusing. She even considered jumping down, brushing past him, and running on to the safety of the ranch house that seemed so very far away now. But such a reaction would only point a condemning finger at her. And as of yet she didn't know what he accused her of—if anything.

Stay cool, Lacey. Stay cool. Smiling stiffly, she accepted his assistance to the ground.

And then she noticed the unnatural glint in his normally gentle eyes, the downward slope of his mouth.

He was on to her. She had played enough cons in her life

to realize when the mark had figured it out and her bluff was called.

"Silas, I can explain," she said in a faltering voice, lifting her hands defensively and taking a step backward, but she found the buggy a barrier impossible to skirt around, especially with him blocking her.

"Can you?" He grabbed her by the arm so roughly she cried out in pain. "Can you explain to me again how it was that Joss McRae found you wondering, lost on the range— all alone?" He shook her so hard that the back of her head thumped against the side of the carriage. "Or was that planned, deLacey?"

"No, it wasn't," she denied.

"I knew you were seeing Annie McRae, and I tried to be open-minded. I know she's the only girl for miles around your own age. I wanted you to be happy. I wanted you to stay."

"I do want to stay, Silas."

"Why?" He raised his hand, threateningly, and she thought for sure he was going to strike her. "So you can meet with Joss McRae behind my back again?"

"No, Silas. It's not like that." Closing her eyes, she could still envision in her mind his intimidating stance, and she waited for the inevitable blow.

"Then how is it?" Agony rang in his voice. He shook her again—but at least he had not hit her.

Lacey teetered on the edge of total confession, tears gathering in the corners of her tightly closed eyes. How much to tell him? How much would satisfy him? How much would save all that she had worked so hard to gain?

"Joss McRae . . . is blackmailing me."

She couldn't explain the terrible pain that racked her body and soul as she again deliberately betrayed Joss to save her own neck. And yet wasn't that exactly what he'd done to her all along, used her, forced her against her will to participate in a deception she had no desire to be a part of? So why was it so terrible that she lay the blame, and the ultimate consequences, where they duly belonged? Why was it wrong that she think of herself—her survival?

All of her life she had played men against themselves, against each other, and had never thought twice about it. She now felt as if she committed the worst of crimes.

But now she had sullied the one aspect of life she had always found sacred and above reproach. Above her own self-worth. The one thing she had clung to, had looked to as her eventual salvation. Love. One day it was to have lifted her out of her sordid existence, washed away her past. Instead she had destroyed the dream by bringing it down to her own base level.

She wanted to cry; she wanted to rail, to take back her words so hastily spoken. Instead she staunchly held her silence, for if the truth be known, she feared to do otherwise. The cards she had been dealt were the hand she must play.

"Blackmail?" Abrams sounded doubtful. "Just what does he know that's so terrible?" He pushed her to her knees before him.

It was a fitting posture for the confession came tumbling out in broken sentences. Call it momentary weakness or the overwhelming need to unburden herself, to find acceptance for who she was that loosened her tongue, but even so she chose her words with care. She would reveal only what she had to.

"You . . . must understand, Silas. After my daddy's death life wasn't . . . easy for me. I was forced to make my own way, with the best means I could. I picked up a trick or two about playing cards, and I became quite proficient."

"You're a gambler?"

"I managed to win a few hands." She couldn't help it that the lies were beginning to slip in slowly. But he looked so angry. "Enough to eat, Silas. Nothing more than I had to do to survive." That was the truth. She paused to judge his reaction, finding his stone-faced glare unreadable.

"Then you're not who you say you are. You're not from New Orleans society, are you?"

At first she didn't answer. She feared to.

"Are you?" He shook her so hard she thought her neck would snap in two.

"What does it matter, Silas?" she finally cried. "No one knows otherwise except you and me . . . and Joss McRae." And Billy Howell, she didn't say. And possibly Theodore Roosevelt. Who knew how long the list might be, but she couldn't let him know that.

"You lying little bitch." He shoved her away.

His rejection crushed her. Blinking back the tears of disappointment, of desperation, she edged forward, touching the hem of his jacket. Somehow she had to make it all right again. She had to make him realize that all was not lost.

"Silas, please listen to me. On my way here to meet you, I learned that a wealthy rancher was aboard the train. He engaged me in a game of cards and I beat him. I didn't want to arrive completely destitute. I wanted to make a good impression on you. Surely you can understand that."

He was listening, thank God.

"This rancher? Who was he?" he demanded.

"Joss McRae."

"You beat Joss McRae?" The most incredulous look crossed his face, momentarily softening it in the flicker of the lamplight.

Encouraged, she nodded. "Actually," she confessed with a giggle, "I sort of cheated him."

"Cheated?" His eyes narrowing once more, his hand clamping down her shoulders painfully.

Perhaps she shouldn't have used that particular word. She scrambled to cover her mistake.

"Silas, if you could have seen him. So arrogant. Flaunting his wealth. I . . . merely took advantage of the situation. I . . ."

"How much, Lacey?"

"Ten thousand dollars," she whispered, unsure just how he would take the information.

"You took Joss McRae for ten thousand dollars?"

She nodded, and swallowed so hard the sound was deafening. "He was so angry—livid."

Silas's look never changed. Oh, how she wished now she had never revealed so much.

But then laughter erupted from the little man.

"How rich. How very befitting, my dear. I wish I could have been there to see you make a fool of Joss McRae. I bet he was fit to be tied." Then he frowned. "So in order to keep his mouth shut about what you had done to him, the son of a bitch forced you . . . forced you to do what?"

The fact that Joss wanted to pin the charges of cattle rustling on Silas, had ordered that she find incriminating evidence, seemed more ludicrous than ever to deLacey. If Silas thought the gambling incident humorous, he might find Joss accusing him of theft just as funny. Since she had never fulfilled her end of the bargain, had never even attempted to supply Joss with the proof he demanded, surely Abrams would find her unwillingness to cooperate a sign of her loyalty to him.

"It seems, Silas, he wanted me to find evidence that you are rustling cattle from him." She attempted to make a joke of it, but her stilted laughter was more of a nervous titter. And then when he failed to respond in kind, she rushed on. "Don't you see? He tried to prove that *you* were the one stealing cattle—not him."

"Tell me, Lacey, did you give him what he asked for?" He grabbed her by the shoulders and dragged her up, shoving his face into hers.

"How could I? I couldn't find any evidence."

"Ah, my dear." His eyes narrowed knowingly. "But you did look, didn't you?"

"No," she cried. Oh, how had he managed to entangle her in her own words so neatly?

"Don't lie to me again." He shook her so hard she bit her tongue, causing tears to spring up in her eyes.

And then it struck her. Abrams was truly concerned that she might have found something to indicate his involvement. And if he feared the possibility, then it must be a possibility. If Silas Abrams was guilty, then Joss must be innocent.

"Oh, my God," she choked, lifting her gaze, still blearly with pain, in accusation. What had she done?

"You're to meet him, aren't you? You have the proof he

wants, don't you?'' There was murder in his beady-eyed glare, and she knew then the bitter animosity between the two men that she had thought one-sided ran deep as a blood vendetta. It would not end until one of them was dead.

"No, Silas." And it was the truth. Billy's plan never intended that she actually meet Joss, just lure him out to the line camp. "I don't know what you're talking about." If Silas were to find Joss now, there was no doubt in her mind what he would do.

"I saw you pass that note to Annie today. I know it was intended for Joss." Jerking her to her feet, he forced her up into the buggy seat.

"Please, Silas, you're hurting me." Casting about, she staring longingly into the darkness. If only she had some-place to run. But there was nowhere except Silas's house in the distance. She was no safer there than here with Abrams. Somehow she must talk her way out of this, must calm Abrams down, must convince him he was wrong.

"When, deLacey?" Ignoring her plea, he climbed in beside her. "When and where are you supposed to meet him?"

Surely he must already have that information, for no doubt Billy Howell was working for him not only as a ranch hand but as a spy. Silas himself had to be behind the plan to make it look as if Joss was the cattle thief, most likely to cover his own involvement. She set her jaw, refusing to cooperate, to be used by him any further in this confusing game of thimblerig.

"I should have known, when it came right down to it, you would protect your lover."

DeLacey paled. Denial leapt to her parted lips and then, suddenly, she found she could no longer continue on with the lie, to him—to herself.

Joss McRae was her lover. . . .

But more important, Joss was the man she loved with all of her heart.

"Ah, Miss deLacey. You daughter of Eve. It's a shame you couldn't be happy with paradise when I offered it to you." The back of Abrams's hand slid down the side of her face, ever so gently. He laughed, soft and sinister, dropping his hand to draw the pistol quickly from the holster strapped to his hip. His action reminded deLacey of how skillful he was with a gun. Carefully he checked the bullet chambers, one by one, then satisfied, he spun the weapon by the trigger guard about his finger and slipped it back into its cradle. "I'm sorry, my dear. Your misplaced allegiance comes too late and too little. You see, I already know when and where you are to meet McRae. I read that note long before you ever delivered it. My plans for him befit the snake that he is. I just wanted to prove to myself where your loyalties lie. Well, now we know, don't we?"

With that he reined the buggy and horse about and slapped the lines across the animal's spine, sending them rolling back down the road, away from the ranch house.

"Silas, where are we going?" she demanded, clinging to the seat of the speeding vehicle, wishing she had the courage—or perhaps the sense—to jump.

"Why, where else, Miss deLacey? We're going to meet your sweetheart just as you so carefully planned it."

"No," she cried in horror. She didn't want to go there, she didn't want to be a witness to the betrayal in which she had been so foolishly entrapped.

But she could think of no way to stop him or the confrontation—or the inevitable conclusion.

CHAPTER 16

Joss read the message once more and didn't know quite what to make of it. Lacey requesting that he meet her at the line camp, tomorrow, alone? Why?

Don't question your good fortune, you fool, he chided. *Why else?*

But he did question it. The gushy manner in which the missive was worded just didn't sound like deLacey. And yet he recognized her handwriting, the way she curlicued her *s*'s and elongated the tails of her *y*'s and *g*'s. It was the same as that first note she had sent him on the train out of St. Louis.

Why he had kept that particular letter, that bold, deceptive challenge to meet and play against the infamous King Honeycutt, he wasn't sure, but now for comparison he took the sheet of linen paper out of the desk drawer where he had stashed it.

Yes, Lacey had penned them both. There was no doubt, even if her reasons for wanting to meet with him weren't so clear-cut. Joss frowned. Just as there was no doubt that he would do what she asked of him, no matter what her intentions.

"I thought you would be tickled to hear from Lacey."

"Tickled?" he murmured, looking up and spying Annie, still standing there, her face as inquisitive as a kitten's that had stumbled upon a rattlesnake den for the very first time and had no idea the danger. He had forgotten her presence. His frown deepened. If she wasn't careful, she was well on her way to becoming a full-fledged busybody as well as a flagrant hussy. Yes, he had caught her and Rusty Chapin out in the barn.

"You'd do well to mind your own business, little girl," he warned none too gently, brushing past her. "You had better mind your manners, too."

"Well, it's time you stopped refusing to see the truth, you big lummox. Not only about me, but about Lacey."

Truth? Joss turned to confront her. What did Annie know of truth? He had spent his whole life shielding her from its ugliness, trying to even the odds so that truth didn't have one up on the McRae name. Regardless of his efforts it seemed whenever he did face reality it disappointed him.

He would like to think that Lacey yearned for him as much as he hungered for her. And perhaps she did, but it wasn't enough. She wanted more. Wanted anonymity. Sought to escape her past and who she was as surely as she wanted the many pleasures life offered.

Her goals were no more or less contemptible than his own ambitions. Power and money. Those possessions had enabled him to rise above his origins, had made it impossible for others to judge him or criticize the deeds of his forefathers—at least not openly. Not that he gave a damn what others thought of him, only how they treated him to his face.

Not so deLacey. How like a woman to want the fairy tale, not just the trappings that went along with it. But like the gambler she was and would never escape no matter how hard she tried, she was willing to let it all—her heart, her future, her happiness—ride on one shuffle of the cards. She had bet all she owned on Silas Abrams. In the end she would be the loser—as surely as he would himself if he ignored her request to meet with him one last time.

"Ah, Lacey," he sighed, and knew then that he loved her no less for the reckless manner in which she pursued life. In fact, he would want her to be no other way, for she would not be Lacey otherwise.

''Go to her, Joss.'' Though it was Annie who spoke out loud, she merely mimicked the urgings of his own heart.

''What if she disappoints me?'' McRae men had never had much luck with their women.

''She won't.''

How could Annie, so young and untried, be so sure? But then a deeper fear emerged, although he didn't voice it. *What if I should disappoint her?*

It was a chance he would have to take, for what was the value of life, of love itself, if not for the risks involved? Hell, deLacey Honeycutt was worth it.

He turned, gathered up his saddlebags from the back of the overstuffed wing chair where he had carelessly thrown it days before, and began to pack. A clean shirt, his slicker, an extra box of cartridges—just in case.

Just in case. He paused just a moment in indecision, then continued. He refused to allow his natural sense of caution to take that thought any further.

By the time they reached the isolated line camp deLacey was cold and stiff and exhausted. The thin wrap she had worn over her off-the-shoulder gown had not been intended for such long exposure to the elements, even at the beginning of June, nor was the one-horse buggy built for the rough trail across rugged terrain.

The cabin with its lone outbuilding was dark and deserted—austere as a burial crypt. It was hard to believe that it was here that she and Joss had . . . had shared something so wonderfully passionate.

Lacey pushed such sentiments to the back of her mind. It was necessary that she maintain a gambler's mien, not only outwardly but inside as well. She must never let Silas know her weaknesses, since he would only use them against her.

The buggy seat squeaked as Abrams got down. As silent and intimidating as their surroundings he came around to assist her. It was hard to believe this was the same man she had thought was so kind and caring, so . . . unthreatening.

"Miss deLacey," he said, offering her his hand with unfaltering patience—the patience of a snake just about to strike. He had murder on his mind, he had as much as insinuated that, and still he continued to pretend to be the perfect gentleman.

A terrible fear for such calculated dispassion shuddered through her. Glancing out over the horizon she sought some means to wiggle out of this one. The full moon illuminated the horse trail along which they had just traveled, stark, offering no cover, no hope to her or anyone unsuspecting who came along.

Somehow, she must find a way to stop him.

Somehow, she must figure out how to keep Joss away or to alert him to the danger if and when he did arrive.

But nothing came to mind short of throwing herself bodily on Abrams and wrestling him for the gun so that she could fire it into the air as a warning.

It was a little too early for so bold a play. Joss wouldn't show up before sunrise, still a few hours away. For the moment she must simply stand pat, even if the hand she'd been dealt was a lousy one. Watch and wait. That was what she would do, what her daddy had taught her was the best way to overcome even the toughest opposition. If nothing else, there was always the chance she could bluff him.

She placed her fingers in his, the feel of his hand covering hers as revolting as reptilian skin—oh, how could she have ever considered marrying him?—but she didn't allow her feelings to show on her face. Daddy had always told her that one day she would find herself involved in the greatest game of all, playing against unbeatable odds, and she had to be prepared. Well, it seemed, at last, that day had come.

Dear God, let her have what it took to get through this ordeal—to win.

Just what would it take? she wondered. Determination? Her confidence wavered, just for a moment. Desperation?

Don't ever gamble with what you can't afford to lose, Lacey, girl. Her father's warning rang in her mind. *Oh, Daddy,* she cried inwardly even as she made her lips smile, her feet take the next step and then the next, as she entered the cabin and heard the door slam behind her, snaring her in her own trap.

There was only one possibility to cling to, as desperate as it was—perhaps Joss wouldn't come. He cared nothing for her, only what she could ferret out for him—what he had attempted to bully, then buy from her—information she would now gladly give him if she could. How foolish to have thought she could lure him into so obvious a pitfall.

Yes, foolish, and now it might be her ace in the hole. If only she could convince Abrams that he was wasting his time waiting for Joss, who would never show up.

"Silas," she murmured, confronting him, hope welling where just moments before there had been nothing but a void.

He was busy raising the sashes and lowering the bits of burlap that served as blinds over the windows.

"Sit down, deLacey, and shut up," he ordered, never once glancing in her direction.

But she was not so easily brushed aside.

"He's not coming," she announced with confidence as she settled in one of the two straight-back chairs in the room. From the corner of her eye she watched him stiffen.

That had gotten his attention.

"What do you mean?" Silas shot her a threatening look.

"I mean, Joss McRae would never put himself in such jeopardy." She took a deep breath, and spread out her hand, studying it as if it were the most fascinating thing, as if she hadn't a care in the world. "You know I only wrote that note to him because I was forced to, not because I thought it would do any good."

"Forced to?" He crossed the room in three strides and jerked her to her feet. "By whom?"

Oh, he was most convincing, but surely he was more than aware of Billy Howell's plan to frame Joss, no doubt had plotted it himself since she knew now he was involved in the rustling. She narrowed her eyes. He was bluffing, and she wasn't going for it.

"You know as well as I do, Silas."

Silas Abrams would never make a decent poker player.

When cornered, confused, he revealed his feelings much too readily. He raised his hand to her. She shrank backwards. His intentions were obvious, too.

Lacey wrenched free of his grasp and darted across the room putting the table between them.

"Who?" he demanded again, skirting around the barrier in an attempt to snag her, as his reach was much too short merely to grab her across the table.

She shook her head, refusing to speak.

"Answer me." He whipped out his gun and pointed it at her, unwavering.

Her eyes widened. Would he really shoot her? Perhaps, eventually, but not yet. He still needed her.

The sound of a horse's hooves rang out, coming closer, running hard.

Joss. He had come. Her heart soared with joy even as it lurched with a terrible dread.

"He's early." Abrams dashed to the window and shoved aside the burlap with the barrel of his gun, pulling back the hammer as he did.

This was her chance, perhaps her only one. If ever she thought to be brave . . .

"Joss, watch out," she screamed a warning. Throwing herself against Abrams, she knocked him against the wall, the gun flying across the room. Dazed, she landed in a heap on the floor at his feet.

Her head hurt, her lungs ached, but she hoped she had raised the alarm in time. Although she would now no doubt suffer the consequences for her actions, she had finally done something truly noble in her life, and she didn't regret it for a moment.

The click of the hammer of a gun being drawn back penetrated the fog in her brain. It was no less than she expected, but it didn't matter anymore. She had saved the man she loved more than life itself.

"Mr. Abrams, Miss Honeycutt, what are the two of you doin' out here?"

She knew that voice. It didn't belong to Joss. Turning her

head, she focused on the speaker. All of her hard-earned self-respect dissolved into bitter ashes.

"Billy Howell? What are you doing here?" Silas sounded just as genuinely surprised as the cowhand.

But she knew what he was doing here. How could she have forgotten?

Unfortunately, it was all part of the plan. His plan, however, not hers.

Bound and gagged, deLacey listened helplessly as Silas Abrams spun his web of lies with the finesse of a crooked politician.

"Apparently Miss deLacey rode out here to warn Joss McRae. I followed her, and she told me, with a bit of persuasion, about her part in the plan to catch McRae red-handed. I figured you could use a little help." He glanced at her, his expression cool and calm as it raked over her. "A little reliable help."

Fighting her bondage, she tried to speak around the red neckerchief stuffed in her mouth to silence her. Her protests came out garbled. She had told Abrams nothing of the sort, and, just as she suspected, he knew what Howell was up to.

She stared at the cowhand pleadingly, hoping to convey her secret by the only means she had left to communicate— her great blue eyes. It was no use. Just like everyone else in this godforsaken territory—everyone but Joss, that is— Howell was taken in by Abrams's mild-mannered charm.

"That's right decent of you, sir," Billy replied, "but I'm not expectin' much resistance. McRae is just one man, after all. Besides, you've been enough help already, tipping me off to the rustlers' location. There's a small herd of Elkhorn cattle trapped up in Sioux Coulee, just like you informed me they would be, the branding irons just waitin' to be heated up. My intentions are to leave another note tellin' McRae to go there—that she's waitin' for him." He jerked his head toward Lacey. "Then, once he goes down to check it out—well, it'll be easy enough to get the draw on him—to arrest him red-handed for cattle thievin'."

Arrest him? Lacey's eyes widened. Just who was Billy

Howell? She had thought him merely some two-bit cow-poke, a flunky for Silas. But it seemed he was more—much more. Again she tried to protest against the gag, but it was useless. Her words came out as grunts and groans that both men chose to ignore.

"I'm always more than happy to help out a federal marshal, Billy. McRae has been leeching off all the ranchers in this part of the territory for too long as it is. We'll all be relieved to see the rustling stopped. And we'll be just as glad to see the arrogant son of a bitch knocked down a notch or two—or maybe even three." Abrams laughed. "Hell, nobody really likes him around here, they just put up with him because of his money. Arrest and trial is better than he deserves. If it was up to me, I'd have him horsewhipped and hung from the nearest cottonwood, and left to rot."

"The days of range justice are long past, Mr. Abrams. If the territory ever wants to become a state . . ."

Silas held up his hands in protest. "I know, Billy. We're civilized now." He smiled.

No, no, Lacey cried inwardly, her head shaking in disagreement, tears of frustration gathering in her eyes. How could anyone think it civilized to set a man up with false evidence? What kind of lawman was Billy Howell to stoop to something so dishonest?

But no one was listening, for apparently no one cared how it was gone about as long as they caught their man.

A terrible sinking feeling formed in the pit of her stomach. Who was she to criticize another's tactic? They were no better, no worse than what she had done to more men than she cared to count. The fact that she was a woman on her own, the daughter of "the King," didn't make what she'd done any less corrupt.

She darted a look once more at Silas Abrams and knew that mere arrest and ostracism of his most hated enemy would never be enough for him. He wanted Joss dead and would go to any extremes to obtain his goal.

Including murdering a federal officer?

She glared at Howell, who still refused even to acknowl-edge her presence. Whether he realized it or not, he was in just as much danger as she was herself, even more, perhaps. She had to warn him, had to make him see the truth—before it was too late for all of them.

Until then, she could only hope that she was right about Joss. He didn't care. He wouldn't come.

"I think, Mr. Abrams, you should take Miss Honeycutt home and allow me to handle this."

Yes, yes, Lacey thought. Even if Joss was arrested she could come forward afterwards and clear his name . . . even if she had to confess to her own misdeeds. It wouldn't matter as long as he was alive.

"All right, Billy. If that's what you want," Silas agreed much too readily. "We'll leave."

She stared at one man and then the other. Abrams was up to something. But what? Why couldn't Billy see he was being too obliging?

"In fact, I'll just take her with me now," Abrams continued, "out to the shed, while I harness the horse to the buggy." He pinned her with a cold, decisive glare that left no doubt in her mind that her first instincts were correct. He was up to something.

Her knees began to knock uncontrollably. She would never reach that shed alive.

The moment Abrams's fingers gripped her arm she began to fight in earnest, for her very life. Biting back a sob, she refused to be led to the slaughter like some dumb range critter that had nothing better to look forward to. After all, she was deLacey Honeycutt, and she couldn't die like this, trussed up and helpless.

Using the only tactic she could think of at the moment, down she went. Abrams jerked her back to her feet and began to drag her toward the open door. Spying a nail protruding from the woodwork, she raked her face across the sharp head, praying her aim was good and it would catch the neckerchief, yanking it free, yet miss her cheek underneath.

And then the gag was gone.

"Billy, you must listen to me. Joss is not the rustler," she cried, even as Abrams hauled her up and planted his beefy

hand over her mouth and nose. Gasping for breath that
wasn't there, she continued her struggle. Never would she
give up until there was no air left in her aching lungs, no
hope in her heart.

"She's lying, Billy. You know that." Abrams's fingers
dug viciously into the flesh of her face, a warning of things
to come if she didn't remain still. "She'd say anything to
save Joss McRae's thieving hide. Who else could it be if not
McRae?" he demanded.

Lifting her foot, she kicked backwards, clipping Abrams
on the kneecap.

He howled and momentarily let up the suffocating
pressure on her face.

Deep breath. "Billy, Silas is the th—"

Abrams's palm clamped hard over her face once more,
cutting off her accusation midword. With his other hand he
wrenched her bound arms high against her back.

DeLacey whimpered and went limp with the pain. Try as
she might she couldn't stop herself.

"Billy, you know what she is, her reputation as a
cardsharp. No better than a thief herself. Who are you going
to believe? Her or me?"

It seemed eternity for deLacey, those moments of light-
headedness as she fought for another breath, of agonizing
pain as her shoulders felt as if they were being torn from
their sockets, as Howell, his face reflecting his indecision,
mulled over his choice. His hand that hovered just above the
butt of his pistol flexed once.

Draw, Billy, draw, she prayed silently.

In response, or so it seemed to her, his fingers flexed
again. He had to believe her.

"There's no question, Mr. Abrams." His arm relaxed and
drifted downwards. "I believe you, of course, so there's no
need to smother the poor girl."

Oh, Billy, no. Tears of hopelessness gathered on her
lashes, even as the pressure of Abrams's hand let up enough
for her to take a breath. It was evident by the look on
Howell's face there was nothing she could say, even if she
could manage to speak, to change his mind.

"I tell you what, Mr. Abrams," Billy offered. "You just wait here while I go out and harness up the horse for ya."

"Why, thank you, Billy, my boy. That would be right kind of you."

No, Billy, don't leave me here alone with him, Lacey pleaded inwardly.

But it was too late. Howell was already headed out the door where even now the first tinges of sunrise painted the distant horizon.

How will Silas do it? she wondered morbidly, wishing he would just get the deed over with. Closing her eyes, she swallowed with a fear that left her knees weak and trembling. Would he clamp his hand over her face once more? Strangle her, perhaps? Or maybe he would shoot her in the back.

What difference did it make how he went about the gruesome task? Her life, as miserable and unworthy as it was, would be over before it ever really had a chance to get started.

In those few moment of cold sweat she thought about Joss, his handsome face, his strong yet sensitive hands, his mouth that had given her both pain and pleasure. And she thought about what was never to be.

She wondered if her death would be for naught. Would he even care?

And then a sound, a thundering clatter, penetrated her terror. Hooves. The running hooves of a horse.

Joss. Who else could it be?

"I knew he would come," Silas whispered in a delighted viper's voice that sent a new fear, a stronger fear than she had felt for her own life, slithering along the column of her neck.

The gag was stuffed back into her mouth even as she began to scream. And then she was helpless to do other than watch through the open door, working the gag back out of her mouth, as the rider, tall and commanding on the back of the powerful buckskin, galloped closer and closer.

The cold barrel of Abrams's pistol pressed against her bare neck. He was using her as a gun rest to steady his bead upon his target. When she tried to twist away, Abrams forced her arms so high up her back she thought for sure the bones would snap at any moment.

Cr-r-rack!

The buckskin wheeled and went to its knees, its loud whinny of pain rending the air. The rider, thrown to the ground, staggered to his feet like a drunkard.

Joss. He was still alive. So close she could see the confusion, the disbelief on his handsome face.

Cr-r-rack! Cr-r-rack!

Seconds after the horrible noise, Joss crashed backwards, and then she could see no more for her eyes filled with tears, running rivulets down her cheeks, blinding her.

He was dead, her beloved Joss, lying in a pool of his own blood. He was dead, and she had killed him as surely as if she had pulled the trigger herself.

"Oh, Joss," she cried against the gag, a great sob tearing through her, leaving an unbearable pain in its wake. He had died, no doubt, cursing her name, thinking she had been the one to betray him. And it was true. She had. Nothing she had attempted to do after she had delivered that ill-fated note could ever change that fact. He had come here because she had asked him to. And now he had died because she had selfishly thought only of her own wretched hide.

Then it seemed as if the air were alive with fireworks going off all around her. An arm grabbed her about the chest and jerked her backwards so hard it knocked the wind from her lungs, but she didn't resist. There was no reason to fight anymore.

There was no reason to live.

There was nothing. Nothing but the blade of icy defeat that stabbed her broken heart.

CHAPTER 17

It was unbelievable to Joss that he was lying there, sprawled on the cool spring range grass, his blood hot and sticky, his life essence seeping from his body like red tidewater. He had been close to death many times in his life, a near goring by a heat-crazed bull, a stampede, even an Indian raid once in his youth, and always he had brushed mortality off as impossible. Even so, he had never thought he would go like this.

Gunned down, just like his love-befuddled father.

Slain by the whims of a greedy female.

DeLacey.

He should have known better than to trust her, to trust any woman, should never have raced blindly, joyfully into her well-laid trap.

Who else could his murderer have been, if not deLacey? She had penned the note that had lured him here, had been standing there in the cabin doorway as he had ridden toward her, a love-blinded fool.

Because his demise was of her doing, because of this ultimate, unforgivable betrayal, he couldn't, didn't care to look for the strength to fight on. What was the use?

Odd, although he had always found life lonely and a bit of a disappointment, he had expected more from death.

True, he could hear the fireworks heralding his departure, but he had thought there would be lights, lots of them, and voices—a choir of encouraging spectators to guide him down the path.

But there was only one calling to him, sweet as an angel's to be sure, yet frantic and earthy as it cried out his name.

"Lacey?" Ignoring the pain and the cynicism that knifed through him, the defeat that told him not to bother, he rolled his head at the sound of that voice, seeking its owner, searching for hope where there was bound to be none.

He ran his hand over his face, and it took his eyes a few moments to adjust. There was the cabin, the front door thrown open just as it had been when he had ridden toward it, a flash of a pale yellow dress framed in the entrance. DeLacey waiting for him with arms flung wide in welcome.

Yellow, yellow, the delicate, deceptive color of a Dakota cactus flower and a loving woman.

Only it wasn't just yellow anymore. A streak of red across her neck contrasted sharply with her gown, clouding his vision, almost seemed to come to life. Joss squinted, straining to make sense out of what he saw.

How had his spilled blood managed to splatter her way over there? But it wasn't blood. Instead he realized it was a red bandana. That was significant, but he couldn't recall why.

Wearily he closed his eyes trying to keep from passing out from the dizzy waves of pain. For reasons he couldn't fully comprehend, he knew he had to hang on—just a little longer, if only to reassure himself that it was Lacey who had killed him. Then the exploding fireworks sounded all about him, so close, yet there was nothing for him to be alarmed about anymore for he was already dead.

DeLacey. Someone was shooting at her. He grunted in satisfaction. Justice swift and sure.

"Joss." He heard her scream his name once more, the final sibilance like crashing cymbals that reverberated in his head, her terror as thick as a child's left in the darkness all alone. It tore at him, refused to release him to his peaceful surrender—made him care, when he didn't want to.

"Lacey," he mumbled, his own voice sounding thick and distant to his ears.

He opened his eyes, and his focus cleared sharper than ever. The woman, her gown, the red bandana . . .

The man crouched behind her, using her as a shield as he fled across the open ground between the cabin and the shed. She stumbled; he jerked her up roughly and forced her to continue on. His arm raised and took aim.

Silas Abrams. Joss would have recognized that son of a bitch through the fires of hell itself.

A shot exploded, follow by a mocking retort from the shed.

Suddenly he realized he couldn't die now, if only to defy the wish of his most hated enemy, Silas Abrams. DeLacey. Her safety meant nothing to a man like Abrams. She needed him.

Ignoring the pain in his chest, the rising queasiness in the pit of his belly, Joss rolled to his side and groped for the gun strapped to his hip. He must get up. He must get . . . He must . . .

Even as his fingers closed about the pistol handle, a wave of blackness swamped over him. He fought it with everything he had.

Nonetheless, it drew him down, down, deeper into its frigid depths.

Gasping for breath, Lacey dropped her head back against Silas's shoulder. His arm was draped across her chest, his hand crushing her breast was all that held her upright.

Let 'em look, missy, but never let 'em touch. Her daddy's words of warning that he had assured her would always see her through anything seemed ludicrous now. What did it matter if this man or any other ever touched her? His hand, her breast. Power and submission. She doubted Abrams even knew that he clutched her so intimately.

"Stand up, damn you, woman," he ordered, his breath hot against her neck, his red bandana tickling her throat. But even as he dragged her toward the shed where Billy Howell was hidden, taking shots at them, she made no attempt to comply or defy.

"Let her go, Mr. Abrams. Give yourself up. It will go a lot easier for ya."

She heard the excited rush of air escape from Silas's mouth as he squatted behind a rain barrel, forcing her down in front of him. "Come out and drop your gun, Billy, and I will," he promised.

She didn't believe him, not for a moment, but what about Howell?

"You know I can't do that," the lawman replied. "But the girl. No need to involve her any further in this. McRae is dead, so you don't need her anymore."

Hauled to her feet once more, Lacey had no strength or will to resist upon hearing her greatest fear spoken aloud. Joss was dead. Billy had said so. Biting back the sob that formed in her throat, she squeezed her eyes closed. When they reached the door of the shed, she still remained silent even as Abrams untied her hands and shoved her forward through the opening.

"Here if you want the bitch, you can have her."

A shot rang out so close to her left ear that it seemed to go deaf from the concussion. She screamed.

Billy Howell stood up from behind a bale of hay, his gun still smoking, his face contorted with dismay upon discovering it was her. Then, as he lowered his gun, he expressed his relief that he had not hit her.

"No, Billy," she cried. "It's a trap. He's right behind me."

Abrams's pistol went off so close she could smell the burnt gunpowder. Billy slumped forward, a broken rag doll draped across the hay, blood oozing from his right temple.

And now there was no one left but Silas and herself. She was the only witness to what had taken place there in that isolated line camp. Even as she faced him, she heard the click of the hammer as it was drawn back, and knew it was meant for her.

"I'm sorry, Miss deLacey, but I can't allow you to betray my trust again." There was something of the old Silas, the gentle Silas, radiating from his eyes, but now there was also a mad gleam.

Funny. Staring down the barrel of that loaded gun did something to her. Sparked a fear of dying if not the desire to live.

"Silas, please." She lifted her hand in a gesture of entreaty, unable to tear her gaze from the weapon, unable to stop the terrible panic from gripping her about the heart and squeezing until she thought she could stand it no more.

"First my mother and McRae's father." Abrams laughed. It was an ironic sound. "And now you and him." His mouth slanted down in anger. "Tell me, Lacey, what is it about McRae men that all the women in my life find so damned attractive?" A sob tore from his throat, raw and tormented; his hand shook, but still his finger squeezed, squeezed the trigger so slowly.

What could she say that would stop him? What could she do? Nothing. Nothing.

"We're real men, Abrams."

With a cry of surprise Lacey glanced up.

Joss. Swaying, he was slumped in the doorway to the shed, one hand pressed against his bloody shirtfront, his gun drawn and aimed at his enemy, his face unreadable except for the pain. But he was alive. Alive.

She took a step toward him, to help him, to tend to him, to tell him . . .

Joss held up his hand, dyed red, insisting that she come no closer.

"Joss?" she asked in frustration, for if he didn't get help soon . . .

He didn't reply. Instead his attention was riveted on Abrams, who had turned to confront him as well. The hatred, the determination to end it here and now was irrevocably etched on both of their faces.

"You son of a bitch," Abrams growled. He leveled the barrel of his pistol on Joss. A stalemate. "What is it bastards like you have that's so irresistible?"

"You really don't know, do you, Silas?" Joss laughed. It was evident that the effort hurt him for he stopped abruptly, his hand clutching at his chest, his brows knitted. "Men like

me, like my father, we know how to live, how to love.'' He
glanced at Lacey fleetingly.

As roundabout as he made his avowal, it was enough. He
was saying that he loved her.

''We know how to die,'' he finished, uncocking his gun
and pointing it skyward.

''No,'' she cried, lurching forward, but Joss silenced her
with another look.

''Tell me, Abrams,'' he goaded. ''Do *you* know how to
die like a real man?'' He shoved his gun back into its
holster, his hand flexing just above it—issuing a challenge.

For the longest moment she thought Abrams would
simply pull the trigger and be done with it.

''We will see who is the victor, McRae.'' Abrams
lowered his gun as well. ''Which of us dies like the dog that
he is.''

Lacey glanced beseechingly at one man and then the
other as they moved out of the shed. What did this mean?
Was this some kind of code of the West? Well, she knew
about codes and ethics—men who put their pride, their
honor, before all else, even life itself. Had she not been
forced to watch such a noble misconception destroy her own
father?

It was true. Kingston Honeycutt had invented the small
device she had used so often to cheat at cards, only he had
employed it merely for parlor tricks. ''The King'' had
always won every card game fair and square, using nothing
but pure skill and talent. And in the end, as his eyesight had
dimmed, his sharp mind had begun to wander, even then he
had refused to lower his standards.

Pride, he had called it. A gambler's honor. What good
had those lofty ideals done him when he had died in a
wretched hole, starving and broke, no one giving a damn
that he had once been great, or that he had been an honest
man all his life. He had deserved a little respect. Instead no
one had even believed him when he'd claimed to be ''the
King.''

Now Joss wanted to risk his life. For what? For a misplaced
sense of honor that was no more meaningful than her

daddy's. In her heart she knew Silas Abrams harbored no such foolish notions, had only accepted the challenge because he truly thought he could win. Having witnessed his skill with a gun, how quickly he could draw, how steady his aim, she feared he was probably right. And even if Joss happened to be as proficient, he was injured.

Like her father he could never equal the opposition in his present condition.

She glanced about and spied Billy Howell draped over the hay bale, his pistol still gripped in his hand.

She had no silly pride, no code of ethics, to prevent her from doing what had to be done. All she knew was that she wanted Joss alive—at any cost.

Scurrying across the shed, she knelt before Howell and tugged at the weapon in his hand.

Billy moaned.

He was still alive.

She should help him. But more important, she must save Joss. Again she pulled at the pistol. Finally managing to free it, she sat back and checked to make sure there were bullets in the chambers. There were three. It was enough.

"Don't interfere, Lacey." Howell's hand, now empty, reached up and gripped her arm with the strength of a fragile bird's claw. Though the bullet had only grazed his temple, there was still a lot of blood, and the wound needed attention.

"I have to." Ignoring the pangs of conscience, she hugged the gun to her heart, refusing to give it up. "Someone has to stop Silas before, before . . ." She scrambled to her feet, aiming toward the shed door.

She could see them. Joss stood off to one side with his back to her. Tall and straight, his hands dangling at his sides, as if he didn't care whether he won or lost. Abrams was in the distance, his stance crouched, his hand hovering just over his weapon. Ready, eager, so eager to be done with it. Hidden in the shadow of the shed, Lacey lifted the gun and took aim. She didn't care what it cost her, she couldn't stand by and watch Joss make such a sacrifice.

"That's cold-blooded murder, miss. Do you think afterward McRae will be grateful to ya? Do you think I will just stand by and do nothin' about it?''

"I don't care,'' she cried. She didn't want Joss's gratitude, nor did it matter what eventually would happen to her. Nor did she give a damn about Billy Howell's sudden attack of integrity. Where had that been when he had so callously plotted to frame Joss for cattle rustling? But regardless of her convictions, her hands began to tremble, and she hesitated.

Just long enough. Billy moved up behind her and took the pistol from her hands.

"Please, Billy, stop them,'' she implored.

"No.'' He slid his gun back into its holster. "There are some things that just have to be settled between two men. This is one of 'em. For neither one will rest until it is. It's a shame, for everyone knows Abrams is the fastest with a gun in these parts. And if Joss tries to draw first and manages to beat him . . .'' He shrugged. "I'll have no choice except to take him in.''

What kind of justice is that? she wanted to scream at Billy. But she realized such an outburst would do her no good. What a fool she had been. She should have pulled that trigger, ended it there and then, when she'd had the opportunity. Joss would have then been free. But now, no matter what happened, now that she had discovered how much she needed him, wanted him, she was going to lose him.

A deadly calm enveloped Joss, like the eye of a tornado, the damage already done strewn all about him, the promise of more yet to come like the distant howl of the wind. Now that he was finally to have his revenge, the revenge he had waited a lifetime for, nothing was black and white any longer. No right and wrong, no good and evil, only varying shades of gray.

His father. Abrams's mother. It had been a scandal that had rocked the community for miles around. When Silas's father had heard the truth from his own son's lips, he had called out his rival. The ensuing gun battle had been inevitable. What had followed had been too, he supposed.

It could have ended there, the betrayed husband avenged with the death of his adversary. And although there would have always been bad blood between himself and Silas, the true victims of their parents' deeds, there would not have been this all-consuming vendetta. But it hadn't happened that way. The passions and naïveté of youth had seen to that.

He glanced at his opponent, a man now, and remembered instead a youth of fourteen, himself no more than twelve. Joss recalled rushing to his wounded father's side, crying for him not to abandon him. At that time there had been no one else for him, only a father who had been unable to make anything work in his life, not even love. Holding the dying man in his arms, Joss had helplessly watched a life, as disillusioned an existence as it had been, slowly seep away.

It had been then, still clutching the warm body, still refusing to believe that his father was gone and he was all alone, that Silas had come up to them.

In those days the Abramses had owned a small but prospering ranch with a few hundred head of range cattle, the McRaes had claimed a patch of barren land that they struggled to scratch a mere existence from. Had his father lived no doubt they would have eventually moved on; they always did. To this day he remembered the jingle of Silas's spurs as he'd approached, towering over him.

When he'd looked up, Joss wasn't sure what he'd expected from the other boy. Contempt perhaps? It was to be anticipated under the circumstances, but tempered by compassion. Instead Silas had kicked his father's still body with the toe of his boot and spit on him.

"Good riddance to bad trash. The world's better off without one more loser. If you're smart, Joss McRae, you'll hightail it outta here as fast as you can. Otherwise, I'll fix you, too. I'll run you out with your tail tucked 'twixt your legs like the cur's whelp that you are."

"I'll get you for that," he'd retaliated, vowing then he'd never leave, no matter what. Scrambling to his feet, he had

rammed into the older boy's gut with his head, knocking
him to the ground. He'd wanted to kill Silas then, and might
have, if some of the spectators hadn't pulled him off.

Ironically he had left the Dakotas for a while after his
father's death and had not returned until he'd had the money
to buy a spread bigger and better then Silas Abrams owned.

Even so, money hadn't tempered his anger or his need for
revenge. Joss still wanted to kill the son of a bitch. Staring
Abrams in the eyes, he knew the other man's opinion of him
hadn't changed—not one iota. He still considered all
McRaes the scum of the earth, no matter how much money
and power they accumulated.

In response to the raw emotions coursing through him,
Joss flexed his hand slightly, a challenge that Abrams didn't
miss. This fight was no longer over the past transgression of
youth, wasn't over cattle rustling or worldly possessions—it
was over a woman.

They both acknowledged that. But Joss wasn't sure
deLacey could appreciate a man's need to win such a
primitive battle. He wasn't convinced that any woman did,
not after what had happened between Abrams's mother and
his own father.

He had known from the beginning that somehow it would
eventually come to something like this. When he had gone
to intercept the arrival of the future Mrs. Abrams, to take
Silas's woman away, he had planned his revenge—his
sweet revenge—well aware of what he was doing.

Or so he had thought. He had expected Abrams's
mail-order bride to be some simpering, wide-eyed female
easily diverted by who and what he was. Never had he
expected a woman anything like deLacey Honeycutt. And
never had he expected to get caught in his own web.

From the beginning he had wanted her in the worst way
and not only for his original reasons. Yes, to foil Abrams's
plans, to show him that the McRaes were not men to be
taken lightly, to steal the bastard's hopes and dreams from
beneath his very nose, to bring him down with a deception
that would surely destroy him.

But deLacey had refused to cooperate, to be merely a

pawn in another's scheme. Instead she had strutted into his life with her own plans of deceit, had lassoed and branded him before he'd known what had happened, and then had refused to be tamed herself. Ah, yes, the impregnable Miss Honeycutt had known exactly what she was doing from the very start.

As if his thoughts of her manifested in flesh and blood, he caught a glimpse of her from the corner of his eye. Now what was she up to? No doubt she plotted even now.

"Joss, please don't do this."

"DeLacey, get back," he warned, casting his gaze in her direction for just a second, remembering that she had twice before foolishly interfered.

But it was a second too long. He sensed his mistake, the exposing of his one vulnerability, the moment he made it. Silas recognized it, too. Not that the man gave any outward indication; he didn't make a move, but the evidence was there nonetheless. It was like watching a conniving coyote, famous for selecting the easiest prey to attack, turn to consider the unprotected calf over the wounded cow—a much less dangerous target. Joss knew without a doubt how it was that Abrams planned finally to even the odds. The very thing he had thought to use to destroy Abrams would now bring about his own downfall.

DeLacey. Oh, deLacey, you little fool.

Even as he pivoted to brush her out of the way of Abrams's line of fire, he saw his opponent make his move. It was like a nightmare, slowing motion down until it seemed there was time enough between heartbeats for him to recount every mistake he had made in his life.

He heard the great rush of indignant air from Lacey's lungs as he landed on top of her, crushing her, yet shielding her. Felt the searing pain in his collarbone from the bullet wound acquired earlier. Heard the retort of Abrams's gun, saw the flash from the barrel even as he fired his own weapon in response, most likely too late, at least as far as he would ever know.

And then it was like something from the netherworld. Silas Abrams howled like a wounded beast, spun around, and collapsed on his knees, doubled up, and hugging his right arm to his chest.

Joss rose, and sucking in a labored breath of his own, he staggered across the yard, kicking the other man's pistol well out of his reach. Staring down at his nemesis there on his knees before him, he aimed his gun at the back of his bowed head and cocked it. Yes, this was all that he'd ever wanted, had dreamed of for years. Silas Abrams at his mercy and begging him for a reprieve.

"Please, Joss, don't do it."

Abrams lifted his face and stared up at him. Odd, he didn't look like a man pleading for his life.

"Please, Joss."

And then he realized it wasn't Abrams that was asking for leniency.

DeLacey.

He turned to examine her and her reasons. Why did she implore so sweetly for Silas Abrams's wretched life? Was it all that important to her? Did she care so much for him?

"Get back, Lacey. This is between him and me."

He took aim once more, placing his finger on the trigger. Odd, now that he had the power, the right to square the score between them, he discovered it just wasn't that vital anymore.

Uncocking his gun, Joss stepped back. "You aren't worth it, Silas. You never were. You're not even worth the price of the bullet it would take to put you out of your misery." Then he turned to Lacey, giving her an ugly glare. "He's all yours, honey. May the two of you live happily ever after."

"Joss." Her cry rang out like a shot, piercing him to the heart.

What more did she want from him?

"You have to listen to me. If I'd known the truth, I wouldn't have chosen to deceive you."

Choices? She dared to speak to him about choices? The only thing she had ever had to choose between was Abrams's money and his. Well, it was apparent who had won that contest. She had come here with Silas Abrams, had enticed him out here for reasons he could well imagine.

"You've lied to me more times than I care to count. So give me one good reason why I should believe you now, Lacey." He anticipated what her answer would be, and it would be good, no doubt, and he prepared himself not to be swayed.

"I . . . I love you, Joss. I . . . need you."

He laughed. "You mean you need my ten thousand dollars now that Abrams is on to you." He frowned. "Or did he offer you a lot more to entice me out here?"

"No. That's not how it happened. I didn't write that note for Silas but for . . ." Her eyes widened, and she clamped her mouth shut.

"For who, Lacey?" he insisted, grabbing her by the arm and jerking her to him. "Who, damn it?" He glared at her.

"She did it for me."

Joss looked up over the top of Lacey's head, for the first time seeing Billy Howell.

"What is your part in all of this?" he demanded, lifting his pistol once more.

"No, Joss." She put her hand on the gun barrel and pushed it away. "Billy is a federal marshal. He knows all about the rustling. He's here to arrest those responsible."

"All right, Mr. Abrams, let's go." As if on cue the lawman crossed over to where Silas still knelt on the ground, handcuffing his wrists and hauling him to his feet. Joss knew that justice would punish Silas Abrams in ways he never could have—much better ways.

"This ain't over with, McRae."

"Yes, it is, Silas," Joss responded, watching Howell put his prisoner into the buggy. "Like it should have been years ago."

Billy a lawman? Now so much began to make sense. The telegrams he had seen the man send from town time after time. Howell's insatiable curiosity about the different cattle operations, going from one ranch to another. That night he had been inspecting Lazy J cattle, obviously he had been looking for signs of brand tampering.

"You thought I was responsible for the rustling, didn't you?"

"I have to admit it looked that way for a while, Mr. McRae," Billy confessed.

"What changed your mind?"

"Miss Honeycutt. It took some doin', but she made me see that it was Abrams here that was behind the thefts, not you." He tipped his head towards his prisoner.

DeLacey had convinced him? Joss turned on her. "Then you had the proof all along, didn't you?"

"No, Joss. I swear. I only discovered the truth last night. By then it was too late to stop you. I could only hope that you wouldn't come, that you didn't care."

"Ah, hell, Lacey. How could you think that?" Reaching out, he drew her forward, savoring the feel of her slender warmth against his heart as he held her close. "I couldn't get here fast enough."

"How unlike you to be so reckless."

"That's what love does to you, honey."

Smiling broadly, she buried her face against his shirt-front. "Oh, Joss," she gasped when he flinched with pain. "Your wound." She pressed him down on an upturned rain barrel, and taking charge, fussed over him as if he were quite helpless. "You can't take foolish risks like that anymore. Do you here me? I won't have it."

She wouldn't have it? Already she sounded like a wife, trying to tell him what to do. A wife? Oddly enough, the idea sounded mighty good.

"It's nothing, Lacey. Nothing at all." Even so, he winced when she drew aside the bloody shreds of his shirt.

And in truth the injury to his flesh was nothing by comparison to the healing of his soul. Now that he had learned how to let go of the past, and if not to forgive, then at least to put a proper perspective on it; now that he had found a woman worth loving, the kind of love that with-stood the rigors of human imperfections, nothing else mattered.

He looked up at her, so petite, her eyes so gloriously blue, her hair the color of ripening wheat, her face like that of an angel, and he couldn't get enough of her as he watched her ply her gentle touch upon his wounded flesh. Yes, a woman's touch—that was what he needed.

But then an unsettling thought dampened his newly discovered happiness. Lacey loved him . . . today, but what about tomorrow? Or a month from now when she was forced to face the scandal that would surely erupt? A year from now when it finally died down? Would she feel the same then? Could he give her enough to keep her content? Could he keep the howling wolves from their door long enough to show her she could trust him? Always trust him?

Love, at least to his way of thinking, was such a fragile thing. Even if she didn't realize it herself, Joss knew deLacey needed a sense of security to go along with the constant challenges life presented. She was a gambler by nature, always was and always would be. But she was a woman, too.

Perhaps that was what he loved about her most, her unflagging spirit, the way she took on life, weighing her odds and forging ahead.

He knew then, if he wanted to hang on to her, he would have to keep the game varied and interesting. But just as important, he must shield her from those who would try to hurt her.

CHAPTER 18

Lacey sat in the middle of the big brass bed, her legs crossed, one foot bare, the pile of discards in her skirt spread over her lap. Joss was there, too, staring intently at the cards held in his left hand, for his right arm was still in a sling.

"I'll see your stocking and raise . . ." She gazed over her own cards, studying with all seriousness what items of clothing he was still wearing. "I raise you a pair of pants and . . . your shirt."

"My pants and shirt?" One dark brow jutted upwards. "You must have quite a hand there, darlin', for in my book pants and shirt are worth all a lady's unmentionables."

"Not so," she argued. "My skirt and petticoats at best, sir."

"Agreed. I call, for I think you're bluffing."

It was a rather silly card game that they played, one Joss swore he'd just invented for their amusement on such a rainy day in September, although Lacey suspected that some bawdy house resident had taught it to him. And she further suspected that if indeed he had made up these outrageous rules, it was to be sure that she wasn't cheating him. His first bets had been for her stockings, forcing her to reveal her legs, proof that she had nothing hidden beneath her skirt.

She giggled. Little did he know, but she was waiting for

just the right moment. Earlier she had managed to slip three aces from a matching deck beneath the pillow beside her. Separating her cards, she slapped the ones she didn't wish to keep face down on the coverlet.

"Three please," she requested.

He dealt them, and when he wasn't looking she slid her hand beneath the pillow, exchanging them for the ones she had stashed there earlier. Quickly she added them to her hand.

Smiling, she was quite pleased with herself, knowing he couldn't possibly beat her four aces. What fun it would be to watch him strip off his clothing, protesting no doubt when he had thought it would be the other way around.

"Your bet, darlin'."

How strange. He was grinning back at her, as if he knew something she didn't. As if he were confident he would win.

Impossible. There wasn't a hand in the world to beat hers unless he held a straight flush or higher. The odds, and she knew well how to calculate the odds, were one in almost sixty-five thousand in her favor.

"I raise you . . ." She peeped over the rim of her cards.

"Careful, Lacey," he warned, "you just might lose, you know."

"At cards, against you? Not likely." She giggled.

"Little witch." He lunged for her with his good hand.

Lacey didn't mean to look, but she couldn't help it. He practically flashed his cards in her face.

A royal flush?

Even as he pressed her back against the pillow, she snagged his wrist to take a better look.

"Joss McRae, you're cheating," she declared indignantly.

"Am I?" He grinned wickedly. "You can't prove that."

"Yes, I can." Taking up her own cards, she fanned them in front of his face. "See."

They both held the ace of hearts.

"Those aren't the cards I dealt you." Joss frowned, grabbing her hand. "Where are they, Lacey?" he demanded. "Where did you stash them this time?" His hand began to roam freely over her, traveling up her bare legs.

She slapped his fingers away. "How do you know what

you dealt me unless you were the one cheating?'' she accused. In turn, she ran her hands into his shirt looking for her own evidence.

Instead, she discovered something much more rewarding. The card game was forgotten, even as the scattered deck she'd held in her lap crackled as he covered her, his intent most obvious.

Winding her arms about his neck, she welcomed his advances, the feel of his mouth on hers, the heat of his urgency.

It was so wonderful being here, being with Joss over the last few weeks. He was kind, and considerate, and generous to a fault. He had even promised that as soon as he was able, he would take her on a tour back East, even on to Europe if she would like. The way he was using his injured arm now, she suspected he was quite able.

But there was something missing in their intimacy, almost as if he hesitated to step over a certain line, as if he were waiting for the day when she would decide to pick up and leave.

But she didn't want to leave. She had everything she wanted or needed here with him—everything and more.

So why did he make no move to cement their relationship? What was he waiting for?

''Lacey, what is it, honey?''

She looked up into his concerned face. He knew her so well, probably better than she knew herself.

''It's nothing, Joss.'' But, oh, how she longed to ask him the same probing question—to tell him her news.

But before she could screw up her courage to do so a knock sounded on the door.

''What do you want?'' Joss growled at the intrusion.

''The gentlemen are here again, sir,'' Henry's ever so proper voice announced.

''Tell them to come back later.''

''They say they won't leave this time until they're given the opportunity to speak with Miss Honeycutt directly.''

''Me?'' Lacey asked.

''Wait here. I'll take care of this.'' Even though his

mouth turned down at the edges, Joss didn't seem the least bit surprised. But he did look worried as he rose up off the bed.

She was sorely tempted to comply with his demand, just to let him handle whatever it was, but something inside of her wanted to know what was going on. Who wanted to see her? How long had they been trying? What was Joss attempting to shield her from?

"No, Joss. It's me they wish to see, not you." Sitting up, she straightened her clothing, gathering up her stockings and pulling them on along with her shoes. "Why didn't you tell me I've had visitors?"

For a moment she thought he was going to deny her permission to go downstairs as if she were a child that needed protection. But then his face softened.

"Lacey, you don't understand."

"No, I don't, but I'm about to find out." She flounced past him to the door.

"Henry, show my guests into the drawing room." She stared pointedly at Joss. "Tell them *I* will be there in a few moments."

"As you wish, miss." The servant bowed respectfully.

Even so, she couldn't help notice the angry looks that passed between Joss and Henry as she skirted between them.

With a sinking heart Joss watched her go. At last the wolves had forced their way in, spoiling the utopia he had so carefully built just for the two of them. It was bound to happen sooner or later, he supposed. If only he could have held them at bay a little longer—just a little longer.

Damn Henry. He turned on the servant. "You're fired."

"Yes, sir." The valet never even blinked an eye. "I'll begin packing right away."

"Why, Henry?" Joss demanded. "Why did you go against my explicit orders?"

"Because, sir, I believe in the lady's intentions even if you don't. She'll see this through."

"How can you be so sure?"

The servant smiled. "If you could have seen her that first day on the train when she appeared at the doorway, so determined, you'd know it, too. Besides, Mr. Roosevelt is with them this time. Even if you'd not agreed to let them see her, they would have subpoenaed her. Her involvement was inevitable, sir. She could use your support right now, don't you think?''

''Face it together, you mean?''

''It would seem the proper thing to do.'' With that the unflappable servant returned to his duties.

Joss watched him go, and didn't bother to remind him that he'd just been fired. It seemed that Henry was a permanent fixture in his life—always would be. If only he could be so sure of deLacey.

There were six gentlemen altogether waiting for Lacey downstairs. Two of them she recognized. Billy Howell and Teddy Roosevelt. They all rose somberly when she entered the drawing room, removing their hats as if she were truly the lady that she so much wanted to be.

A debilitating fear overtook her. Perhaps she should have let Joss handle them.

''Gentlemen,'' she said with as much grace and dignity as she could scrape together. ''I'm sorry you have been kept waiting for so long. What can I do for you?''

''Miss Honeycutt, we appreciate your finally agreeing to see us.''

She didn't know the man speaking, so she looked to Teddy Roosevelt for an introduction.

''Howard Blount, Miss Honeycutt, prosecuting attorney in Bismarck, the territorial capital. He's in charge of the legal case against Silas Abrams.''

''I see,'' she responded calmly. Inside she felt anything but calm. She had thought the whole sordid affair with Silas Abrams was over and done with.

''I'll come right to the point, ma'am,'' the lawyer said briskly. ''My evidence against Mr. Abrams is strictly circumstantial. In order to give credence to the charges of cattle rustling and attempted murder, I require your testimony.''

''Me?''

''Yes, ma'am. Apparently you are the only person to

whom he made a confession. With you on the witness stand I can prove his involvement beyond a shadow of a doubt.''

Lacey paled. If she was forced to go into court, to reveal her part in this affair publicly, all of Medora as well as the entire territory would know who she was, what she was, and what she had done. The humiliation, the ostracism she no doubt would have to face, it was too much to ask.

''I'm sorry.'' She took a step backward, the terrible urge to turn and run seeping into every bone in her body.

But then a hand curled about her arm just above her elbow, ever so gentle, yet enough to check her flight. She glanced up to find Joss standing beside her, a deep frown marring his handsome face. He was ashamed of her, who she was—what she had done. Not that she could blame him. No wonder he had never asked her to marry him. If he only knew the truth, the whole truth, how irrevocably they were tied.

''I-I-I can't do this,'' she tried to explain, tugging at his restraining grip.

''No, I suspect you can't, Lacey.'' His voice was calm, emotionless, but there was a determination in his steely gray eyes the likes of which she'd not seen since that very first time she had seen him in the St. Louis train station when he had been looking for Abrams's mail-order bride.

Battling the lump that clogged her throat, she closed her eyes. At last. Here it came—the ultimate rejection that she had known all along was inevitable. She just couldn't handle it. Not now . . . now that . . .

''Not alone,'' Joss continued. ''But if you're willing, if you'll let me . . . trust me, Lacey, we can face this together. This is as much my battle as yours. We'll overcome this, honey, I promise.''

Her eyes flew open, not sure she had heard him correctly, praying that she had. Anxiously she studied his face.

''That is, if you can see fit to have me,'' he finished up on a hesitant note.

Joss McRae unsure of himself? It seemed unreal. She had only seen him that way once before, and it had been then at that very moment she had fallen helplessly in love with him.

''Have you?'' Her face lit up with undisguised joy. ''Oh,

Joss, I couldn't do without you. I wouldn't want to. Haven't you figured that out yet?'' There in front of all those men, she threw her arms about his neck and pressed her mouth to his.

What did it matter what they or anybody else thought of her? What did it matter if she broke the age-old code of the gambler and revealed her hand before the final showdown, if she displayed her feelings openly in front of others. She loved Joss McRae, had won him fair and square, and wanted the whole world to be aware of it.

For a brief moment he kissed her back, then he gently pulled away. ''Then it's settled. How soon do we have to be in Bismarck?'' he turned and asked the lawyer.

''A week from tomorrow.''

''So soon?'' Joss frowned. ''That means we only have a few days to plan a wedding. Can you manage it, Lacey?''

''Manage it? Of course.'' She laughed. ''I could be ready in an hour if need be.''

It took more than an hour. Three long days of working around the clock and still all the details of the spur-of-the-moment wedding were not attended to. Thank goodness Teddy Roosevelt had so graciously offered the use of his spacious veranda to hold the ceremony, insisting that he be allowed to give the bride away. And Miss Bertalli, bless her nimble fingers, had worked miracles, creating a wedding gown out of a bolt of ice blue taffeta that surpassed even Lacey's wildest hopes.

Nonetheless, it was all down to the wire. Even as Lacey donned her dress less than an hour before the actual ceremony was to take place, Mrs. Anderson, the banker's wife, had arrived with several basketfuls of blue cornflowers from her garden to decorate the banisters.

''Matches your eyes,'' she had said as she entwined several into Lacey's hair, then had set about concocting a lovely bouquet for her to hold.

''Suck in, deLacey,'' Miss Bertalli ordered, as she added a last few stitches to the gown's waistline that she'd been obliged to let out at the last moment. ''If I didn't know better, dear,'' she muttered between the straight pins in her mouth, ''I would wonder at the reason you are getting rather thick around the middle.''

But that was Lacey's little secret.

''Raspberries and cream,'' she murmured.

''Well, then, you've been eating an awful lot of them, child.'' As she took the final stitch, the seamstress frowned her disapproval. ''You had better slow down if you don't want to get as big as a barn. Joss McRae doesn't strike me as the kind of man who would care for a plump wife even if it was pleasing.''

Lacey turned to inspect her profile in the mirror, her hands molding to the barely perceptible swell of her waistline. Was what the seamstress said true? How would Joss feel about her once her slender body grew misshapen? What would he say when he found out that she? . . .

''Mr. McRae, you can't come in here now.''

Lacey glanced into the mirror, discovering Joss standing right behind her, his turbulent gray eyes taking in all of her, a furl creasing the bridge of his straight, masculine nose.

''Why not,'' he demanded, his frown deepening. ''You ladies keeping secrets in here?''

Dropping her hands, Lacey faced him. Her heart slammed to a halt when her eyes met his. He knew. With that uncanny ability he possessed, he had figured out the truth. Was he angry with her?

''It's bad luck for the groom to see the bride before the wedding,'' she blurted, hoping to distract him.

''What a pile of poppycock.'' He swept further into the room. ''Excuse me, Miss Bertalli, but I would like a few moments alone with Lacey.''

''Well, I never.'' Indignantly the spinster stuck the last of her pins into their cushion and marched from the room.

The moment they were alone, Joss turned to confront her. ''Do you think she ever has?'' he whispered, his eyes taking on a mischievous glint. ''Every time that woman says that to me, I can't help but wonder.''

''Joss,'' Lacey chided, surprised at his crassness, but she couldn't stop the spurt of laughter that erupted from her lips.

Then he pulled her to him, his arm about her, his broad

shoulders enveloping her as one of his hands moved down to cup her belly. "Does she know?"

There was no sense in trying to deny the truth. Lacey shook her head. "She thinks I've eaten too many raspberries."

"Raspberries?" He threw back his head and laughed. Oh, how she loved his laugh, so full of life and promise. "No doubt she still thinks babies come from the cabbage patch."

"Shhhhh." Lacey glanced around him to make sure no one, especially not Miss Bertalli, had heard him. "She'll be one of the first to count the months on her fingers."

"So what? Let 'em count."

"But they'll soon figure out that this child was conceived out of wedlock."

"It was conceived in love, Lacey. What else matters?"

"They'll wonder if it's yours or . . ."

"Nobody will dare question the paternity of my son." He gripped her arms so tightly she feared the bones would snap in two.

"Not to your face, perhaps," she retorted, still not convinced.

"Listen, darlin', what's done is done." He pulled her close, so close she could hear the steady, comforting beat of his heart.

She wanted to believe him, wanted to trust that their future, hers, his, the baby's, would turn out all right. But it was hard, so very hard.

"We are who we are," he assured her. "Now, we can spend the rest of our lives trying to cover it up and offer excuses, or we can just go on and make the best of it. To hell with those who don't approve. We'll do what makes us happy."

"And what about the trial, Joss?" Even though today was the happiest in her life, she couldn't stop thinking about what lay ahead for her—for them, she corrected herself— never once doubting that Joss would stand by her no matter what transpired.

"Just tell it as it happened."

"All of it?" she asked in a small, uncertain voice.

"Well, you might make that little peashooter you held me

up with sound a bit larger, much more dangerous, protect my manly image, but otherwise, yes, Lacey. All of it.''

''Oh, excuse me, I didn't mean to . . . Joss, what are you doing in here?''

Together they turned to discover Annie standing in the doorway. Annie, her maid of honor, was dressed in a peacock blue gown meant to complement the icy paleness of deLacey's dress.

Annie. So saucy, so innocent, so in love herself. It was such a shame that her brother was being so obstinate about her feelings toward her cowboy-artist. Glancing at Joss, Lacey caught a glimmer of the trouble, the anger and confusion, brewing inside of him. But Annie's was another problem altogether—one she was determined to solve just as soon as she could.

''Come on in, you're not interrupting. Your brother was just leaving.'' She gave Joss a little shove toward the door. ''Otherwise, he'll miss his cue, and I'll be left standing at the altar.''

As soon as he was gone, Annie turned to her, presenting her with a brown paper-wrapped package she had hidden behind her back. ''Did you get a chance to talk to him?''

''Not yet, but I will. What's this?''

''A present from Rusty.''

Lacey tore the paper off, revealing a pen-and-ink drawing. It was Joss, riding his favorite buckskin, roping a steer, just the way she remembered him from that day of the roundup so long ago.

''Oh, Annie, it's wonderful. I had no idea Rusty was so talented.''

''He is, isn't he?'' The girl's pride was evident in the way her eyes softened. ''And that's why you have to talk to Joss right away. Rusty was offered a commission in Chicago. He's got to leave soon . . . and he wants me to go with him as his wife.''

''Don't worry, Annie, we'll turn Joss around. You tell Rusty yes.'' She put her arm about her sister-in-law-to-be and squeezed.

"Oh, thank you, Lacey. I knew I could depend on you."
Annie hugged her back.

In the distance the wedding music started up, at first slow,
then building.

"Oh," Annie exclaimed, straightening. "That's my
cue."

Then the girl was gone, leaving Lacey by herself.

Dependency. Trust. Wasn't that what this was all about?
Was she not an intricate part of Joss's world, his family, this
community?

Then she experienced a sudden flutter in her belly.
Gasping, she pressed her fingertips to her stomach and felt
the spasm again. Butterflies? No, it had been the new entity
growing there inside of her that had stirred, her ace in the
hole in this great game called life, reminding her that it, too,
expected her to make the way smooth for its entry into her
circle of interdependency. In return, she knew it would be
there to comfort her.

"Miss Lacey, are you ready?"

She glanced up to find Theodore Roosevelt standing in
the doorway—so dignified in his Eastern attire, his intelligent blue eyes offering his approval of who and what she
was—past and present. She knew then that he was destined
for greater things. And if he, a man history would no doubt
expound upon, could accept her, respect her, regardless of
all that had gone before, could those of lesser stature do any
less?

Let 'em look, but never let 'em touch. Her father's sage
advice suddenly took on a new, much clearer meaning,
perhaps the one he had been trying to convey to her all
along. Don't let the opinions of others deflect her from her
course.

"Yes," she said, standing straight and eager to meet her
future, both the obstacles and the rewards, head on. "I'm as
ready as I'll ever be."

Placing her hand in his much larger one, she moved
forward, toward the happiest moment in her life.

The moment when she became the unbeatable Mrs. Joss
McRae.

SPECIAL PREVIEW!

If you enjoyed *Hearts Are Wild,*
you won't want to miss . . .

SWEPT AWAY
by Jean Anne Caldwell

Book Two in the enthralling
"Brides of the West" series.

*Here's an exclusive excerpt
from this exciting new romance—
available from Jove Books
in August 1993 . . .*

Although Jennifer Fairchild knew that she had made the right choice in leaving Philadelphia, her legs did not share her courage. They felt distinctly wobbly and threatened to give way. She clutched the letters of introduction to her breast and stepped down tentatively from the train. Within minutes, she would be meeting her new employer for the first time. She hoped Mr. Morgan wouldn't be too terribly upset when he learned that she had applied for both positions: housekeeper and his mail-order bride. But maybe he wouldn't discover her deception just yet.

Her wide brown eyes took in the weathered buildings and the dirt road that passed in front of the stationhouse. Gold Shoe, Colorado, was even smaller than she had envisioned, and she hadn't been imagining anything grand, but perhaps that was a blessing. Jenny searched the nearly empty platform, uneasiness settling heavily in her stomach. Where was Mr. Morgan? Surely the employment agency had notified him to meet her. *Miss Emily's Positions For Young Ladies* had appeared to be an efficient agency. Jenny frowned. Yet how efficient could they be if they had unknowingly hired her to fill both of Mr. Morgan's advertised positions?

Her father would have said the situation she found herself in was no more than she deserved for running away from home—right after he called her those awful names and locked her in the attic. Well, no more. She was never going back to Philadelphia. Her father would be wasting his money to send someone to fetch her home. Nothing short of marauding Indians would make her give up. She had taken too many risks in getting as far as she had.

This was 1888 and a woman of eighteen should be able to make her own decisions without fear of retribution. If the stories in the *Philadelphia Times* were to be believed, in the West most women her age had already made names for themselves. While Jenny's own skills were limited, her young heart warmed to the romantic notion that with time and training she could be anything she wanted to be—a rancher, a miner, or even a stagecoach driver.

Neither of the positions she'd actually been hired for—Mr. Morgan's mail-order bride or his housekeeper—quite fit her dreams of independence, but she firmly shoved those doubts aside.

With a gloved hand, Jenny readjusted the ribbons on her new silk bonnet, then straightened the front of her yellow and black dress. Jenny was well aware that the brightly striped gown was a bit much for a housekeeper, but a willful streak of vanity had prompted her to dress well. Gently she tugged at the corner of the matching jacket, being especially careful not to disturb the money she had sewn into the lining.

While she continued to check the road for Mr. Morgan, Jenny tried her best to ignore the grumblings of the men unloading her luggage. They kept muttering something about train schedules and other such nonsense. She could see no reason for them to turn so nasty merely because she had a few more bags than most of their passengers. It wasn't as if she could send back to Philadelphia for the rest of her things. It was bad enough that she had had to leave her sister Izzy behind until she was settled.

Jenny walked the entire length of the wooden platform and back before again checking the watch pinned to the bosom of her yellow jacket. The sun was nearly down. Where was Mr. Morgan? She stopped beside the pile of luggage and unfolded one of the letters from the agency.

She carefully reread the instructions. Her memory hadn't failed her. It clearly stated Mr. Morgan or someone from his ranch would be at the station to meet her.

A large lump slowly made its way up her throat. *What if Mr. Morgan already discovered her deception and intended to leave her stranded here without a chance to explain?* It wasn't as if she had deliberately set out to cheat him. She had had more than enough money to meet her needs when she had left Philadelphia, and she certainly hadn't counted on being robbed by that dirty little man the moment she stepped off the train in St. Louis.

If she hadn't been desperate, she would never have resorted to such duplicity.

When Jenny had gone to the agency, she had only thought to check out the possibilities. She hadn't expected the clerk from the agency to all but force her to take the bride position. It had seemed so simple at the time. They would give her a train ticket to Colorado and all she was obligated to do was talk with Mr. Morgan. If they didn't suit, she was on her own.

It wasn't until she had signed the agreement that she discovered Mr. Morgan was also seeking a housekeeper. Jenny let a reproachful sigh escape her lips. Why hadn't she merely told the clerk that she had changed her mind? But no, she had let her need for money overcome good sense. The money she could get from cashing in the second ticket would help recoup her stolen funds.

It still amazed her that not a twinge of conscience asserted itself when she planned her scheme. She had merely taken the small, jeweled comb her mother had left her and pulled her long thick black hair back into a tight knot. Then perching a thick pair of discarded spectacles on her nose, she returned to the agency to claim the house-keeper's position as well.

She had to admit finding those cracked glasses on the bench outside the general store had been a godsend. While she could barely see to walk, the lenses lent Jenny's brown eyes a distorted look that kept the overworked clerk behind the desk from noticing that both her last two customers had worn the same blue traveling gown.

After the second theft of one of her bags, the journey from St. Louis had gone off without a hitch. The ruse may have gotten her to Colorado, but if Mr. Morgan refused to hire her after all this, what good had it done? What would she do if he had changed his mind? She might have enough money to return to Denver, but what was to become of her after that?

For the hundredth time since leaving St. Louis, Jenny's fingers traced the square outline of bills sewn into her jacket. Thank goodness, she had it. If Mr. Morgan didn't come soon, she would be forced to look for lodgings. She cast a wary eye down the long line of buildings. One of the weathered wooden shingles swinging in the evening breeze read "hotel."

She had heard that most merchants situated close to the stations catered to people who flocked to the mining areas hoping to strike it rich. The privilege of room and board were said to run high. If the rumors were correct, Jenny couldn't afford to stay long. A modest boardinghouse might be all her funds would allow.

Resigned to the fact that she would need directions, Jenny stepped into the station. Except for the stationmaster behind the glass partition, the room was empty. He looked up from a stack of invoices as she approached. Although he continued to thumb through the papers, his watery blue eyes followed her progress across the wooden floor. His unwavering gaze set the small hairs on the back of Jenny's neck to prickling. She wanted to turn and run, but Jenny was stubborn and wasn't about to let the man's rudeness scare her. It was something she had learned from dealing with her father.

"The gentleman that was supposed to meet me is late and I was wondering if perhaps there was a boardinghouse you could recommend?"

Carl Turner licked his dry lips at the sight before him. He'd been watching the little lady pace the narrow platform for the last hour and wondered when she'd finally be forced to come to him. And here she was, prettier than a mountain flower, asking him where she should go. He couldn't believe his luck. It wasn't often a woman was stranded in Gold Shoe and he was already going over what he would do with the money for selling this one.

Having found the invoice he needed, Carl shoved the rest of them into a drawer and again focused his attention on the young woman. She wore no ring on her finger but Carl had learned to be cautious.

"You married?" he asked.

Jenny did not care for the look of greed that suddenly flared in his eyes. Although the question seemed innocent enough, his delivery of the words hinted at more than common curiosity.

"Does the quality of the room depend on the existence of a husband, sir?" Jenny asked stiffly, determined to humble the man by remaining a lady.

He grinned. "It might."

Jenny started to give him her views on such a statement when his eyes suddenly narrowed, bringing a lump to her throat. Evil seemed to seep from his pale blue orbs. Instinctively, Jenny stepped back.

Carl savored her apparent fear of him. This was going to be easier than he thought. "You one of Em's girls?" he demanded.

Jenny let out the breath she was holding. If this despicable little toad thought just because she had been reduced to seeking employment through Miss Emily's Positions For Young Ladies that she was no longer to be treated with respect, she would soon set him straight. She lifted a delicate brow. "You know Miss Emily?"

The question appeared to humor him for the obnoxious man tossed back his head in laughter. "Miss Emily," he crowed. "Now don't that beat all. Is that what she calls herself back East?"

Apprehension washed over Jenny. What had she gotten herself into? "If you would please tell me of a boarding-house, I will let you get back to your work."

Carl leaned across the counter. "Won't you be wanting to stay at Em's place?"

The agency had not mentioned having a hotel in Gold Shoe, but then why should they? After all, Mr. Morgan should have been there to meet her. Perhaps they would know what had detained him. The mocking smile on the stationmaster's face was beginning to irritate her.

"Yes, of course," she said with more conviction than she felt. "Now if you would kindly show me the way."

Carl didn't bother to hide his disappointment. Em had sure bagged herself a pretty one this time. A shame she had found this little black-haired dove on her own. With her combination of fire and innocence, she would have fetched him a pretty penny at one of the more exclusive brothels in Denver.

Well, no matter. He should have known. Only the other day Em had told him she was expecting a couple of new girls. He gave his fingers a quick lick, then ran them through the greasy strands of his lank, brown hair.

"Name's Carl, miss. Carl Turner. Em's place is a might hard to find for a stranger. I get off in an hour," he offered, displaying a mouthful of yellowing teeth. "I'd be more than happy to take you there."

The foul odor of his stale breath curled the inside of Jenny's stomach and she stepped back. "You need not bother, Mr. Turner," she said through clenched teeth.

"No trouble. No trouble at all. Em told me to expect you. I always watch out for her girls."

"Thank you, but Miss Emily said there would be someone to meet me."

Carl couldn't hold back the loud snort. "Said that, did she?" He gave her a broad wink. "Em has her good intentions, but I'd not be countin' on them if I were you. More than likely some miner with a bag of gold and an ache in his pocket distracted her."

His words set a warning ringing in Jenny's head. What if there were no Mr. Morgan? What if . . .

No! Jenny decided. She refused to allow herself to draw such a conclusion until she talked with Miss Emily. There was no sense borrowing trouble.

She had no more shored up her confidence when the stationmaster suddenly straightened his shoulders and looked past her to the door.

"Wasn't there to be two of you?" he demanded.

Jenny could feel her newly formed conviction crumble with the trembling of her limbs.

"Where's the other one?" he insisted.

Jenny took a deep breath. She was a fool to think she would get away with her deception unscathed. Even so, she wasn't about to make her excuses to this man. "She missed the train from Denver," she lied.

"Em won't be pleased. No, ma'am. Not pleased at all."

The sly grin on his lips belied any real concern on his part, but Jenny didn't let it upset her. At this point, she could care less about what Miss Emily thought of the absence of Mr. Morgan's bride. It was more important to settle her position as his housekeeper. All she wanted to do now was get somewhere where she could buy a cup of strong tea and think things through.

"If you don't mind, I think the matter best discussed with Miss Emily. Now if you would please show me the way."

Carl sobered at her curt dismissal. His blue eyes narrowed. If Em didn't give him a break on the price of the pretties upstairs, he'd send this dark-haired beauty to the far end of town and let her spend the night with the coyotes. But he had other plans for this high-and-mighty miss. She thought she was too good for the likes of him. Well she'd soon learn you didn't mess with Carl Turner. He had connections. Em would have this little lady spreading her legs for him before the night was out. It had been a long time since he had roughed up one of Em's girls, but it would be worth incurring Em's wrath to have this one beg for mercy.

He pointed to the window. "You'll be wantin' to take Eighth Street to Parker. Em's place is down on your right."

After getting Carl to agree to look after her things, Jenny left in a swirl of petticoats. After his appalling manners, she didn't feel the need to thank him. Once outside, she hurried across the street.

The sun perched precariously on the distant mountain ridge and cast long shadows across her path, quickening Jenny's pace. It wouldn't be wise to tarry. Already the walkway lay in darkness.

Now that she was getting close to her destination, she couldn't seem to justify her duplicity quite as easily as she had managed to do so far. Even her footsteps seemed to echo her guilt with each step.

The housekeeper . . . the bride . . . the housekeeper . . . the bride.

The walkway appeared to grow in length, the censorious words keeping ominous time with her slow progress.

Perhaps it was better that Mr. Morgan had been late for suddenly her rehearsed explanations did not seem adequate. While Jenny was not above bending the truth when the occasion demanded, she much preferred to cleverly weave her harmless white lies into a seemingly solid fabric of truth. She had learned when dealing with her father that it was the smartest way. Over the years, it had become the only method Jenny found effective to save both herself and her sister from his unforgiving wrath.

The sound of shattering glass pulled her up short. She looked around. Somewhere along the way, night had fallen and the brightly painted shop windows now lay cloaked in darkness.

Surely the boardinghouse was not much further, she told herself as she hurried down the deserted street. The sun had taken its warmth with it and Jenny shivered in the cool night air. Despite her brave assurances, it wasn't until Parker crossed Eighth Street that she began to relax.

An abundance of lights poured from the windows up and down Parker. Jenny found herself drawn to the music and laughter that drifted from the many storefronts.

An elegant coach lumbered past and she watched it weave its way between the wagons that lined the narrow street, coming to a stop in front of a large house. Before the driver had time to climb down, several young men rushed forward to assist a beautiful red-haired woman from the coach. While the revealing cut of the woman's green gown brought a warm blush to Jenny's cheeks, she was nonetheless fascinated by the woman's striking beauty.

The men seemed quite taken with the lady as well, for they appeared to hang on her every word. Jenny smiled to herself. She had made the right choice. It was obvious in Colorado a man respected what a woman had to say.

So intent was Jenny on her study of the strangers that when the door suddenly burst open beside her, she gasped. Before she could step back, a man lay sprawled at her feet.

She lifted the hem of her gown and tried to step around him without attracting his notice, but it was too late. He was already crawling to his feet.

"What have we here?" he asked, his words baptizing her with a fine spray of cheap whiskey.

A cold finger of fear traced an icy path up Jenny's spine when he reached for her. His hands grasped the corner of her jacket, the fabric ripping. Jenny watched in horror as the last of her money fluttered to the ground. A gust of wind picked up the bills and threatened to carry them away.

She reached for them when another man came charging out of the saloon. The light from the doorway outlined the huge, ugly man in a dark silhouette. Jenny's wide brown eyes were drawn to the table leg he clutched in his massive hands. She watched as he lifted it over his head. A loud angry roar rolled from deep down inside him and all thoughts of retrieving her money fled.

Jenny couldn't move. Her feet were frozen to the boards. With a wide arc, the big man swung.

Dark blond hair hung nearly to his shoulders. That along with a deep tan and startling blue eyes gave people who first met him the impression that here was the epitome of what every gentleman should be. Rugged, good looks, a smile that could melt a woman's heart, and shoulders that could fill a suit coat to perfection.

It took only a frown and an arrogant toss of his head for Cade Morgan to quickly dispel any such theory. He was a man who shared few of his feelings but counted many his friend. With no conscious effort on his part, he demanded respect and got it. There were not many who crossed him and did not suffer the brunt of his swift revenge.

"The fool," he silently cursed as he ducked his six-foot-four-inch frame through the doorway of the train station. It was bad enough he was late, then to have the stationmaster send his bride to Em's place was beyond belief.

But then Cade had never liked Carl Turner and had often wondered how he had managed to keep his job as station-master. Did the man think every woman traveling alone was a prostitute? If Miss Fairchild came to any harm, Cade would personally see to it that the railroad learned of the man's incompetence.

Cade started to climb back onto his buckboard, then thought better of it. As narrow as the street was in front of Em's place, he'd have a hard time making his way between the drunks that wandered from saloon to saloon. He'd make better time walking.

It wasn't until Cade reached Parker Street that he realized he hadn't overtaken Miss Fairchild. He stepped up his pace as he searched both sides of the street.

If not for the yellow and black striped dress, Cade might have missed her. A drunk had Miss Fairchild corralled outside Mac's Saloon and she did not appear at all pleased. No lady should have to deal with such ruffians, especially not his bride-to-be.

Cade shouted but no one paid him any heed. The idiots were treating her as if she were one of Em's girls. With powerful strides, he broke into a run. Before he could reach her, another man burst through the doors of the saloon.

It had been months since Cade had last seen Bear, but it wasn't difficult to recognize the huge miner. There weren't too many men who could match Bear for size. Even from this distance, Cade could see the anger that twisted his friend's scarred face.

When the Bear drew back his club and swung, his assailant ducked and ran.

"No, Bear!" Cade shouted.

Bear checked his swing, but not soon enough. The table leg caught the young woman's brow. She fell like a shoring log cut too short for the shaft. Bear dropped his club.

"Cade?" he asked, confused that a woman lay where that no good claim-jumper, Elmer, should have been. "Did I kill her?"

Cade found himself staring. With hair as black as a raven's wing and skin an alabaster-white, Miss Fairchild was everything he had hoped for. Breathtakingly beautiful and a figure that made a man impatient with society's polite rules that said he should marry her first. It wouldn't do to let himself dwell on the fact that she didn't look old enough to be a widow, he told himself. A lot of women married young.

Cade knelt beside her and examined her rapidly purpling eye. "She's not dead, Bear," he told his friend, "but she'll have quite a shiner when she wakes."

Unconvinced, Bear dropped to his knees. It wouldn't be the first time he had killed someone in his anger. Leaning over, he peered into the young woman's face.

"Are you sure she's not dead, Cade?"

Cade nudged her shoulder. "Miss Fairchild," he urged. Getting no response, he shook her again. "Wake up, Miss Fairchild."

Jenny winced at the demanding voice that echoed in her head. She tried to open her eyes, but only one seemed to want to obey. Forcing it open, she blinked at the huge, ugly man bending over her.

It was him. The man who had hit her. She lay perfectly still. He no longer wore a fierce scowl on his scarred face, but with that unruly mane of wild red hair, he looked every bit as frightening as when he'd come rushing out the door.

"Who are y-you?" she finally managed to choke out.

"I'm Mr. Morgan," Cade answered.

Jenny blinked her good eye again. Odd how the words came out but the man's lips never moved. She closed her eye against the pain. It was no wonder, her mind was playing tricks on her. Her head felt like someone was using it for a church bell. A thousand iron clappers each vied for a chance to strike their own tune.

"Are you Miss Fairchild?"

Oh Lord. This was going to be more difficult than she had imagined. Such a cultured voice for such a primitive face. Surely there had to be some mistake. No one could ever bring themselves to marry such a man.

Jenny struggled to find the right words, but try as she might she couldn't seem to formulate a single coherent sentence. Guilty conscience or not, now was not the time to try to conduct a clever interview. She certainly didn't want to offend a man who was capable of breaking her in two without any great effort on his part.

Jenny gently rubbed her swollen brow. ''I'm Jenny, your housekeeper,'' she managed to say before a black curtain descended again.

Cade stood. His housekeeper! The agency had sent a beautiful young woman like this to be his housekeeper. They must have been out of their minds. She wouldn't be with him a week. Once word got out, every miner for miles around would be on his doorstep asking for her hand. Even so, he couldn't just leave her lying here. The wind was beginning to pick up. At this time of year, it could be harboring either spring or winter. Cade knelt down and gathered her up in his arms.

''Can you help me get her home, Bear? I'll have Albert make up a bed and you can spend the night.''

Cade started to say more when he felt Jenny stir in his arms. All he needed was her to raise a fuss to add more color to the story Carl was bound to be cooking up.

''Lie still,'' he warned. ''We haven't far to go.''

Jenny opened her eye and stared. The scarred face had been replaced by the handsomely rugged features of a bronzed warrior. Pale blond hair shone like silver in the light of a crescent moon. Handsome enough to make one's heart skip a beat, she told herself. Even so, Jenny was not one easily drawn to such things. She had learned from experience that it was best to remember handsome is as handsome does. Many a deceiving smile hid a determinedly squared jaw of an unforgiving nature.

Jenny pushed against his broad chest. ''Who are you?'' she asked.

''Didn't I tell you to lie still?''

At the sharp command, Jenny immediately ceased her struggles.

''That's better,'' he said as he stepped off the boardwalk. ''It sure would wound my pride if the stationmaster were to see me drop you.''

Jenny tried to turn in his arms. ''He's watching us?''

''Every move.'' Cade smiled at her frown. ''With your torn jacket and that black eye, you're quite an attraction. I'll have a hard enough time explaining to all my friends that I didn't hit my new housekeeper.''

Jenny froze. "Your housekeeper? I'm your housekeeper? Then who . . . ?"

Cade nodded to the big miner behind him. "Meet Charlie Wise. We call him Bear."

"Oh!" was all she managed.

Having dispensed with the introductions, Cade turned his attention to the pile of luggage stacked on the train platform. It was no wonder Carl was working late. Someone had left him a mountain of bags to look after.

"Which bag is yours?"

"Th-the ones on the platform," she answered, still trying to sort out her mistake.

Watching them haul her possessions to the buckboard, Jenny almost wished she had admitted to being the bride. Mr. Morgan surely wouldn't have begrudged his bride her things.

As they worked, Jenny found her attention drawn more and more to the taut muscles that worked beneath the snug fit of Mr. Morgan's white linen shirt. The light from the station revealed more than just a fine set of shoulders. While lacking the massive girth of Bear's barrel chest, Mr. Morgan was every bit as intimidating. Jenny couldn't remember when she'd met someone quite so tall before. With eyes bluer than the skies over Colorado, he was most pleasant to look at. A girl could easily find herself drawn to him. Much more so than the man her father wished her to marry. A shame she wasn't in the market for a husband. Otherwise, she might have been tempted to marry the tall, handsome rancher just to show her father that she could make her own decisions.

Jenny gave herself a brisk shake. What in heaven's name was she thinking? She was to be the housekeeper, not the bride. This job was to be the beginning of a new life for her. One of independence. One she had only dreamt about until a week ago. If she was going to succeed, she couldn't be slipping back into the ways of her father's upbringing. She had secured this position on her own and she was determined to prove to everyone a woman didn't need a man. If a woman wanted, she could . . .

The thought lodged in her throat when Mr. Morgan pinned his brilliant blue eyes on her. It was almost as if he had guessed that she was to have been his bride and was awaiting an explanation. She had meant to explain, but not here. Not now.

"Ready?" he asked.

Jenny let out the breath she was holding. He sounded irritated, not mad. He didn't suspect. But she would still have to explain. As for the money she owed him, well that would have to wait. After all, she had tried to go back after it. It wasn't her fault he had refused to let her. Perhaps there would be an opportunity on the ride to his ranch to bring the subject up.

Her conscience very much relieved, Jenny smiled brightly at Mr. Morgan as he lifted his jacket from the seat and climbed up beside her. After slipping into his coat, he nodded at Bear. To Jenny's dismay, Bear stepped up on the other side and calmly waited for her to move over. How was she to have the privacy she needed to apologize to Mr. Morgan?

"There's not room enough for the three of us," Jenny protested.

Cade, who had lost his patience somewhere around the tenth bag, glared down at her. "Bear would ride in the back but your luggage took up all the room. It's either the three of us on this seat or you can walk."

At his uncompromising words, Jenny slid over to make room for Bear. Mr. Morgan might be handsome, she decided, but he was certainly no gentleman. She was all but wedged between the two men on the narrow seat.

Jenny scrunched her shoulders forward, trying to make room. "I c . . . an't br . . . reathe," she protested.

"Stand up!" Cade snapped.

"What?"

"I said, stand up."

"I can't r . . . ide like th . . . at."

"Stand!"

Jenny shot up off the seat.

After a shuffling of feet, Cade pulled her down on his lap. She opened her mouth to protest, but he quickly cut her short.

"One word and you stay," he growled.